SUNSET AT ROSALIE

Also by Ann L. McLaughlin

Lightning in July

The Balancing Pole

Sunset at Rosalie

A NOVEL BY

Ann L. McLaughlin

John Daniel & Company
PUBLISHERS
Santa Barbara • 1996

Design & typography by Jim Cook

Published by John Daniel & Company, Publishers
A Division of Daniel & Daniel, Publishers, Inc.
Post Office Box 21922, Santa Barbara, California 93121

LIBRARY OF CONGRESS CATALOGING-IN-PUBLICATION DATA
McLaughlin, Ann L.
Sunset at Rosalie: a novel / Ann L. McLaughlin.
p.   cm.
ISBN 1-880284-15-4 (ppbk.: alk. paper)
I. Title.
PS3563.C3836S86   1996
813'.54—dc20   95-37387
CIP

To the memory of my mother,

STELLA MCGEHEE LANDIS

ACKNOWLEDGMENTS

I want to express my thanks to the Virginia Center for the Creative Arts and to Yaddo for time to work on this novel in those beautiful settings. I want to thank my Southern family: my aunt, Mrs. Howard B. McGehee; my cousins, Mary McGehee and John and Cameron Napier for their help; also my friend, Ernestine Hunt.

I want to thank the Writers Mentor Group once again for their thoughtful criticisms and support over the years. As always, I am indebted to my family: John and Ellen, and especially my husband, Charlie.

This novel was inspired by a collection of stories my mother wrote about her childhood on a remote cotton plantation in Mississippi. I am particularly grateful to my sister, Ellen Landis McKee, who transcribed my mother's stories and encouraged me to write this book.

Sunset at Rosalie

1

CARLIN pushed back her brown braids and squinted down the long drive, hoping to see Papa and Uncle Will riding up to Rosalie. The ball of sun had turned the sky yellow-white beyond the pine trees, and she lifted one hand to shade her eyes from its slanting light. They were late. The dark live oak trees that lined the road made a shadowy tunnel between the plantation's cotton fields stretching out green and white on either side. But there was no sign of Papa on Graylie, his tall mare, nor of her uncle, whom her father had gone to meet at the train station.

Soon Uncle Will would dismount right there, Carlin thought, and sucked in her breath as she stared at the black hitching post at the end of the red brick walk. He would glance up at the white house for a moment with its columns and wide front gallery, and she would jump up from her seat here on the top step and rush down. "Carlie!" he would shout and stoop, opening his arms wide to enfold her.

Of all Uncle Will's returns, from Paris or from New Orleans, this was the most exciting because next Saturday he and Carlin's Aunt Emily would be married. Carlin could see the slanting letters on the ivory wedding invitations, with Uncle Will's and Aunt Emily's names at the top, the name of the church, the date, August 28, 1909, and Warrington County, Mississippi, at the bottom. The whole plantation was getting ready. Mama and Aunt Lucy were finishing the flower girl dresses in the big house, the stable boys were polishing the harness brasses in the barn, and out in the kitchen house Aunt Georgia was making meringue kisses for the reception. It would be exciting to have the party here, but it had to be at Felicity Grove, Aunt Emily's plantation, because the Grove was bigger than Rosalie.

Carlin raised her eyes and gazed out across the north field toward the stand of pines which marked the line where their fields ended and the Grove's began.

"Carlie." Her brother Tommy ran out onto the gallery. "I've got the telescope."

"Be careful," Carlin warned. "Don't drop it."

"I won't." Tommy grabbed a column and pulled himself up on the balustrade, causing some flakes of white paint to fall on the gallery floor. He straightened cautiously, and Carlin watched him open the jointed sections. His brown curls hung down over the collar of his shirt, which looked babyish, Carlin thought, for a boy of nine. But Mama had promised she would let Aunt Ceny cut his hair in time for the wedding. "I don't see them," he whined. "They still haven't come."

"Don't worry." Carlin paused, surprised by the comforting note in her voice, which sounded almost grown-up. "The train was late, probably. They'll be here soon." She looked down at the book in her lap, but the story seemed remote amidst all the excitement and uncertainty swirling around them now. Putting the book down beside her, she stretched out her legs above the steps and stared at a dark red scab on her knee and her dusty bare feet. She settled her feet on the step below her again and pulled her gingham dress away from her sticky armpits. It was still so hot.

The sound of violin notes came from the library window behind, dropping past her down into the dark ivy of the garden below. Carlin lifted her head. Mama was practicing the Bach air she would play at the wedding. It would be the signal for Carlin and her little sister Evie and her cousin Amy to start down the aisle, scattering the rose petals.

Uncle Will was to arrive tonight, then Grandfather would come tomorrow, for he was performing the service. Family and friends from all over the county would be in the church and at the reception afterward.

"Hey!" Tommy shouted. "There's Papa. I can see him way off."

"Where?" Carlin scrambled to her feet and grabbed the telescope. She turned the focusing ring and caught the distant image of her father on his horse, wearing his wide-brimmed hat. "But where's Uncle Will?" Her voice trembled. "What's happened? Papa's all alone."

"Let's run meet him," Tommy shouted and leapt down the gallery stairs to the front walk. "He'll tell us where Uncle Will is." Carlin put down the telescope and rushed after him. Sam, the graying house dog, rose from the ivy and loped along behind.

Carlin felt her pigtails slap her shoulders as she ran. Tommy was even with her at first, the strip of weeds in the center between them, then Carlin shot ahead. She ought to be able to beat him, she thought. She was ten, thirteen months older than he was, after all. A stitch began in her side, but she kept on. When she reached the edge of the south field, she leaned against the fence, panting, and waited for Tommy to catch up. Papa raised his hat as he trotted toward her, and Carlin waved back. His white shirt looked gray in the growing dimness, and his big tan hat seemed dark.

"Good to have a welcoming committee," he said, reining Graylie in beside them.

"Where's Uncle Will?" Carlin looked up at her father through the dust cloud that had trailed him and now enveloped them all. She turned and gazed down the empty drive to the board fence that marked the county road, hoping to see her uncle on his black mustang.

"He's not coming tonight," Papa said.

"But why not?" Carlin asked. "We've been waiting for him for hours." Her voice shook, and "hours" came out like a sob. She glanced down at the dirt road, annoyed.

"He's been delayed," Papa said. "He'll be along soon, darlin'." The familiar endearment touched her, and she looked up at her father again. He was disappointed too, probably. "He sent a telegram," Papa went on. "He's coming."

"When?" Tommy demanded.

"Tomorrow or the day after." Papa threw the reins over Graylie's withers and slid to the ground. "Come along now, children. Your mama'll be waiting." He lifted Carlin first and she hung in the stirrup a moment, then threw her leg up over the big plantation saddle and settled behind the pommel. Why couldn't Uncle Will come tonight, she thought, as she watched her father lift Tommy, who squeezed in front of her while Graylie stood, switching her dusty tail. Carlin saw Sam greet Papa's bird dog in the tangle of weeds at the edge of the field and felt pleased all at once at her sudden elevation.

Her father mounted, and as he reached around her legs to gather the reins, Carlin felt his warmth behind her, wrapping her in the familiar smells of his pipe tobacco and his perspiration. "Giddyap," he called out.

Carlin tipped her head back as the horse began to move, so that her father's soft moustache touched her forehead. He smiled down at her and moved his head a little, making the moustache tickle. She let out a low laugh, then straightened abruptly. "I just wish Uncle Will had come tonight," she said and looked out at the long field beside them. The cotton plants were full and bushy, and here and there she could see light splotches where some of the bolls had opened. But there were no men in overalls hoeing in the field now. "I like lay-by time, don't you, Papa?" she said, turning her head. "I like it when the fields are all empty, and the colored folks have time to fix their roofs and hold their baptisms before picking begins."

"And have weddings," Tommy added, twisting to look back at his father. "Uncle Will's wedding's going to be in lay-by time this year."

"Yes. Lay-by is a nice quiet time," Papa said. Carlin felt him turn to squint toward the horizon where the long field ended. "Let us pray that God follows it with a good picking and gives His blessing to your uncle's wedding."

They clomped along in silence awhile, the silence that always seemed to follow Papa's calls upon God. "Papa," Carlin began, breaking the quiet. "Do you think Uncle Will will like being a father to Amy and Hugh and Ted?"

"Oh yes, darlin'. Your uncle loves your cousins. He'll be a fine father." Carlin frowned at the horizon. Please, God. Don't let Uncle Will love Amy more than me, she prayed, visualizing her ten-year-old cousin with her blond pigtails. That was a bad prayer, she thought, shifting her gaze to a dark space under a live oak tree, bad and mean.

The lighted house grew closer, and Carlin could see the dormer windows in the roof, the six fluted columns supporting the front gallery, and the orange half-moon of the fanlight window above the front door. It was pretty from here, though most people would say that Felicity Grove was prettier. Everything was kept painted and neat at the Grove, unlike Rosalie, where the front gallery sagged and mildew stains spread up the dining room wall, despite vigorous scrubbings by James the house man.

"I just wish Rosalie was as rich as the Grove." Carlin said.

Her father let out a little snort as he guided Graylie past a dark grove of pines. "Well, that would be nice, darlin'. But it's not."

Carlin studied the house again as they grew closer. Rosalie wasn't poor, really, and yet . . . "Papa," she said and twisted to look back at her father. "We won't ever leave Rosalie, will we?"

She felt her father's chest lift, then settle behind her as he let out a deep sigh. "No, darlin'," he said slowly. "God willing, we'll never leave Rosalie, if I can help it."

Carlin gazed out at the field again. If the cotton was good this year. . . . Everything depended on the cotton, of course, and if it was good, then everything would be fine. She watched as they passed a dark clump of weeds beside the road, then a cotton shed in the shadows, and then she saw the short paved part of the drive ahead that led up to the house.

They paused at the gate and Papa leaned down. "Evening, Toe," he called out as Plato the colored boy, who was waiting by the gatepost, swung the wide gate back so that Graylie could trot through. Her hooves rung out on the paved section. Toe could go home now, Carlin thought, for theirs would be the last horse to come through the gate tonight. "Here we are, children," Papa said. "Home again."

Papa slid from his saddle, threw the reins to the stable hand, and lifted Carlin and Tommy down. They stood on the brick walk a moment, then rushed up the steps, across the gallery, and into the brightness of the wide front hall.

Carlin saw her mother hurrying toward them in her long flowered dress. "Oh, there you are, dears." She bent down, holding out her arms. They ran to her, and Carlin inhaled the scent of cologne as Mama pulled them close. "I knew you must have run off to meet your papa." Mama straightened as they heard their father cross the gallery, and Carlin watched her pat the twist of dark hair at the back of her head. "Thomas," she called, and moved toward him lightly. She lifted her face and then, in a movement that Carlin had seen so many times before but still made her stare in fascination, her parents kissed. Their lips brushed together, and she saw her father slip his hand around her mother's waist. "Where's Will?" Mama asked, leaning back. "Did he go straight to the stable?"

Papa shook his head. "He's been delayed. He'll be here tomorrow or Friday."

"Oh dear." Carlin watched her mother pull back as a crease appeared in her forehead. "We have a thousand things to do, what with the reception and Father coming tomorrow."

"I know." Papa took a folded yellow paper from his breast pocket. "Here's the telegram."

Mama read it then looked at him, hesitating. The crease between her dark eyebrows had deepened. "Thomas, you don't think it's his old trouble, do you? I mean, do you think he . . . ?"

"No, no, my dear." Carlin felt her father's glance fall on her, then Tommy, then move back to Mama. "I'm sure it's not that. Will has business in New Orleans, you know."

Carlin saw her mother frown again, then nod. "Go get cleaned up, children," she said. "Aunt Georgia has supper ready." Carlin grasped the banister, feeling its sticky film of humidity, and climbed the curving staircase slowly, wishing she could hear what Mama and Papa were saying about Uncle Will.

⚜

Supper was over and it was time to gather in the library for evening prayers. "Papa," Carlin began, as they crossed the hall. "Is it true that we'll be the only two plantations in all of Warrington County that are bound together twice by marriage? I mean two sisters, Mama and Aunt Emily, married to two brothers, you and Uncle Will?"

Her father smiled down at her. "You're a little thinker, aren't you?" he said. "It might be true, darlin'. I expect it is."

She wanted to ask more about marriage bonds and plantations that were related to each other, but mainly she wanted to delay the boredom of evening prayers. When Papa opened the door to the library, Carlin saw her mother standing by the desk reading the *Daily Picayune,* which Papa had brought from town.

"Prices are down again," she said, looking up at Papa. "It's that cheap foreign cotton, isn't it?"

"Let me have that, Belle," her father said. "Please." He reached one hand out for the paper. "You let me worry about the crop. You take care of the household."

Carlin saw her mother purse her lips. Then she stepped into the hall to signal the servants that it was time to come to the library. They took their regular places in front of Papa. Carlin knelt in the first row between Mama and Tommy. Aunt Lucy, Papa's sister, who lived with them, knelt behind. Their teacher had always knelt beside her. Carlin drew in her breath, remembering that the new teacher would come in September. Suppose they didn't like her? Still, September was a long way off. She stared at the fringe on the rug, then looked up as Papa began to read.

To everything there is a season, and
A time to every purpose under the heaven:
A time to be borne and a time to die,
A time to plant, and a time to pluck up that which is planted;

God was talking about setting out the new cotton plants in the spring and picking the bolls clean in the fall, Carlin thought. God could see them all, white people and colored people. He could see Papa with his spectacles on, reading from the thick Bible by the light of the coal lamp, and He knew Papa was worried about the crop. That's why he had been cross with Mama just now. Through her half-closed eyes, she saw her mother glance past the bookcase with its dark red row of Sir Walter Scott to the shaded window. Did she think Uncle Will might still come tonight?

Carlin looked back at Aunt Georgia, their cook, who knelt in the back row, her eyes closed, her large black face fixed in a look of concentration. Next to her was thin little Aunt Ceny with her freckles and her queer reddish hair. She had just slipped in after putting Evie to bed. Evie didn't have to come to prayers since she was only five. James, the Rosalie house man, was kneeling near the door. Carlin turned back to the front, saw Papa frown at her, and lowered her head again. Please God, make the cotton good this year, she prayed, so Papa will be happy.

✿

Carlin sat on her wide windowsill in her nightgown, looking out at the moon above the dark magnolia tree. A piece of cloud had drifted over it, but the glowing half circle underneath was tipped upward in the evening sky. It was waxing, she realized, and might be full by Uncle Will's wedding. She tucked her nightgown around her ankles and looked down at her open diary. "Uncle Will didn't come today," the penciled words read. "But Papa says he'll be here tomorrow or Friday. Part of me still wishes he would never marry. But that is a bad wish, especially right now."

She looked out at the moon again. Why did Uncle Will want to marry and move to the Grove? He had always come home to

Rosalie from New Orleans where he did his architecture work or from Paris where he used to be a student. He had been born at Rosalie and he always came back. His room was at the end of the hall, his napkin ring was in the sideboard, and his wide-brimmed hat hung on the hook beside Papa's in the back gallery. Why did he want to marry and leave?

Mama said they would see more of him now because he would be nearby all the time, not off in New Orleans. And they would all do things together and have fun. But Carlin would have to share him with Amy and Hugh now, and Ted too, when he was home from school. Of course, it was good that Uncle Will would have children, but. . . . Would he sit on Amy's bed at night and read *The Swiss Family Robinson* to her and Hugh, the way he had read it to Carlin and Tommy? He'd read the father in a French accent, the oldest son in a Mississippi accent and so on, until Carlin and Tommy, who were supposed to be growing sleepy, had fallen back on the pillows shouting with laughter.

But Uncle Will was in love with Aunt Emily. Carlin closed her eyes partway and saw her uncle in the rose garden putting one arm around her pretty aunt, touching the dark curls above her ears with the other hand. Then she saw him lean forward and cover her mouth with his.

"Carlie." Tommy's whisper was urgent. He was standing in the doorway of her bedroom in his white nightshirt. "There's something in my room. It flew onto the wardrobe. But it's not a bird."

Carlin hurried down the hall after Tommy. A bat was clinging to the side of the wardrobe in the corner, its half-closed body pulsing with its frightened breathing.

"Don't touch it," Tommy yelled as Carlin approached.

"I have to get it out," she said. "You don't want to sleep with it in your room, do you?"

"We could call Papa or James."

"I can get it," Carlin said. "I think." She pulled a towel from the washstand. The bat did look scary, with sharp thorn-like things sticking up out of its wings and queer skin-colored ears. She paused a moment, then flung the towel over it, gathered the ends quickly, and rushed to the window. "Open it all the way," she shouted and flung the end of the towel through the open window. They leaned on the sill together watching as the dark thing slipped from the white cloth, spread its blackish wings, and skimmed off into the night.

"Ooh," Tommy said. "That was scary." He shivered and his shoulders rose with a jerk. "Bats can get in your hair, you know." He put one hand to his curls and squeezed them for a moment, then shivered again. "I should have gotten it out." He twisted the side of his nightshirt. "Girls aren't supposed to be brave."

"It doesn't matter," Carlin said. "It's gone now." She sat down on the window seat and gazed out at the shadowy drive. "I wish Uncle Will would come. The wedding's so soon."

"I know." Tommy sat down opposite her and leaned back against the side of the window frame.

"It's going to change a lot of things," she said.

"I know," Tommy said again. He leaned forward and picked at a scab on his ankle. "I wish he could just get married and then come back to Rosalie." Carlin gave a snort, but Tommy went on. "'To fall in love' is a funny saying."

"It is, sort of." Carlin thought of a fly falling into a vat of molasses, getting its wings sticky so it couldn't get out.

"Carlie." Tommy twisted a button on the worn cushion of the window seat. "What did Mama mean about Uncle Will's old trouble?"

"I don't know. Maybe she meant those times when he gets sort of sad and quiet." She paused, remembering a summer when Uncle Will had sat on the back gallery not talking, not playing with them on the lawn, not even reading to them at night. "But now he's happy, and Mama and Papa are glad he's marrying Aunt Emily," Carlin continued. "It's good. I mean Aunt Emily's needed a husband ever since Uncle Royal died."

"Oh, but Uncle Royal was really different from Uncle Will," Tommy broke in. "Remember how he spanked us when we got straw on the rug? Uncle Will would never do that."

"No, he'd never spank anybody," Carlin said. "Marriage'll be good for him," she went on slowly, imitating the way her mother might talk. "His architecture business isn't doing very well, and I heard Papa tell Mama that he used up a lot of his money in Paris."

"All of it?" Tommy asked.

"No, not all. I don't think. Grandpapa gave him money and—"

"I know how it went," Tommy broke in. "Papa got Rosalie when Grandpapa died, and Uncle Will got money so he could be an architect."

"But now he'll be a planter," Carlin put in. The idea was reassuring, yet dull.

The room had grown shadowy, and Tommy's face across from her was dim. Carlin glanced out of the window, thinking of the bat flying back to its family in the dark.

"You know what I think it is," Tommy began. Carlin looked back at him. "I think what it is, is that Uncle Will just wants to stay close to Rosalie and us. I mean maybe he has fallen in love with Aunt Emily and everything, but I think it's mostly that he loves us all and wants to stay close by."

※

Amy had come to Rosalie for the afternoon. Carlin sat watching her as she stood on a stool in front of the wardrobe mirror while Mama pinned up the hem of her bridesmaid's dress. Amy's blond hair fluffed out around her ears, and her pigtails had curls at the end. Mama said she had lovely eyes. "Stand up straight. That's it." Mama was more patient with Amy than she had been with Carlin. "Hold still just a minute more."

At last it was over. Carlin led the way, running barefoot down the front staircase to the gallery. "Let's go swing," she said and ran out into the garden and over to the big oak tree. Two rope swings hung side by side, motionless in the afternoon heat. Carlin pumped fast, grateful for the rush of air on her face after the stuffy sewing room. She swung out and back, until she was climbing high into the oak leaves, then glanced across at Amy who had begun to pump slowly. She joined Carlin's rhythm, and they swung up into the leaves together and back again.

"It's too hot for swinging," Amy complained after a moment and slowed. They dragged their feet and hung, staring down at the scuffed dirt. "By this time next Saturday," Amy said, "my mama will be married to your uncle. Frankly, I'll be glad when it's all over."

"Why?" Carlin twisted in her swing to look at her cousin. "Aren't you excited about the dresses and the sashes and the guests and everything?" She waited. It seemed impossible that Amy was not. "We'll look like twins, almost."

"But we're not twins," Amy said. "We're only cousins and anyway I'm two months older." She leaned back in her swing. "You're lucky the reception's not going to be here."

"Oh, I wish it were," Carlin said. "It would be so exciting."

"It couldn't be here." Amy looked back at the house. "Mama says Rosalie looks shabbier every time she visits."

"Shabby?" Carlin stopped her swing and stared at her cousin. Had Aunt Emily really said that? Amy swung out a little, as if to escape Carlin's stare.

"Rosalie's smaller." Carlin heard her voice tremble. "Anyway," she said. "Uncle Will's going to stay here first when he comes tonight or tomorrow."

"He has to," Amy pointed out. "He can't stay overnight at the Grove until he and Mama are married." Carlin gazed at the veils of Spanish moss hanging down from the live oak tree. Why not? Why couldn't Uncle Will stay at the Grove if he wanted to?

"Evie goes down the aisle first," Amy said, "then me, then you, then Tommy with the ring, if he doesn't drop it."

"Mama's going to sew it on the pillow with a loose thread so he won't," Carlin said. "Has your mother's dress come?"

"Yes. It's yellow, you know. Not white, because this is her second wedding." Amy tipped her head back and looked up into the leaves. "I remember the night my papa died. His heart just stopped. I woke up when Dr. Dabney came, but Papa had already died."

Carlin stared down at the dirt, feeling guilty. She never thought of Uncle Royal anymore. He had died four years ago when he was fifty, much older than Papa or Uncle Will, and she could hardly remember him. He wore spectacles and a brown vest that smelled of cigars. Carlin pushed her heel into the dirt, making a hollow, aware suddenly that in the midst of all the wedding excitement there was this sadness. She lifted her head and looked at Amy. "You'll like Uncle Will," she said softly. "He'll be a good papa, I bet."

"Maybe he will." Amy spun herself slowly in the swing. "I hope so anyway."

❁

When Carlin opened her eyes, the early morning light was slanting through the blind at her window and someone was talking on the front gallery down below. Carlin started to swing her legs over the edge of her bed, but stopped and sat counting as the grandfather clock downstairs struck five, which meant it was really six.

She pushed back the mosquito netting that hung over her canopied bed and ran to the window. The voices were low. She heard a man's cough and then a familiar voice. "I'm sorry to disturb you so early, Belle, but I had to talk. I mean we've always been friends, you and I, and. . . ."

It was Uncle Will, Carlin realized. He was the only man beside Papa who called Mama Belle. He had come at last. "Uncle Will," she started to shout.

"You mustn't act too quickly," Mama was saying. "This could be a terrible thing to do."

Carlin pulled the blind up quietly and leaned across the window sill. "I know that, Belle. I know the pain and humiliation I'll cause." Carlin leaned out further. What were they talking about? What pain?

Never mind. She turned from the window and ran bare foot along the hall and down the stairs, pausing a moment at the bottom. Uncle Will's wide-brimmed hat lay on the marble-topped table in the downstairs hall. Carlin touched the soft crown lightly before she crossed the rug to the front door, which stood half-open to the gallery. Uncle Will, she wanted to call out. Carlin pushed the door open an inch and peered through the opening. He was sitting forward in one of the rockers, his elbows on his knees, his head in his hands, staring down at the floor.

"I love your sister, Belle," he said in a hoarse voice. "I love her deeply, but I tell you the black beast is on me again and I can't do it. I can't go through with it. I can't." He raised his head, and Carlin saw that his face looked pale and blotched.

"This is just one of your bad times, Will," her mother said. "You've had them before, and they always pass, you know."

Uncle Will nodded, then let his head drop again. "This is different, Belle. I can't put this on Emily and the children," he said. "Don't you see that?"

Carlin waited, holding her breath. "Will, dear," her mother began. "This is a time when you need Emmy and the stability of marriage. Her love will help you. Don't you see? To cancel the wedding now would only. . . ."

Carlin took a step back and glanced around the hall. Cancel the wedding? He couldn't do that. What about the dresses and the cakes and all the invitations? She turned and fled up the stairs and down the upstairs hall to her room. Back in her bed, she sat with the covers pulled up around her shoulders. Cancel the wedding? What was Uncle Will thinking? What was wrong?

She heard Graylie's snort, then her hooves on the paved drive. That was Papa back from the fields. "Will," she heard him call out below, his voice muted, so as not to disturb his sleeping family. "Welcome, brother. Welcome home." Carlin got out of bed again and leaned across the window sill to listen. There were greetings, and then the sound of the three grown-ups settling in the rocking chairs below. Their voices grew low, their words indistinct. Carlin leaned out further and clutched a leaf of the old red maple that brushed the side of the house. She heard phrases: "the family honor," "God-given responsibilities." She shouldn't be listening here at the window, but she stayed.

Papa's voice grew louder after a while. "That's right, Will," she heard him say. "You're making the right decision, I'm sure." The rockers creaked as they stood. "Be of good courage, brother. You love her. That's the crucial thing. We'll work together, you and I, and fight this black beast of yours. . . . You know, Will, sometimes I think this sadness is in the McNair blood. But you'll conquer it. With God's help, I know you'll put it down." Carlin heard their boots on the gallery steps, then she saw her father and her uncle on the brick walk. Papa had his arm around Uncle Will's shoulders.

Carlin watched them cross the drive and stand near the pecan orchard where Fancy, Uncle Will's black mustang, was munching in the high grass. Papa stroked his shank as Uncle Will put on his hat and mounted. "There's never been a bridegroom worth his salt that didn't have doubts," her father said.

"I thank you, Tom." Uncle Will leaned down to grasp Papa's arm a moment. "And you too, Belle, dear," he said nodding to Mama, who had come down the gallery stairs and stood beside Papa. "I thank God for bringing me back to you again."

Carlin bit her lip as she watched her uncle walk Fancy along the box hedge slowly beside Papa. "Don't worry about me, Tom." He straightened, and for the first time that morning, she saw him tip back his head and give his wide, happy smile. "Everything's going to be fine now. You'll see, brother. Just fine." He slapped the reins and smiled again, then turned Fancy and trotted down the drive.

Carlin stood at the window, watching her uncle's figure grow small as he disappeared down the long corridor of live oak trees.

※

As soon as breakfast was over, Carlin ran across the courtyard to the kitchen house. She needed to talk to Aunt Georgia, but when she pushed the door open it bumped against Feely, Aunt Georgia's granddaughter, who was crouched down beside a box full of kittens near the stove.

"Hey, Carlie," she said. "Look. Ain't they cute? Kitsy had 'em in the night." Carlin drew her breath in and stooped down to look at the tangle of mewing fur bodies. They must be Kitsy's fourth or fifth family. She reached to touch one soft little body, excited about the kittens, yet uneasy about the presence of Feely, her best friend. Right now she needed to talk to Aunt Georgia alone.

"This one's my favorite," Feely said and stroked a striped head

27

with her brown forefinger. Any other morning it would have been fun to stay here and play with the kittens, Carlin thought, but today there was something urgent she needed to know.

Aunt Georgia was standing at the long oilcloth-covered table, turning the handle on the side of the sifter, as a white cascade of sugar poured down into a tan bowl. She looked large in her white apron, its bib covering the shelf of her heavy breasts, her dark face damp with perspiration.

"Me and Hamlet's goin' fishin'," Feely said, referring to her twin brother. "Tommy comin'. He's gone back to git his pole. You come too."

Carlin opened her mouth to answer, then looked down at the kittens again. "Maybe," she said and squeezed her hands together. "First I . . . I need to. . . ." She stopped.

"If you all's goin' fishin'," Aunt Georgia said to Feely, "you better go dig you some bait now, Feely, while them crawlers is still out." Her eyes moved to Carlin, and she picked up an egg and held it a moment as she studied her.

"But I. . . . Yes'm," Feely said and stood. She looked up into her grandmother's dark face. "I'll go get me the bait bucket."

Carlin watched Feely leave, then turned back to Aunt Georgia, grateful but mystified. How had she known that Feely's absence was exactly what Carlin wanted?

Carlin sat down on the bench beside the table and swung her bare legs back and forth. She looked up at Aunt Georgia, then down at the table. How should she start?

"I got all these cakes to make for the weddin'," Aunt Georgia said. "And Miss Emily she say she want another six batches o' them meringue kisses too." She paused and looked at Carlin, making a space for her to speak, but Carlin continued to hesitate. "You wanta pound me them almonds there?" she asked after a moment. "They's all blanched."

Carlin rose and took the mortar and pestle from the sill. She'd better begin, she told herself, as she poured the nuts into the wooden mortar. Feely might be back soon. "Aunt Georgia," she said. "Is there something wrong with Uncle Will?"

She watched Aunt Georgia take another egg from the basket beside her. She cracked it smartly on the side of a bowl and held up the two pieces of shell to let the white slide down. "Wrong, honey?" She looked over at Carlin. "How?"

"Well, I heard him . . . I heard. . . ." Carlin hesitated. "He told Mama he had a black beast on him. It was early this morning. They were talking on the front gallery, and I heard them from my room." Carlin paused. For a moment she saw a large animal behind her uncle, its black furry arms clutching his shoulders, its huge dark head leaning down over his. She shook her head to erase the image and went on. "He said he didn't want to marry Aunt Emily. But then Papa came, and he and Mama talked to him, and he said he would." She stopped again. "What did he mean by a black beast?" she asked.

Aunt Georgia put both hands on her hips and shook her head. "Oh, that's just your uncle's way of talking, Carlin. Mister Will goes up and down. Always has, all the twenty years I known him. Some weeks he's just so happy, then come times when he's real sad and dark-like. Don't even want to get outta his bed sometimes." Carlin nodded and waited for Aunt Georgia to go on.

"Mister Will, he always been that way. Put your hand over that mortar, honey," she said, interrupting herself. "So them almonds don't jump."

Carlin moved her hand. "But he said he didn't want to have the wedding," she insisted.

"You heared him say that?" Carlin nodded. "Well, of course your uncle's taking on a lot with that big family. Three chillun and the Grove too, and he ain't had no time to learn much about cotton plantin' yet, what with his architectin' and all."

"But suppose he doesn't marry Aunt Emily," Carlin said. "Suppose at the last minute, he says he just can't." She looked down at the mortar and clutched the pestle more tightly. How queer she was, she thought suddenly. Just last night she had been secretly wishing that Uncle Will wouldn't marry, and now she was all upset that he might not.

"Carlin, you stop your worryin'." Aunt Georgia's voice was

stern. "Your uncle is a feelin' man. He goes up and down, like I say, but he's gonna be all right. Fact is, he's gonna be better than he ever was, 'cause your Aunt Emily, she's gonna be a good wife for him, real sweet and steady. Miss Emily'll help him even up his feelin's and set things right."

Carlin let out a long breath and felt her shoulders slump forward with relief. If Aunt Georgia said that Aunt Emily would make a good wife for Uncle Will, she would, because Aunt Georgia knew. She tipped her head back and studied the row of copper pots hanging on the wall.

"Yes, honey," Aunt Georgia went on. "Your uncle's weddin's gonna be good for everybody. Your Papa'll teach your uncle all about cotton, and Mister Will, he gonna be a fine planter. Might be your Papa'll use that big gin at the Grove sometime, and. . . ." She paused. "Yessir. This weddin's gonna be good for everybody. Your Uncle Will and your aunt, your three little cousins, and Rosalie too."

Carlin nodded and looked around at the kitchen.

"There's gonna be a fine big wedding with flowers and punch and pretty dresses and all these here cakes. And you and your cousin Amy and little Miss Evie, you's goin' be the prettiest flower girls ever."

Aunt Georgia turned to the cupboard behind her. "Now where's that nutmeg run off to just when I's fixin' to use it?"

Carlin pounded the last almond and put the pestle down. "I've finished," she announced. "I'm going to go help Feely dig bait."

"Put yo' hat on then, you hear? That sun's fierce. You make those boys wear theirs too. And Feely. I don't want no heat-struck chillun in my kitchen this afternoon, not with this weddin' 'bout here."

✿

Carlin stood in the crowded vestry, twisting the pink ribbon that hung from her basket of rose petals as she listened to the deep notes of the organ reverberate in the church beyond. She imagined the guests being ushered down the aisle into their pews, the kin from Vicksburg and those from Jackson.

"Can I start now?" Evie pulled at Carlin's arm. "Now?"

"No. Not till I tell you."

"Just a little bit longer," said Aunt Lucy, Papa's sister, who was in charge of the flower girls. She patted Evie's head.

But Carlin felt they had been waiting in the stuffy vestry for hours, watching through the narrow window as the buggies drew up outside and ladies descended in their wide veiled hats. The men had reached up to help, handsome in their dark suits, some in high silk hats. Now the crowd of arriving guests had thinned. Almost everyone was in the church.

Carlin stood on tiptoe to peer through the little window in the door that led into the church. The pews were full, even in the back. She turned to see if Aunt Emily had come into the vestry, but she must be waiting still in the minister's office with her two sons.

"Fix my sash, Carlin," Amy ordered. "It's come loose again." As Carlin pulled Amy's sash into a tight bow in back, the violin notes began. That was Mama starting the Bach air.

"Now," Carlin whispered and gave Evie a little push, just as Aunt Lucy leaned over and tapped her shoulder. Carlin watched her sister start down the aisle, smiling and sprinkling the petals from her basket exactly as they had shown her in rehearsal. She felt so relieved at the ease of Evie's performance that for a moment she couldn't think what she was supposed to do. Then Amy started. "Now you," Aunt Lucy whispered, and Carlin followed, feeling tall and trembly as she began. The pink rose petals stuck to her damp fingers, and Uncle Will and Papa seemed a long way off down by the altar, in front of Grandfather, who stood holding the large red prayer book.

She took her place next to Amy and stared straight ahead. Grandfather looked imposing in his Prince Albert frock coat and his pointed white beard that almost hid his clerical collar. After a moment, she turned her head to glance at Uncle Will. He wore a black suit with a white waistcoat, and a single white rosebud protruded from his buttonhole. She wished he would glance down at her, but he was staring straight ahead at the carved wooden altar. Carlin glanced at Tommy as he took his place beyond them, holding the pink cushion with the ring sewn to it.

All at once the organ rang out, "Here comes the bride." Carlin could feel Aunt Emily approaching, but she knew she mustn't look back. When she saw the yellow silk folds of her aunt's skirt close by, she knew that Aunt Emily had taken her place beside Uncle Will. Carlin reached down to stop Evie, who was swinging her basket, and they stepped back. Now only her aunt and uncle stood in front of Grandfather.

"Emily," Grandfather said, looking at his younger daughter. "William." He encompassed Uncle Will in his serious blue gaze. His long hands, holding the prayer book, were freckled and thin. "You have come here today to seek the blessing of God and of His church upon your marriage. I require, therefore, that you promise. . . ." Carlin looked down at the rose petals in her basket. " . . . to fulfill the obligations which Christian marriage demands. . . . William." Grandfather's voice was stern. Didn't he like Uncle Will? "Do you promise to love her, comfort her, honor and keep her, in sickness and in health?"

Carlin looked up at her uncle. His face was white, and she saw his jaw tremble. She drew in her breath, waiting. At last he whispered, "I do."

Grandfather asked Aunt Emily the same question. "I do," she said, and her voice seemed to ring out, a loud confident sound.

Uncle Will took the ring from the pillow and pushed it onto Aunt Emily's finger; then he bent and kissed her. When he straightened, he was smiling. It was all right, Carlin thought with relief. Now everything would be all right.

As the wedding guests stood clustered on the steps of the church with others coming out behind, Carlin watched Uncle Will help Aunt Emily up into the special surrey that was waiting by the walk. Two big bunches of white roses were tied to the brass lanterns, and white ribbons trailed down. Carlin stood on tiptoe as Aunt Emily waved her bouquet at the crowd. She wanted to see Uncle Will, but he must be leaning back out of view.

When Carlin and Tommy and their cousins arrived at Felicity Grove, the stable yard was already filled with buggies and surreys. They ran up the front steps into the main hall, moving quickly through the guests who had gathered there. The French doors in the parlor had been pushed open, and people were lining up to move out onto the terrace where Uncle Will and Aunt Emily and the rest of the wedding party stood shaking hands.

Amy darted out to them, but Carlin paused to stare up at the candelabra in the dining room, where all the candles were burning although it was still light outside. Tall vases of pink and red roses stood on the sideboard, and Mama's special white roses were arranged in a long silver bowl at the center of the lace-covered table. A few guests, who had already gone through the line, were selecting pieces of cake or meringue kisses from the china platters, while others sipped tea from Aunt Emily's Limoges cups with their gold-painted handles.

Carlin slipped out onto the terrace. Mama and Papa were standing on either side of Uncle Will and Aunt Emily, receiving guests, and beyond them were two stone urns filled with white and lavender petunias. Holton, the Grove house man, who looked handsome in a black suit and white tie, and James, who had come from Rosalie for the day, moved among the guests with silver trays, offering glasses of fruit punch or iced tea.

"That soft yellow is lovely on you, dear. You look just beautiful," Carlin heard an elderly relative tell Aunt Emily. Her aunt did look pretty, with pearls at her neck, and her hands and forearms covered in long white gloves. Papa beckoned, and Carlin ran over to stand beside him and Amy at the end of the receiving line. A large woman in a lavender hat with a veil bent down to speak to them. "Such pretty dresses, girls. You look just precious."

"Thank you," Carlin said and curtsied. "My mother made them. The sashes come from New Orleans." She made the same speech three times and was grateful to see that the line was finally petering out. "You can go along now and have your supper," Mama whispered.

After supper Amy, who had gone upstairs, came running back

to Carlin. "Hurry up," she said. "Mama's changing her clothes. It's time to get the rice." They hurried out to the front gallery where Carlin's mother was arranging little net bags of rice on a tray, each bag tied with a white satin ribbon.

"Here you are, girls," she said, straightening, and smiled at them. "Oh, you look so nice, and you did beautifully too, coming down the aisle, not too fast, not too slow." Carlin stood drinking in her mother's praise. "It was a perfect wedding. Has your Papa Will gone upstairs to dress yet?" she asked Amy.

"No," Amy said. "Just Mama."

"Run find him, Carlin. Will you?" Mama said, touching her arm. "Tell him to hurry. Here. Take a bag of rice."

Carlin looked in the library and out on the back gallery, then she glanced into the cloakroom. Uncle Will was standing alone at the narrow window, staring out at the big oak tree in back. His elbows rested on the high sill, and he held his chin in his hands. He was still wearing his wedding suit and his white waistcoat, but the rose in his buttonhole had drooped.

"Uncle Will," she called and hesitated. Her uncle turned. His face looked gray and strange. "Mama says it's time for you to go dress." She stopped and looked down at the collection of top hats on the day bed.

"Yes, dress and leave," Uncle Will said. "Your Aunt Emily is my wife now," he added slowly. "I'm taking her to Paris."

"I know." Carlin squeezed the bag of rice with both hands as she stood looking up at her uncle. "I know," she said again.

"I wish you could come with us, Carlie." Carlin frowned and looked down at the hats. You were supposed to be alone with your wife on your wedding journey, weren't you? You weren't supposed to take other people, not children anyway.

"This where hats go?" A fat man in a mustard-colored jacket stood in the doorway, clutching a black bowler. "Ah, Mr. McNair." He straightened and put out his hand. "My hearty congratulations to the bridegroom. Sorry I had to miss the service. Business, you know."

"Mr. Marvin." Uncle Will bowed slightly and shook the man's

hand. "Glad you could come. Do you know my niece, Mary Carlin?"

Carlin curtsied awkwardly, and turned to duck around them and leave. But she felt her uncle's hand on her shoulder and waited. The man cocked his head toward the hall with its lighted candelabra and the line of portraits beyond. "Felicity Grove is a fine plantation, Mr. McNair. You've done very well."

Carlin saw her uncle's jaw tighten. "How about some punch," he said. "Some cake maybe, or a sandwich." He kept his hand on Carlin's shoulder.

"Being a planter is far better than being an architect nowadays," the man went on. "More money, more security."

Carlin felt her uncle's hot fingers press into her shoulder, and she felt she must say something. "Please." The word sounded squeaky. She raised the bag. "It's time for the rice."

"Ah. Excuse me." The man bowed to Uncle Will. "You have my very best wishes for the future. You've made an excellent marriage." He turned and left the room.

Uncle Will dropped his hand, and Carlin looked up at him, wanting to comfort him somehow. But Uncle Will stood silent, staring at the empty doorway. "Go tell your aunt I'll be ready in a minute. All right?" He moved to the door, then turned back. "Thanks for staying with me, Carlie," he said and left. Carlin stared after him a moment, then hurried out into the hall, still clutching the bag of rice.

※

The Vicksburg kin, who had stayed at Rosalie for the wedding, had left. Only Grandfather was staying until Saturday. His presence always brought a heavy formality to Rosalie, Carlin thought. James, the house man, had to wear his black suit coat all day and set the table with the good silver, even for breakfast. Evening prayers were much longer because Grandfather not only read from the Bible, but talked about each of his selections, while the nap of the rug pressed into Carlin's knees, and she ached to stand and run. Aunt Georgia was so busy in the kitchen she had no time to talk.

"Mary Carlin," Grandfather said one morning. "I want you to come into the library with me." Carlin looked up. Grandfather's stern blue gaze seemed to envelop her, making her feel scared and small. Last year when he had asked her to recite two Bible passages, she had stumbled and couldn't get them right. But this year she was more prepared, she told herself, as she followed him into the library and watched him seat himself in Papa's chair.

"Now stand there, child," he said, pointing to the space in front of him, "and say your Beatitudes."

Carlin swallowed and stepped into the space. She lifted her head and began. "Good," Grandfather said when she had finished. "At least you've learned that, Mary Carlin." He turned to the desk. "This is for you," he said, and handed her a small black book. Carlin reached for it eagerly, thinking perhaps it was a book of poems or a play. But it was only a Bible, of course.

"Thank you very much, Grandfather," she said. "I'm glad to have my own Bible. I'll read it often." It was scary how easily the polite lies came. Carlin stared at her grandfather, who was looking down at some papers on the desk. Did he believe her? Did he know her at all?

※

Carlin and Feely were kneeling in a patch of dry dirt near the kitchen courtyard. They had poked several small holes in the ground, and short broomstraws were sticking out of two of them. Feely lifted one straw to her mouth, spat on the end, and rolled it a moment until her saliva formed a ball. Then she poked it back in the hole, stirring the straw slowly as she whispered, "Doodle bug, doodle bug, come out of your hole. Your house is on fire and your chillun'll burn." She waited and then lifted the straw, but it was bare. "Ain't no doodles today," she told Carlin and shook her head. "Sayin' that rhyme always make me kinda sad anyway." She sat back on her heels and looked at Carlin. "Know what I mean?"

"I know." Carlin nodded. "Besides, hunting for doodles seems sort of dumb after all the excitement of the wedding." She sighed and looked around her. "It feels like now there's nothing left to look foward to."

"Dat's it. Dat's de feelin." Feely tipped her head back.

Carlin followed her gaze to a hawk circling slowly in the late afternoon sky. "I wonder where Uncle Will is in Paris now?" Carlin said. "I wonder what they're doing?"

"Don't he write no letters?" Feely asked.

"Yes, but they take a long time to get here from France. Papa says it's too early to hear anything yet."

There was a sound of running footsteps, and Tommy and Hamlet came rushing toward them across the courtyard. "A man's come," Tommy announced, panting. "He went in the kitchen house to talk to Aunt Georgia."

"I seen him from the field," Hamlet said. "Seen him comin' down the drive, way off like a little bug. No horse, nor nothin'. See?" He pointed. "There he come. Now."

Carlin stared as a short man in baggy pants and a dark jacket stepped from the kitchen house and stood glancing around the courtyard. The lining of his coat hung down below the pocket, and he held a broken derby hat in one hand, then put it on his head, half-covering the long gray hair that rested on his collar.

"He's a peddler," Carlin whispered. "See his pack?" She pointed to the black shape that rose behind his shoulders. "I bet he wants to stay the night and sell his things in the morning."

The man waved and crossed the courtyard to where they were playing.

"You must be hunting doodle bugs," he said, looking down at the holes. Carlin nodded. "I just got here. Your cook told me to wait outside for your father. I want to ask him if I can stay the night and show my wares tomorrow."

Carlin got to her feet and brushed the dirt from her knees. "You must be tired walking." The man smiled at her, and the tanned creases on either side of his mouth deepened. He leaned to one side and pulled a strap from his shoulder so that the pack hung loosely. "Why don't you sit down there on the bench," she said.

"Thank you kindly, little lady. I'd like to sit, but I'm going to get me a dipper of water first." He lowered the pack to the brick surface of the courtyard and walked over to the well.

"Listen," Carlin whispered to Feely and the boys. "Remember those blazes we saw down by the road, the ones the peddlers make? Let's ask him what they mean. Surely he'll know."

"He just better not steal nothin'," Feely warned. "One o' them peddlers stole a big chicken last year what Gran was fixin' to cook."

"I think this man's different," Carlin said. "He has a nice smile."

They watched the peddler mop his chin then put both hands to his back and stretch. He walked over to them and settled on the bench. "Ah. Sitting feels good," he said. He leaned back and looked up into the chinaberry tree.

Carlin knelt down in front of him. "We want to know about the blazes," she said. Feely leaned in close beside her and the boys stooped down. "The cut places on the trees. Could you please tell us what they mean?"

The peddler bent forward, putting his tanned hands on his knees. "Well, there's lots of kinds of blazes," he began. He took off the derby, put it down beside him, and pushed back his gray hair. "I followed the half-moon blaze here. It means a small plantation. Nothing big or rich, but worth stopping. It tells you you'll get a good supper—molasses and biscuits maybe—and a real bed, not a hay loft, and it says the dogs won't bite."

"You can tell all that from a half-moon sign? That's amazing, isn't it, Feely?" Feely nodded at Carlin.

"Feely," the peddler repeated. "I don't think I've ever heard that name before."

"It's short for Ophelia," Carlin told him. "Her twin brother's Hamlet." She pointed to Hamlet sitting on the ground beside Tommy in the semicircle they had made around the peddler. "My mother named them," Carlin said. "She names lots of plantation babies, mostly from Shakespeare, but Greek and Roman names too. Their cousin's Plato."

"But we call him Toe," Feely put in. She looked at Carlin and they giggled.

"My name is Mary Carlin," Carlin announced. "Carlin's my mother's maiden name, and everybody calls me that. My brother's Thomas Junior, but we call him Tommy."

"Well, well," the peddler said and smiled. "My name's Mr. Mishkin, Isaac Mishkin."

"Mishkin." Carlin whispered the foreign-sounding name to herself, as she studied the peddler. She was staring, she realized, and looked down. "Do you like being a peddler?" she asked.

"Oh, yes," Mr. Mishkin said. "But business isn't so good as it was once, especially here in Warrington County. Cotton's gotten risky, you know. A lot of small plantations around here have failed."

"Failed? How?" Carlin clenched one fist and leaned forward.

"Well, there's a lot of competition, what with the foreign cotton. Yes," he hesitated. "Cotton's a difficult crop right now." The peddler took a pipe from his pocket, and a pouch like Papa's. Did he think Rosalie might fail, Carlin wondered. Did the half-moon sign say a small plantation that might fail? She watched him pack the tobacco into the bowl.

"I'll get a light," Tommy said, springing up. He disappeared into the kitchen house, then dashed back across the courtyard with a burning twig from the stove.

"Thank you kindly, sir," the peddler said and lighted his pipe. "I was at Felicity Grove last night," he told them as he got the bowl of his pipe glowing, then let out a stream of sweet-smelling smoke. "Just three miles from here. That's a fine prosperous plantation."

"Did you see our cousins?" Tommy asked. "Did Hugh buy anything?"

"Is Hugh the boy that's about your size?" Tommy nodded. "Seems to me he bought a pocket knife, if I remember correctly."

"Have they heard from our uncle?" Carlin broke in. "Or from their mother, I mean?"

"Oh it's your uncle who married the widow there, isn't it?" Carlin gripped her knees.

She did not want the peddler to say that Uncle Will had been smart to marry a rich widow. If he did, she would just get up and leave, she decided.

Mr. Mishkin breathed out another fragrant stream of smoke. "A wedding's a wonderful thing," he said. "Gives you memories for years to come."

Carlin looked down at the peddler's dusty boots. He must have come a long way. "Do you ever go to Memphis?" she asked.

"Oh, yes," the peddler said. "Memphis is a lively city."

"Tell us about it," Carlin asked. "Does it have trolleys? Does it have any department stores?" She leaned closer to Feely and put one arm around her waist. The blue and red plaid dress Feely was wearing had been Carlin's two years ago when the colors were still bright. Feely moved Carlin's arm, tucking it under hers, and clasped her hand. Aunt Lucy said that next year when Carlin was eleven, she must end her friendships with her colored playmates. But she wasn't going to, Carlin thought, and tightened her fingers on Feely's. Aunt Lucy could never make her do that.

The peddler was telling about the crowds, and Carlin could almost see herself and Feely mixing with them on the Memphis sidewalks. They would jump on a trolley car together and hear the conductor pull the bell. Or would they be together then? Was Aunt Lucy right?

"Have you ever been to Paris?" she asked, distracting herself.

"No, I never got there," the peddler said. He sucked at his pipe a moment making the bowl glow more brightly. "But I walked all the way across Europe. I come from Odessa, you see."

"Odessa," Carlin repeated. "Where's that?"

"In Russia," the peddler said. "A long way off. A beautiful city on the Black Sea, with parks and birds and cafés looking out on the water."

"I'd like to see it," Carlin said. "When I grow up, I'm going to travel." Carlin gazed out across the cotton field, which was shining in the evening light. "Someday I'm going to see the Black Sea."

"Me too," Feely said. "I wants to see that Black Sea too." Carlin felt a familiar twist in her stomach, and she stared down at the bricks. She might really travel someday, but Feely never would, probably.

᠀᠐

Carlin and Tommy went down to the kitchen courtyard early the next morning to watch the peddler spread out his goods. "This knife's broken," Tommy said, opening a small pearl-handled pocket knife that the peddler had placed beside a tortoise-shell comb.

"Yes, but the case is good," the peddler said. "Sometimes a gentleman'll buy a broken pocket knife when he's got a good knife and needs a new case to put it in." He nodded to himself.

Carlin watched as he brought out a collection of bracelets, some rings set with pieces of blue and red glass, and a bunch of palmetto fans, inscribed, "Collins Funeral Home, Jackson, Miss." He draped lengths of ribbon and slightly soiled lace across the end of the table and arranged two piles of little gold pins and some spools of colored thread beside them.

"Oh, Lordy. How I wish I could buy me that," Aunt Ceny said, pushing close to Carlin. Her freckled face twisted into a look of longing, as she stroked a piece of pink ribbon. "Make my Sunday dress real pretty."

Feely let out a giggle from the other side of the table where she and Tommy were bending over something. Carlin looked up, and Feely pointed to a blond hair piece nestled near the necklaces. She held it to her head, covering one of her short black braids, and Carlin laughed.

"Mama gave us each five pennies," Carlin reported to Feely. The fact seemed both natural and embarrassing. She and Tommy could each buy something, but Feely and Hamlet could not, for neither Aunt Georgia, their grandmother, nor Violet, their mother, had pennies to give away to children for foolish presents. Yet by tomorrow, they would all four be trying on or playing with whatever Carlin and Tommy had bought. Carlin picked up a small pair of scissors. She opened them, then tried to squeeze the handles back together, but they were stiff. She put them down and chose a necklace instead with six blue beads in front.

"Mama," she said, holding the necklace up to her mother who stood watching on the back gallery. "Mama, look what I bought."

Her mother was leaning against the balustrade in a white lawn dress with a lavender sash. "What do you think, Mama?" Carlin asked and pulled the necklace over her head, settling the beads on the white yoke at the front of her dress. The catch was broken, she noticed, and the ends of the necklace were tied together with a black thread. She slid the broken section around to the back, hoping to hide it under her braids.

"Do you like it, Mama?"

Carlin waited a moment, then raised her hand to the necklace again. She felt an ache in her chest. If only Mama would look down.

Her mother's eyes seemed to sweep over her slowly. "Oh, Carlin. The clasp on that thing's broken," she said. Carlin bit her lip, feeling tears start, but she lifted her eyes to her mother's face. She was gazing out across the cotton field. Was she thinking about her sister, far away in Paris, Carlin wondered, or about how remote and poor Rosalie was with this peddler and his broken wares? Her mother looked down, as if she had seen Carlin's thoughts. "Wait a minute, dear," she said and stepped back. "I think the clasp on my old bead necklace would fit that. Let's go look in my jewelry box."

Carlin stared, startled at her mother's change. Then she twirled around and followed her into the hall.

⚜

Picking began in the last week of August, for the cotton was finally ready. Men walked up the paths to the fields in the pre-dawn light. Women left their wash tubs and their vegetable gardens, strapped their babies to their backs and followed. Feely and Hamlet had no time to play with Carlin and Tommy, for they were in the field picking with their mother. Aunt Ceny put on her battered sun hat and went out to help. James appeared in overalls, looking unfamiliar without his suit coat, and went off to pick. The big house seemed strangely empty to Carlin. She and Tommy played with some Confederate money they had found in an old trunk in the attic, but the game grew dull.

Early one afternoon when Carlin heard the big bell ringing in the courtyard for work to begin again, she held a whispered conference with Tommy in the hall, then went to the doorway of her mother's sewing room and stood a moment looking in. "Mama, please. Could Tommy and me—Tommy and I, I mean—go picking this afternoon? We won't stay long. Please."

Her mother stopped pedaling her sewing machine and looked up at Carlin. "All right," she said. "It might be good for you two to see what it's really like. You ought to know what hard work picking is. Go find the twins. Violet'll put you to work."

Carlin and Tommy flew down the stairs, snatched their straw hats from the hooks in the back hall, and ran across the courtyard, up the path past the barn, to the north field. They stood a moment squinting in the sun as they searched for Feely and Hamlet. The long rows were crowded with people bent over picking.

"There they are," Tommy said. "There's Hamlet." He pointed to Hamlet's fringed hat, and Carlin recognized Violet further on with Feely. Tommy ran down the row, moving around several bent figures to reach Hamlet. But Carlin stood a moment longer taking in the scene. There were "stoopers" or "crawlers," she knew, and Violet was a stooper—also Feely, it looked like. The two black mules stood waiting beside the wagon, switching their tails and swinging their heads back and forth to swish off the flies. She saw Mr. Rayley, the overseer, in the wagon throwing a gray sack down to a latecomer. Her eyes traveled along the rows, the bent backs, the sweaty brown arms and shoulders, the faded straps of overalls. There must be eighty pickers, maybe more. She ran up the row to the place where Violet and Feely were picking. "Hey," she called.

Feely straightened and took in Carlin, standing in the row with her hat on. "What you doin' here?" she demanded.

"I came to help." Carlin looked down at the cotton plant beside her, feeling uncertain suddenly.

"We don' need no help from you, Carlin," Feely said. "You don't know nothin' about pickin'." Carlin caught her breath and looked around her. Had the other pickers heard? Feely turned and stepped past her mother, then stooped down beside a plant a yard or so beyond. Carlin stared. What had she done? Why was Feely so mad? She looked at Violet, who touched her shoulder and said,

"Now what you do is just pull this." She pointed to a soft spray of cotton in an open boll. "Stuff it in my sack as quick as you can and pull some more. See?" Carlin nodded, but she felt singed by Feely's anger, and she stood staring up the row, where Feely was picking with her back to Carlin. "When we finishes this plant," Violet said, "we moves to the next. Quick. Being quick's important when you're pickin'." Feely thought she was intruding, Carlin realized. Violet was being kind to Carlin, but maybe she felt the way Feely did too.

Carlin reached for the silky white clump, but it clung to the hard shell of the open boll and then to her fingers, so that she had to scrape it off before she added it to Violet's sack. Feely was mad because she thought Carlin had come to play at picking when she had to do it all day long, whether she wanted to or not. And yet Papa was the planter, the owner of Rosalie, and Feely didn't have a papa, and none of that was new. Carlin had been friends with Feely ever since she could remember.

"Come on you, Carlin," Violet said, leaning down. "If you goin' pick, you gotta hurry." Carlin worked on the plant beside her, trying to catch Violet's rhythm—reach and pick, stuff in the sack. Reach and pick, stuff in the sack. Would Feely ever play with her again? Brambly weeds were mixed with the cotton plants. She cut her hand and noticed a long bloody scratch on Violet's arm. Maybe if she lent Feely her doll, Joan. She tried to hurry, but Violet was almost three plants ahead and Feely was beyond her. Carlin kept her eyes on the plant, picking as fast as she could. It was because they were being watched, Carlin decided. If they could keep their friendship secret, it could go on. The sun was hot on her back and her straw hat felt sweaty on her head. She picked the plant clean and moved on. If Feely saw that she was picking hard, not playing around, but serious, maybe she would forgive her and come back to this part of the row. She yearned to straighten and look up at the sky. She kept on picking, but Feely did not come.

Tommy and Hamlet were in the next row now. "It's good when they goes to pour it all into the wagon at the end," Hamlet was saying, "and it go off to the gin. That wagon hold a whole bale, about. Them bales is real heavy when they git all pressed down and strapped with them metal things." Carlin straightened partway and glanced at the wagon, but it was Feely she was thinking of. She turned to look for her, but Feely was way up the long row, her back to Carlin still.

"You there, Carlin," Aunt Ceny called down their row. "You and your brother, you gotta go home and get cleaned up for supper."

"We want to see the cotton loaded into the wagon," Tommy shouted, but Carlin straightened and pushed her hat into place. Never mind about the wagon. She was glad to stop.

Carlin was too tired to talk at the dinner table that night, and she felt she might fall over as she knelt in her place during evening prayers. Tommy went back to the north field the next afternoon, but Carlin went to her room to read. She wanted to be in the hot field with the others, but Feely's scorn was scary, and she did not go the next day either. When Papa came up to say good night that evening, Carlin asked, "What's it like in the early morning when the picking starts, Papa?"

"You want to come see, little one? I'll take you with me tomorrow if you like." He paused and she could feel him studying her in her high four-poster bed, her white nightgown buttoned at her neck. "We'll go to the north field, darlin'. Your friends Feely and Hamlet'll be picking in the pond field tomorrow."

"Oh good, Papa. Then I'll come."

"You'll have to get up real early."

Carlin nodded and hugged her knees. "I will."

⁂

The quiet stable yard seemed eerie to Carlin as she watched her father guide Graylie to the mounting block in the bluish light. Beyond them the row of dewy locust trees was shrouded in a white mist. When Papa lifted her up onto the big plantation saddle, she tipped her head back to look at the sky. "The stars are all gone."

"Time to start picking then," her father said. He swung himself up behind her and took the reins. Carlin held onto the pommel with both hands as they started up the bumpy path to the north field.

"Someday I won't have to ride on your saddle," Carlin said. "Mama says she's going to teach me how to really ride soon."

"You'll be a good rider, darlin', and maybe one of these days when I sell an extra bale of cotton, I'll buy you a pony."

"Oh, Papa." Carlin looked back at her father, but he had turned to nod at one of the men walking along the path. When, she wanted to ask. When?

"Morning, Joseph." The men stood back to let them pass.

"Morning, sir. Morning, miss." They wore faded overalls and battered straw hats. Some carried water jugs, cornbread wrapped in a cloth, and Carlin could see a baked sweet potato sticking out of the back pocket of one of the men's pants.

"Morning, Walker," Papa said. "Thaddeus." Papa knew all the men's names, and most of the women as well.

Mr. Rayley had parked the mule wagon at the side of the field. Carlin could see the tangle of long gray sacks inside. "Got enough?" Papa asked. Mr. Rayley nodded, but did not speak. He was not one for conversation, Papa said. Her father reined Graylie in, and he and Carlin watched as two men came up. Each chose a sack, then a row, and started down between the lines of plants.

Men and women began to crowd around the wagon now. Some took sacks, others had their own. They fixed them over their shoulders or tied them to their belts. A dozen pickers were already strung out in the field. The two men Papa had greeted first were well ahead of the others, bent figures far up the row. Feely's older sister had arrived with her new baby strapped over her breasts in a blanket, and behind her Ella Mae was carrying her youngest on her back. Carlin saw Toe and Macbeth start down the row behind their mother. She turned her head, hoping Toe would not notice her sitting up high in front of her father.

"There's Aunt Looley." Papa nodded to a squat little woman with wiry white hair pushing out from under her dark bandanna, who limped up to the wagon and greeted Mr. Rayley. "She's about the fastest picker of all. Watch." She held a three-legged stool under one arm as she bent over to choose her sack.

"Mornin', Mister McNair," she said, looking up at Papa.

"Morning, Aunt Looley. I hear you picked a lot of cotton yes- terday. It was a hundred and two out here by midday, they say."

"It was warm all right, Mister McNair. That's the truth. Be warm today too, probably. But when that cotton's ready, we gotta pick it." She stared at Carlin a moment. "Up early this mornin', ain't ya, Miss Carlin? You and your brother gonna come back and help us pick again this afternoon?"

Carlin nodded, surprised that the old woman had noticed their presence. But then they were Mr. McNair's children, after all. Aunt Looley was a neighbor of Feely's and had once yelled at them for upsetting her hens. "She's remarkable," Papa said, moving Graylie along the row. "She argued with Mr. Rayley about how much her sack weighed last week and she won."

Carlin looked back at the old woman, who was surveying the rows near her. She started toward one in her heavy, uneven walk, then stopped and claimed the next one instead. She settled herself on her low stool and began on the first plant. Her fingers were quick and certain, pulling out the fluff, stuffing it into the sack, reaching out and back, out and back in a steady rhythm. She fin- ished the plant, pulled her stool forward, and sat again. "She's so fast," Carlin whispered.

"Experience," her father said. "Aunt Looley's been picking for fifty years, maybe fifty-five."

Carlin looked out at the long field. All the work of the year led up to picking time—the spring plowing and planting, and the long hot weeks of summer hoeing. Everything that had been done came together for better or worse at picking time. The field was filled with bent figures now, and at the far side she could see clumps of goldenrod, low yellow clouds in the early morning light.

"Wouldn't some of the men rather work in the gin, Papa?" she asked as her father guided Graylie around the fence at the end.

"Some would," Papa said. "But we can only use four men there, plus the foreman, of course. And it's dangerous work. Every gin has accidents."

Carlin looked up the dirt road leading toward the high wooden building beyond the pine trees, and back at the scale with its long steelyard weighing arm, its marking lines, and the black hook at the end. At the Grove they had two scales and three mule wagons, Carlin thought, and their gin was bigger and never broke down.

"I know what a sucker man is, Papa," she said.

Her father smiled. "What is a sucker man?" he asked.

"He's the one at the gin that works that big vacuum pipe that reaches down over the wagon and sucks the cotton up."

"That's right, darlin'. That's just what he does."

"I told Amy we made lots of good middling cotton, but she said, no, we only make low middling at Rosalie."

"Well, your cousin's pretty much right for the present," her father said. "But we got some good middling cotton a couple of years ago, and God willing, we'll have some more."

Carlin glanced toward the quarters where a light singing sound was rising. It couldn't be more than five in the morning, but the children, who had been left behind, were playing games now before the fierce heat of the late morning enveloped the whole plantation.

> *Lipto, Lipto join the ring,*
> *Lipto, Lipto dance and sing.*

That was Dodie's voice, Carlin thought. She imagined the thin little boy, standing in the circle with his bird-like arms outspread, as the others danced around him. The high young voices continued, an incongruous sound, rising from the cabins at the far side of the field.

> *Dance and sing, laugh and play,*
> *For this is now a holerday.*

Carlin glanced back at the stooping figures in the row beyond her. A holiday? In an hour their backs would be aching, burned in the sun, their arms scratched, their hands roughened, and their minds dazed with the monotony of it all. Reach, peel, and stuff, she thought. Reach, peel, and stuff. Hour after hour. She had done it for barely three hours on Monday, but they would do it all day long, this week, next week, and the week after. In another year, surely in two, Dodie would be behind his father, working his own way down the row.

"Picking's hard work, isn't it, Papa?"

"It's very hard work, darlin', and the price's gone down in Liverpool. New York too." He sighed. "It's not easy to make money from cotton anymore."

"What's Liverpool, Papa?"

"It's a big city in England where they set the price on cotton from all over the world—Egypt, China, and other places. When America buys cheap foreign cotton, it brings the price of our own cotton down." Carlin nodded. If the foreign cotton was bad, why couldn't America just stop buying it? "But with God's help, we'll have a better crop this year," Papa said.

He slapped the reins and Graylie moved on. A flock of black birds rose from a pile of manure as they approached and fluttered up into a red bud tree. The fields seemed full of life now—the pickers, the birds, the insects droning, and the mules standing by the wagon, switching their heavy tails. Ella Mae's baby whined and was hushed.

"I'll give you a little view of the whole thing," her father said and turned Graylie toward the pine ridge.

Carlin heard the weariness in her Papa's voice and looked down. They had reached the pine ridge, and he reined in Graylie and sat gazing out. The long north field stretched to the horizon. The pickers looked tiny now, bent over, moving along the rows. She turned to look back at the big white house with its galleries and the kitchen house behind, a trail of smoke rising from its chimney. She could see the barn with its lightning rod, the stable, the chicken house, the necessary, the tool houses and sheds, the gin, and, to the left, the quarters with its double line of cabins and the wide pounded path in between. A rooster crowed far off. That was Aunt Ceny's Gabriel, probably.

She felt her father's sleeve brush against her arm and heard him sigh. "I would give anything to keep this," he said softly. "To make Rosalie go on. God knows that." But Rosalie is going on, Carlin wanted to protest. She thought about the way the front gallery sagged and needed painting. She would never have a pony, probably, but Papa would not leave Rosalie. He had promised that.

"Papa," she started, and paused. Her father had been born here, she remembered. He had lived at Rosalie all his life. "Papa," she began again, not knowing what she wanted to say.

Her father slapped the reins and Graylie moved forward. "We've got to get you back, darlin'," he said. "You need your breakfast, and I've got to get to work."

※

Carlin was excited when Mama announced that she was going to teach her to ride. Carlin sat high up on Johnny Boy, surveying the riding ring and the line of locust trees beyond. She glanced down at her mother in her long riding skirt, her high-buttoned blouse, and her jaunty straw hat with its feather, startled at how elegant her mother looked, like a woman in a magazine.

"All right," Mama said. "Giddyap." She held a lead rope in one hand, and as Johnny Boy began to trot, she ran along beside him. "Up, down, up, down," she called out. "Don't touch the saddle." Mama was panting, but she continued to run. "That's the way. Good. Good." They continued around the ring, then Mama pulled Johnny to a stop and leaned against the fence, breathing hard.

Carlin tipped her head back. The heavy heat had lifted, and the air seemed to hold a new freshness. A swallow flew past, swooping down to the pecan trees at the side of the meadow, their leaves turning a soft orange.

"Belle." It was Papa's voice. Carlin twisted in the saddle and saw Papa riding up to them on Graylie. He stopped beside the weathered fence. "Just got the mail," he called out. "A letter from Paris. It's good news." Mama led Carlin and Johnny Boy closer, so that the two horses stood side by side with the fence between them.

"Listen to this." Papa held up several thin sheets of paper with small slanted writing in black ink. "My dear brother and sister, I have wonderful news to report." Papa paused and glanced across at Carlin, as though uncertain whether he should continue when she was listening, but he went on.

"All at once on the second day of our wedding journey I became better. So much better that it was like a miracle. You remember how sudden these changes of mine can be. Emily is kinder and more beautiful than ever, and I am deeply in love with my dear wife. I sleep well and am eating heartily again, enjoying the marvelous French cuisine in all its wonderful variety. But best of all, I am alive once more, in love and blissfully happy. So, my dear brother and my dear Belle, you must not worry about me anymore. You were so wise and right to urge me to go through with this marriage. It is the happiest decision of my life. On Tuesday, we drove to Versailles, and, dear Tom, you will be glad to hear that I engaged a French peasant there in a long discussion about crop rotation and learned much of French farm methods."

Papa looked up from the letter and laughed. "Oh, Lord," he said. "Now he's going to want to start growing grapes at the Grove, or truffles." He laughed again and glanced back at the letter, then up at Carlin. "You take Johnny back to the stable now, darlin'."

Carlin walked Johnny Boy around the manure pile and into the sudden dimness of the stable as her father continued to read Uncle Will's letter. Why wouldn't Papa let her stay? What was in the rest of the letter? What did Uncle Will mean by a change that was like a miracle?

When Carlin came out of the stable, her father was holding out a card. "It's a postcard from Paris for you," he said. "It came with your uncle's letter."

"For me?" Carlin reached for the card. She read the message in the thin, black writing silently, then aloud. "We are having a lovely time in Paris. I will have lots to tell you when I return. Keep reading, and write in your diary everyday. Hug Tom for me and give Evie a kiss. Your fond uncle, Will."

"That's nice," Mama said. "Let's see the picture on the other side." Carlin turned it over. "Oh, look," her mother said. "It's Artemis. The goddess of the hunt." Carlin stared at the black and white photograph. The goddess wore a short loose dress, belted at the waist, and she stood quietly, holding her bow, a deer at her side. Her hair was wound in a knot at the back and held with a wide band. She was looking downward as if following some private thought, and her face was serene. The printed writing on the other side said that the statue was in the Louvre, that big Paris museum that Uncle Will had talked about.

Carlin went up to her room and took her treasure box from the back of her closet. Inside was her peacock feather, the French quill pen that Uncle Will had given her, an empty blue perfume bottle of Mama's, and an almost perfect robin's egg. She fitted the postcard on the top, closed the box, and pushed it back into its place. Had Uncle Will sent Amy a postcard, she wondered?

That afternoon, she closed the door to her room, propped the postcard against the mirror, and unbraided her hair. Gathering it loosely with one hand, she studied herself. If she could wear it in a knot like that, she thought, and if she could get a dress with a belt. . . . Would Uncle Will like her that way? Was that why he had sent her the picture of Artemis?

※

Carlin came down to the kitchen courtyard the next morning and saw Tommy and Owen, Mr. Rayley's son, stooped over Tommy's stamp collection. Owen was Carlin's age and she would have liked to have played with him herself, she thought, but he was shy and seldom came to the big house, and then just to play with Tommy. Sometimes Carlin could feel him watching her with his dark, serious eyes, but he said little.

"Hey." She stood looking down at the two heads, Tommy's springy brown hair, Owen's smooth black crown. Tommy was sorting a small pile of foreign stamps that he had torn from various envelopes that Papa had given him, mostly French stamps from Uncle Will's letters. He had mounted some of the stamps on pieces of white paper. Carlin saw a pink English stamp she knew Grandfather had given him. Her eye lit on a triangular piece of paper with a familiar French stamp. It was her postcard. For a terrible moment she thought Tommy had found her treasure box, then she remembered she had left the postcard on the schoolroom table overnight and had only retrieved it this morning, barely glancing at it, as she stuffed it into her pocket. She pulled it out and stared down at it. The top was bent and the whole corner had been snipped away.

"You cut my postcard," Carlin shouted and turned it over. The goddess's face was unharmed, but part of the dark knot of her hair had been cut off so that she had lost part of her head. "You cut Artemis. You cut her . . . you. . . ." Carlin clenched her fists as she stood glaring down at her brother. "You . . . you. . . ." Words churned in her mind. Thief, robber, criminal.

"I only wanted it for my stamp collection," Tommy began. "I don't have any French postcard stamps. The others are all for letters." Tommy gazed up at her. "I didn't hurt the picture."

"Yes, you did. You did!" Carlin looked back at the girl on the postcard, her friend. "You cut into her head." She could feel Owen's hot eyes boring into her. "I hate you," Carlin shouted at her brother. She clutched the postcard and jammed it back into her pocket, feeling her face grow hot. The pile of stamps seemed to spin in a whirl of color. "You and your stupid stamps!" Owen had had nothing to do with the theft, probably, yet his presence felt insulting. Carlin jerked her head forward and spat, meaning to hit Tommy, but the string of saliva flew outward and caught on Owen's shoulder. She saw him reach up to brush it off, then his staring eyes settled on her again.

A tumult of crying twisted inside her. She turned and rushed up the stairs to the back gallery and into the front hall just as Evie came whining out of the dining room, dragging her doll. Carlin stopped for a moment and stared. She was acting like Evie, she thought, and yet a roaring had begun within her that she couldn't stop. She rushed toward the library, startled by the angry choked noises rising from her.

"Carlin, what's the matter?" Her mother came to the library door, holding her violin. "What's happened?"

"Tommy cut my postcard," Carlin wailed. "He. . . ." She stood a moment, clutching the edge of the marble-topped table in the center of the hall. "The postcard Uncle Will sent me."

"Well, for goodness sakes. That's not the end of the world." Aunt Ceny appeared from the back gallery, twisting a dish towel. She caught Evie by the shoulder and held her as she stood staring at Carlin.

"I didn't mean to hurt the picture," Tommy shouted from the doorway of the back gallery where he and Owen were standing. "I just wanted the stamp."

Carlin turned to the staircase. Her face was burning, and she could feel her jaws shake. "It was my picture," she shouted. "Uncle Will sent it to me. Me!" She clenched her hands into fists as she mounted the staircase, then turned. Her mother was staring up at her, her hands clasped. Aunt Ceny was behind her, holding Evie's shoulder, and the boys were watching from the doorway. Even Sam, who had been sleeping on the floor beside the grandfather clock, had raised his furry head to look up at her. They were all waiting for her action. She turned and pounded the wall beside her with one fist, then the other. Her hand met the framed engraving of the Roman coliseum that hung above the carpeted stairs, and she hit it with her fist once, twice. She raised her arm and stared, amazed at the spiderweb of cracks that she had created in the glass.

"Carlin," her mother cried out, hurrying up the stairs. "Stop that. Stop."

"You don't understand," Carlin shouted. "You don't understand." She turned and rushed up the remaining steps, down the hall to her room, and flung the door shut.

"Carlin." Mama opened Carlin's door and stood there stern-faced. "Let me see your hands." Carlin held them out, but neither was hurt. She dropped them and leaned against the bedpost, feeling her teeth chatter. "Carlin, you must learn to control yourself. You cannot act like that. You've been very bad. I want you to come to the library before dinner. Your father will talk with you."

"Yes, Mama," Carlin said. Her voice was muffled by the loud sound of her breathing.

"Stay here and compose yourself," Mama said. "Then come down to the library as soon as you hear your father." Her mother turned and left the room.

Carlin moved to the mirror above her washstand and stared. Her face was blotched from crying, her nose red, her eyes swollen. Who was that stranger, she wondered? What had she done? She thought suddenly of Owen, watching from the doorway, and let out a moan as she covered her face with her hands. Owen had seen it all.

✼

The library door was open, and Carlin could hear her parents talking within. "Of course Tommy must be reprimanded for taking the stamp, but with Carlin it's partly Will's influence, Thomas," her mother was saying. "There's an intensity about her friendship with him, you know."

"Mama," Carlin said, coming into the room. "It's not Uncle Will's fault. It's. . . ."

"Come sit down, Carlin," her father said, pointing to a place on the horsehair sofa. "You mustn't listen to conversations you're not a part of." Carlin took her place on the sofa.

"We all have moments of anger," her father began. "But you allowed your anger to take over this morning. You did something very destructive, and you scared your brother and sister, as well as the servants."

"I know," Carlin said and looked down at her limp hands lying in her lap.

"We all have feelings we don't understand," her father continued. "But we have a responsibility to the people around us, the people we love, to try to control our anger."

"I know, Papa." Carlin felt her jaws shake. "I want to be good. I want to. . . ." She was crying, and her voice shook too much to finish.

"If you ask for God's help, daughter, He will give it." Papa bowed his head a moment, then looked up at her again. "You must believe that your mother and father love you and want to help you."

Carlin looked down. Her tears were making dark splotches on her blue skirt. She raised her hand to mop her nose, remembered her handkerchief, and pulled it from her pocket. There would be a punishment now, and it would be much harder than just cleaning up the playroom as she and Tommy had to do last summer when they had crawled up on the roof of the toolshed and had eaten almost half the bananas spread out there to dry.

Papa pulled his glasses from his breast pocket and opened the Bible on the desk. "I want you to memorize chapters three, four, and five of Ecclesiastes. You will start by writing out all twenty-two verses of chapter three and tomorrow night you will recite them to me without a mistake. Chapter four will be for the next night, then chapter five. Those verses will help you and they will be with you for the rest of your life."

"Yes, Papa." Carlin said. Three whole chapters, she thought, and looked down. She would stay in her room and learn them until she could recite all of them perfectly, she resolved, and maybe as she learned them she would begin to really believe in God the way Papa did. Then she would be able to press down that awful anger when it rose up, so that it would never, ever come back again.

❧

"Carlie?" Tommy opened Carlin's door.

"What?" Carlin asked, looking up at him from the book she was reading in bed.

"The new teacher's come."

"What? But she wasn't supposed to come till day after tomorrow. Did you see her? What does she look like?"

"I only saw the buggy," Tommy said. "But it's her. I heard Mama talking to her in the hall." Tommy gripped the bedpost and pulled himself up on the bottom of the bed. "What if we don't like her, Carlie? What'll we do?"

"I don't know. Tell Mama, I guess." Carlin looked toward the window. "Mrs. Coates wasn't bad, really," she said, thinking of their last teacher. "She was just so boring. I wish we could go away to school like Ted. Amy's going next year, maybe. But Papa hasn't got enough money for that."

"I wish we didn't have to have lessons at all." Tommy pushed his legs out straight. "It's easy for you. You always read everything. But I have to puzzle and. . . ." He stopped.

Carlin looked up at the pale folds in the canopy above. Tommy's slowness in reading made her feel guilty about her easy access to the stories and novels she loved. "Her name is Miss

Betts," she said. "Mama told me. Bets, bats, buts. It sounds as though she's fat and fussy." She paused. "But Mama said she wanted to get somebody young, who'll teach us a whole lot." Carlin looked toward the window. "Mama thinks we're not getting as good schooling as she and Aunt Emily did."

"We're learning other things," Tommy said.

There were sounds in the hallway. Mama was talking, showing the teacher her room across the hall. Carlin put one finger to her mouth and looked at Tommy. Someone had lit the big lamp in the hall, and an orange line had appeared under the door. They heard James bring up a trunk. There was more talk, then a door closed. They waited. They shouldn't be in here talking together, Carlin thought, but nobody would know.

There was a soft knock on the door. Carlin frowned at Tommy and sat rigid in the bed as the door opened.

"Hello, I'm Mollie Betts." A short young woman stood in the lighted doorway. Little tendrils of blond hair framed her face, and a locket that hung down over her high-necked shirtwaist gleamed in the light as she stood smiling in at them. "I heard you talking, and I thought I'd just come in and introduce myself. Did the buggy wake you?"

Carlin nodded, though it had not. Was this really a teacher? She looked so small in her dark blue jacket and her long skirt. Carlin stared at the locket. Were there pictures in it, she wondered? Whose?

"I had a beautiful trip out here from town. Those great dark trees along the road are wonderful with all the moss." She smiled again. "Well, you'd better go to sleep now. We'll get acquainted in the morning. Good night."

"Good night."

Tommy went off to his room and Carlin lay back on her pillow and stared out at the dark. Miss Mollie Betts was very different from what she'd imagined. "Ooo-whit," an owl called outside in the pecan orchard, a silvery sound circling down through the shadowy trees.

Carlin watched their new teacher plump two books down on the schoolroom table the next morning, then take her place at its head. "This is for history," she said. "The history of England." She pointed to the dark red volume. "That's for Carlin. But this. . . ." She picked up the green book. "This is geography, and it's for both of you."

"What's geography?" Tommy pronounced the new word with a worried caution.

"You see, we haven't done any geography," Carlin began uneasily. The book looked interesting, tall and green, but she wanted to protect Tommy. Miss Mollie mustn't judge him as slow before she had even begun teaching him.

"Geography is very important," Miss Mollie said. "And it's exciting too." She opened the book to a brightly colored map of the United States that spread across two pages.

Carlin paused, then leaned over the map with Tommy. "I see Mississippi." She pointed to a long rectangle outlined in pale green.

"Where does it say Rosalie?" Tommy demanded and leaned over the map too.

"The plantations aren't marked." Miss Mollie smiled. "But let's see if we can find Greenwood." Carlin watched her lean forward and pause. "No. It's not marked either," she said.

Carlin glanced at Tommy over Miss Mollie's bent shoulders. How could Greenwood not be marked? It was their town.

"Look how big the river is," Miss Mollie said as if it would compensate for Greenwood's humiliation. "See how all the other rivers pour into it." Carlin rolled her eyes. They knew about the Mississippi River, for heaven's sake.

"Hey." Evie pushed open the door to the schoolroom and stood looking in, her hair messy with uncombed curls, as she held her doll by one arm. Miss Mollie turned and smiled at her, and Evie seemed poised to enter, but Aunt Ceny scurried up and led her away.

"Eva's five. Is that right?" Miss Mollie asked. Carlin nodded. She could remember how excited she had been in the weeks before Evie was born. She had been eager for a sister, but now Evie was just a part of everyday life, and the eagerness of that dim time seemed strange.

Miss Mollie turned to a map of the European continent. "Where's Paris?" Carlin asked.

"Here," Miss Mollie said, putting her forefinger down beside a large red dot. "Why are you interested in Paris, Carlin?"

"That's where our Uncle Will is on his wedding trip. He studied architecture there, and now he's showing it to our Aunt Emily."

"Your uncle sounds like an interesting man."

"He's our favorite uncle," Tommy announced.

"Why?" Miss Mollie asked.

Carlin looked up at the new teacher, startled by her question. Why? "Oh, everybody loves Uncle Will," she began. "He's handsome and kind and funny and. . . ."

"He brings us presents," Tommy broke in.

"That's not why we love him, though," Carlin said sternly and paused. The look of Uncle Will standing at the window in the cloakroom after the wedding came back to her with a sudden vividness. She saw his white face, his darting troubled eyes. "I wish you could come with us, Carlie." He had said that. She clutched a button on her blouse remembering her promise to herself: she would not think about that time in the cloakroom, and she would never tell anybody about it ever.

"Uncle Will tells us a lot about Paris," Tommy went on. "About the big long loaves of bread they eat, and about all the buildings there and the parks."

"He loves France," Carlin explained and felt her face flush, for Miss Mollie had tipped her head as if what Carlin was saying really interested her. "You see, he was in Paris a long time, but he used to come back every summer, and sometimes at Christmas too."

"And when I hear Fancy—that's his horse—out in the drive, I run downstairs," Tommy put in. "I slide down the banister," he continued, talking fast, as if he too were aware that they had gained an unusual listener. "And Uncle Will picks me up and says, 'How's my man?'"

"Not always he doesn't," Carlin corrected. "Sometimes we go

meet him at the station when he comes up from New Orleans. Once he took a steamboat straight up to Natchez."

"He hides his presents, and we have to hunt for them," Tommy continued. "He pretends he can't remember where he put them, and Carlin and me have to look in all his pockets, which tickles him, and last time he brought me a real pocket knife."

"Is your Uncle Will your father's brother?" Miss Mollie asked.

"Yes," Carlin answered. "He's the youngest son in the family and Papa's the oldest. There are two daughters too, Aunt Lucy, who lives with us, and Aunt Tazey, who lives in town."

"Uncle Will's going to be papa to our three cousins," Tommy put in. "They're Aunt Emily's children from when she was married to Uncle Royal."

"Ted's the oldest," Carlin explained. "He's thirteen and he's going away to school this year. Then comes Amy. She's my next best friend after Feely. Then comes Hugh, who's just Tommy's age." Carlin stopped. She was talking too much. She studied a cluster of freckles on Miss Mollie's nose and breathed out slowly.

"I was in Paris last summer," Miss Mollie said.

"You were?" Carlin caught her hands together and stared at the wisps of blond hair spraying out around Miss Mollie's face. "What was it like?"

"It was very beautiful. You'll have to go there someday."

"Oh yes," Carlin said. "That's what I want to do."

❧

Carlin sat watching her mother talk with Miss Mollie over the breakfast table. "We had such a nice letter from Paul," she said as she poured a cup of coffee. Miss Mollie took the cup in its saucer and looked up at Mama.

"You did?" she said, and her face took on an expectant look. Paul was a second cousin of Papa's, and he had written to Mama about Miss Mollie, but there was more, Carlin thought.

"Do you know Paul well?" she asked Miss Mollie later, when they had settled around the schoolroom table.

"Yes, indeed." Miss Mollie laughed. "We're engaged."

60

"You're what?"

"We are engaged to be married."

"Oh." Carlin put both elbows on the table and held her chin in her hands in order to study Miss Mollie more closely. "Where is he?" she asked.

"Right now he's in Germany." Miss Mollie sat forward and looked eagerly from one to the other of them. "He's a wonderful man." She slipped the gold locket over her head, opened it, and pushed it across the table to them. "Isn't he handsome?"

"He's a doctor," she went on while Carlin studied the small sepia photograph of a dark-eyed man with a moustache. "He's at the University of Berlin doing research on diseases. It's where some of the most advanced work in the world is being done. They're studying things like bacteria." She paused and clasped her hands together.

"Bacteria?" Carlin repeated the unfamiliar word slowly. "What's that?"

"They are tiny living things that cause diseases."

"What kind of diseases?" Carlin asked.

"Well, tuberculosis for one. That is one of the most terrible diseases of our time, and if they can understand what causes it, then maybe they can prevent it. You see?"

"But couldn't he catch the disease that he's working on, or one of the others?" Tommy asked.

"That is a danger. But they're very careful, of course."

"Will you go to Germany to marry him?" Carlin demanded. "Will you have your wedding there, or will you be married in New Orleans?" she asked, feeling knowlegeable since Mama had told her that Miss Mollie came from New Orleans.

"We'll have the wedding in New Orleans. That's where Paul comes from, too. My father's a cotton broker there, you see."

Carlin wondered whether Miss Mollie's father had passed on the cotton bales from Rosalie, testing the cotton in his fingers, deciding which was good middling or fair.

"Paul and I will marry in our church," Miss Mollie went on, "and have the reception at my parents' house." Carlin nodded and dressed her new teacher quickly in a white dress with a train and fixed a veil around her hair. "After the wedding, we'll sail to Germany," Miss Mollie said.

"It's just like Uncle Will," Tommy said. "You and Paul are going to Berlin, and Uncle Will and Aunt Emily are in Paris."

"Yes, except we'll live abroad a few years, probably."

"Have you ever been to Germany?" Carlin asked.

"Oh, yes. I was there last summer, studying and seeing Paul."

"What did you study?"

"Literature and philosophy, mostly. I want to continue when I get back."

"Why don't you go now?" Carlin said. "Why don't you marry Paul right away so you can go back to Berlin?"

"Well, I'd like to, of course." Miss Mollie laughed. "But he needs to get settled in his work there, and I want to make a little money for my passage and my studies."

Carlin nodded, then let her breath out slowly. One wedding was over and one was just ahead, and she had two romances to think about, four people to imagine kissing. She hugged her arms around her. It was almost too much.

⚹

Carlin gazed out the schoolroom window as she memorized the list of Stuart kings. "James the first, Charles the first," she whispered, keeping one hand over the page in her history book. Something red was moving up the drive. Carlin stared. "The Commonwealth, Charles the second." It was a buggy, but not the Rosalie one. No. Wait. It was a surrey. The body was painted a deep red and there were two seats, one in front and one in back. She rose partway and saw the sun glinting on one of the brass lamps at the side. That was the Grove surrey. It had to be. "It's Uncle Will," she shouted and turned to Tommy and Miss Mollie at the table. "He's back. He's coming with Aunt Emily. They're back from Paris."

"Where?" Tommy rushed to the open window.

"Out there. See the surrey."

"That's them," Tommy shouted. "I can tell the horses. That's

Hunter. I know it is, and Blackie. It's Uncle Will. They're back."
He leaned on the table with both hands and stared at Miss Mollie,
as if to make sure she understood the importance of this event.

"Sit down, children. They're not here yet," Miss Mollie warned.
"You can go down when they come, but not before."

"But . . . ?" Carlin and Tommy sat down. How could they do
lessons now? Didn't Miss Mollie see that this was the day they had
been waiting for? Carlin squeezed the fingers of one hand with the
other and listened. After a while she could hear the buggy wheels
turning on the dry gravel in the drive and then on the paved space
in front. There was a sound of horses snorting, and Eben shouted
as he ran down from the stable.

"Whoa there." That was Uncle Will's voice. Carlin gave Miss
Mollie a pleading look. Surely she wouldn't insist that they go on
sitting in the schoolroom now?

Miss Mollie nodded. "All right, children. But go quietly. It's
bad manners to whoop and yell when relatives appear, no matter
how excited you feel."

Carlin and Tommy rushed to the stairs, then paused a minute
on the landing to stare down. Mama was already out on the front
gallery laughing and calling out as Uncle Will helped Aunt Emily
out of the surrey and lifted Amy and Hugh down. Aunt Emily
hurried up the brick walk in a blue-sprigged dress while Uncle
Will, who had a funny-looking cap on his head, pointed to something in the back of the surrey that Eben, the stable boy, was to
bring in. Aunt Emily and Mama hugged, and then Uncle Will
hugged Mama. Mama leaned back and touched his queer cap and
laughed as they turned toward the front gallery. Amy and Hugh
ducked around the adults and ran into the hall.

Tommy threw one leg over the banister. "Look at me, Uncle
Will," he shouted as he rushed backward down the smooth rubbed
wood to the heavy newel post at the bottom, where the curving
banister stopped. Uncle Will leapt across the hall with a laugh and
caught Tommy before he landed on the rug.

"You're getting so big," he exclaimed and held Tommy high.
"Both of you." He looked from Tommy to Hugh, who was stand-

ing beside his new stepfather, staring up at his cousin. "I can barely swing you up anymore. Either of you fellows."

"Why're you wearing that hat?" Tommy demanded as Uncle Will put him down.

"It's a beret. Lots of men wear them in Paris."

"Oh." Tommy stepped back.

"Carlin," Amy called out. "Where are you?"

"Here," said Carlin, coming down the stairs. But she was looking at her uncle, surprised again at how much younger Uncle Will seemed than Papa. It wasn't just that there were no threads of gray in his soft brown moustache or lines on his forehead. He was somehow taller, springier than Papa, and he had changed back to his old self since that time at the wedding, for his face was full of color and he looked ready to laugh. He wore a red silk cravat at his neck, which must be French too, she thought, but otherwise he seemed familiar in his riding breeches, his tan shirt, and polished boots.

"And how is the beautiful Miss Eva?" Uncle Will asked. Evie, who stood in the back doorway, holding Aunt Ceny's hand, smiled and hung her head. But Uncle Will stepped forward and stooped down. "You're getting big too," he said "and so pretty." Evie turned and buried her face in Aunt Ceny's apron, but let herself be gathered up in his arms as Carlin watched.

"They came back last night," Amy whispered to Carlin. "We got to stay up really late, and Mama and Papa Will brought us lots of presents from Paris. Look." She held up a large doll. "She has three petticoats, and look at her boots. They're real kid." Carlin looked down at the doll's smooth china head. She had never heard her cousin say Papa Will before. "Her name's Marie. That's French."

"Come on out on the front gallery where it's cool," Mama said. "I'll have Aunt Ceny bring us some iced tea. Or would you rather have lemonade?"

Uncle Will turned. "You girls go on out and get comfortable. I'll be with you in a minute. I've got a little business in here first." He pointed to a large box that Eben had brought from the buggy and put down on the marble-topped table. "Carlie," he said, letting his gaze settle on her at last. "How are you?"

Carlin felt herself grow warm as she stared up at her uncle, and her smile seemed to quiver. "Fine," she told him. "Was it a good wedding trip?" She paused, worried that that wasn't quite the right question, so she added, "Was Paris as beautiful as ever?"

"More beautiful, if that's possible," Uncle Will said, smiling. "More beautiful because I could show it all to your wonderful aunt."

"They came last night after supper," Amy continued to Carlin. "We stayed up till ten o'clock almost, maybe eleven." Amy pushed back one blond pigtail. "That box has presents for you and Tommy and Evie." Amy raised her eyebrows. "Everything they got is French, including Marie, of course." Carlin glanced down at the doll's static face, the parted china lips, the staring blue eyes.

"There's a box here," Uncle Will began. "I don't know what's inside, but let's just see." He laughed and moved to the table.

"I hope you get a doll too," Amy whispered. "Then they can be friends."

"Now where's my pocket knife?" Uncle Will began a search of his shirt pockets and then his trousers. The knife was in his trouser pocket, as he probably knew, Carlin thought. Uncle Will was like an actor, always making funny little dramas about where his pocket knife was or where he'd put the presents. She watched as he cut the string on the package, then opened the flaps of the box which had foreign writing on the side. "Wait now," he cautioned Tommy, who reached to open the final flap. "These things can't be rushed, you know." He took out a layer of straw, then pulled out a rectangular box with more foreign writing on the top and handed it to Tommy. Tommy squatted down with Hugh close beside him. He opened the box and let out a shout as he lifted a red metal fire engine from the tissue inside. It had two water barrels on the back with two tiny black hoses attached. There was a ladder that came off and one that was painted on, and the engine had a little brass bell in front that made a pinging sound.

"There's more," Uncle Will said. He dug in the box and brought out a little metal man, then knelt down beside the boys. "Now these men go in front," Uncle Will said. "See? And that one goes in the back behind the ladder," he explained, "and this one. Let's see. He's the driver."

"I got a steam engine," Hugh said. "It's green." He took off one of the men, then fitted it on the fire engine again. "The train and the fire engine can meet," he told Tommy. But Tommy was too absorbed to answer.

Uncle Will pushed the fire engine, watching as it rolled across the dark polished floor and nosed up against the baseboard. Tommy straightened and stood up. "Mama," he shouted and ran out to the front gallery. "Uncle Will brought me a fire engine from Paris."

"Now let's see what there is for Miss Evie," Uncle Will said, returning to the box. He lifted something soft and bulky, wrapped in white tissue paper, and held it out. Evie ran to him and raised her arms to take the package. She pulled off the paper and let out a cry as a brown teddy bear emerged.

"Say 'thank you' to Uncle Will," Carlin instructed, but Evie was busy raising the bear's arms. She squeezed him, then glanced around her and gave her uncle a shy smile.

"And now Carlin." Uncle Will bent over the box and pulled out something flat.

"That's not a doll," Amy said. Carlin stepped forward and lifted the tissue paper from something that looked like a book bound in soft gray leather.

"It's a diary," her uncle said, watching her. "A Parisian diary. I know you already have one, but I thought you could move to this one when that one's full."

"Oh," Carlin breathed. The diary had a square gold lock on one side, and a bright little key dangled down on a white string. There was a gold border all the way around and raised bands of gray on the spine. Carlin pressed it against her chest.

"Open it," Amy urged. "Let's see what it looks like inside."

Carlin fitted the key into the little lock and turned it. She lifted the cover slowly. The flyleaf was a pale blue with water markings. She turned to the first page and stared down at the cream-colored page with its thin gray lines.

"Oh," she said again. "Oh, Uncle Will, thank you." She closed the book and locked it, as the others watched. Then she unlocked it and gazed at the flyleaf once more.

"Do you really like it?" Amy asked.

"I love it," Carlin said. "Oh, Uncle Will." She looked up at her uncle, who stood with one hand leaning on the marble-topped table. "I love it."

"You're sure?" he said, smiling down at her. "If you don't, I could sail back to Paris tomorrow and get you something else."

"No, no." Carlin laughed and heard Amy's laughter beside her. "It's perfect." She stepped forward and stretched up to to give her uncle a kiss.

"I thought you'd enjoy writing in it," Uncle Will said. "A nice book can make diary-keeping more fun."

"Oh, yes," Carlin said and squeezed the book against her chest again.

"It's a funny present," Amy told Carlin in a low voice. "I wish they'd brought you a doll like Marie. Look." She rocked Marie back so that her hinged eyelids closed.

"She's wonderful," Carlin said, but she, Carlin, had been given a true grown-up present. Uncle Will had brought her a leather-bound diary from France. She would begin writing in it tonight, she resolved, and the first thing she described would be Uncle Will's return from Paris.

※

Carlin lay in bed listening to the sound of a violin melody Mama was playing as it rose above Aunt Emily's piano accompaniment. The music floating up from the parlor seemed to lift Carlin and she felt she could sail out over the shadowy lawn on its wings. It stopped, and Carlin waited for it to go on again, but when it did not, she pulled her knees up and looked down at the book she had been reading.

"More coffee, Will?" That was Papa. He and Uncle Will must have taken their coffee out onto the front gallery below. "You know, sometimes I don't know how Father did it," she heard Papa say. "One good harvest after another, bales of good middling, year after year, improvements here, new mule teams. Remember when he built the new stable? Paid for it all, and I . . . I can't even seem to keep things balanced. I've got to get another middlebuster plow, and I had to repair the gin three times during this past picking. Of course, if I'd had good middling cotton, but it was low middling again, and we barely made six hundred bales."

"The problem could be the crop, brother," Uncle Will said. "This one-crop system."

"Well, the system has its flaws, certainly," Papa said. "But God has given us this crop to work, and this land, this life to live."

"Maybe that isn't all God's doing," Uncle Will said and Carlin heard him give a low laugh. "God might be in favor of a few changes."

"Father didn't change," Papa told him, "and Rosalie prospered under him."

"Different times, different economies, brother," Uncle Will said.

"I don't know," Papa paused. "I don't know. Father passed Rosalie on to me, and I don't want to fail it or him."

"Ah, brother, you mustn't worry so. It won't come to that. There are things we can do."

Carlin closed her book and blew out the candle. If only Rosalie were as rich as the Grove, she thought. But Uncle Will was home, and now everything would be better.

✿

Carlin sat at the upright piano in the parlor, staring at the title of the music in front of her, *Sonata Facile* and underneath in smaller letters, *Für Anfanger, von Wolfgang Amadeus Mozart.* The "u" in "Für" had two little dots above it. That was German writing, Mama said. It meant "for beginners." This was Carlin's first sonata and it didn't seem facile to her, but it was exciting. This was her first piece written for piano and violin, and Mama had said they might play it to the Tuesday morning club later on, when all the ladies came to the Grove to hear music.

She stretched her fingers, then bent them one by one as Mama had taught her. Sam groaned and shifted on the bare floor below her. The October morning was hot. One-two-three-four, one-two-three-four, she whispered to herself, then lifted her left hand and began the bass. She must keep it even, Mama said, as smooth as oil. Carlin thought of the coal oil sliding from the metal pitcher each morning as Aunt Ceny poured it down into the cleaned lamps.

Way up the drive, one of the bird dogs was barking. Sam raised his head and rose with a scratching of his toenails on the wooden floor. He stood a moment, ears cocked, then bounded through the open French door onto the front gallery, down the steps, and out to the drive. Somebody shouted. Blue had treed a possum maybe, or a chicken had escaped. She heard Tommy running down the stairs. He was supposed to be doing his geography lesson; but Miss Mollie had gone into town, and any disturbance would be enough to distract him.

Carlin continued the bass, then added the right hand cautiously. The music book had been Mama's when she was a girl, and this was the first piece by Mozart that Carlin had ever played. She must work to learn it so that she could play it well, not in a silly little-girl way that would make the ladies smile. "One-two-three-four," she whispered to herself, making her left hand rock as she continued the melody in the right. "One-two-three-four." There was more barking. Carlin paused to listen. The sound of scales on the violin had stopped in the library. Had Mama interrupted her own practicing to go investigate the commotion?

"Boop-boop." What was that? The queer noise came from somewhere down the drive. Carlin hurried out onto the front gallery, where Mama stood holding Evie with one hand, shading her eyes with the other as she stared at the tunnel of live oak trees. Tommy had climbed the gate and was waving excitedly. Carlin squinted. A huge machine on wheels was roaring toward them down the drive. There were people inside—Uncle Will behind a sort of glass plate and Aunt Emily, maybe. At least Carlin thought it must be Uncle Will, though he had some kind of huge glass things over his eyes, and a funny hat blowing up. Aunt Emily's arm was raised in a wave, and her wide hat was tied down with a veil.

Amy and Hugh stood behind them, waving and shouting. Carlin pulled at her mother's arm.

"What is it, Mama? What is that thing?"

"It's a motor car, dear. Your uncle's trying out a Model T."

"What? What's a Model T?" Carlin demanded as Tommy jumped from the gate with a yell and dashed toward it down the drive. "What is it?" she began again, but her voice was drowned in the noise of the machine and the queer boop-boop sounds which lifted above it.

Papa appeared on Graylie. "Hold those dogs, children," he shouted as Graylie swung her head and whinnied, a high frightened noise above the puttering of the machine. There were shouts from the field and the stable yard. Men in overalls came running as the motor car approached the gate. Graylie whinnied again. "I'll stable her," Papa yelled. "Hold onto those dogs. They could get hurt."

Tommy caught Blue, then Bessie, the spotted bitch, who strained and squirmed, and Carlin leapt forward to catch Sam's collar and hold him tight as the noisy machine bore down on them.

It was painted a shiny black, and Carlin could see big round lights on either side of the high wheels and a square sort of grill in front. There were curved metal guards that rose on either side, and the wheels were turning so fast that the black spokes seemed to blur together. The machine passed through the open gate and on up the drive to the hitching post at the end of the front walk.

Carlin heard Evie cry and turned her head, but Papa had said to hold the dogs. There was Uncle Will, smiling his familiar smile. He looked funny with the huge glass things covering his eyes and that cloth cap that kept billowing up. Aunt Emily sat beside him in the front seat, holding her hat with both hands as they came to a stop beside the front walk.

"Goodness gracious," Mama said. She leaned close to look at the machine, jiggling Evie in her arms. "I can't believe it. You talked about it last week, but I had no idea you were really going to try one out so soon. Where did this come from?"

"Jackson," Uncle Will shouted. "I drove it all the way down to the Grove yesterday. Wait a minute." He reached down on the big column that held the black wheel and switched something. The roaring softened. "That's the throttle." His laugh echoed in the relative quiet. Carlin, who was still half-stooped holding Sam, stared at the machine in astonishment while Mama and Aunt Emily laughed.

"Can I do the horn, Papa? Please," Hugh pleaded from the back seat.

"All right." Uncle Will laughed. "You'll be driving it yourself soon at the rate you're going." Hugh leaned over the back of the front seat and did something by the door beside Uncle Will's arm which made the boop-boop sound again, a more cheerful noise now that the machine itself was quieter.

"Papa, may we . . ." Carlin longed to stand upright and look into the machine, but Sam was still straining to get away and Blue and Bessie were pulling Tommy.

"Hold onto those dogs a minute more," Papa said. "I don't want them to jump up and scratch the paint, or get themselves killed either," he added."

"Why don't you put them in the tack room?" Uncle Will said. "And hurry back. I'll take you all for a ride."

Carlin slammed the tack room door, and she and Tommy ran down the stable path to the drive, ignoring the barking of the imprisoned dogs behind them. Mama had squeezed into the front seat beside Aunt Emily, holding Evie on her lap, and Uncle Will had gotten out of the car. He was wearing a brown bathrobe-like coat, and he was stooped down beside the engine. A sort of metal screen was folded back, and Uncle Will was pointing to something inside as Papa leaned over beside him. Carlin stared at the brass section above the grill. The word "Ford" was written in cursive letters. What did that mean?

"Get in," Amy shouted. "Hurry up." Tommy had already crowded in beside Hugh, but Carlin held back a moment, looking at the black step and the bright brass. Uncle Will got back into his place behind the long stick with the wheel on top. He pulled the huge glass things down over his eyes again and glanced back at Carlin as she started to mount the black step. "That's called the running board," he shouted. "Step up on it and get in."

Carlin sat down in back and ran her hand over the black squares of the soft leather seat. "It's like a parlor sofa," she said and stood up again to look some more. On the floor beside Uncle Will's feet were pedals almost like the organ pedals at church.

"And see, there's a top, too, for when it rains," Hugh explained. He reached up to the metal frame above them, then pointed to the black folds behind. "You can ride anytime. Rain or wind or anything, and it'll go everywhere. To the Grove, to town. It'll even go to Jackson."

"Of course it'll go to Jackson, silly," Amy said. "That's where Papa got it. Let's go, Papa," she shouted. "Let's go." Carlin watched Amy pound Uncle Will's shoulder. She had dropped the "Will," Carlin noted. It was just plain Papa now.

Uncle Will grasped the wheel in his gloved hands. He clicked the throttle so that the machine's noise grew loud again. Evie whimpered, then broke into a loud wail. "It's all right, darling," Mama said, rocking her.

"It's all right," Carlin repeated, bending toward the front seat, but she felt the sound of Evie's fear pluck at something within her.

"Come on, brother," Uncle Will shouted to Papa. "Let me show you how she rides." Carlin saw Papa glance at the machine with the women crowded in front, Aunt Emily in her wide hat, and Mama with Evie in her lap, and the row of children behind.

"You take this crew on a spin. I'll wait my turn," Papa said.

"No, Papa. Please," Carlin called out, startled at her own urgency. "You have to come with us now." She squeezed closer to Amy, making a space for him on the black seat.

Papa laid one hand on the door and looked down at them. "Well, brother, if you're going to kidnap my whole family in this wild contraption, maybe I'd better come too." He opened the door and perched on the patch of black seat Carlin had uncovered. "Squeeze over a little more, girls," he said and laughed as he pulled in his legs. "We're sardines back here, but we're all in, I think." Carlin felt her father's warm thigh pressed against her side, and she breathed out slowly. Now they would be safe, she thought.

All at once they were moving. There was a shout from the stable yard where a group of field hands had collected. Toe and Hamlet had climbed the fence and sat clapping their hands over their heads, cheering. Aunt Georgia was on the brick walk, waving her white apron, and Aunt Ceny was leaning out of a bedroom window upstairs, waving a feather duster. Carlin and Amy waved back, and Papa lifted one hand. Everybody in the car was waving except for Uncle Will, who was watching the road through his big glass eyes.

"Oh my," Mama cried out and squeezed Aunt Emily's arm. "Oh, my gracious. It's so fast." Carlin twisted to look back at the house and then up at the stable as the motor car rushed down the back road toward the pond. Leaves blurred into streaks of green and brown. Birds rose up from the field and flew ahead of them, frightened by the noise. They reached the road to the pond and paused, and Uncle Will turned the switch on the long stick in front of him so that the noise got softer again.

"Well, what do you think?" Uncle Will asked and looked back at Papa. "Pretty amazing, isn't it?"

"It is that. But are you going to buy it?" Papa asked.

"I already have," Uncle Will announced. "Paid in full." Carlin saw her father press his lips together and look down.

"Of course, it was expensive," Aunt Emily explained. "But, as I said to Will, it'll pay for itself in no time when you think of what a help it'll be getting around at the Grove."

"What about repairs?" Papa asked. "And parts?"

"Oh, that shouldn't be a problem," Uncle Will said and tipped his head back. "The man who sold it to me said it's easy to repair."

Amy gave a bounce on the leather seat. "Try it," she said. "It's fun." Carlin bounced, then leaned back and looked out at the trees and the field beyond. This was her first ride in a motor car, she thought, the first motor car ever to come to Rosalie.

※

Carlin glanced around the empty plantation store, feeling guilty but pleased. The store was closed in the mornings when the workers were in the field and did not open until late afternoon. But

Carlin and Tommy had sneaked in through a back window. They were going to play store, although Mama had told them they must not go in when the store was closed. Behind the wide wooden counter were three shelves crowded with goods. On the bottom shelf were straw hampers and baby baskets and two shiny new buckets. A line of tan cookie jars stood on the middle shelf, and beyond them was a jumble of butter molds and mouse traps. On the shelf above were bolts of material wrapped in brown paper. A pickle barrel sat on the floor at the end of the counter, and beside it was a cracker barrel with NATIONAL BISCUIT stamped across the wooden staves in large black letters.

Tommy took a rubbery-looking licorice stick from a jar on the counter, stuck it between his lips, and put his hands on his waist. "You want half a pound of flour, Roxie?" he asked Carlin.

She laughed. With the licorice stick protruding from his mouth like a cigar, Tommy really did look like Mr. Rayley, who ran the store. They shouldn't be here, but they didn't have lessons today, and if they were quiet, they wouldn't get caught. Carlin took a licorice stick for herself and squinted at the line of barrels on one side—flour, sugar, cornstarch, molasses. She shook her head.

"Wait," she said and scurried behind the counter to pull a large rush basket from the bottom shelf. She hooked it over her arm and stooped forward as she looked at the shelves again. "I think I'd like to have a little look-see at some of them yard goods up there," Carlin began and paused, pleased with her acting. "I got me a baptism comin'."

"For you?" Tommy said. "Haven't you been baptized yet?" He laughed and covered his mouth with both hands, bending the licorice stick.

"It's my granddaughter, silly. She needs a new dress. You can put it right on my account. Fats'll be sure and pay end of the month."

"Well, I don't know, Roxie," Tommy began and crossed his arms over his chest. "Pickin's over now, and you and Fats still got an account to pay here. This store's not a charity, you know."

"But my granddaughter. . . ." Carlin hesitated.

Tommy turned to the dusty shelf behind him where three bolts of material were stacked. "All right. Let's just see." He stretched and lifted down one of the bolts and shoved it crossways over the counter, holding the end up with one hand.

The glass panes on the front door shook suddenly, and the bell on the back made a tinkling noise. Tommy let the bolt fall to the counter with a thud, and they both turned. Miss Mollie stood beyond them, wearing her wide-brimmed straw hat. She must have seen them climbing in the window, Carlin thought, and stared, realizing that the door had been unlocked all along.

"So you're selling yard goods, Thomas," Miss Mollie observed and took off her hat. "Do you know the price?" She laid the hat on the rolltop desk beside her and settled herself in a cane rocking chair.

"We were just . . . ," Carlin started. "We. . . ."

"What's the price of that material per yard, Thomas?" Miss Mollie asked again, and Carlin saw a smile flicker around her mouth.

Tommy leaned over to read the ticket hanging down from the side of the bolt. "Eight cents a yard, ma'am."

"And how many yards do you think you need for a dress, Carlin?"

"Four, maybe. Perhaps I could get by with three and a half. My granddaughter's not very big." Carlin smiled, eager all at once.

"Then how much will you have to pay?"

Carlin laughed and swung her basket as she began to multiply. She used to tell Mama that she wanted to go to school in town with other children, but Miss Mollie was fun. She had been at Rosalie almost two months now, and lessons had still not gotten boring.

The bell tinkled again, and the door opened partway. A thin colored woman holding a baby on her hip hesitated on the threshold. She wore a skirt made from a feed sack and a white shirt with the sleeves torn out. She took a step and stood tentatively, one bare foot poised on the dusty floor, as though she might turn back. "I thought," she began. "I thought maybe the store was openin' special. That Mr. Rayley were here." Carlin felt her troubled gaze sweep over them, then settle on Miss Mollie by the desk.

"Oh, ma'am. Please. Could you fix it for me to git just a little flour and a cup of molasses? I want to make my baby a cake for her birthday." She shifted the child on her hip. "And I ain't got nothin' to make it with."

"I'm sorry. I can't," Miss Mollie said. "I don't keep the accounts."

"You can't?" the woman repeated and stared at her. "You can't fix it no way?"

"I'm sorry," Miss Mollie said and rose. "The store's closed. Mr. Rayley's not here now, you see."

The woman nodded slowly and turned. Carlin stared, taking in the horse blanket pin on the side of her skirt and the thick black hair greased back. She might be the wife of that field hand Aunt Georgia had told her about, who had brought his wife up from Louisiana just a month ago. The bell made its high tinkling noise once again as the woman pulled the door shut behind her.

"Why couldn't we give her some flour and molasses?" Carlin demanded, turning back to Miss Mollie. "She didn't want much."

"I can't give away something that isn't mine, Carlin."

"But she only wanted to bake a birthday cake for her little girl."

"When you take something that isn't yours, it's stealing, Carlin. You know that. We would set a bad example."

"But we're setting a terrible example now," Carlin protested. "It looks as if we don't care." She clutched the edge of the counter, feeling tears start. "I hate it when people are so poor. I hate it that we're rich and won't do anything." She paused, frowning. "We are rich compared to her." She stopped, startled at the loudness of her voice. "Why does this happen?" she demanded. "Why do people have to be so poor?"

"Let's take a walk," Miss Mollie said and opened the door. "We shouldn't be in here anyway." They started across the barnyard and down the back road. "Poverty is a complicated thing," Miss Mollie said and put one hand on Carlin's shoulder. "People need jobs to get enough money to buy food and clothes and pay for a roof over their heads, and they need to learn to read and write and cipher, so they can get better jobs, you see? Poverty's a huge problem. We just have to keep working on it."

"Here at Rosalie?" Carlin asked.

"Definitely here at Rosalie, and all over the world."

⚉

A new book of music that Uncle Will had ordered from Paris had arrived at the Grove, and Mama and Aunt Emily were trying out some of the pieces. Carlin sat on the rug with Tommy and Evie and her cousins watching Mama draw her bow back and forth across the strings of her violin, bringing out a sad, slow melody as Aunt Emily played the piano. Carlin studied her mother, then her aunt, wondering if she would ever enter that intimate world of music that they shared.

There was a sound of footsteps on the front gallery and they all turned. "Sounds wonderful. Wonderful," Uncle Will said, striding across the room in his brown boots that gleamed in the afternoon light. A silk cravat was pushed into the neck of his white shirt and his breeches looked freshly pressed. He put one hand around Aunt Emily's waist, bent to kiss her cheek, then smiled at Carlin's mother. "How's that collection?" he asked and glanced over Aunt Emily's shoulder at the book of music on the stand. "Anything good in it?"

Aunt Emily slid down the bench and patted the space beside her. "We've just started," she said. "You come play. You're a better sight reader than I am."

Uncle Will sat down on the piano bench and began leafing through the book. "Aha," he said. "Strauss. *The Vienna Woods.*" He ran his fingers up and down the keyboard, making rippling chords. Mama leaned forward, found her place, and began to play, as Carlin sat watching. The music swelled. She could feel the pulse of its rhythm within her, and she beat the three/four time on Evie's shoulder. Uncle Will whipped over one page, then another.

"Let's see," he said, stopping. "They must have *The Beautiful Blue Danube.* Ah. Here it is."

77

He began playing, swaying as he did, singing da-dee-dee-da-da. Aunt Emily laughed and began the bass. Mama worked away with her bow, a little behind now, laughing, then catching up.

"Wait. Wait." Uncle Will lifted his hand and the happy pulsing music stopped. "We can all play," he said, glancing down at Carlin and the others on the rug. He swung one leg over the bench and started across the room. "Come on, you all."

They scrambled to their feet, and Carlin took Evie's hand as they followed Uncle Will into the wide hall. "Now here's a tambourine," he said, reaching up to take the round instrument from a line of molding that ran along the back of the hall. "You've got those drums I brought from Paris," he said to Hugh as he handed the tambourine to Amy.

"I've got my bird whistle, Uncle Will," Tommy spoke up. "Would that be all right?"

"Great, Tom. That'll be fine. Now the two Rosalie ladies." He looked down at Carlin and Evie. "I know. We'll use glasses. Pansy," he called to the colored girl who was sweeping the back gallery. "Bring two glasses of water. One half-full, and fill the other a little less." He turned back to Carlin. "Now we need a couple of spoons."

They gathered around the piano with their instruments. "I'm the conductor," Uncle Will announced. "You all have to watch me." He raised both arms, then turned back to the piano and played a chord.

The waltz began. Uncle Will pointed to Amy, who shook her tambourine. "Good girl." He pointed to Tommy, who blew the bird whistle so loudly that Aunt Emily stopped playing and put one hand over her ear. They all laughed, and the waltz plunged on. Hugh made heavy thumps on his drum, and Carlin and Evie banged their glasses, making ringing sounds. The first time Evie came in too early, but in their second entrance she watched Carlin and rang her glass on time.

"Now we've almost got it," Uncle Will announced. "Everybody know what he's doing?" Carlin felt hot with excitement.

Uncle Will began to play the bass part, Aunt Emily the melody, with Mama keeping up on her violin. Amy entered, then the drums

and the whistle, then Amy again, and Evie and Carlin. The piano
was loud as the waltz rocked on. Carlin felt as though the whole
plantation was pulsing with the music. Pansy and Aunt Philadelphia would be listening in the kitchen house, and the stable boys
would hear it as they worked in the stalls. Even the hands out in
the field would hear if a wind rose. She glanced over at Amy who
had lifted the tambourine to rattle it. Why hadn't Uncle Will given
her the tambourine? She was better at music than Amy.

Uncle Will stood. "You ladies keep on playing," he said to
Mama and Aunt Emily. "I'm going to dance with one of these fair
maidens in the orchestra." He held out his hand to Carlin and
bowed. She stared a moment, then flushed as she rose and took his
arm.

"I'm not sure how," Carlin said, but she and Feely had practiced
waltz steps together in the kitchen courtyard and she did know,
sort of.

"Just follow me. I'll lead." He stepped back, and Carlin followed. She dipped and turned in the shiny space of bare floor
beyond the rug as his warm hand pressed against her ribs. The
music pounded on, wrapping them in its rhythm, the crash of the
tambourine, the drums, the whistle, and the ringing notes of the
glass that Evie was making all alone.

Carlin glanced up and saw that her uncle's forehead was damp
with perspiration, but he seemed to have no thought of stopping.
They whirled past the French doors and the antique highboy, past
the ferns in the corner. Then Uncle Will slipped. His elbow
banged against the what-not stand, and it crashed to the floor with
a shattering noise as he fell.

"Oh, Willy." Aunt Emily ran to him. "Are you all right?"

"Yes, of course, I'm all right." Uncle Will turned over on one
side and put his hand to his back.

"Did you hit your shoulder? Your head?"

"I tell you, I'm all right, Emmy." Uncle Will stood and brushed
at his breeches. "Take a look at that what-not stand. That's the
casualty."

Mama and Hugh righted the stand, but the antique teacup and

its saucer, that always stood on the top shelf, were broken and the little vase with the blue and white stripes was cracked.

"What a mess." Uncle Will stood looking down at the smashed bits of china.

"Oh, Willy. That's nothing," Aunt Emily said. "If you're all right."

"Emmy." Uncle Will stood with his hands on his hips staring at her. "You've got to stop mollycoddling me." He pushed open the French doors and strode across the gallery and down the steps.

Mama touched Aunt Emily's elbow. "You girls, go out to the swing," she directed, "and boys, you go play in the barn." Carlin and Amy moved slowly down the gallery steps, trying to hear what their mothers were saying.

⚜

The rest of the family went home to Rosalie after supper, but Carlin was to spend the night with Amy. They sat on Amy's big bed in their nightgowns whispering together as they waited for Uncle Will to come up and read to them. But it was Aunt Emily who came finally and read from *The Child's Garden of Verses,* which Carlin thought was boring.

She woke suddenly at the sound of a voice in the hall. "Stop worrying about me, Emmy," she heard her uncle say. "I just want to finish this book." There was a pause, then his voice continued. "I often used to work until four or five in the morning in Paris when I was a student. It's natural with me. You go back to bed. Please."

There were some whispered sentences, then the sound of footsteps in the hall. An early rooster called far off, and a door closed. Carlin glanced at Amy, but she was turned on her side, breathing steadily. Carlin lay back in the darkness. Was it bad for Uncle Will to stay up all night? He used to do that at Rosalie. Was there something wrong with him? No, no. Aunt Georgia had said everything was going to be fine. Carlin turned over and slept again.

⚜

80

After breakfast the next morning, Carlin and Amy took the new hoops that had come from Paris out to the back road to try. The hoops were made of a light wood and painted with pink and lavender stripes, and there were two white sticks to use as pushers.

"Be careful," Amy warned as they set them down on the dusty road. "I don't want them to get dirty."

"We can't help getting them dirty, if we roll them," Carlin said. "We'll wash them off afterwards. All right?"

Amy nodded dubiously and watched as Carlin lifted her hand from her hoop and gave it a tap with the white pusher. It rolled a foot or so, then met a rut in the road and fell over. "Wait," Amy said. "We need to find a smooth place."

They walked past the smokehouse with its lattice where bees were moving in and out of the honeysuckle vine, then on past the dairy with its heavy walls. "Here. This is better," Amy said and pointed to a stretch of road that had fewer bumps. "Wait. We have to read what it says." She pulled a folded paper from her dress pocket and spread it out. There was a drawing of two girls in belted dresses with embroidered collars, rolling hoops. The paragraph of writing underneath was in French.

"Pshaw," Amy said and stuffed the paper back in her pocket. "That's no help." She balanced her hoop in front of her and pushed it with the stick, but the hoop fell over. Carlin tried. Her hoop went a couple of feet, met a clump of stones, and collapsed. Amy tried her hoop again, but it barely got as far as Carlin's.

"It's not going to work," Amy said. "The roads are all too bumpy, even this one." Her voice quavered. "Stupid hoops." She let hers fall into the weeds, dropped her stick, and sat down on a tree trunk beside the road. "They're silly." She kicked at the hoop with her shoe.

"I guess they're really for the city," Carlin said and sat down beside her. "But maybe there's somewhere we can use them."

"No, there isn't. They don't work here. I wish Mama had never bought them."

Carlin looked back at the honeysuckle vine. "They probably work in Paris," she said. "Uncle Will says he's going to take you all to Paris someday."

"Not me," Amy said. "I don't want to go." She pushed the hoop with her foot again. "I don't like French things."

"What about Marie, your doll?" Carlin asked.

"Her name's Mary Sue now, and she's not French anymore."

"Oh."

"I'm going away to school next year," Amy announced. "It's all decided. Mama said so." She looked up into the leaves. "Of course, I might not like school, but at least I'll be away from here." She propped the two hoops against the fence. "Let's go to the graveyard."

"All right." The family graveyard at the Grove had become Amy and Carlin's private spot. They could sit on a favorite flat stone and talk in the shade of the Spanish moss.

"Wait. I've got a stone in my shoe."

Carlin shaded her eyes with one hand as she waited, and looked across a weedy field where a single column stuck up among the scrub firs. "There's Uncle Will's temple," she said, pointing to it. The column looked odd and forgotten, towering over the undergrowth. "Let's go over there, not the graveyard."

"No. It's all weedy," Amy protested. "There might be snakes. Holton saw a cane brake rattler here last year."

"Oh, those big ones don't come around much," Carlin said. "We'll be careful. Come on." She climbed the low fence and waded into the tangled vines.

"If Mama sees us, she'll be mad," Amy said, plowing along behind Carlin.

"She won't. Nobody'll see us." Carlin stepped around a tangle of blackberry vines, avoiding the briars, and strode on until she was in front of the wooden platform with the column beside it. She crawled up and looked around her. White paint was peeling from one side of the column, and the light filtering through the leaves made shadows on the weathered surface of the platform. "I love this place," Carlin said and patted the column, then picked off some flakes of paint. "It's so secret and quiet." She turned back to Amy, who struggled up onto the platform and stood. "It could be our place. It's closer and more private." She turned and stared up into the dark green of the pine tree close by. "We could come here to talk instead of going to the graveyard. I mean, until it's finished."

"It's never going to be finished," Amy said. "Mama says it costs too much money."

"Never?" Carlin stared at her cousin. "But why not? This was going to be a Greek temple for Uncle Will."

"It wasn't going to be just for him," Amy corrected. "My real Papa asked him to build it. That was when Papa Will first came to the Grove."

"Was that when he built the front gallery?"

"I guess so. I can't even remember when we didn't have the long one," Amy said.

"I can't either." Carlin sat down and leaned back against the column. Amy settled beside her, and they pulled up their bare knees. A mourning dove sung its sad complaint somewhere amidst the leaves. "I wish he'd finish it," Carlin said. She tipped her head back and looked up at the top of the column. "It would be so pretty."

"But it costs too much," Amy said.

Carlin put out a finger and traced an oval of light on the wooden surface. "Why does everybody think about money all the time?" she complained. "I thought the Grove was rich."

"It is," Amy told her. "Papa was rich, much richer than your Uncle Will."

"I know." Carlin kept her eyes on the oval, feeling a flush of shame spread through her, as if the fact that Uncle Will wasn't rich were her fault somehow.

"Everything's different now," Amy said. "I mean, Papa Will is always doing things, thinking up expeditions and games. He and Mama hold hands and sit close together on the gallery. I saw them kiss last week in the front hall."

Carlin squinted a moment, changing her imagined picture from the rose garden to the hall. She put Uncle Will under the chandelier and watched him bend down to Aunt Emily and press his mouth to hers. "Do you think they'll have babies?" she asked. The idea startled her.

"I don't know," Amy said. "Maybe."

There was a sound of footsteps on the road, and they turned. Through the branches, they could see Uncle Will walking along the back road, scowling. "He's mad because the Model T broke down. He spent a whole morning trying to fix it yesterday," Amy said, "but he couldn't."

"What's the matter with it?"

"Oh, it's the engine or something. He's going to have to take it all the way back to Jackson to get it fixed." Amy stood up and called out, "Hey, Papa. We're in the temple, Carlin and me." There was a sound of crackling as Uncle Will moved through the weeds toward them.

"What're you doing here?" he demanded.

"We came to see how the temple was coming along," Carlin said and looked down, sensing that was the wrong explanation.

"It's not coming along at all," Uncle Will said, and his voice was angry. "I stopped the work on it months ago. And it's not a good place for you girls to play. Come on now." He climbed up on the platform. "I'll see you back to the road."

There was a thrashing noise in the thick leaves behind them all at once, and they turned as an old colored man emerged from the undergrowth. He was beating the branches back with a heavy stick, but he stopped when he saw them, stared a moment, then continued toward them slowly.

"Mornin', Marsa Will," he said and bowed. His kinky gray hair was bound with a red cloth, and a raveled old undershirt showed beneath the bib of his ancient overalls. "Mornin' to you, little ladies." He nodded, his Adam's apple working visibly in his thin throat. "Jest tryin' to beat them bushes back a little, so they won't come suckin' up around your buildin' here, Marsa Will."

Uncle Will gazed at the man and frowned. "That's fine, Reuben. I thank you." He drew a leather change purse from his back pocket and took out some coins. "Here's something extra for your trouble," he added and gave the man the change. Carlin looked away, uncomfortable that Uncle Will should give a colored man money that way, even an old one. Papa would never do that.

"Thank you, Marsa. Thank you kindly," the old man said. He turned and moved back into the undergrowth, making a softer thrashing sound.

"Lord, how I hate that." Uncle Will breathed in and struck one fist into the palm of his other hand. "Marsa. Oh my God." He stared down at the dry stalks of goldenrod beside the platform.

"Reuben must be about the oldest darky here at the Grove. Born in slavery and now look at him. Free?" He gave Carlin, then Amy, a challenging look and paused. Carlin waited, not knowing what she should say. "He's not free," Uncle Will went on. "He's a sharecropper. Do you know what that is?" Carlin nodded. There were no sharecroppers at Rosalie, but there were some at the Grove, and most of the farms on the way to town belonged to sharecroppers. "The fact is there's no real difference between share-croppers and slaves," Uncle Will announced. A long moment passed. Uncle Will stood still, his hands opening and closing at his sides. "That terrible system comes from our one-crop economy. See?" Carlin nodded again, not knowing what else to do, as she and Amy stood there before him.

"It's got to change. We've got to diversify. Plant different kinds of crops. We're bleeding our land. Bleeding it." Carlin stared. Beyond the fence was a cotton field, ragged and brown now after picking, with leaves still clinging to the stalks. Was it bleeding? Could a field bleed?

"Oh, listen to me." Uncle Will stooped to their level all at once, putting his hands on his bent knees. "Sometimes I just get up on my soapbox. Come on now. Let's go back to the road."

Uncle Will strode ahead, making a path through the weeds for Carlin and Amy. When they got to the fence he lifted them over. "What about those?" he asked, pointing to the hoops they had left beside the road. "Do they work?"

"No. It's all bumpy and rutty here," Amy said. "They keep falling over."

"Ah." Uncle Will lifted a hoop and ran his fingers down the side of the smooth wood. "In Paris, you see lots of children playing with these in the parks. They have beautiful smooth allées there for rolling." Carlin watched him turn the hoop. Did he miss Paris? Was that what was making him sad?

"I know what we'll do," Uncle Will said all at once and turned back to them smiling. "We'll try them on the front gallery." He pulled the hoops over one shoulder and began walking rapidly toward the big house. "We'll move the rockers and the long table," he said, speaking quickly, as the girls half-ran to keep up with him. "We can clear a wide space, I bet. That gallery's good and long. I ought to know." He laughed. "I designed it."

Carlin had to stop to slap a mosquito on her leg, and she stood a moment watching her uncle, leaping ahead with Amy half-running beside him. Was this what Aunt Georgia had meant? One minute Uncle Will was angry about Reuben and the bleeding field, and the next he was hurrying to the front gallery to roll their hoops. Right now he was almost flying.

※

Mama came into the schoolroom on a gray November morning and bent over to touch Miss Mollie's shoulder. "Mollie, there's a telegram for you." Her face was serious, her eyes focused on the teacher.

"Me?" Miss Mollie rose at once. "Where?" She looked small and bird-like standing next to Mama. "Where is it?" she asked, and Carlin drew in her breath, inhaling her teacher's fear.

"Come down to the library, dear. Thomas has it." Carlin stared. She had never before heard her mother address Miss Mollie as "dear." Mama led the way, leaving Carlin and Tommy staring at each other on opposite sides of the schoolroom table.

"It's bad news," Tommy said. "Telegrams always are."

"Maybe her papa's sick or her mama," Carlin began.

"Or Paul," Tommy added.

"Not Paul," Carlin said. "They can't send telegrams across the ocean." But maybe they could. "Let's go to the landing," she said.

There was not much to see from the stair landing. The library door was closed, and they could not make out the low voices on the other side. Miss Mollie did not return to the schoolroom. Mama came up instead.

"Miss Mollie has had some sad news," Mama said.

"What sad news?" Carlin asked. "What's happened?"

Mama stood a moment, looking at them. She sat down in Miss Mollie's place at the head of the table and stretched out her arms, taking Carlin's hand in one of hers and Tommy's in the other. "Paul has died," she said slowly. "It's very sad."

"Paul?" Carlin looked at her mother open-mouthed. "Oh no."

"Yes. It's a shock."

"But how, Mama? How did he die?" Carlin thought of the sepia photograph in Miss Mollie's locket, the deep eyes, the drooping moustache. How could Paul be dead?

"He died of influenza in Berlin."

"Oh no," Carlin said and heard Tommy groan. "We must talk to her, Mama." She pulled her hand back and rose. "We must go cheer her and . . . and. . . ."

"Yes, dear. In a little while. Tomorrow maybe. But today, this evening, we'll let her be by herself. That's what she wants." Carlin sank back onto the bench. If Miss Mollie really wanted to be alone, she thought, as her eyes filled with tears, they would wait.

Miss Mollie's sorrow pressed around them. Aunt Ceny took a tray of supper to her room and another tray at breakfast time, and her absence from the table seemed ominous. Would she go home to New Orleans? Would she ever return? When Carlin looked out of the schoolroom window in the afternoon and saw Miss Mollie walking slowly past the row of camellia bushes toward the marble bench at the end, she pulled her sweater on and flew down the stairs and out into the garden.

Miss Mollie was sitting on the bench, her back toward the house, when Carlin came running up to her.

"Miss Mollie," Carlin panted. "I . . . I. . . ." Miss Mollie turned and Carlin saw her red, swollen eyes. "I'm so sorry," Carlin said. "We all are. I mean . . . I mean, is it really true? I can't believe it."

"I know, dear. I can't either," Miss Mollie said and held out her hand. "But I guess I must."

"Wasn't influenza one of the diseases he was trying to cure?" Carlin asked and clutched her teacher's hand.

"It's all so ironic," Miss Mollie said and sighed. "He was study-ing the bacterial diseases, and he died of a disease they still don't understand, one of the most common of all."

Carlin pressed her lips together to keep from crying as she stood looking down. She sat down on the bench, and Miss Mollie put one arm around her shoulder, and they hunched close together on the damp marble seat. "He was tired and he was working so hard. He said in his last letter that he wasn't feeling well, that he might take off a few days, but—It happened so fast. A high fever and then—Oh!" The exclamation came out in a moan. "If only I could have been with him."

Carlin reached over and squeezed Miss Mollie's knee, causing a network of wrinkles to appear below in her long dark skirt. "I never thought he would die," Carlin said, feeling tears start down her cheeks. "I never. . . ." She lifted her hand from Miss Mollie's knee and smeared back the tears. What could she possibly say? What could she do?

"It's such a waste, Carlin," Miss Mollie began. "Not just for me. Paul was such a bright, kind man. The world needed him. He could have done so much good." She covered her face with both hands as Carlin sat watching. "I wish you had met him." Miss Mollie brought her hands down to her lap again. "You and Tommy and Evie. He would have liked you." She clasped her hands together tightly below her chin.

"I wish I'd met him," Carlin said slowly, but she felt as though she had. She thought again of the photograph in Miss Mollie's locket, for it seemed to her that she knew Paul well, his eyes, his hands, the way he sat forward to stare into that microscope that Miss Mollie had described, and most of all the way he gathered Miss Mollie to him and kissed her mouth.

"I'm going home to New Orleans for the funeral," Miss Mollie said.

"Will you come back to us afterward?" Carlin asked, and sucked in her breath and waited for her crucial reply.

"Yes," Miss Mollie said. "I think so. I've been happy here. I'll stay with my family through the holidays and come back in

January, I think." She hugged Carlin's shoulders again and started to rise.

"Me and Tommy," Carlin began. In her relief, she felt a sudden need to express their sympathy in a grown-up way. "We want you to know that we're very sorry," she continued. "We wish he was still alive."

"Thank you, Carlin," Miss Mollie said. "But start that sentence again."

"Me and Tommy. . . ." Carlin stopped. "Tommy and I," she said. "Oh, I wish I could get that right. It sounds so babyfied the other way."

"You'll get it. You already have. It's just a matter of hearing the right voices in your head."

"We'll do our lessons while you're gone," Carlin promised. "And our chores, and keep the schoolroom neat until you come back." They started up the front walk together. Carlin glanced up at the library window and thought all at once of the Bible on Papa's desk. "Why did God do this, anyway?" she demanded suddenly and looked up at Miss Mollie. "It doesn't make sense. It isn't fair."

Miss Mollie put her arm around Carlin again and pulled her close. "A lot of things in this life are unfair, Carlin," she said quietly. "That's one thing I'm learning, and you'll have to learn it too."

❀

"Mama, did you know there're only five more days till Christmas?" Carlin sat on the carved rosewood bench beside her mother's dressing table, watching Mama pull her long black hair forward across her shoulder and pick up her silver-backed brush. "I've got so much to do," Carlin continued. "I've got to make presents for the dolls and all the animals too." She saw her mother smile and stared down at the rug.

"Sam's easy since all he wants is a bone." She tugged at her wrinkled stocking. "But I have to make catnip balls for Kitsy and Fo' Bits, and I haven't finished Papa's present yet, or Tommy's either." Carlin hesitated. She couldn't tell Mama that she was bored with the present she was making for her—a soft blue cloth to wrap around her violin, with red cross-stitched initials in the center. She had told Aunt Lucy, who was helping her, that some girls just weren't meant to hem and stitch. "Wrong," Aunt Lucy had said. "All well-bred young women know how to sew."

"I wish we had better presents for Hamlet and Feely, Mama. I wish we could give them some oranges too."

Her mother put down her brush, wound her hair into its soft twist in back, and anchored it with some hairpins. "You're such a worrier, Carlin." She reached out and patted one of Carlin's stockinged knees. "Christmas is supposed to be a happy time, dear, especially for children. Not a time to worry." Carlin stared at her mother. It was useless to remind her that she was not a child anymore.

⚜

"Children?" Carlin looked up from the mounds of catnip that she and Tommy were wrapping on the rug to see Papa standing in the doorway of her bedroom. "Come with me," he said. "I want to show you something." Carlin stared. Papa's voice had a quiver of excitement and his eyes looked bright. What did he want? What was happening? "It's a secret," he whispered and put one forefinger to his lips. "You've got to promise not to tell anyone."

"What is it, Papa? What?" Carlin and Tommy clustered around him, Carlin in her nightgown, Tommy in his long nightshirt.

"Come downstairs with me. Your mama's in the parlor with Grandfather, so be very quiet." Grandfather was staying at the Grove for the Christmas holidays, but he had come to dinner and would be at Rosalie on Christmas Day.

Carlin and Tommy followed their father down the stairs, moving stealthily across the hall in their bare feet. Papa closed the library door behind them, then bent down and lifted a box from the floor beneath his desk. He opened it, and Carlin and Tommy crowded close, watching as he took out a black case. He clicked the catches on the side and raised the lid. A violin lay nestled in the blue plush lining. Carlin drew her breath in with a little gasp as she stared down at the glowing amber wood. There was a delicate ivory inlay around the edge of the sound board, and the carved bridge looked elaborate and old. Carlin stooped down to look. It was clear that other chins had settled into that smooth black chin rest, for the whole instrument seemed polished with time.

"What do you think?" Papa demanded. "Think your mama'll like it?"

"Oh, Papa," Carlin said. "She'll love it. She really will."

"It's old, but it has a lovely tone. I bought it last week in New Orleans. Your mama saw it when we were there together a year ago. She tried it out in the shop, and I knew she wanted it." He made a little clucking sound. "It cost more than I should be spending now, but. . . ."

Carlin gazed up at her father, thinking of how he had planned and saved. Mama would protest that he shouldn't have, but she would be pleased. "You really think she'll like it?" Papa said and tugged at his moustache. He was so proud of himself, Carlin realized, and so excited.

"Oh, yes. She will. She will," Carlin said.

"She will, Papa," Tommy echoed. "I know it." The room glowed, and they were here in secret, Carlin thought, as Papa shared with them the gift of love and music that he would give to Mama on Christmas morning.

Carlin and Tommy took Evie with them when they were excused from the table after Christmas breakfast. The wide hall was fragrant from the boughs of pine that wound around the banister railing. There were sprays of smilax above the portraits in the hall, and the front looked curiously dim, Carlin thought. The long pocket doors to the parlor, which stayed pushed into their compartments on either side of the doorway for months on end, had been pulled shut, cutting the parlor off from view. She stared at the dark mahogany surface of the doors, thinking of the tree inside, which Mama and Papa always decorated together on Christmas Eve and kept as a surprise for Tommy and Evie and her on Christmas morning.

"Let's just push the doors open a little bit," Carlin said "and have a peek. They won't know. They're still having breakfast." She let go of Evie's hand and curled her fingers around the brass fixture.

"We shouldn't," Tommy said as Carlin tugged, but he crowded into the crack she had made, making room for Evie in front as Carlin craned over them. The big pine that James had cut stood in the bay window, its branches bright with decorations, red wooden apples, elves with peaked hats, and the white lacy strings of popcorn that Carlin and Tommy had made. Carlin thought of her father and mother hanging the wooden apples and deciding where the gold horns and the red Santas should swing. Had they laughed as they unpacked the ornaments and talked of other Christmases, or had they been rushed, thinking of Grandfather's arrival the next day, worrying about Rosalie's shabbiness, and the presents they couldn't afford?

"Look, Carlie." Tommy pointed to the carved white angel pinned to the top of the tree, her glittery wings outspread. Her face looked stern, Carlin thought, as if she might wing off to some other tree or family celebration if this one proved not to her liking.

She heard voices down the hall. "Crop rotation is important, of course." Grandfather was talking to Mama as they started up the hall. "But sometimes I think Will does more talking than planting, you know."

Carlin pulled the doors shut quickly, and they stood with their backs to it, watching Mama take a large basket from the hall table. "Now, if you'll take that, Father." She pointed to a larger basket on the floor. Grandfather bent and lifted it, and followed her out to the front gallery. "You come along now too, Carlin. I need your help," she said. Carlin followed and watched them set the baskets on the long gallery table where two other baskets were waiting.

"Put the chewing tobacco there," Mama directed, and Carlin lined up the packages of Red Coon on one side, then the little clusters of pins and curls of ribbon on the other side along with a jumble of dress goods. Six magnets, a bunch of lollipops, some firecrackers, several tiny bags of marbles, some wine balls, and a clump of licorice sticks went in the center. James brought out two large boxes, one marked shoes, the other gloves, though both seemed crowded with other woolen things as well, sweaters, and dark scarves, and socks that Aunt Lucy had knitted.

The paved section of the drive and the lawn in front were already full of people, laughing and calling to each other in the gray mist of the winter morning. The family gathered on the front gallery, Carlin and her parents, Grandfather, Tommy, Evie, Aunt Lucy, and Aunt Tazey, Papa's younger sister, who always came in from town to spend Christmas at Rosalie. Papa put on his spectacles and held up the list Mama had made.

"I think we should begin," he said in a loud voice. "Tyson, I see there are some presents here for you." Tyson, a thin dark man in overalls, came forward followed by his two boys, both in shoes, though one lacked laces. "A magnet for you, Errol," Papa said, bending down to smile at the child, "and marbles for Macbeth. Beth, that is."

"Thank you, sir. Thank you, ma'am." Tyson bowed to one and then the other. Carlin looked down. She wanted the colored people to get their presents, and yet this part of Christmas seemed embarrassing somehow, almost wrong. Papa looked back at the list and continued. Carlin watched as the spread of objects on the table got smaller. Only one packet of Red Coon was left, then none, and the boxes of shoes and woolen things were empty.

Papa moved to the top step of the gallery. "Reverend Ambrose," he said. "Would you come forward?"

Reverend Ambrose was Aunt Ceny's husband, and he had been at Rosalie as long as Carlin could remember. He was standing in the center of the semicircle of people, between Aunt Georgia and Aunt Ceny, looking unfamiliar in the silk top hat and black cutaway coat that Grandfather had given him three years ago. He removed the hat, and, holding it carefully in the crook of one arm, he mounted the steps to the gallery and bowed first to Mama, then to Papa and Grandfather, smiling his double-chinned smile as he inclined his fuzzy gray head. "Would you kindly say a few words to the group this morning, Reverend?" Papa asked.

The Reverend nodded. "This is the day, Lord," he began, and

his deep voice rang out in the moist chilly air. "This is the day when Your son was born to this world."

"Amen," Aunt Georgia shouted from the group on the lawn and other voices joined her. "Amen, Amen."

"We thanks you, Lord, for this gift—a Christmas gift of which we is proud."

"Amen," the voices broke in again.

"Lead us in the footsteps of Your son, the Lord Jesus, and to Heaven when we die. We think of Heaven, and we needs to think how we's gonna get there, how we's gonna make ourselves ready for that time of paradise," the Reverend continued, "but. . . ." He smiled his huge white smile and turned to look back at the family. "Not now," he said and smiled down at Evie, who was holding Mama's hand. "There are children here who want to get to their Christmas presents, like little Miss Evie and Master Tom and Miss Carlin. And all of our own," he added and looked out at the crowd beyond him in the drive.

"Hallelujah," voices shouted. "Amen."

The Reverend bowed to Papa and Mama, then to Grandfather, who bowed in return. Grandfather looked grave and dignified in his black suit, which might well become the Reverend's someday.

"Thank you, Reverend," Papa said as Reverend Ambrose stepped down from the gallery and returned to his place on the lawn. "Stop by the kitchen now, everybody, and get a drop of Aunt Georgia's toddy before you start home." There was laughter and applause at this announcement, and the group began to move off toward the kitchen house. "Merry Christmas to you all," Papa called out. "We'll see you at the creek tonight for the Christmas fireworks."

⚜

Bunches of tissue paper were burning wildly in the fireplace behind the brass fender in the parlor, and ribbons were strewn around the rug, for all the presents had been opened. Carlin gazed down at her atlas with the gold writing on the front and lifted its cover gently. There were pages and pages of colored maps inside, hundreds of places she could read about and visit someday. She glanced over at Tommy, who was fitting a new train together on the rug. Just beyond him, Evie was trying to push the arm of her stuffed rabbit into a red sweater Aunt Lucy had knitted for him. Carlin looked up at the circle of family above her: Grandfather in the big armchair, the aunts on the horsehair sofa, and Mama in the carved rosewood chair, holding her new violin. Carlin sighed. It was all over. The dizzying time of the presents had passed. Soon they would have Christmas dinner, and tonight there would be fireworks by the creek with the cousins and Uncle Will and Aunt Emily. But the exciting part of Christmas had come and gone.

James appeared in the parlor doorway, bowed slightly, and spoke to Papa, who was standing at the fireplace. "Excuse me, everyone. I'll be right back," Papa said and followed James out of the room.

Carlin opened the atlas to France and found the big red dot marked Paris. "Carlin," Papa said from the doorway. "I want you to come outside a minute."

Carlin looked up at her father. "Outside? Now?" She rose from the rug and straightened the ribbon at the back of her dress. Why did Papa want her to go outside now?

"Come out, everybody," Papa ordered. "There's a surprise."

Carlin hurried across the hall behind her father and out onto the front gallery. Mama and Evie followed, and Carlin could hear Aunt Lucy ordering Aunt Tazey to push in the fire screen tightly before they left. "We don't need to have the house catch fire on Christmas morning."

Carlin stopped and stood beside her father at the top of the steps. There in the drive was a trim little black pony. Eben, the stable boy, stood beside him, holding his bridle, which was decorated with a large red bow. The pony turned his head, displaying a white streak on his nose. He wore a new saddle, and a brand new riding crop hung down from the pommel. A white card dangled below the pony's chin. Carlin pulled her breath in and turned to her father with a questioning look.

"Go see what the card says, darlin'," her father directed. "It just might be for you." Carlin stared at her father a moment, then leapt down the gallery steps.

The pony laid his ears back and took a step sideways as she ran toward him. "Easy, boy. Easy," Eben said, tightening his grip on the bridle. He untied the tag and held it out to Carlin.

She recognized her uncle's small slanting hand and caught her breath. "It's from Uncle Will," she called to the others. She glanced back at the group watching her from the gallery and felt her face flush as she read the message. *Dear Carlie, I'm sending this pony to be your very own. You must name him soon, and I hope you'll ride him over to Felicity Grove often.*

"Oh, oh," Carlin cried out and threw one arm around the pony's neck, inhaling his horsey smell.

There was a sound in the drive beyond her and she stepped back to see Uncle Will coming toward her on Fancy. He must have been watching from under the pecan trees. "Uncle Will," she shouted. "Is he really for me?"

"He's all yours, sweetheart. All yours to ride and ride. Isn't he pretty?"

Uncle Will rode up close, dismounted lightly, and handed his reins to Eben as he took the pony's bridle. Carlin started to give her uncle a hug, but stopped and smiled instead, conscious again of the family watching her from the gallery.

"Oh, Uncle Will." Carlin squeezed her hands together as her uncle stroked the pony's neck. "I can't believe this." She reached up and patted the black hair, following the path of her uncle's hand.

Uncle Will turned toward the gallery, smiling. "A pretty sight, isn't it? A little girl with her first pony."

Carlin glanced down at her red velvet dress, then turned to the gallery. "Can I go change, Mama?" she asked. "I want to ride him right away and—" She stopped.

Grandfather had stepped forward. He looked tall and stern as he stood gazing down, one hand clasping the balustrade. "Isn't this Christmas morning at Felicity Grove, William?" he asked.

Uncle Will turned. "I beg your pardon, sir?"

"The master of the plantation stays on his plantation on

Christmas morning, doesn't he? He doesn't go visiting around among his relations giving large presents."

Uncle Will turned back and took Fancy's reins from Eben. He slung them over the saddle and mounted quickly. "I'm on my way back to the Grove right now, sir," he said. "I just rode over to make sure the pony was all right."

"Will," Mama called out. She leaned across the balustrade. "Will. You're coming here tonight, aren't you, for the fireworks down by the creek?"

Carlin glanced from her mother to Uncle Will, sitting high on Fancy, remote-looking now under his wide-brimmed hat. Her throat tightened.

"Yes, we'll be here," Uncle Will called back. "We're looking forward to it." He pulled on the reins. "Goodbye, all. Merry Christmas."

"Uncle Will," Carlin started. "Wait. I haven't said thank you." Her uncle lifted his hand to wave at her, then trotted down the drive toward the live oak trees. She saw him pass the hedge with its dry tangle of jasmine vine and break into a canter as he started across the field to the pine woods and on to Felicity Grove.

Carlin stared at her grandfather, then back at the pony. Eben handed Carlin a piece of sugar cane. She held it out and felt the pony's soft mouth fill her hand, his lips nibbling. Was he really her own? Should she keep him, or should she give him back to Uncle Will so that Grandfather wouldn't be mad? Carlin turned to her father, who had come down the gallery steps, and started to ask, but Papa put his arm around her.

"Don't worry, darlin'," he said. "It's all right." But Carlin heard the tension in his voice and squinted, feeling tears rise. Why did everything have to be so mixed up and sad? Anyway, he's mine, she thought, and leaned her head against the pony's neck. Mine.

❧

It was time to get up, but Carlin stayed curled under her quilt. She hated winter. It was just day after day of boring mud, no rides on her pony, no visits to the Grove, and no trips into town, just mud

97

everywhere. Miss Mollie had still not come back, and with Christmas over, there was nothing to look forward to anymore.

The door opened and Tommy stood in the doorway, looking waiflike in his nightshirt. "There's funny white stuff all over the garden and the drive. It's coming down like rain. But it isn't rain."

"What?" Carlin sat up in bed and twisted to look out her window. A fine white powder had turned the gallery roof from copper-brown to gray-white. It had covered the top of the balustrade and edged the bare wisteria vine. Carlin flung back her covers and dashed to the window. "That's not rain. That's snow."

"Snow," Tommy repeated. "Snow in Mississippi?"

"It must be," Carlin said. "That's the way it is in stories. Come on. Papa'll know."

Their father was standing on the front gallery, wearing his brown coat and wide-brimmed hat. "It's snow all right," he said. "Happens about once a decade here. Get dressed, you two, and get some caps and mittens on. I'll show you how to make a snowman."

"A man out of snow?" Carlin and Tommy rushed up the stairs to dress. They found scarves and unmatched gloves in the battered chest in the hall and ran outside.

Carlin paused on the top step of the gallery and stared. The world around her was changed, silent and white. The dark leaves of the magnolia tree were sprinkled with whiteness, and the box hedge, usually a network of bare branches, was rounded with snow.

"Look, the fence posts have hats," she shouted. She gathered some snow in her glove and stared down at the queer crystal-like powder.

"You start with one of these. See?" Her father patted a snowball in his hand. "Then you roll it like this." He stooped and pushed the ball a foot or two on the ground, leaving a little trail of wet black weeds and twigs behind.

Carlin and Tommy worked fast, panting as they rolled the balls and carried them back to Papa. The fact that Papa was playing with them in the morning before breakfast was almost more startling, Carlin thought, than the white rain drifting down.

They had already used or trampled the thin layer of snow

around the chinaberry tree, so they had to cross over beyond the rose arbor to roll the third ball for the head. They ran to the kitchen and brought back two chunks of coal for the eyes. "You need a carrot for the nose," Papa told them, and Carlin turned to run back. But the sound of beating hooves came from the snowy drive.

A man was riding toward them under the white canopy of the oak branches. "It's Uncle Will," Tommy called out. "Look. He's come in the snow."

Carlin and Tommy ran up to him as he stopped at the hitching post and slid down. "Isn't this exciting?" Carlin shouted.

"Yes. Fine, fine." Uncle Will tied Fancy and glanced back at Papa, who was standing on the gallery steps.

"Look at our snowman, Uncle Will. I'm going to make a nose with a carrot and. . . ."

"I need to talk to you," Uncle Will said, looking up at Papa. He brushed the melting snow from the shoulders of his jacket.

"Of course," Papa said and opened the door. "We'll go in the library and build up the fire."

"Can't we finish the snowman, Papa?" Carlin called out. "We want to finish his face."

"Not now," Papa said. His voice was firm. "It's time for you two to come in. Take off your wet things and go have your breakfast. Tell Aunt Ceny to bring a tray with coffee to the library."

Carlin put her mittened hands on her hips. "But Papa, the snow," she said and heard her voice rise with an angry quaver. "We might never get to make a snowman again!"

"You heard what I said, Carlin." Papa looked stern. "Come in right now." Carlin stamped and kicked at her loose boot, but she followed Tommy, who had already started up the steps.

"It's not fair," she muttered and heard the tremble of crying in her voice as her father closed the library door.

"It's because Uncle Will came," Tommy whispered. "Something's wrong."

Carlin forgot about her uncle, for suddenly Miss Mollie was back. Carlin, Tommy, and Evie rushed down the stairs and she hugged each one in the front hall. "Oh, it's so good to have you here again," Mama said. "How's your family in New Orleans?"

"They're fine. Just fine." James brought in her trunk and took it upstairs. Then he returned from the buggy carrying a wooden box and a big black horn. "Those go in the library," Miss Mollie directed.

"Mollie. What in the world?" Mama turned to stare.

"Well, my father bought it last year, and since he and Mother are going to be in Europe for the next two months, I thought I'd just it bring it to Rosalie for a while. It was Father's idea actually. When I told him how you loved music and how you always wanted the children to hear more, he insisted I bring it, and the conductor was very helpful on the train."

"Oh gracious," Mama said. "How generous."

Carlin and Tommy stared as James put the wooden box carefully down on the desk in the library and rested the huge black horn in Papa's empty chair.

"What is it?" Carlin demanded. She watched Miss Mollie attach the horn to the top of the box, then she bent to stare at a metal plate attached to the front. It showed a little dog listening to a horn. "Oh, I know what it is," she shouted and gave a jump. "I know. It's a talking machine. A Victor Talking Machine. Is that right?" Miss Mollie smiled and nodded as Carlin clapped her hands. "I've seen that dog picture in *McClure's*. Oh, Miss Mollie. Can we play it now? Please."

"Please," Tommy joined in. "Please."

But Miss Mollie shook her head. "Tonight. After prayers," she told them.

"Now?" Carlin said when prayers were finally over. "You're going to play the Victor Talking Machine now, aren't you?"

She and Tommy clustered around the desk. Mama was standing just behind them, and Papa, though he remained in his chair, was watching intently. There was a round plate covered with dark green felt and a shiny metal arm that stuck out across the plate. Carlin stared into the huge black horn with its scalloped edges which reached out almost to Papa's chair.

"Oh, Mollie," Mama said. "To think we have this all to ourselves for two whole months. How good of your father."

"Isn't it wonderful? Now what shall we start with?" Miss Mollie asked. "Oh, I know what you'd like." She pulled out a thin black platelike object from a leather case and fitted it down onto the machine. "Now, this is a record," she said. "Let's hope it works." She leaned down to wind a metal handle on the side of the box. The record began to turn. Miss Mollie straightened and put the arm down on the outer edge. Carlin and Tommy hovered close, watching the spinning black circle. There was a grinding noise, then a whine.

"Oh, wait. I didn't put the needle down right." Miss Mollie picked up the arm again. "Sit down, children. You can hear better." Carlin and Tommy sat on the rug and hugged their knees. The grinding noise came again, then all at once the sound of a man's voice singing. Carlin stared.

"Oh, it's Caruso," Mama said and clasped her hands together. "Thomas. It's Caruso."

"*Che gelida manina se la lasci riscaldar,*" the man sang.

"That's Italian," Miss Mollie explained, looking down at Carlin and Tommy. "It's from *La Bohème,* a famous opera. He wants to warm the hand of a girl he loves because she's cold. She's sick with tuberculosis, you see."

Carlin pulled her breath in with a jerk and looked down at the rug. Wouldn't the song remind Miss Mollie of Paul? Still, she had picked out the record herself. Carlin looked up at Miss Mollie, who was smiling at Mama.

"*Ma per fortuna,*" the man was singing. He seemed so in love and so sad, Carlin thought, as she cupped her chin in her hands.

"How does it make the sound?" Tommy asked and stood up to bend over the machine again.

"The record has little grooves," Miss Mollie explained. "They vary according to the sound and they make the needle vibrate, you see."

"But how does . . . ?"

"Shh," Carlin said and stared up at the black horn as Caruso sang on. She didn't want to know to know how the machine worked now. She didn't even want to know what the Italian words meant. Caruso, who lived in Rome perhaps, was here at Rosalie and he was in love with this lady with her cold hands.

Had Uncle Will loved Aunt Emily the way Caruso loved this lady? Would a man ever love her that way? Carlin tightened her elbows against her sides. "*Aspetti signorina*," Caruso sang on in his beautiful voice. What did that lady feel? What was she thinking? Love, love. What was it like?

⚘

Uncle Will was sitting at the breakfast table, but he had not touched the sausages or the mound of grits on his plate. He sat with one elbow on the table, talking to Papa in a low voice as he drank his tea. Carlin could hear him only in snatches over Evie's chatter on her other side. There was something about his failure in architecture, his failure in something else. Was it planting? Carlin couldn't hear.

It was almost time for lessons. Carlin excused herself to go upstairs, but stopped on the staircase landing and looked out of the arched window. Beyond the chinaberry tree, the sky was bright and the lightning rod on the stable roof gleamed in the February sun. She stood staring out for a moment, then ran back to her room for her sweater. There was time for a ride if she hurried.

"I'm going to take a quick ride. Want to come, Uncle Will? Lightning's really lively in the morning." The pony's name had come to her suddenly one morning when he broke loose from Eben and tore down the drive. "I want to show you how well I can ride now." She waited, half-expecting rejection.

Uncle Will glanced back, then looked down at the table again. "Your uncle's talking to me, Carlin," Papa said. He pulled his watch from his vest pocket. "You don't have much time. Just up to the north field, then straight home. You mustn't be late for Miss Mollie."

"I won't be," Carlin shouted and ran out to the back gallery and across the brick courtyard.

"Hey, Carlin." Hamlet and Beth were kneeling over a clutter of muddy boots by the kitchen door. Scrapers, cans of polish, and dirty rags lay spread around them.

"Hey," Carlin called back, but she did not stop. She ran down the path to the stable yard, leaped over the ruts, ducked between two weathered boards in the fence, and stopped at the manure pile beside the barn, where Eben was shoveling. "I'm going to ride Lightning now. Just a quick ride before lessons."

"It's only eight, Miss Carlin, and I ain't got the stable horses fed yet."

"Please, Eben. He won't mind. He likes to be ridden before breakfast."

"Just listen to that little missy now." Carlin looked through the wide door into the dimness of the barn and saw Aunt Julia, sitting on a milking stool beside one of the cows, her petticoats dripping down between her large knees. She laughed and turned back to Eben, holding one teat in her hand. "You might jest as well let her ride, 'cause she gonna get her way anyhow."

"All right." Eben glanced from Aunt Julia to Carlin. "But the fact is, that pony don't like to be ridden 'fore his breakfast." He jammed his spade into the manure. "Still, if you're set on it, come on."

Lightning trotted toward the north field slowly, reluctant to leave the stable, but when Carlin emerged from the pine grove and turned him toward home, he broke into a canter, wanting his feed and the warmth of his stall. Carlin leaned forward, feeling his shoulder muscles churn. He was plunging down the back road, his metal hooves drumming on the hard ground.

Carlin squeezed her knees and pulled hard at the reins, meaning to slow him down as he approached Reverend Ambrose's garden at the corner. The Reverend stood leaning against the fence, smoking his pipe as he watched Aunt Ceny hoe. At the noise of Lightning's beating hooves, they both turned to stare. "Just look at that," Carlin heard Aunt Ceny call out. "Just look how Miss Carlin can ride."

She felt the blood hot in her cheeks as her braids blew back and heard a shout from the kitchen courtyard. "That's a way, Carlin," Beth yelled, and Carlin looked up to see him standing on the bench in the courtyard with Hamlet, cheering. "Keep a' comin'," Hamlet shouted. A shutter was flung open, and Carlin saw Miss Mollie with Tommy on one side and Evie on the other, staring down at her from the schoolroom window.

"Hang on, Carlie," Tommy shouted. "Hang on." Carlin's breath was coming in noisy pants, and she started to twist to glance at the dining room window. Surely Papa and Uncle Will would hear the shouts and look out too. She would rush past them and then she would stop sharply at the mounting block at the stable door, slide from her saddle in one smooth movement, and hand the reins to Eben with a little slap. "Thank you, my man," she would say, just the way a friend of Uncle Will's had done when he had dismounted there a few weeks ago. She would show them all what a stylish rider she was.

All at once Lightning veered from the path and plunged past an abandoned tool shed, across the back yards directly toward the stable. Carlin jerked hard on the reins, trying to pull him back to the road, but he was intent on the short cut through the weeds and up through the yard. He certainly wasn't going to stop at the mounting block to let Carlin dismount decorously. She would be lucky if he let her off before he charged straight into his stall.

"Lightning," she yelled, keeping her voice low in the hope that she might still look like a daring rider. "Light!" She heard Star, her mother's Morgan, whinny, welcoming the pony home. Carlin tugged at the reins, but she knew she had lost control.

As they came pounding toward the yard, Carlin glimpsed Aunt Millie, the laundress, sitting in an old kitchen chair beside the iron laundry pot. She was gripping a long stick, stirring the boiling sheets as steam rose in a thin gray column. At the sound of Lightning's hooves, she turned her head in her soft faded hat and for a moment Carlin saw the whites of her terrified eyes as the pony galloped toward her.

A burning hand caught Carlin under the chin. A clothesline, she thought, as she felt herself yanked backward. It was Monday washday, and Aunt Millie had crisscrossed the yard with lines. She kicked one foot free and felt herself fall backward over Lightning's haunch. She shook her left leg, but it was caught in the stirrup. She was being dragged, she realized. For a long moment she could see the veins in a brown oak leaf just above her, then it was dark.

"Whooee, Carlin," Hamlet shouted. "What a fall." The yell came to Carlin from a long way off. She opened her eyes, closed them, then opened them again. The oak leaves were dipping way down. She put her hands on the damp earth beside her and pushed herself up to a sitting position. Her back was on fire, and one thigh seemed numb. But it was the swaying of the trees around her that made her groan.

"Lordie, Miss Carlin." Aunt Millie was bending over her. "You all right?" Carlin stared up at the dark wrinkled face, framed by the cloth hat.

"I think so," she said and raised one muddy hand to touch her burning neck.

"Them lines got her good," Hamlet announced as he came running up. "She didn't even see 'em." Carlin clutched one knee as she glared up at him.

"She was showing off how good a rider she be and then, wham," Beth said, joining him. Carlin grimaced as she leaned forward. She would stand, she resolved. She would stand right now and walk to the kitchen house, even if her back were broken.

"You all right?" Carlin felt a pain shoot through her neck and down through her shoulders as she turned her head. Owen stood above her; his crest of black hair looked higher than usual, and his eyes were dark with alarm.

"I'm fine," she mumbled. "Where's Light?"

"He ran straight to the stable," Owen said.

Carlin stood. The house beyond her was rocking, the laundry tub, the fence. Her backside felt open. She reached behind her quickly and touched bare skin. Clutching her ripped overalls together, she turned, hot with the fear that Owen or the other boys had seen. The skin underneath was wet, maybe bloody. She took a step, then another. She was going to the kitchen house, and she wasn't going to cry or faint either, not in front of those boys, not in front of Owen.

"You all git out of here. Git," Aunt Georgia shouted as she hurried down the path toward Carlin. "You go back and finish them boots," she told Hamlet and Beth. "Now don't you walk none," she said to Carlin. "You got a blow on your head, honey. You gotta rest." But Carlin moved on. The kitchen house had settled, and the fence was two steady lines of weathered rails now, not wobbling gray shapes moving up and down. She stepped onto the path.

"All right, then, Miss Smarty," Aunt Georgia said. "If you bound you gonna walk, put your arm around my waist."

Carlin put one arm around Aunt Georgia. "Did Uncle Will see?" she asked. She did not look up, fearing another jab of neck pain. "Was he at the window in the dining room?"

"No, no. He didn't see nothin'." It was Aunt Ceny's voice. She had joined Aunt Georgia and Aunt Millie as they moved across the courtyard, surrounding her in a little group, Carlin realized. "They was in the dining room, talkin'. They weren't watchin' you."

Aunt Georgia held open the door to the kitchen house and Carlin stepped in. The warm room smelled of baking bread, and the big lamp glowed beside the floured board. "Come here and bend over," Aunt Georgia ordered, pointing to the oilcloth-covered table. "Let me see that backside."

Carlin moved to the table, but the kitchen house felt crowded. She glanced from the three dark faces to the window. "No," she said, clutching her torn pants with both hands. "Not here."

"Go pull that curtain," Aunt Georgia ordered.

Carlin heard the ring of the hooks as Aunt Ceny jerked the curtain along the rod. She bent over obediently and took her hands away from the torn overalls.

"You got a big rake scrapin'," Aunt Georgia said, staring down. "That's what you get when a horse drugs you. It'll hurt a while, but it'll heal, honey. We just got to clean it good. That's all."

"I gotta get back to them sheets," Aunt Millie said, watching from the far end of the table. "Look like it's not too bad, Miss Carlin. You be all right soon."

"I'se goin' too," Aunt Ceny said. "I'll tell your papa and the teacher you's goin' be all right. Good thing your mama's over at the Grove, or she'd be right here worryin' around." She followed Aunt Millie to the door and pulled it shut behind her.

Carlin let out a long breath, relieved to be alone with Aunt Georgia. She pushed down her overalls, stepped out of her bloomers, and leaned across the table, wearing only her shirt and sweater. With one cheek pressed against the oilcloth, she watched Aunt Georgia take a stack of clean white cloths from the corner cabinet and fill a speckled blue basin from the iron kettle on the stove. Carlin felt the soft warmth of a cloth pressed first on her buttock, then on the back of her thigh, and she raised her head to watch as the water in the basin turned pink.

Aunt Georgia took a little bottle from behind the row of spice jars and put it on the table. The label read IODINE, and displayed a drawing of a skull and crossbones. Aunt Georgia unscrewed the top, held up the glass dropper, and bent over Carlin's buttock again.

"This gonna smart some," she said as Carlin felt the glass touch her skin. "That hurt?"

"No," Carlin said, but she shuddered and bit her lip hard as Aunt Georgia moved the dropper in a wide area. The liquid ignited the wound. Her buttock and leg were on fire now. Brown-orange flames seemed to encircle her whole back.

"Now I'm going to bandage it best I can," Aunt Georgia said. Carlin heard the sound of cloth ripping and felt the material against her skin. Aunt Georgia pulled narrow strips around her upper leg and fastened a larger one to her waist. She put an arm around Carlin and helped her straighten. "You're a brave girl. You know that? You done good. No fussin', no cryin'. I'm proud of you."

Carlin felt tears jump to her eyes. She had managed not to cry from the pain of the fall or the cleaning of her scrape. She mustn't start crying now just because Aunt Georgia said she was brave. She took the clean overalls that Aunt Georgia held out and stepped into them awkwardly. "I shouldn't have lost control," she said. "Lightning wanted his breakfast. In the end, all I could do was try to hold on, and I didn't even do that."

"That pony got a mind of his own." Aunt Georgia chuckled. "Stubborn little beast. But you gonna learn him soon. You'll see."

"I don't know. I wanted to show Uncle Will how well I could ride." She straightened and looked around her.

"You gonna be a fine rider. Now you just sit down there and rest yourself a minute while I get these loaves in."

Carlin eased herself into the rocker by the window and sat half-turned so that her weight rested on her less damaged side. She gazed at the tan mixing bowl that stood on the table beyond the clutter of the bandage cloths. Aunt Georgia lifted a soft mound of dough from it, put it down on the floured table top, and shaped it into a loaf.

"The black beast is on Uncle Will again, isn't it?" she said and looked up at Aunt Georgia's face. "I mean he's so quiet and sad, and he keeps coming over to talk to Papa."

"Yes. Your uncle's sad." Aunt Georgia nodded. "And that worries your papa and mama, and your Aunt Emily, too, of course. It'll change though. It's bound to change."

"But when?" Carlin asked.

"You never can say exactly. But I feel it's comin' soon. I mean, I knowed your Uncle Will a long time," she said, "and I say one of these days he gonna be talkin' and singin' and playin' the piano and makin' plans again. You just wait."

Carlin nodded and looked down. "Aunt Georgia," she began. "Do you ever get a little. . . ." She paused, not sure that she wanted to go on. "Do you ever get a little mad at Uncle Will? Why can't he act like other people?" She stopped. The question seemed mean.

"Well, honey," Aunt Georgia said. "He just ain't like other folks. That's all." She paused and wiped her hands on her apron slowly. "We all gets cross at Mister Will now and then. But we love him dearly, and that's the truth."

❧

Carlin eased the door shut behind her and started across the back gallery. Mama was practicing and didn't like people making noise.

"Carlin, what's that you're carrying?" Carlin turned at the sound of Aunt Lucy's voice. She had forgotten about her thin aunt in her black dress out here on the back gallery, doing the accounts. Her lap desk with its green felt cover lay open on the wicker table, and Aunt Lucy sat peering at her through her metal-rimmed spectacles.

"Just a doll, ma'am," Carlin said.

"Let me see."

Carlin hesitated, holding the doll, which was wrapped in a small patchwork quilt.

"Show it to me, Carlin." Aunt Lucy put her pen back in its holder and snapped off her glasses. Carlin lifted the stocking doll slowly, knowing a scene lay ahead. "That's a darkie doll, Carlin. That's not yours."

"No, ma'am. I mean yes, ma'am. Her name's Daisy." Carlin clutched one of the black arms and looked down. Daisy's white button eyes stared up at her in a pleading look, and her short straight mouth seemed stretched into a scream. "Me and Feely like to—" Carlin stopped. It wouldn't help to tell Aunt Lucy that Josie, Carlin's stocking doll, had spent the night with Feely while Daisy had slept on the trundle bed beside Carlin. "Aunt Georgia made me and Feely both dolls, and we changes 'em sometimes, you see."

"Heavenly days, Carlin, listen to your language. Now: Aunt Georgia made dolls for Feely and for me, and we exchange them from time to time. Doesn't that sound better?"

"Yes, ma'am." Carlin nodded and squeezed Daisy's arm. She knew that more than grammar was involved in the lecture her aunt was about to give.

"In my opinion, Mary Carlin, you spend entirely too much time with that little darkie. And really, playing with a black doll."

"She's just a stocking doll," Carlin began. "Aunt Georgia made her and. . . ." Carlin left the sentence unfinished. There was no point in arguing with Aunt Lucy. There had been a long dull time after picking when Feely wouldn't play at all. Then sometime in November they began again with the dolls. She thought of Aunt Georgia, sitting by the kitchen house door, selecting a black stocking and then white one from the big straw mending basket on the ground beside her. "These here stockings don't have no mates, so your papa ain't never gonna wear 'em again." She had stuffed each stocking with short rags as Carlin and Feely hung over her, watching the dolls' bodies grow plump.

"They need eyes," Carlin insisted, and she and Feely had spread out the contents of the button box on the brick surface of the courtyard, searching for the best pairs of eyes. The black one was for Feely, the white for Carlin. They had names before they had dresses, and they were best friends.

"Don't you see, Carlin," Aunt Lucy continued. "You can get diseases playing with those darkie children's toys. They're dirty. They're not right for you to play with."

"But Feely's my best friend." Tears smarted in her eyes, and she clenched her free hand at her side, feeling hot. "I can too play with her, if I want to, and I will." Her heart was pounding, and she could feel her jaw shake. "You can't make the rules here," she added. "You're not my mother."

"Carlin." Mama was standing in the doorway. "Apologize to your aunt this minute," her mother said. "Then go take that doll back to Feely."

Carlin looked from her mother to her aunt and back to her mother again. Whose side was Mama on anyway?

"I'm sorry, Aunt Lucy. I didn't mean to say that." She clutched Daisy against her dress and started down the gallery steps. Was Mama really mad at her, or was she mad at Aunt Lucy? Carlin hesitated at the bottom, feeling hot. Aunt Lucy was mean, mean.

"Lucy, I have to tell you," Carlin heard her mother begin. She ducked behind the box hedge at the side of the gallery and crouched down to listen. "I don't like you to discipline my children." Mama sounded weary. "I know you mean well, and I appreciate your concern for them, but—"

"Surely, Isabelle," Carlin heard her aunt break in. "Surely you can see that those toys the darkies play with are dirty. They're bound to be. Carlin could pick up some disease." She made a sound in her throat. "Of course, they're your children. I'm only the widowed sister-in-law who keeps the household accounts."

"I appreciate all you do, Lucy. You know that. I've never been good at figures."

Carlin watched her mother move to the edge of the gallery and stare into the distance as she raised her hands to massage her long fingers. "This is a lonely place, Lucy," Carlin's mother said and sighed. "My children have almost no friends outside of their cousins, and they only see them once or twice a month. If they can find some amusement and happiness playing with the colored children, for Lord's sake, Lucy, let them do it."

Aunt Lucy said something that Carlin couldn't hear, then she rose and went into the house. Carlin watched her mother stand by the balustrade a moment longer, staring out across the field, then she too turned and left.

Carlin crept out from behind the hedge and started running toward the quarters. Why was everything so sad and complicated all the time? A sob had risen in her throat, and she stopped beside the toolshed and sank down on a weathered bench, letting Daisy slide to the ground. Aunt Lucy was mean and unfair. What did it matter that Feely was colored? Feely was her best friend. The real trouble was that nowadays Feely didn't always want to play. Carlin covered her face with her hands, feeling tears leak out between her fingers. Aunt Lucy wasn't supposed to tell her how to talk and who to be friends with. That was Mama's job.

As Carlin bent to pick up Daisy, she saw Uncle Will coming toward her across the barnyard. He'd come to see Papa, she thought. He waved, stepped over the low fence, and strode toward her.

"Hey, Carlie." He stood looking down at her a moment. "How are you?"

Carlin pressed her lips together and looked up. She needed to wipe her nose. He would see that she'd been crying. Papa would have given her his handkerchief, but Uncle Will just stood there smiling.

"Mind if I sit with you a minute? I'm waiting for your papa." Carlin nodded, not trusting her voice. Uncle Will sat and crossed his legs in his long brown boots slowly, so that Carlin had time to raise one arm and wipe her nose with the back of her hand before he looked at her again.

A rusty middlebuster plow lay in a clump of purple vetch beyond them. Her uncle nodded at a yellow-bellied sapsucker that had lighted on the sidebar and leaned forward to watch it. He was ignoring her tears on purpose, Carlin realized, giving her time to get over them. She pushed back her braids and looked at him. Did the fact that he had come to sit with her mean that he was feeling better?

"It's awful to say," she began and looked down at her feet. "But sometimes I hate Aunt Lucy. She doesn't like me and she tries to boss me around. She doesn't like me playing with Feely. She doesn't like the way I talk, and she doesn't like colored people, and what's more, she comes to Rosalie every year and stays for months and months, and it makes Mama sad. I know it does."

"Yes," Uncle Will said and looked off across the weeds toward the stable. "Lucy can be hard to live with. She's lonely, and that makes her difficult sometimes. But she's not alone in not liking colored folks, you know."

"Yes, but she. . . ."

"There're a lot of people like Lucy in the South, Carlie. Slavery was wrong, but it was around here for a long time, and it's taking years to recover from it." He leaned over and pulled up a blade of meadow grass from a tuft beside the bench. Carlin held still. This was the longest talk she had had with Uncle Will in weeks, since before Christmas maybe. He was definitely feeling better. Aunt Georgia was right; the black beast had gone.

"You know when I was in Paris studying, I used to think I could never come home again, never live amidst this hate and violence. But I was born here. I love Mississippi. In the end, I knew that I had to come home."

Carlin looked at her uncle, waiting for him to go on, but he was silent, staring at the plow. Maybe she was wrong. Maybe he was still sad. "Do they have colored people in France?" she asked, eager for him to talk again.

"Yes, but there they're treated just like anyone else."

"Really?" Carlin twisted to look at her uncle. "They are? Like white people, you mean?"

"Yes, like white people." Uncle Will looked at her, then back at the weeds.

"Do you miss Paris, Uncle Will? Do you want to go back?" Carlin sucked in her breath. Maybe the question would make him sadder. But Uncle Will smiled and twisted the long strand of grass.

"Sometimes," he said. "Sometimes I miss it a lot. I miss the parks and. . . ." He stopped and turned to her. "You know everybody gets sad sometimes, Carlie, and angry too. The trick is to find ways of lifting yourself up out of your sadness so you can go on." He sat a moment looking down at the scuffed dirt between his boots. "I keep a diary too," he said, still looking down. Carlin drew her breath in. He did?

"Turns out, I mostly write in mine when I'm feeling sad. Sometimes when I was feeling sad in Paris, I'd take my diary and go to the Luxembourg Gardens. It wasn't far—a nice walk, really. There's a special little pond there I used to head for. Not the big one, a little one further off with a fountain. There's a statue there back under a chestnut tree. I used to sit on the marble bench and look out at the pond and up at the dark red leaves of that chestnut tree. There were birds, city sparrows mostly, but finches too. I'd hear them above me as I sat writing. That chestnut tree, that *arbre châtaigne*, became a friend just like that *petit oiseaux qui chante*."

Carlin sat silent a moment, seeing the pond, the fountain, and the dark chestnut tree. "Does *'oiseau'* mean bird?" she asked.

"Yes and *'chante'* means sing." He smiled.

"And the chestnut tree?" Carlin asked. "What did you call it?" She would ask Miss Mollie about French, she resolved. She wanted to learn more words and real sentences too.

Her uncle did not answer. "It was beautiful there," he said. "Peace. Freedom, and yet, yet. . . ." He broke off another piece of grass and folded it over. "I want to help Mississippi recover. That's my vision, Carlie. To help Mississippi recover and grow strong. Do you see?" Carlin nodded. She was not sure what Uncle Will meant by a vision, but she knew he had confided something important to her, and she sat up straight, feeling quiet and more grown up suddenly.

Aunt Georgia had told Carlin to call her parents to dinner. It was past noon, and the ham was getting cold. But when Carlin ran to the door of the library, she stopped and stared. Her father was sitting with his elbows on the desk, his head in his hands. Her mother stood close by looking down at him. "I can't believe it's this bad, Belle," he said and lifted his head to stare up at her. "I just can't believe it. There was no sign of them at all yesterday afternoon, and then this morning, everywhere. Not a square on any one of those plants in the north field. Not one square."

Carlin stared. A "square" meant a bud on a cotton plant. She knew that. But what had happened? Mama nodded as she stood with her arms folded across her breasts. "We lost about a bale last year," Papa continued. "But now . . . now it's the whole north field. The whole field," he repeated and looked at Mama again. "I've got the men picking up the squares so we can burn 'em, the way Mr. Knox from the Extension Service told us. He was right when he predicted that we'd see that bug again this year, Lord knows. Leapt the river in 1908, he said, and now it's here in Warrington County. I was upset when I saw it last year, but oh, Belle, when you see that north field. Those plants were coming right along too, squares on almost every one of them." He let his head sink into his hands, and Mama moved to put her arm around his shoulders.

"We can save the south field, I think, the pond field too, maybe. But the north field, I don't know. I think it's gone."

"What about that spray dust that Mr. Knox talked about," Mama asked. "That Paris Green?"

"Yes, yes. We'll use that and anything else he can think of, but. . . . Oh, Belle. Pray. We've got to have the Lord's help now if Rosalie is to survive."

❧

Carlin fled to the north field after rest time. She had run along the path just yesterday, noting the buds poking up from the cotton leaves, the "squares," as they were called. She climbed the fence and held onto the top rail as she looked out. But the field looked the same, just rows and rows of cotton plants with men bending over, raking or hoeing. Papa was wrong. The boll weevil hadn't come to Rosalie. She looked again and realized all at once that the squares were gone at least none of the plants near where she stood had squares. Then she saw them. They were scattered along the dirt rows between the plants like bits of paper. She jumped down, ran up the path, and looked out at the field again. Once more the rows were full of the tiny dead buds.

"Hey," she called to Tyson, a thin colored man stooping over near the end of the row.

"Hey there, Miss Carlin." He straightened and pushed one hand under his overalls straps to rub the small of his back. "You come to see Mr. Weevil, our visitor?"

"Yes, but I don't see him," Carlin said. "All I see is the squares on the ground."

"That's where he's at. Right in them squares there." Tyson stooped and picked up a cotton bud. "See here." Carlin moved close to study the bud in his hand. "See, he's just a little eensy spot. But now, there. See that?" He separated the thin leaves of the bud. "That green thing there. That's him. That's Mr. Weevil all right. That's what they call the larva."

"But it looks so little," Carlin protested. "How could it hurt a whole cotton field?"

"Oh, he grow fast, Mr. Weevil do. Pretty soon he be a grown bug with gray wings and crawly legs and a snout, even though he not much bigger than these here larva."

"Oh," Carlin said and nodded. "But how can these little ones hurt the squares like they do?"

"They don't just hurt 'em," Tyson said. "They strikes 'em. Strikes 'em dead. See that?" He pointed to the long row with the buds sprinkled on the ground. "Your papa says we's got to gather all them squares now and burn 'em fast so's they don't turn into them big critters. 'Cause if they do, they's gonna make more trouble, real trouble." Tyson looked out over the field toward the quarters, then back at the big house behind them. "Trouble for colored folks and trouble for white folks too."

Carlin watched her father when they gathered after dinner for evening prayers. His face looked tired, she thought, and he had trouble finding his place in the Bible. Her mother moved out to the gallery with Aunt Lucy afterward, both of them taking their sewing. Papa came and sat down. But Carlin, who was sitting cross-legged on the floor beyond them, reading, watched him stand up again after a few minutes and go back into the library. Poor Papa, she thought, and rose quietly. She stood in the doorway to the library, looking in, wanting to say something, not knowing what. Her father sat close to the oil lamp, the Bible open on his knee. His spectacles were balanced low on his nose, and it seemed to Carlin that his lips were moving as if he were murmuring a prayer. Oh God. Please, help Papa, Carlin whispered to herself as she tiptoed up the stairs. Make the boll weevil go away. Please.

✠

An acrid smell of smoke from the piles of burning squares hung over the courtyard and seeped into the house during the week that followed. The north field was abandoned, except for a few patches, but the work of hoeing went on as usual in the pond field, and in the south field too. Standing at her window in her nightgown in the early morning, Carlin saw her father ride out to supervise the work as always. Despite the weevil, the routines of Rosalie life were continuing, yet they all knew that the loss of the north field was bad.

"Will Papa have to sell Rosalie, do you think?" Tommy asked Carlin one evening as they lay in the hayloft, talking. "I mean, next year if the weevil comes back and takes the south field too."

"Sell?" Carlin repeated and looked at her brother. "Why would he sell? Things aren't that bad." But maybe they were, she thought. "If the end comes," she said and frowned, "it'll be slow, probably. Miss Mollie says a lot of plantations get by with less cotton than Rosalie grows."

"The weevil didn't even go to the Grove," Tommy said. "And they're rich. They could afford to lose a field, but we can't."

"I know." Carlin looked down at the jumbled straws of hay.

"It's not fair," Tommy said. "Papa works a lot harder than Uncle Will, but he's the one that got the weevil."

Carlin drew her breath in with a hissing sound. The comparison seemed wrong, put into words that way. She pushed her feet out straight in the hay and looked down. "If Uncle Will would buy that new gin he and Papa went to look at. . . ." She paused. "That would help. I mean, our gin keeps breaking down, and if Papa could just take the cotton over to the Grove. . . ." She paused again and they sat silent a moment.

"Carlie?" Tommy bit down on his thumbnail and looked over at her. "What would we do if we had to leave Rosalie?"

"I don't know," Carlin said. "I don't know."

※※

Spring moved into summer, and June was hot. Carlin swung the egg basket back and forth as she ran to the chicken house. She opened the door and was engulfed in the smell of feathers, dust, and excrement. She looked around her quickly, sensing that someone was there.

"Hey, Carlin," a voice said.

Carlin turned sharply and saw Owen, Mr. Rayley's son, scrubbing the window with a wet rag. "Hey," she said. "Why're you doing that?"

"Punishment," Owen said. "I cursed."

"Oh." The window, which was cracked at the bottom, was clouded with bits of feathers and droppings that clung to the surface. "That's a hard job. Have you got to clean the whole place?"

"Yeah," Owen said. He dipped the rag into the bucket beside him, squeezed it, and went on scrubbing.

"I know where there's a knife." Carlin put down the basket and poked behind a pile of feed sacks in the corner. "Here. The blade's bent, but it'll get some of that ick off."

"Thanks." Owen took the knife and turned to scrape. A wad of feathers and dried excrement dropped off. He continued scraping.

Carlin bent to gather some eggs from the empty nests. Owen's scraping and the low settling sounds of a hen nearby were the only noises in the quiet. "I'm going to the town school next year," Owen said.

Carlin straightened to look at him. His dark eyes seemed to burn into her as if there were worlds of other things he could tell.

"You are?" she said.

"I'm going to live with some town people my papa knows."

"Oh." Owen was leaving. He was going to school, the way she had always wanted. He would leave Rosalie in the fall, and Carlin might never see him again. She stared a moment, then picked up the egg basket. "Aunt Georgia's waiting for these," she said and opened the chicken house door.

✿

The long hot summer was almost over. Guests were coming for dinner, and Carlin was sitting on the rosewood bench beside her mother's dressing table, watching her mother lift a string of coral beads from a velvet-lined box and hold them to her neck. "That looks pretty," Carlin said and paused. "Mama, I'm worried about. . . ." She hesitated. "About the harvest. I mean, what if it's bad again? It can't be good with only two fields." She waited.

"Carlin, your father manages the plantation, and he doesn't need you worrying over it too," her mother said. She leaned toward the oval mirror, considering the look of the reddish beads against her pale neck. Then she turned to look at Carlin directly. "I know you worry," she said in a different voice. "We all do, and you're right. It is serious. The harvest will be bad." She sighed and put the beads on the dressing table. "There are so many things that need repair or replacement or . . . and right now there just isn't enough money."

"But . . ." Carlin hesitated, reluctant to threaten this moment of direct talk with an annoying suggestion, and yet. . . . "Why don't we borrow some money from Aunt Emily and Uncle Will, Mama? They're rich, and the weevil didn't bother them at all. Uncle Will's going to buy a new gin for the Grove, isn't he? And then Papa can use that."

"Yes. Maybe," her mother said. "I'm not sure." Mama paused.

118

"Your father doesn't want to borrow if he can help it. Rosalie is better off than many other plantations, you know. We'll get through this somehow." She took a puff from the cut-glass jar on the dressing table and dusted her neck quickly, then picked up the beads again and fastened them. "Try not to think about it, Carlin," she said and reached over to pat Carlin's knee. "And above all, don't let your father see you're worried."

"Yes, Mama."

"And Carlin." Her mother put a hairpin in her bun and frowned as she turned back to Carlin. "There's something I've been meaning to mention." She paused and glanced at the window. "It's time now that you begin to put a little distance between you and Feely, you and Hamlet, you know. They've been good friends for you as a little girl." She let her breath out and squeezed her hands together. "But you're becoming a young lady now."

"But Mama," Carlin started.

"Oh, Carlin. Let's not argue." Her mother put her fingertips to her forehead, hiding her face as though a headache had started. "A lot of things don't make sense. You just have to do them anyway."

Carlin ran down the worn path between the cabins. Mama's injunction about not playing with Feely still boiled within her. She could never tell Feely what Mama had said, so now she would have to lie and sneak off all the time. She stopped in front of Aunt Georgia's cabin and wiped her forehead. Her skin seemed covered with a slime mixed with gnats and weed pollen. "Hey," she called and opened the door, but the dim interior looked empty.

"You lookin' for Feely?" Hamlet backed out from under the house. "She ain't here. She's helpin' with the chickens."

"Oh." Carlin nodded.

"You wanta see our little piglet? Mama bought him with her sewin' money. He's gonna taste mighty good come Christmas."

"You've got a piglet?" Carlin stooped and followed Hamlet as he crawled back under the cabin.

"We'se keepin' him in a cage till he get bigger." It was almost cool down on the packed earth, and Carlin could make out a wooden crate in the dimness. Hamlet removed a wire mesh, picked up the pig, and backed out into the light. "He's the best little piglet we ever had." He held the little pink and tan animal close, rocking him lightly. "Ain't he cute?"

Carlin bent closer and scratched behind the soft ears. The pig squirmed and scrambled against Hamlet, its tiny hooves scratching his shirt, then he twisted suddenly and jumped to the ground. He turned to glance back at them and tore off down the path into the undergrowth.

"Oh, holy Jesus," Hamlet shouted. "My Mama'll skin me alive if I lose that pig."

They turned and rushed after him. Carlin could see the piglet yards ahead as he scooted on through the vines toward a little branch of the creek. Hamlet plunged into the weeds, cursing as he trampled. Carlin followed, then paused a moment. She could hear the hum of gnats near the creek and the soft trickling sound of the water. All at once she saw the piglet, hesitating by a little crepe myrtle tree half-covered with honey suckle vines. If she could just get a little closer, she might be able to corner him there or by the crumbling log further on. She moved into the undergrowth, forgetting snakes, ignoring the brambles that clawed at her ankles, keeping her eyes on the pig, who was still poised by the low tree.

"Here piggy, piggy," she whispered and crept a few steps closer. She saw his pointed ears move, sensing her behind him. "Here we go," she said and lunged forward, catching him under her chest. The pig squealed, but Carlin clutched him in both hands and gathered him close. "I caught him. I caught him," she shouted to Hamlet, who was all the way up to the stream.

Carlin stood, holding him, as Hamlet rushed back through the weeds. "Oh, Carlin. Thank God," he breathed. "My Mama woulda skinned me. I mean it." He breathed out heavily.

"I was lucky. Here." Carlin handed over the pig and stood beside Hamlet a minute, panting. "It's so hot," she said, pushing the hair back from her forehead. "Let's get a drink." She moved through the brambles and knelt down in the moss beside the little rivulet that ran down to Carter's Creek below. Cupping her hands together, she scooped up some cool water, gulped thirstily, then sat back on her heels and held her wet hands to her face. "Want some?" she asked, turning back to Hamlet. "I'll hold him a minute while you drink." Hamlet handed her the pig, then leaned over the water.

"They's some what say this water ain't good to drink from," Hamlet said as he mopped his mouth with the back of his hand. "What with runnin' through the pasture and all. But I say when it be this hot, ain't no water can hurt you. It's the thirst what hurt you. Here, you bad piggie, you." Hamlet sat and put the piglet down between his outspread legs, holding a fold of the pinkish hair on his back, and Carlin sat down opposite him. "Put your feets out, Carlin," he directed. "We'll make him a cage."

Carlin spread her legs, but as her bare feet touched Hamlet's bare soles, she tightened a moment and glanced around. Mama wouldn't like her doing this and Aunt Lucy would be furious. She looked down at the piglet who was nosing the barriers of flesh enclosing him; Hamlet's long dark legs with their roughened knee caps and Carlin's smudged whitish ones, sticking out from her old dress, one of them with a bloody scratch. She was disobeying, but who would know? She watched the piglet snuffle his way into the middle of the enclosure, then turn and flop against Carlin.

"He's so cute," Carlin said, pleased all at once to be sitting in the moss with Hamlet as if the piglet was their child. She leaned back on her hands and smiled as a mockingbird called from a willow tree nearby.

"Pickin' time soon," Hamlet said.

"Lay-by in a couple days," Carlin added.

"It sure was bad about that weevil. My mama say your papa— Mister McNair, I mean—he gonna get a loan from his brother over at the Grove, and that mean Rosalie be all right soon."

"A loan? Is that what your mother said?"

"Well, stand to reason if your papa's goin' save Rosalie, he got git money somewhere. Why not from his own brother, what he love?"

"Maybe." Carlin scratched behind the piglet's ears, then leaned back and looked up into the leaves. Sitting here in the moss with the trickling creek nearby, Rosalie's problems seemed far away.

❧

Lay-by time had come again. Carlin loved the sudden easy feel of the plantation when even her father seemed to relax. The cotton yield would not be good this year, but it would be better than Papa had first expected, Mama said. Had there been a loan? Carlin didn't know. She was just enjoying lay-by, thinking of the field hands fixing their houses or sitting on their stoops, talking, before the heavy work of picking began.

The dining room was dim, the lamps unlit, and it felt almost cool in the evening quiet. Aunt Lucy had left that morning to visit kin in Memphis, and all at once there was just the family at Rosalie.

Aunt Ceny had taken Evie upstairs to bed, and Tommy had been excused, but Carlin sat listening to her parents talk. She had turned eleven in the spring, and as she sat gazing at her mother, then at her father, it seemed to her that they were her friends now, not just the powerful heads of the family. She looked at the familiar bowl of wax fruit in the center of the table and up at the portrait of her great-grandmother staring down. Carlin knew a cricket was nestled in the shadowy fern that stood in its iron holder near the half-open window. Maybe it would sing tonight.

Her mother glanced around the table where the only remaining signs of the meal were the cut-glass water goblets standing on the white tablecloth and her parents' two demitasse cups in their flowered saucers, each holding a small silver spoon.

"How about a little poetry tonight," Mama suggested. She smiled at Papa at the other end of the long table and thrust her chin up in a teasing challenge.

> *On either side the river lie*
> *Long fields of barley and of rye,*

She paused, then continued:

> *That clothe the wold and meet the sky;*
> *And thro' the field the road runs by*
> > *To many-tower'd Camelot*

Her mother waited, her eyes bright. Carlin turned to look at her father, eager to see if he was going to join this game, which Carlin loved. Papa smiled at Mama, put his napkin on the table beside him, and began in his deep voice.

> *And up and down the people go,*
> *Gazing where the lilies blow*
> *Round an island there below,*
> > *The island of Shalott.*

"*Willows whiten, aspens quiver,*" Mama broke in. "*Little breezes dusk and shiver. Then something, something runs for ever, Flowing down to Camelot.*"

"Oh help," she laughed. "We can't get stuck this soon." She rose and hurried across the hall to the library. Papa smiled at Carlin and leaned back in his chair. "I've got a story to tell you about your mother and poetry."

"Here it is," Mama said, coming back to her chair. "Listen." She held an open volume bound in green, and Carlin could see the name ALFRED, LORD TENNYSON written in gold script on the cover. "Here we are. '*Four gray walls, and four gray towers,*'" she continued.

> *Overlook a space of flowers*
> *And the silent isle imbowers*
> > *The Lady of Shalott.*

Carlin put one elbow on the tablecloth and sank her chin into her hand as she watched her mother, then her father, continue, reciting bits, laughing and glancing down at the book again. How smart they were, how elegant. "*God in His mercy lend her grace,*" Papa said, reaching the final line. "*The Lady of Shalott.*" Mama laughed and flung herself back in her chair. Papa looked across at Carlin, his face flushed and smiling. "That's the way I met your mother," he said. "It was all Tennyson's fault."

"Oh, no, Thomas. You said you liked my dark mysterious eyes."

"I did. I did," Papa protested. "But the way you quoted Tennyson made me look at them in the first place."

"Oh, you're such a romantic," she laughed. "Now me. I just saw a handsome man who lived next door to Emmy at the Grove, and I thought to myself, now if I married him I'd be close to my sister."

"But didn't you . . . ?" Carlin stopped. There was so much more that Mama could tell, if she would.

Her mother turned and smiled at her. "Didn't I love him?" she said and looked at Papa tenderly. "I certainly did, his quiet way of standing, his hands. I loved his hands and. . . . Oh, it was embarrassing. I knew that first evening that I'd just have to get that man to propose to me."

"And when did he?" Carlin asked, watching her mother so intently that she did not hear the footsteps behind them in the hall.

"How's my favorite family?" Uncle Will's voice was loud. Carlin saw her parents turn their heads abruptly. His face looked flushed and he seemed large, hulking in the doorway in his tan breeches and riding boots. A blue silk scarf that matched the stripes in his shirt hung twisted on one side. Carlin saw her mother glance at her father, then turn to Uncle Will with a deliberate smile.

"What a nice surprise," she exclaimed. "Come in, Will. Would you like some pie? Some coffee?"

"A little coffee would be perfect." Uncle Will sat down at Tommy's place. "You look beautiful tonight, Belle," he told Mama. "But then you always do."

Carlin's mother smiled and shook her head so that her coral earrings trembled. "How are you, Will? Getting ready for picking?"

"Oh, cotton, cotton." He groaned. "I want to get some new crops started at the Grove, and at Rosalie too next spring. But right now. . . ." He smiled at Mama. "I've written a play." He looked around the table, smiling at them all. "It's a play about the Grove and the war." He put his forearm on the table. "I want you all to come and see it." He turned to Papa with a laugh. "I want lots of clapping. Lots of praise. Six o'clock tomorrow evening on the front lawn at the Grove. All right?"

"I'm not sure about tomorrow, Will." Papa had risen. He turned from the sideboard where he stood holding the silver coffeepot. "The gin saw's gummed up again, and Porter's driving out from town late tomorrow afternoon to take a look."

"That won't take more than an hour. You can be at the Grove by six." Uncle Will turned back to Mama. "You see, it's a play about the Grove—the old story of its burning in the war."

"I see." Mama nodded uneasily.

"I got started last night after supper and I wrote all night. Emmy showed me her father-in-law's journal the other day, and I was amazed. It goes right through the war and it's really vivid, even though he never left the Grove. I've built the play on it mainly, but I've used some other histories too. I really think I've written quite a remarkable little drama."

"That's lovely, Will. But staying up all night. . . ." Mama paused.

"Don't worry, Belle. I'm fine, and it's quite a play, if I do say so myself. It really is."

"But who'll be in it?"

"All the children, principally Carlie, of course." He swung around to face her. "You're the heroine. You've got the most lines."

Carlin felt a flush rise and she swallowed. The heroine? Mama reached across the tablecloth and encircled Carlin's wrist with her hand. "What about Amy, Will? She'd make a lovely heroine too."

"Don't worry, Belle. Amy has an important part, but she's not as good at learning lines as Carlie is. They'll be sisters actually." He turned to his brother. "I drove to Natchez early this morning and bought one of those new arc lights they use in the theatre there. It's really bright. Two carbon electrodes. Perfect for the stage. I'll be able to get great effects with it for the fire. I'm going to use a red scarf and . . . I rented a gasoline generator from Morton's." He paused and gave a quick laugh. "I brought it home this afternoon on the mule wagon. This way I can really do the fire, which is the big scene," he said, turning back to Mama. "You know the terrible fire at the Grove when the Yankees arrived? The lamp's crucial. I've got the costumes all lined up too. Aunt Philadelphia's going to run up Amy's skirt tonight and she'll do Carlin's tomorrow."

"You rented a gasoline generator?" Papa paused a moment behind Will's chair, holding a demitasse cup in its saucer.

"It's important, Tom." Uncle Will glanced up at Papa, who frowned as he put the coffee down in front of his brother. "You see, the thing is, with this light and the red scarf. . . ." He turned back, took a small spoon from the saucer, and stirred his coffee briefly. "You see, with the light and the scarf I can get fantastic effects. I tried it an hour ago, and even in the daylight it's marvelous. It's going to be spectacular at night."

"Renting a generator's a big investment." Papa's face was grave as he returned to his place. He took a sip from his water goblet and leaned back in his chair. "By the way, Will. Have you had a chance to look through those bank forms I brought over? Mr. Marvin needs to have all that done before we go any further."

"Marvin, Marvin. I get sick of Marvin's needs. I'll do the forms when I'm ready." He looked at Papa again. "I'll do them, Tom," he said in a quieter tone. "I'll get to them tonight." He turned back to Mama. "You see, the thing is, the audience has to be convinced about the fire. The fire is what gives the play its power, its ultimate meaning."

So there was to be a loan, after all. The thought flicked through Carlin's mind, but the play pushed it aside. She was to be the heroine and would have more lines than Amy. Carlin stared at her uncle's hand, chopping the air as he talked. There had been a magic in this room just before he arrived, with Mama and Papa reciting poetry. Now it was gone. Carlin looked up at the portrait, then at the fern by the window. It seemed to her that the room was grieving.

"I want the children there right after breakfast," Uncle Will said. "Nine sharp, if possible."

"But what about their lessons?" Mama said.

"Oh, forget the lessons this one day. The play will be a grand history lesson."

"The fact is, I can't spare the buggy horse in the morning," Papa said and looked at Mama.

"Then I'll send Holton with the surrey," Uncle Will said. "He'll be here at nine." He pressed his lips together a moment as if he knew they were thinking of the Model T, still awaiting repairs in the Grove stable. Uncle Will drank down his coffee and rose. "Get a good sleep, Carlie," he said. "You have lots of lines to learn tomorrow." Carlin looked up at her uncle, suddenly hot with excitement.

"We're going to make it into a party," he said, glancing back at Carlin's mother. "The Randolphs are staying with us for the week, you know, and Emmy's invited the Dabneys and two other couples."

Mama raised her eyebrows. She glanced down at Papa, then back at Uncle Will. "All right," she said, "I'll make sure Carlin and Tommy are all ready for Holton when he comes. And tell Emmy I'll have Aunt Georgia bake an almond cake."

"Good." Uncle Will bent to kiss Mama. "Goodbye, everybody. It's going to be an evening to remember. I can feel it in my bones."

They sat silently, listening as Uncle Will crossed the hall and went down the gallery steps. There was the clatter of Fancy's hooves on the paved part of the drive, and then Uncle Will's voice as he called, "Night, Toe," at the gate, and the sound of hooves dying away in the evening quiet.

"Good heavens," Mama said. "What a whirlwind." She looked at Papa and twisted her water goblet. "I just wish he wouldn't do things so fast. Buying that fancy lamp and renting that generator. Gracious. As you said, that costs a lot of money."

"Yes." Papa stared down at the tablecloth. Carlin looked at her father, then her mother. The times when Uncle Will's black beast was with him were worrisome, of course, but his happy times seemed worrisome too.

"Belle." Papa looked up at Mama. "Will you go over to the Grove with the children tomorrow morning?" He paused. "It would relieve my mind."

"Yes, of course," Mama said. "I was going to propose that myself."

The cricket made a thin chirruping noise in the fern. Carlin waited, but it did not sing.

It was exciting at first, sitting on the rug in the Grove library, listening while Uncle Will read the play. They rehearsed all morning, but Aunt Emily appeared just before dinner, and she and Uncle Will walked out to the rose garden together. "Amy's not going to be such a quiet sister," Uncle Will announced when he returned. "I'm going to rewrite her part so she'll have more lines."

"But that's not fair," Carlin whined. "I've learned all my lines and. . . ." She would have continued, but something about her uncle's eyes, shiny, yet tired-looking with gray pouches underneath, made her abandon her protest midway.

When they started on the revised play, Ted, who was supposed to play the old father, wouldn't come down from his room to rehearse. When he finally did, he mumbled his lines, getting them wrong both times they did the big scene. Uncle Will clenched his fists and yelled a bad word at him. He stamped off to the library, and Carlin and the others stood on the gallery looking at each other, uncertain whether the play would happen at all.

"Come on," Amy said, and she and Carlin ran down the drive to the graveyard. Carlin felt strange to be there that afternoon for the moss-covered obelisks marking the graves of the two sisters they were impersonating stood in the corner by the iron fence: Lila Baldwin, 1821-1868, Amy Baldwin, 1823-1869. Would the sisters approve of Uncle Will's play, or would they rise and shake their bony fingers at Carlin and Amy, and stare at them with accusing eyes as their white hair blew out around their ghostly faces?

Carlin settled beside Amy on their usual gravestone under the Spanish moss that dripped down from the elm above. "Uncle Will ought to remember that Ted's been away at school all year," Carlin said and scratched at a scabby patch of moss on the stone. "He isn't a child. I mean he's different from the rest of us."

"Oh, school doesn't matter to Papa Will," Amy said. "He and Ted just don't like each other."

"But they have to get along," Carlin protested.

"Ted doesn't like having a new papa. He liked our real papa more."

"Well." Carlin paused. "It's hard for Uncle Will too." She drew in her breath. "I mean, sometimes he feels like he has a black beast on him."

"I know," Amy said and wound a piece of grass around her wrist. "Sometimes he's all happy and fine, and sometimes he gets so grim, he won't even talk."

"He goes up and down," Carlin told Amy. "Aunt Georgia says he always has."

"My real papa didn't go up and down," Amy said. She gazed up at a rope of gray moss and frowned. "We better go back," she said and jumped down from the gravestone. "Maybe there won't be a play, if we're lucky, that is."

Uncle Will came out of the library when Amy and Carlin returned. His face was flushed and he still looked angry, but he ordered them to rehearse all the parts where Ted didn't appear. Amy and Carlin were sure of their lines. It was really a pretty easy play.

⚶

Carlin peeked through the long brown curtains at the audience which was seated in wicker chairs on the front lawn. Holton, the Grove house man, had hung the curtains along the edge of the front gallery as Uncle Will had directed, making the middle portion of the gallery into a stage, which was set with a small table and three rush chairs. Pewter goblets stood at each place beside a pottery bowl, a spoon, and a folded napkin.

Carlin turned and glanced past the stage into the big hall behind her with its crystal chandelier and the line of portraits on the wall. The Grove was bigger than Rosalie, of course, but it had a sprawling feeling. The house had been burned by some of Grant's troops during the war and rebuilt later.

Carlin turned to stare at the three columns at the end of the front gallery, the only remnants of the original Felicity Grove. They looked tall and shadowy in the evening light. Each was built of special triangular-shaped bricks, made by skilled slaves at the Grove long ago. Uncle Royal used to tell the story of how the columns had survived, and a lady artist from Greenwood had made a painting of them that hung in the library. Carlin stared out at them. They had towered over the house all these years since the war, dwarfing it and guarding its story, a story that Uncle Will's play was about to retell.

Carlin shivered and gazed out at the lawn again. She felt hot and her head ached, and as she looked at her mother sitting in the front row talking to Doctor Dabney in the row behind, she thought for a moment of running out to her and saying that she didn't feel well and didn't want to be in the play after all. The doctor sat fanning himself with his straw hat, his brass-topped cane hooked over the back of an empty chair.

"I was looking forward to seeing your lovely wife here tonight," Mama said.

"Too busy getting ready for picking, you know. It's wonderful how you and your sister can take off time right now for a party. But that's youth for you—youth and energy."

"Well, I'm not so sure, doctor. The play's a sudden idea of Will's, and you know how Will is when he gets an idea."

Lighted candles shone within tall glass chimneys on the long refreshment table where Holton was ladling punch from a wide Chinese bowl. Lightning bugs made little dots of orange above the hydrangea bushes, and Papa's pipe was a larger, redder dot, as he stood talking with Mr. Randolph.

"What about this fever, doctor?" Carlin heard Mama asking. "This typhoid? They say it's serious this year. I heard that they're two cases in the quarters over at Elmcrest."

"Typhoid's always serious, especially if you're the one that gets it. But it comes every year, like the heat and the rains."

Mama laughed and flipped open her black lace fan. "Oh, doctor, you're quite a philosopher."

Uncle Will was showing a lady in white and a gentleman the gasoline generator parked on the mule wagon in the side drive. Carlin had gotten used to its intermittent whirring as the day went on, but the lady put both hands over her ears as they came around to the front lawn. "I just hope we can hear the play over that roar," she said, laughing.

"I've instructed the children to speak out," Uncle Will told her and repeated, "Speak out," enunciating the words in such a loud voice that she laughed again. Carlin glanced back at the stage and shivered, feeling poised between the life of the play and the life on the lawn.

"Is my hair pinned up right?" Amy demanded. She dropped her side of the curtain and turned to show Carlin the back of her head. "I wish Pansy hadn't twisted it so tight. It pinches."

"It's all right," Carlin told her. She let the other edge of the curtain go and raised her hands to the knot of her own hair. Would the hairpins hold when she had to shake her head and stamp her foot? Carlin glanced down at her long taffeta skirt. Aunt Philadelphia had turned it up, but the hem was heavy. Her lace blouse smelt of Aunt Emily's lavender cologne, which seemed to wrap Carlin in an uneasy adulthood. She was Great-aunt Lila and Amy was Great-aunt Amy, and they were the beautiful maiden sisters who had lived at Felicity Grove during the war.

Ted came out on the gallery, and Carlin saw with relief that he was wearing his costume, a white shirt with a stand-up collar, a vest with a gold pocket watch, and dark pants. Aunt Philadelphia had powdered his hair with flour, turning it a convincing gray, and the wrinkle lines she had drawn around his mouth and eyes made him look like a tired old man. He must have made some truce with Uncle Will, she thought, and let out a grateful sigh. She watched him lounge against the balustrade and felt a twist of envy for his show of disinterest in the whole elaborate effort of this play. Could he do his part without rehearsing, she wondered. Would he?

"All right, everybody." Uncle Will mounted the gallery steps and stood on the stage. "It's almost time." Carlin could hear the quiver of excitement in his voice as he stood in front of them surveying the cast. She noticed once again the shiny eagerness that had replaced the old look of sadness in his deep-set eyes. "Places everybody," Uncle Will said. Carlin sat and glanced down at the tablecloth, feeling her face burn as Ted left the balustrade and settled into his chair between her and Amy. "Everybody ready?" Uncle Will asked. Carlin sat forward and twisted her goblet self-consciously. "Here we go," Uncle Will whispered. He nodded at Holton, who was holding the opposite curtain, then he raised his hand to stop him. "Just a minute," he whispered and leaned over the table to straighten one of the napkins. "All right," he said, returning to the curtain. The brass rings at the top clattered together with a sudden noise that made the audience on the lawn grow quiet and turn toward the stage.

"Oh, mercy. Not dandelion roots for supper again, sister," Carlin began. There was applause, praise for the stage presumably, and the long curtains, and the look of Carlin and Amy with their hair pinned high, and Ted as a gray old man. Carlin waited and repeated her line, then waited again, feeling her blood pound.

"We're lucky to have dandelions, sister dear, with dreadful General Grant battering Vicksburg so terribly, and all those poor people starving," Amy said.

"Grant, Grant," Ted muttered. He flung down his napkin and rose. "But it is that lieutenant of his, that damnable Sherman that will bring us woe." Carlin felt a flood of gratitude pour through her as she sat looking up at her older cousin. He stood partly stooped, glaring out at the audience, as he railed on about the infamous Sherman. Thank goodness, Carlin thought. Ted, who had been so reluctant earlier, was doing his part with gusto. As Carlin spoke her lines about the deprivations of the war, the siege of Vicksburg, and the burnings around Natchez, she twisted her napkin with a feeling of sudden urgency.

"All that is true," Ted said, "but, daughters. . . ." He hesitated. He was making his voice old and throaty-sounding. Carlin widened her eyes and sat looking up at him admiringly. He'd not only memorized his lines, she realized, he'd developed a tone for them too. "You must go into town to read the lists of the slain and see whether your brother, my beloved son, Douglas, has survived."

Carlin nodded. "Yes, Father," she said. "Of course." She rose from the table and curtsied to him, hot with the sense that she really was the dutiful Lila at the Grove in 1863.

"Daughters," Ted said sharply. "You must beware. It is dangerous on the roads now. Yankee deserters and desperate men lurk in the woods around us looking for food. Take the buggy and stay together. And come home as fast as you can."

Amy rose and stood beside Carlin. "Yes, Father," they answered in unison. "We will, Father."

Uncle Will and Holton pulled the curtains together with a ringing noise, and Moose, one of the colored boys at the Grove, lifted the table and pushed it back against the balustrade. Uncle Will pointed to the three chairs that he had lined up on the other side, and Moose placed one behind the other in the center of the stage and put a sawhorse in front of them. Carlin sat down in the first chair with Amy behind. The curtains opened again.

"We've got to hurry," Carlin said and leaned forward to tighten the reins that Uncle Will had tied to the sawhorse. "Giddyap." The dangers that had surrounded Great-aunt Lila and Great-aunt Amy on that August morning as they drove to town seemed real and close.

Moose made a convincing whinny offstage, and Tommy rustled some pine branches against the gallery floor, then rose at the side, stage left. He looked disheveled in a dark unbuttoned jacket with the paper Union insignia Uncle Will had made hanging crookedly at one side. His chin was smudged with ash dust to give him an unshaven look, and one arm was wrapped in a white dish towel. He lurched to the side of the chair buggy.

"I'm wounded, ma'am," he announced. Carlin inhaled sharply and clutched the string of seed pearls at her neck with one hand, holding the reins with the other. "My friend here's worse." Tommy bent to lift one of the branches and revealed his cousin Hugh lying on his side, one leg wrapped in another tea towel, which had been daubed generously with tomato sauce. There was a shocked sound from the audience as someone sucked in breath.

"Please, kind ladies. Help us. A little water. Some food," Tommy begged. His face looked so serious and urgent that Carlin, who continued to twist her pearls, understood the sympathy that Great-aunt Lila had felt for this stranger. "We're only human after all," Tommy added. "Sons and brothers first, soldiers later. Maybe you have a brother yourself."

Hugh, who was lying splayed out on the gallery floor, moaned loudly, and Carlin heard murmurs from the audience. She turned in the chair buggy and met Amy's gaze in a long self-conscious look that they had practiced that afternoon. Carlin nodded. "Get in," she said and left the carriage to help Tommy lift his cousin onto the third chair at the back. She waited for him to get in beside Hugh, then she returned to her seat. "Home," she commanded and stared straight ahead of her, leaning sharply to one side to indicate that they were turning the buggy back to Felicity Grove.

The curtains closed again. "Costume changes," Uncle Will commanded in a loud whisper. "Hurry." He and Holton pushed the chairs to the side and pulled up two rocking chairs. There was a pause. Amy's hair had come down on one side, but Aunt Philadelphia was waiting in the hall with a box of hairpins.

Finally the curtains reopened to show Tommy and Hugh stretched out side by side in the rocking chairs. Amy was bending over Hugh's leg, changing the tea-towel dressing. Carlin entered stage left, carrying a tray which she put down on the table. She handed a soup bowl, a large napkin, and a spoon to each man. Tommy's arm bandage was gone, both men were clean, and Hugh looked cheerful, despite his bandaged foot.

But Ted stood stage right, frowning, his blond hair still gray with flour. "These Yankees," he grumbled to the audience. "They act like nice enough young men. But you can never trust a Yankee. Never." The curtains were pulled together again with the familiar ringing sound and Moose held up a cardboard sign with black letters reading SIX WEEKS PASS.

When the curtains reopened, Carlin was sweeping the gallery. There was a sound of stamping as Uncle Will stepped heavily from one foot to the other offstage left. Moose whinnied again, a high frightened sound. Carlin glanced back at Uncle Will and saw his flushed, excited face, his eyes bright with a queer shine. Tommy, Hugh, Moose, and Moose's brother Doxie appeared to the left on the lawn. The audience turned to take them in. There was more stamping, then Tommy coughed. He wore Uncle Will's wide-brimmed riding hat, which gave him a new look of authority, even though it wasn't strictly Union gear. His dark jacket was buttoned neatly now, the paper insignia pinned on straight, and he carried a wooden rifle. Hugh stood slightly behind him, silent still. The tea towels were gone and they both looked militant and grim. Moose and Doxie stood behind him looking stern.

"Excuse me, ma'am," Tommy said to Carlin. "But we have orders to burn this house immediately." He turned and stared at the tall brick columns beyond the gallery as though he had just remembered that this incident had really transpired in this very place. "Get the family out fast," he commanded Carlin. "The house will be in flames within minutes."

"But you can't do that, Captain Thomas," Carlin shouted at him. "This is Felicity Grove. This is where my sister and I brought you and your friend when you were wounded. You were our guests for three long weeks, recuperating from your wounds before you rejoined your regiment. We fed you and nursed you and cared for you." Carlin felt her voice shake with anger. Her body seemed to be burning up with heat. The horror of what had really happened was all around her, and she clutched at Tommy's arm, hearing her voice break. "Don't you remember?"

"I'm sorry, ma'am," Tommy said, shaking off her arm. "But orders is orders."

"Oh, Captain," Amy shouted, entering stage right. "You can't burn Felicity Grove." She began to weep noisily, clasping at Carlin for comfort, but Carlin turned from her and clutched at Hugh's arm.

"You can't burn our house," she told him. "You would have died or lost your leg if it hadn't been for our care. You know you would." She paused, feeling her blood pound, but Hugh maintained his stern look, shook off her hand, and started toward the house without a reply. "It's not Christian. It's not right," she shouted. "You cannot do this thing."

"It's orders, ma'am. Orders," Tommy said again and pushed past Carlin to mount the gallery steps. "Bring the kerosene," he said to Moose, who came forward, carrying a large can.

Amy ran down the steps. "Please," she begged. "Spare my

piano. Please." But the boys rushed past her into the house with a whooping yell. The generator roared behind them and all at once the area was bathed in a white brightness. Carlin looked back. Uncle Will was crouched down beside the big arc light at the edge of the gallery, flapping a red silk scarf up and down in front of the light. Eerie pink shadows appeared on the white wall, merging and changing. The audience broke into applause and Uncle Will flapped the scarf higher, so that reddish shapes covered the whole wall. Amy and Carlin clung together, but Ted approached Tommy. His shoulders were still stooped, but his face looked fierce.

"One request, Captain." He had to raise his voice, for the gasoline generator was thumping loudly outside. "One single request. Save my daughter's piano. That is the least that you can do."

Tommy hesitated as if uncertain whether he could disobey commands to that extent, then he turned and leapt back into the house, past the pink shadows, and emerged from the hall door pushing Aunt Emily's glass-topped tea wagon. Amy had covered it with a long sheet of paper showing a black outline of piano keys. Someone clapped at the sight, and Moose, who had played a Yankee moments earlier, jumped forward, a tea towel on his arm to indicate that he was now the Grove house man. Together, he and Tommy lifted the table down the steps and out onto the lawn.

"But the library," Carlin wailed. "Your great library, Papa." She made her voice catch and felt real tears start down her face. Had Uncle Will noticed, or was he too involved with the big lamp?

"And the portraits," Amy added. "The furniture, the violins."

Carlin stood clasping Amy's hand, while Ted raised his fists in fury. Then he turned and moved slowly to the old columns on the side. He waited. His were the most important lines of the play, lines that Carlin had seen written in brownish ink in that diary that Uncle Royal's father had kept. The audience turned in their seats so that everyone was gazing toward Ted, who stood in front of the three old columns.

"Only these remain," Ted began and waited for Uncle Will to turn off the generator and stop the flames, so that the audience could concentrate on him. He pointed to the long columns, dark now in the evening light. There was another moment of leaping shadows, then the gasoline generator stopped its whirring and the arc light went dim. "Only these remain," Ted said again in the sudden silence and pointed to the columns. "I decree that they shall stand here through sun and storm for all time so that the generations to come may view this monument to Yankee perfidy."

Applause broke out, and the curtains closed. Carlin and Amy joined hands with Ted, Tommy, and Hugh, standing in an uneven semicircle as Moose and Doxie smiled from behind. Amy and Carlin curtsied, and the boys bowed, while the grown-ups continued to clap. The curtains closed, then opened again for another curtain call. One more, and it was all over at last.

※

"Come to the kitchen house," Amy whispered. "Pansy's made peach ice cream."

"In a minute," Carlin said. "I have to get some lemonade first. I'm thirsty." She felt hot as she stood at the refreshment table, yet she shuddered when she touched the cold, dewy glass.

Uncle Will approached and put his arm around her, enveloping her in the smell of his perspiration. "You were wonderful, sweetheart. A true Sarah Bernhardt." He lifted a cigar to his mouth and exhaled a stream of strong-smelling smoke.

"I almost got confused in that place where the Yankees come and. . . ." Carlin stopped as Uncle Will turned to Dr. Dabney.

"Have one of these," he urged the doctor and handed him a cigar. "They're the best. Cuban, of course." He lit the doctor's cigar and exhaled again. "I want to show you that lamp," he said, leading the doctor to the stage. "Wonderful invention. So bright. Wasn't that fire amazing?"

"Did you see me cry, Uncle Will?" Carlin asked, following them. She had meant to go to the kitchen house with Amy, but somehow she was standing near the light instead.

"Pretty darn convincing," Uncle Will said, stooping down beside it. "The story's absolutely authentic, you know. Part of our heritage, or what we think our heritage is, at least." Uncle Will

137

straightened and faced the doctor. His face looked large in the candlelight. "We Southerners are such romantics, you know. Suicidal in our fascination with the defeats of the past."

The sound of laughter made Carlin look up. Aunt Emily was standing beside the refreshment table with two men from the Elmcrest Plantation and Mr. Randolph, who was staying at the Grove. He had the biggest cotton plantation in this part of the county, next to the Grove, Amy said.

"It could be a good investment," Carlin heard him say. "A modern gin with three stands and a new vacuum sucker. A gin that four or five plantations could use. Give it some thought." Aunt Emily was wearing a pink dress with white panels in the skirt that seemed to swirl and merge together when she turned, Carlin thought.

"We'd all agree, I'm sure, that a good gin is vital to our business," Mr. Randolph continued. "Now, if we were to go in together and invest in one of these new gins those fellows at the Continental Company are putting out, I think we could help ourselves a lot."

Uncle Will straightened and stood staring across the lawn at the speaker. "What does he mean 'help ourselves,'" he muttered. "Gins, gins. Always gins. Another gin is just another step on the road to our enslavement by King Cotton. Doesn't he know that?"

"It's an interesting idea, Jim," one of the other men said. "But—"

Uncle Will marched across the lawn, holding his cigar. Carlin saw her aunt glance over at him and touch Mr. Randolph's arm. "Come in and help yourselves to the buffet, gentlemen," she broke in. "You must be starved." She laughed and pointed toward the lighted gallery.

"Just a minute." Uncle Will's voice was loud. The three men had turned toward the house, but they stopped and looked back at him. "Why are you discussing a new gin?" He looked at his wife, then at the men who stared at him with startled faces. "You came here in the name of art. You came to see an original play about our common past. I want to talk about that, about our heritage, our . . . our. . . ."

Uncle Will glanced at the candles burning within their tall glass chimneys on the refreshment table, then back at the semicircle of men. "As you know, I wrote the play, but my feelings about it are ambivalent—tortured, even, as I suspect yours are too."

He exhaled another long stream of smoke and shook an ash into the grass, then looked around the group again with a searching stare. "This is our drama, our tragedy, yours and mine." He pointed to the columns. "I love those." His voice trembled slightly and he pointed to the stage. "But this is the art of defeat, gentlemen, a romantic delusion, and we must move beyond it." He took a step forward and stared at the men with a challenging look, but no one spoke.

Carlin clutched her arms around her as she stood watching. "We lost the war because our plantation economy was weak," Uncle Will continued. "And we continue to lose—the depression in the cotton market, the weevil again this year. To us the South means only cotton, and the defeats of our past. We shall never be victors." Uncle Will raised one hand in a fist. "We will never even be survivors if we continue this way." He dropped his arm and stepped back. "A new cotton gin is not the answer, gentlemen. Not at all."

Carlin felt her fingernails bite into the flesh of her upper arms. Stop it, Uncle Will, she wanted to shout. Stop!

"We must move to diversification and industry," he went on. "We must. . . ." Aunt Emily pulled at his sleeve.

"Supper's ready, dear." She turned to the others. "Come along to the gallery, and we can go on talking there."

"I want to talk here. Now," Uncle Will protested. "While the play is fresh in everyone's mind." Carlin squeezed her eyes shut, then opened them again. "You want to talk about cotton gins." He made a raking noise in his throat and focused on the balding man. "You only think in terms of cotton. But I tell you . . . I tell you. . . ." He swung from left to right, surveying his silent audience like an animal at bay.

"Willy, darling," Aunt Emily whispered. Where was Papa, Carlin thought frantically and glanced around her. Papa would make Uncle Will sit down.

"We've got to develop new crops," Uncle Will went on. "Cotton is not the answer, nor cotton gins." He put his hand over his mouth suddenly and turned his head. Carlin turned her own head, feeling sick. She saw her mother sitting beside Mrs. Randolph near the maple tree, and she ran along the box hedge to the bench, where they sat.

"Sit down a minute, Carlin," her mother said. "You must be worn out, dear." Mama had been talking to Mrs. Randolph, Carlin realized, and was unaware of what Uncle Will was saying. She sank down beside her on the grass.

"Come in, come in. The buffet's ready," she heard Aunt Emily call out in a high voice. "Come to the side gallery, please." Carlin saw the group of men begin walking across the grass, talking jerkily. The women joined them, and they hurried toward the gallery for food, but mainly for shelter, Carlin thought, from the embarrassment that had erupted on the lawn. Aunt Emily bustled among them, pointing to chairs, directing Moose to move those remaining on the lawn back up to the gallery.

"Lovely," Carlin could hear a woman in lavender saying, "Such a lovely party."

"No need to hurry," Mama told Carlin. "We'll wait until the others serve themselves." Carlin leaned against her mother's knees. She was hot, and she could feel her chest rising and falling as if she were panting. Uncle Will had settled in one of the empty chairs in the first row beside Dr. Dabney, who was leaning forward on his cane. The awful business was over, Carlin thought with relief. Dr. Dabney was old and would not be embarrassed by Uncle Will's talk.

Carlin closed her eyes. "We must fight these sentimental old myths of ours, this sick romanticism." Uncle Will's voice lifted with a sudden passion.

"Oh dear." Carlin heard her mother breathe out and knew she was listening now.

"We must see them for what they are—the loser's art." Carlin turned, wondering if Mrs. Randolph had heard Uncle Will, but she was busy fixing a lace shawl around her shoulders. "That's the real reason for my play tonight." He paused a moment as if he had surprised himself with his own reason. "We must create a new South." He was almost shouting. "A South of economic diversity and new strength."

Carlin covered her ears with both hands. Why had Uncle Will written the play if it was sick and romantic, and why had he spoken in that rude way to Mr. Randolph about the gin, lecturing the men like that? Carlin pressed her hands against her ears harder and felt the earth spin. The sensation scared her and she lowered her hands and stared up at the sky. "Star light, star bright," she whispered, although the evening star had gone. "I wish I may, I wish I might. . . ." The old rhyme felt soothing and she sighed as she stared up into the soft night sky.

"That play's so sad, and it's all true apparently," Mrs. Randolph said, leaning toward Mama. "I remember Royal telling us about those columns years ago. He was very proud of them."

Carlin thought of an afternoon last summer when she and Amy had swung in the wide hammock together, talking about the war. "Suppose the South had won?" Amy had said. "Suppose the Grove hadn't burned and had gotten rich instead? Suppose the real Grove was still standing?"

Carlin reached for the knot of her hair and pulled out a hairpin. But suppose there were still slaves? Suppose Aunt Georgia could be sold? Suppose Hamlet and Feely could be taken away from her and Violet? Carlin pulled out another pin and felt the loop of her hair drop down. Uncle Will was right. They should turn away from the past. Maybe the burning of the Grove wasn't the worst thing. Maybe the worst thing was the way the South held onto its hate. Uncle Will was right, but why did he have to embarrass everybody?

"I'm going to get a little supper," Mrs Randolph said, rising. "May I bring you some?"

"Thank you, no. We'll wait a bit," Mama said.

Relieved to be alone with her mother, Carlin let her head flop forward on her knees and breathed out loudly. "What's the matter, dear?" Mama reached down to feel her forehead. "You're hot." She felt Carlin's face with both hands. "Good Lord. You're burning up." She straightened quickly. "Thomas. Yoo-hoo, Thomas," she called to her husband, who was standing near the doctor now, talking to his brother. "Come here, please."

Papa turned and walked toward them, his lighted pipe in his

hand. "I think Carlin's got a fever," Mama said. "Feel her fore-head."

Carlin felt her father's hand on her face. "I'll ask Dr. Dabney to have a look," he said. Carlin felt him meet Mama's eyes above her head and heard him turn to leave. She let her head fall backward onto her mother's lap. "Star light, star bright." The sky was so big now, so dark.

"Dr. Dabney's going to come take a look at you, dear." Mama stroked the hair back from Carlin's hot forehead. "Then Papa'll get the buggy and we'll go home." Carlin rolled her head a little, to indicate she understood, but the trees above her had blurred together, and even nodding seemed hard.

She heard the men talking and imagined the doctor rising, taking his cane from the back of the chair. "They ignored me, Tom," she heard Uncle Will saying. "They care more about this cotton gin than they do about my play or my ideas for the South."

"No one ignored you," Papa said. "You've exhausted yourself, Will. Get to bed now. Get some sleep."

"You're right, Tom. I am tired." Uncle Will's voice was calm all at once. "Worn out in fact. I'll go to bed soon."

"Let me feel your head, child." The voice was close. Dr. Dabney was beside Carlin, his dry, clean-smelling hand on her forehead. "Yes. She's certainly feverish. Get her home, Thomas. I'll saddle up and follow you." He hesitated, then he added quietly. "It could be just a simple fever, you know. It may not be what we think." He paused. "I'll be at Rosalie in half an hour." Carlin imagined him peering down at his pocket watch in the dimness.

"Much obliged to you, doctor. Stay right here, Belle. I'll bring the buggy around to the side."

Carlin let her eyes close. "Willy." That was Aunt Emily's voice. "Here's Holton, darling. He's going to help you up to bed."

Carlin heard Uncle Will's voice again. "I don't want to sleep. I want to talk." He was close to her now. "I want to get people here thinking about the implications of . . . of. . . ."

Carlin closed her eyes, letting her uncle's voice fade. The others were waiting on the dim lawn, but she was rising, she realized. She was swirling, turning now in some warm yellow space above them all.

"Carlie." Uncle Will's voice was beside her, pulling her down from that light place. "Carlie, sweetheart. Are you really sick?" He straightened. "Don't take her home, Belle. Let's put her in the pink guest room. I'll read to her later."

"Come on, Willy," Aunt Emily said. "Holton's right here."

"All right, all right." But Uncle Will stooped down in front of Carlin, exuding the mingled smells of cigar smoke and perspiration as he placed his hands over his knees. "I'm sorry that the play ended this way, sweetheart."

Carlin turned her head away from him to bury her nose in the silky fragrance of her mother's lap. She wanted to go home with Mama and Papa. She wanted to be in her own bed, amidst the familiar shadows of her own room, away from the play, away from her uncle.

2

AUTUMN 1910 – SUMMER 1911

CARLIN could not remember her first weeks of typhoid fever. Images appeared to her later: Papa sitting by her bed in the dim room, the oil lamp on the bedside table with its pleated shade pulled low, Mama reading aloud, Aunt Georgia wiping Carlin's forehead with a cool cloth. She remembered Dr. Dabney's black medical bag standing open on the bureau near her dolls, but she could not remember the sequence of days and nights. Sometimes she felt that she had risen and her hot, outstretched body was pressed against the ceiling. She wanted to call to those sitting close to her bed below to look up since the bed they were tending was empty.

The taste of the bitter medicine was familiar. She had been sick three weeks, Mama said, and she was better. Then the fever returned, and she was wrapped once more in its burning haze and weak when it receded. Abdominal pains came in the night and often in the day. Sometimes they were so sharp that she cried out and clung to Aunt Georgia's hand, twisting it as she crushed her knees against her chest and heard her screams beat against the walls of the room. Sometimes she flopped over on her stomach, hoping that by lying flat she could ease the scissor-like pains, and there were times when she was so exhausted that she had no energy left to scream and clung to Aunt Georgia, mouth open, eyes half-shut, simply enduring until the awfulness passed.

Once, as her screams died away, she wondered what the noise had sounded like in the schoolroom, where Tommy might be working at some composition on the oilcloth-covered table, or in Evie's room at the end of the hall. As she lay waiting for the pain to return, she watched the hall for someone to come, perhaps Tommy with news of Lightning and the stable or Evie peeping around the doorway to hold up her doll.

Tommy and Evie were staying at the Grove awhile, Mama explained, but Carlin could not seem to remember that. She missed her sister and especially her brother, and in some secret way, she felt she needed them to see her sickness and confirm its importance.

Sometimes when the pains came at night, Papa held her hand or put his arm around her shoulders, while Mama hovered at the bottom of the bed, her dark hair hanging down. Aunt Georgia seemed to be always in the room. She bathed Carlin's hot body and spooned in broth. She sat with her through the long nights, stroking her forehead. Carlin knew the feel of her dark hands with their light palms, her smell, her little clucking sounds. She could tell when Aunt Georgia had arrived without opening her eyes. And she knew her departures, the sound of her feet moving unevenly down the hall in those blue slippers that had once been Mama's.

One evening, in the half-darkness of the room, Carlin heard voices above her, Aunt Georgia's and Aunt Ceny's maybe.

"You sit with Hamlet last night? How's he doin' now?"

"Mighty sick," Aunt Georgia answered, and Carlin heard her sigh. "He be mighty sick. Reverend Ambrose with him this mornin', and Violet. She ain't never left his bed almost. Poor thing.

I tell her it's in the Lord's hands now, poor little fella. He's burning up with fever. Such a good boy too."

"It's that creek water what done it," Aunt Ceny said. "That little pasture creek. Violet think he and Miss Carlin both done drink it. Hamlet should o' knowed that water was bad, but. . . . Ah, Lord, and this child too. Two children strugglin' with the angel."

"Shh," Aunt Georgia warned. "She doze in and out. Might hear you and git scared."

Carlin kept her eyes closed. Would Hamlet die? Would she? She could see Hamlet in his overalls, one leg ripped open at the knee, his head tipped to the side, his mouth in its teasing smile. She thought of them at the creek, their bare feet pressed together, making an enclosure for the piglet with his wet forehead. Aunt Georgia and Aunt Ceny were wrong. Hamlet wouldn't die, nor would she. Dying was for old people, other people, not for them.

A drink of cold water. That was all they had wanted. Just one or two sips. But what if she and Hamlet died? Would she drift upward in a long white dress and play a harp, or would she twist and turn in some gray place, homesick for Rosalie? Carlin opened her eyes and reached for Aunt Georgia's hand. "Aunt Georgia," she whispered. "Don't let me die. Please."

⁂

One morning, or perhaps it was at night, Carlin brought her arm down from her head, and when she opened her fingers, she saw that her hand was full of hair. Why? What had happened? Later, hours or days maybe, she raised her arm and touched her scalp with one hand, then the other, feeling the bones of her skull pressing up against the rough skin. Where were her braids, her hair on the top and the sides? Had it all come out? Was she bald? She asked for a mirror, but Mama said, "Later. Your hair'll grow in," she told Carlin. "It might be curly, or black even. It'll be a surprise." Carlin nodded and burrowed back into her pillow. Her scalp felt itchy and sore, but at least she didn't have to raise her head to have her hair brushed. Right now it was easier having no hair at all.

Her raw throat ached and she yearned for cooling liquids. In her dreams she saw lemonade in tall green glasses with ice chips tinkling together at the top. Yet swallowing was painful. When Mama held her head up to the glass, the cool liquid made her cramps return, and she stared up at her mother through her tears.

Images of chicken marengo on china plates flicked before her. She saw Mama's blue Meissen dessert dishes with thick slices of pecan pie, a cut-glass bowl of peach ice cream with one of Aunt Georgia's brown-edged cookies stuck into the top. But Mama and Aunt Georgia would only give her soups and mushy tasteless mixtures, which they spooned into her mouth from a white custard cup. The walls of her intestine had been punctured by the typhoid, Papa explained. She could not eat ordinary food. Later, he assured her, but right now she must be patient and give thanks to God.

Tommy sat on the end of Carlin's bed talking. He and Evie had come back to Rosalie with Miss Mollie the day before. "Me and Hugh rode a whole lot. We got to trot in the woods, and canter too." Tommy leaned back. "I wish I could have my own pony like Hugh."

"You can ride Lightning if you're careful," Carlin offered. "I can't ride for a while, and he needs exercise."

"I know. Eben told me. But Light's so jumpy." Tommy lowered his head to examine a cut on his bare foot. "It's funny being back here without Hamlet around," he said and stared out of the window. "I keep sort of looking for him, thinking we could play."

"What do you mean?" Carlin pushed herself up on her elbow and stared at her brother. "What about Hamlet? What's happened?"

"Didn't you know? He died Thursday night. They've already had the funeral and everything. Reverend Ambrose preached, and they buried him in the colored folks' graveyard. Violet's real sad, and Aunt Georgia too."

"But nobody told me," Carlin said.

"They didn't want to get you upset, probably. You both got it from that creek water, you know. That's what Aunt Ceny says."

"Oh, I should have known." Carlin let herself collapse into the pillows and covered her face with her arm. "I should have known about the creek," she moaned. "I guess I did, really." She let her arm flop down. "We were so thirsty." She raised herself on her elbow again. "I didn't know he died. I mean, I knew he was really sick like me, but died. . . ."

She collapsed against the pillows again and stared up into the canopy. "Oh," she moaned. "Oh, no."

"It's awful," Tommy said. He leaned toward Carlin as her eyes filled. "Listen, Carlie. Don't start crying. Please. I shouldn't have told you, and if you get all upset and sick crying, I'll catch it from Papa and Aunt Georgia and everybody."

"All right." Carlin wiped her nose with her wrist. "Feely must feel awful too." She studied Tommy. "He was your best friend, wasn't he? Better than me and Feely really. I mean you know Feely gets mad at me sometimes."

Tommy looked down. "I asked Uncle Will if I could come to the funeral, but they wouldn't let me. Uncle Will said it was just for colored people. But I don't see why. Hamlet would have let me."

"Aunt Georgia must feel sad, and all the time he was so sick, she had to nurse me instead of him."

"Not all the time," Tommy said. "She was with him a lot."

"Oh, it's awful," Carlin said. "It feels like everything is awful now. Hamlet dead, me sick and can't do anything, and Rosalie never getting a good harvest." She reached down and gripped her abdomen suddenly. "And now I've got a cramp coming."

"I'll call Mama," Tommy said and slid off the bed.

"Come back," Carlin called out. "I get lonesome up here."

⚜

Picking time was almost over. Papa left for the fields early and came back after dark, but he always sat with Carlin in the evening. Once he brought a perfectly shaped cotton boll and stuck it up above her in the corner of her canopied bed. On the days that she could sit up, Carlin watched the mule wagon lumbering slowly down the drive to the gin.

"Mama," she said one morning. "May I use Grandfather's telescope up here in bed?" Carlin could picture the telescope in its black leather case sitting on the library table with Grandfather's initials, HBC, stamped on the side in gold. "I could watch the mule wagon and see Papa when he comes home on Graylie at night."

"I'm sorry, dear." Her mother frowned. "I can't bring it to you."

"But why not, Mama? I only want to look out at the mule wagon. I'll be careful."

"I can't bring it, Carlin," Mama said again. "Later, maybe. We'll see."

Carlin lay back among the pillows, and as she slipped down into sleep, she saw the telescope sitting in a store window. The pawn shop, she thought suddenly, and opened her eyes. Had they pawned the telescope that Grandfather had given them? She thought of the dusty shop down the street from the bank. There were boots in the window, a scuffed sidesaddle, and a little collection of jewelry spilling out of a blue plush box in front. Was Grandfather's telescope there too?

❧

"Did they sell Grandfather's telescope?" Carlin asked Tommy that afternoon. "Is that why Mama can't let me use it?"

"Papa had to buy a new mule team."

"But. . . ." Carlin paused, grateful that Tommy had not said that they needed to pay Dr. Dabney.

"They took Mama's engagement ring, too," Tommy added. Carlin stared, then closed her eyes, visualizing her mother's hand. She had noticed that Mama was not wearing her diamond engagement ring, the hard bright stone, clasped high in its gold setting. She had noticed her naked-looking finger with only the wedding band, but that had been weeks ago.

"They can always buy them back, you know, when things get better." Tommy said. "It's just for now."

"I know." Carlin nodded wearily. "I know."

Carlin heard Uncle Will's voice downstairs, then Mama's. After a while she heard his footsteps in the hall, and she raised herself up among her pillows and straightened the neck of her nightgown.

"Hey there, beautiful," Uncle Will said, filling the doorway with his shape. "I brought these from the garden," he said and held out a bunch of yellow roses. "They're just about the last ones."

"Let me put them in water," Mama said, bustling in. "Now you sit here, Will. This is a comfortable chair."

She left with the roses, and Uncle Will sat down beside Carlin's bed. "Haven't seen you in weeks," he said. "You were pretty sick the last time I was here."

Carlin smiled. She hadn't known that Uncle Will had visited. She sat up higher, feeling a flush of energy. "How's everybody at the Grove?" she asked.

"Everybody's fine," he said. "Amy sends her love. She's going to leave for school next week." He looked away. "You know how I've talked about Mississippi's one-crop economy?" He crossed his legs and gazed at the canopy above the bed. Carlin nodded and drew in her breath, remembering her hot embarrassment the night of the play. "I've met some men up in Jackson," he continued. "Some fellows that are thinking about these problems too. One of them writes for *The Progressive Farmer*, that magazine your Papa and I pass back and forth. Things are going to change soon, Carlie. Really soon, I think."

Carlin raised herself a little higher in her pillows. She would ask Uncle Will about her own worry, she decided, thinking of the pawn shop, the telescope, and Mama's ring. "Uncle Will, is Rosalie going to be all right?"

"Rosalie?" Her uncle glanced around the room a moment, then up at the canopy again. "The whole answer is crop diversification," he said. "Cotton takes the chemicals out of the soil, you see, and destroys the land."

"But what about Rosalie?" Carlin asked.

"It's going to be all right, Carlie," he said. "Rosalie, the Grove, all the old plantations, if we can just persuade people to plant other crops beside cotton, like clover, alfafa. It's going to be all right."

Uncle Will glanced down at her, then at the window. She looked shocking after her weeks of fever, her thinness and her bald head. Uncle Will was scared, Carlin realized suddenly. He hadn't seen her in a long time.

"You're going to get back to your old self soon, Carlie," he said, looking down at her, as though he had read her thoughts. "You and I will go riding together this spring," he went on and let his gaze rest on her steadily now. "Fancy and Lightning'll get along famously, I bet."

Carlin leaned back and smiled up at him from her pillows. Don't worry about my looks, she wanted to say. When you come back in a week or two, I'll be really well, and I'll look like my old self too.

❧

Carlin heard rain hit her window pane like gravel and saw slippery brown leaves sticking to the balustrade as she lay curled on her side, staring out. It must be November, she thought, or the end of October anyway. Some mornings she could read or even write in her Paris diary. But other mornings she lay on her side with her knees drawn up, breathing noisily, as cramps moved through her abdomen once again. Aunt Georgia held her hand and put warm washcloths on her forehead. "She's been sick four months now," Carlin heard her mother say to Dr. Dabney out in the hall. "When will it end?"

"Hers is a very severe case," the doctor said. "I can't predict. Soon, I hope. Very soon."

❧

"Thanksgiving be next Thursday," Aunt Georgia announced as she bent over Carlin with a cup of broth one morning. If I could just get well by then, Carlin thought. If I could sit at the dining room table and have some turkey and cranberry sauce.

But the cramps returned, and Carlin's yearnings were lost in a tangle of pain and tiredness. "Weren't much of a celebration anyway," Aunt Georgia reported, shaking her head. "All of Rosalie is thinkin' about you right now, wantin' you to get well." But Hamlet would not get well, Carlin thought, and all of Rosalie knew that.

As Christmas approached, Carlin tried to persuade Papa to carry her downstairs to see the tree. But Dr. Dabney ruled against the scheme, and Carlin stayed in bed, staring at the little potted tree that Miss Mollie had arranged on her bureau.

⚶

February came, and pale buds stuck up from the gray wisteria vine that hung over the balustrade. Carlin sat in the chaise longue by the window. The slice of field that she could see was a vivid green, and a new calf was grazing beside its mother. There was a sound outside. She turned to see a motor car emerge from the tunnel of live oak trees and stop beside the hitching post. Uncle Will had fixed his Model T, she thought, and leaned toward the window in excitement. But that was not Uncle Will getting out, nor was that Uncle Will's motor car, she realized. This one had black sides and a canvas roof. The driver who descended was a portly man in a black derby hat and a dark yellow vest. Carlin stared, trying to remember where she had seen him.

"Was that man who came in the motor car this morning the man who works at the bank?" she asked when Aunt Georgia brought her lunch. Aunt Georgia nodded. "He came to Uncle Will's wedding, didn't he, and his name is. . . ." Carlin stopped, still determined to avoid that cloakroom memory. She glanced back down the drive where the machine had been. "He must be rich to have his own machine."

"I 'spect so. He be a bank man, after all."

"Why did he come all the way out to Rosalie? Papa usually sees him at the bank in town."

"Now, Carlin, what that man's doin' here, that's men's business," Aunt Georgia told her. "Nothing for little girls to worry about, 'specially if they been sick near onto seven months with the typhoid."

⚶

153

Papa brought Carlin a little orange kitten from the barn. He had a round loop in the pattern of his reddish fur on one side, which matched a loop on the other side exactly. He kneaded the crook of Carlin's arm, wanting his mother, wanting milk, and Carlin cuddled him in the quilt and let him sleep. "His name is Geoffrey," she told her father as she stared into the kitten's stern little face. He did look like a Geoffrey, but she didn't know why.

Aunt Emily and Mama sat talking in the sewing room across the hall one afternoon. Carlin was glad to hear their voices. She hadn't been able to get up in the chaise that day or even read, because she had had pain again and was lying down among the pillows, staring at the line where the rose-patterned wallpaper met the ceiling and the long plaster crack in the corner began.

"Oh, Belle. Don't worry," Aunt Emily was saying. "Thomas will pay it back when things get better. That's the least of our worries."

"But when will that be? The harvests weren't good before the weevil, and now. . . . ." That was Mama's voice. There was a pause. Carlin heard the clock ticking.

"I don't like that new man at the bank, Emmy, that Mr. Marvin. He's too fancy with his motor car and his derby. I just wish Mr. Humphrey was still there. The McNairs have done business with Mr. Humphrey for over thirty years."

Carlin turned on her stomach. The clock downstairs chimed two, meaning three, but Aunt Georgia wouldn't be up for another hour anyway. She curled up and dozed awhile.

"If only he weren't so restless, Belle," Carlin heard Aunt Emily say. "If only he could be satisfied with life at the Grove." Carlin turned and raised herself on her elbow to listen. They weren't talking about Mr. Marvin now. "If he just wasn't so intense about this crop diversification business and. . . . Oh, I don't know, Belle." There was a pause. "Sometimes I get so lonely and so tired of it all. Not just Will and his talk, but the Grove, cotton, everything. Do you know what I mean?" Carlin imagined her mother nodding. "I think I wasn't really meant for plantation life. I think of the old days when we were at the Conservatory together, our friends there, those concert teas we had. Remember?" Carlin listened, but she couldn't hear her mother's reply.

"I feel so alone at the Grove. I mean with Will up in Jackson half the week now, and Ted and Amy gone. Will thinks politics will solve the problems. He even talks about running for office, Belle."

"Oh, Emmy." Carlin heard the sharp intake of her mother's breath.

"I want him to be happy, of course. But I don't know what would happen if he should run. I mean, you know Will. He's too sensitive to get into politics, all that bickering and manipulation." There was another pause. "It's always hard when Will's down. I try to cheer him and make things pleasant, but Belle, when he's up, it's . . . it's almost harder really. I mean, it can get so embarrassing at times. His speeches and talk. It can be painful. Sometimes I just don't know what to do. It's as though he was a stranger almost and. . . ." The voice stopped and Carlin heard a low choking sound. "I feel so helpless, so. . . ." The choking noise was the sound of her aunt crying, Carlin realized as she felt her own lips tremble.

"Oh, Emmy," she heard her mother say. "Emmy dear." The choking cries grew louder. Carlin pulled the sheet up over her head, wanting the sound to stop. "Oh, Belle, I miss those Conservatory years, just you and me and our friends, before we had husbands or plantations."

"Yes, yes," Carlin heard her mother whisper. There was more whispering, and at last the sound subsided. Carlin lay curled up shivering, still hearing the crying. She had never thought about her aunt's unhappiness, she realized, only Uncle Will's. Pictures of her aunt drifted through her mind: Aunt Emily in a wide-brimmed hat carrying a bunch of roses as she came up the steps to the front gallery, Aunt Emily at the Grove piano, Aunt Emily sitting at the bottom of Amy's bed, reading aloud to them at night. She was a good aunt. A nice aunt. Why had Carlin never thought about her before? Because, she told herself, she was always thinking about Uncle Will.

A cramp began below her ribs, a wave-like pain, moving down. The pain was slight compared to the horrible ones of the fall that had made her scream and left her shaking. But she was tired of being patient, tired of being sick.

"Mama," she called out, her voice querulous and high. "Mama, it's hurting again. It hurts."

※

Planting had begun, and Papa was so busy that Carlin was startled when he appeared in her doorway one morning after Dr. Dabney had made his weekly visit. "I have a surprise for you," he announced and clapped his hands together. "Dr. Dabney says I can take you downstairs."

"Right now?"

"Yes, now," he said. "The whole crew's waiting."

"Oh Papa." Carlin straightened her nightgown and put on her robe. She looked up at him, feeling her jaws tremble with excitement, and raised her hands to her furred head.

"Ready?"

Carlin put her arms around his neck. "Ready," she said. He lifted her and moved out into the hall, which looked smaller somehow and darker, Carlin thought, as she gazed around.

"Hooray, Carlie," Evie shouted. "The great day at last." Carlin turned to see Evie standing with Mama and Miss Mollie in the schoolroom door. It was a great day, Carlin thought, and tipped her head up, flushed with their attention. She was important and this was her moment. She caught sight of Tommy and Aunt Georgia looking up at her from the hall below as Papa started down the stairs. She saw the worn banister and twisted to catch sight of the barn from the landing window, then saw the gray bare places in the carpeting on the bottom steps. The smell of chicory coffee rushed toward her from the dining room, and she saw a long crack in the marble-topped table in the hall. The front door was open, and the sun was glinting on the damp brick walk. She smiled excitedly at Aunt Ceny, who had joined Aunt Georgia, and looked around as Papa carried her into the parlor and settled her on the horsehair sofa.

Carlin turned her head, taking in the room in great searching sweeps, while Mama tucked a blanket over her legs. There was the fireplace with its carved mantelpiece, the long drapes pulled back at the French doors, and the piano in the corner with Evie's music on the stand. She smiled a wide-stretched smile, feeling the family waiting, wanting her approval somehow. "Oh, it's so wonderful," she told them and clasped her hands together. "So wonderful to be down here again at last." The world had opened. Rosalie stretched out around her, spacious, airy, full of colors, sights, and smells. "It's just wonderful," she said again.

❦

Aunt Georgia had baked a chocolate cake for Carlin's twelfth birthday. There would be chicken marengo and sweet potato pie, and then the cake with twelve candles for her years and one to grow on. Carlin sat in the chaise, waiting excitedly for Papa to come carry her down. But Tommy appeared instead. He crossed the rug and sat down on the hassock next to her chaise. "It's the weevil again," he said. "The squares are on the ground." He tightened his hands into fists. "Papa says it's not just the north field this time. They're in the pond field too."

"But. . . ." Carlin thought of her birthday dinner, the cake on the silver platter, waiting below. This was to be her first meal in the dining room. Then she remembered her sight of Papa last spring after the first weevils came. She saw him sitting at his desk in the library, head bowed, the Bible open on his knees. "Oh, not again," she said. "Not again."

"It might not be so bad," Tommy began. "There's the spray that Government Extension man told Papa to use."

"Carlin." Mama was standing in the doorway.

"The weevil's come again, hasn't it, Mama?"

"Yes, dear. Unfortunately." She paused and moved to the chaise. "But Carlin, you're not to worry, you hear? Or you either, Tommy." Carlin felt her mother looking down at her on the chaise and at Tommy on the hassock beside her. Mama knew they had been talking about the weevil's return. "You children are not to worry,"

157

Mama repeated. "Your papa will deal with this." Mama's voice was firm, but her face looked gray. "Now, don't speak of it at supper. We'll just go right on with Carlin's birthday the way we planned. All right?"

Carlin and Tommy nodded.

The coming of the weevil was different this year, Carlin realized. The shock she had seen in her parents last year had been replaced with a kind of tired resignation. She saw the lines around her father's mouth, her mother's stern, almost heavy look, and the silent, dogged way that Aunt Georgia, James, and Aunt Ceny kept on with their work, avoiding any mention of the weevil.

Meanwhile Carlin's long sickness began to ebb at last. Dr. Dabney announced that she could try standing. Carlin held onto Aunt Georgia and stood up beside her bed. She felt awkward and tall, and the rag rug on the floor looked frighteningly remote, its blues and pinks swirling slightly. Carlin was startled. She had yearned for this moment when she would finally stand up, but now, after all those weeks of waiting, it was proving scary. She put one arm around Aunt Georgia's waist and watched as the bureau blended into the dressing table and the slop jar made a wide blue streak.

"It's gonna git better," Aunt Georgia assured her. "Everyday you and me'll stand awhile and take one or two little bitty steps, and when Dr. Dabney come back next Monday, he'll be real proud of how good we done."

Carlin sat at her dressing table one morning while Aunt Georgia stripped her bed. She picked up the hand mirror and stared at her new hair in back, then glanced at Aunt Georgia, who stood studying her as she clutched a bundle of sheets against her chest. "Pretty soon that hair o' yours gonna be just like your Mama's. That's one good thing that old fever done. It give you your Mama's thick black hair, which is real handsome."

"Maybe," Carlin said and put down the hand mirror, but she

continued to stare at her image in the oval mirror on the wall. She thought of how she used to push her brown braids back behind her shoulders with a slap and how she used to twist the tail on the end of the left one around her forefinger when she was reading.

There was a sound of footsteps in the hall. "I most forgot," Aunt Georgia said and glanced toward the door. "I got a surprise for you, a visitor you ain't seen in a long time."

Carlin turned on the dressing table stool. Feely stood in the doorway. "Feely." Carlin caught her breath and half-rose from the chair, then sat again, feeling awkward, aware all at once that they had not seen each other since Hamlet died. Feely looked tall and different. She was wearing a grown-up dress, and her hair was slicked back in a bun.

"How you, Carlin?" she asked. "You feelin' better now?"

"Oh, yes. I'm just about well." Carlin sucked in her breath. Was it her fault that Hamlet had died? Partly. She should have known about the creek. "I can walk a little now," she said, "and Papa's carried me downstairs three times."

"That's good. I got me a job in town. Did Gran tell you?" Carlin shook her head and glanced at Aunt Georgia.

"What kind of a job?" she asked.

"Baby mindin'. It ain't bad and it pay pretty good. I goes everyday though, 'cept Sunday, of course. The babies is bad, though. Real spoiled. It ain't a good job."

"How about a job in Mr. Russell's feed store?" Carlin said and hesitated.

"Uh-uh. He need somebody what can read good and cipher. He don't want no colored help." Carlin saw the angry gleam in Feely's eyes and she looked down. There it was, that old pain that had haunted them from the beginning, always present despite Carlin's determination to defy Aunt Lucy's rules, always unfair. Feely had been quicker learning to read than she had, but when would she have time to practice her reading or ciphering now? Yet couldn't they be friends again, she thought? They had known each other so long. "Could you mind babies here at Rosalie?" she said and drew in her breath, knowing Feely would have thought of that.

"Ain't no work at Rosalie now. Lotta folks is leavin' or fixin' to." Carlin nodded, not knowing what to add. "I gotta go. I'll be seein' you, Carlin. Hear?"

"Feely, did you know that all my hair came out?" Carlin said, calling out the question. But Feely had already started down the hall. "Bye," Carlin called after her. Aunt Georgia carried the dirty sheets out to the hamper, and Carlin gazed around the empty room, listening to the high foolish echo, "bye."

※

The paper dolls Carlin had played with when she was eleven seemed childish. When Evie brought a stack of old *McClure's* magazines into her room, the paste pot, and two pairs of scissors, Carlin let out a groan of boredom. But Evie sat down on the rug and began turning the pages of one of the magazines. She stopped at a picture of a woman in a new fur coat and began snipping. Carlin watched. Evie laid the cut-out woman on the rug, pasted it to a piece of cardboard, and turned to a tall man in a top hat. Carlin slid down to the floor and picked up the other pair of scissors. She flipped the pages of another *McClure's* and found a baby in a high perambulator and a little girl with a straw hat. Soon a large family lay spread out beside them. Carlin snipped out an elegant spangled dress for the mother and Evie cut out a fur coat. When Carlin found a picture of a large black dog, she gave a little shout, cut it carefully, and pasted it beside the family group. In addition to the parents and the baby in the perambulator, there were two daughters and three sons, and Carlin's and Evie's fingers were scabby with paste. They played with the paper doll family again the next afternoon, making additions and arrangements, leaning the whole group in a line against the wall.

"Oh, look at that," Mama exclaimed, coming into the room. "What smart little girls I have." Carlin stared up at her mother. After her months of sickness, was she still just a little girl?

※

Carlin announced that she was going to read straight through the row of dark green volumes of Dickens on the library shelf. She read *David Copperfield* and rushed on to *Oliver Twist*. When Papa suggested *A Tale of Two Cities*, she plunged into that. The fictional worlds felt vivid and enclosing, and she described the plots to Tommy and Evie in detail. She had been to Natchez, but London was much bigger, of course, and so crowded in Dickens's time. She talked with Miss Mollie about the poor that Dickens portrayed. What was done for them then, she wanted to know. What could be done about poverty now?

❧

Uncle Will visited Carlin every week during April and May, but as the summer began he came less frequently. He wrote a note saying he couldn't visit for a couple of weeks, but would come on June tenth. Carlin hurried to finish a story she wanted to show him and then two more. But Uncle Will could not come on the tenth. She kicked the side of the rocker when James brought the news in a note, and turned her copy book on the side to look at the used pages. It was over half full of her stories. But what was the point of filling all those pages, she asked herself irritably, when Uncle Will never came to read them?

❧

As Carlin grew stronger, she was allowed to sit in a rocking chair on the front gallery and read. She was absorbed in *A Tale of Two Cities* one afternoon, when she heard someone walking across the drive.

"Didn't find no greeters in the courtyard this time," a voice said just below her. "Nobody out there playing doodle bug today."

Carlin jerked up her head. The peddler stood on the front walk in his torn, yet oddly respectable-looking jacket, his hair pressed down under the same battered derby, and the pack sticking up behind his shoulders.

Carlin leaned forward. "You're back," she said. "Have you come straight from the Grove?"

The peddler nodded and pulled one strap from his shoulder, so that the pack swung down unevenly. "Yes indeed. That's just where I been." He studied Carlin. "They told me you've been sick a long time."

"Almost a year," Carlin said. "I had typhoid. All my hair came out."

"Well, well." The peddler studied her. "A year's a long time to be sick. Your hair's nice now, though. You look real grown-up."

Carlin flushed and raised one hand to cup the curls over her ear. "Come sit down," she said and put the book on the table beside her. "My parents are away for the afternoon, but they'll be home shortly. Would you like some lemonade? Some iced tea maybe? Aunt Georgia'll fix you some supper." She smiled at him, taking in his dusty boots and sagging shoulders. "You know where the cottage is, if you want to put your pack down first and rest awhile."

"Thank you, little lady. I believe I'll go wash first." Carlin watched him start down the path. His name was Mr. Mishkin, she remembered, and when he was last at Rosalie, Uncle Will had been in Paris on his wedding trip with Aunt Emily. She thought of the doodle bug game that she and Feely had been playing and looked out at the garden. That kind of little-girl boredom seemed curiously remote right now.

"Lovely afternoon," Mr. Mishkin said, coming back up the brick walk. He had shed his pack and coat, and his graying hair was smoothed back. He settled on the gallery steps below her and cocked his head to look at Carlin's book. "What're you reading?" he asked.

"Dickens," Carlin said. "I've been reading a lot of his novels."

"Someday you must read Pushkin," the peddler said and shaded his eyes as he gazed out over the long cotton field. "Alexander Sergeyevich Pushkin. My countryman. A great poet."

"What's his name again?"

"P-u-s-h-k-i-n." The peddler spelled the name slowly. "You may not find him in the town library. But you'll come upon him later. I promise."

"I'll try and remember," Carlin told him and looked down the drive. "You haven't been here for a long time. Almost two years."

"Oh, I was here last September just before picking time. But you were a sick little girl then. Very sick. I showed my wares, but I didn't stay long."

"I didn't know you'd been here then," Carlin said and stared at him. "A lot of things happened that I didn't know about."

"Yes, yes. I'm sure of that," Mr. Mishkin said and stretched out one leg. "Hard times here in this county. The weevil and all. Many things are changing." He looked up at Carlin. "I was real sick in Richmond myself once, and when I finally got well, the world looked different to me. I felt different inside too."

"That's the way it is with me," Carlin said, leaning forward. "It isn't just that certain things have changed, though they have. I mean, our teacher Miss Mollie is going to leave sometime soon, and that's going to be a big change for me because I've been doing my lessons with her every day now since February, and she's been at Rosalie two years almost. Next fall I'm going to start school in town, I hope. If my papa will let me, that is." She paused. "But it's more than that." She looked out at the cotton field. "I don't know what it is, quite, but I feel different inside too."

"Well, of course, you're older now."

Carlin glanced down at her lap, then up at the peddler again. "Yes, I am and yet. . . ." She paused. "Sickness makes you feel apart in a way. I mean, you're alone a whole lot. And now, well. . . . Feely's got a job in town and Amy's gone off to school this year, you know."

Mr. Mishkin nodded. "I heard that at the Grove," he said. "She'll be quite the young lady."

"Tommy and I talk a lot," Carlin continued. "And I play with Evie." She paused. "My uncle used to be a friend to me when I was little," she went on. "But he's gotten very busy now."

"At the Grove, they say your uncle's all wrapped up in politics. Goes up to Jackson pretty much every week."

"He does?"

"He's been spending a lot of time up there, they say, at the legislature, going to meetings and such. Might be he's planning to run for office."

"Oh?" Carlin hesitated, thinking of the worried voices of her mother and her aunt discussing that possibility in the sewing room one afternoon in the spring. "It would be hard on Aunt Emily, having him away and all."

"Hard, and expensive too."

"Why expensive?" Carlin stared.

"Well, politics is a complicated business. A campaign, even a little local one, can cost a lot of money. And there're other problems. Here in Mississippi, you've got the poll tax, of course."

"Oh, Uncle Will doesn't believe in the poll tax." Carlin shook her head and frowned. "He thinks every citizen should vote. He's got lots of ideas to make Mississippi better and. . . ."

"Well, politics can be disappointing," the peddler said.

"Yes, I suppose." Carlin paused and gazed at a cloud of gnats spinning in a shaft of afternoon sun. She looked from the gnats to the long dusty drive. "Maybe he shouldn't be doing politics," she said. "Maybe he should stay at the Grove and do his new crop planting there or maybe, maybe he should have gone on being an architect, the way he wanted to be."

"Carlin McNair," Aunt Georgia said from the doorway. "What you doin' out here, talkin' to the peddler? You still not a well girl, you know. We gotta get you upstairs for your rest so you'll be strong enough to come down to supper with your mama and papa tonight." She crossed the gallery and bent to lift Carlin's feet from the stool. "I got some nice chicken for your supper, mister," she said, looking down at the peddler. "And some mixed greens and spoonbread too. But first I've gotta take this little girl up to her bed. She not completely well yet. And she gotta have her rest."

Carlin looked at the peddler and rolled her eyes upward, meaning to indicate to Mr. Mishkin that she was merely tolerating Aunt Georgia's fussy care. But when she felt that large warm arm around her waist, she sank against it, tired and grateful once again. "I'll see you tomorrow, Mr. Mishkin," she said, adopting her mother's company voice. "I hope you have a very nice evening at Rosalie."

Miss Mollie was to leave that morning. Carlin had told herself for weeks that she was resigned to the event, but when Miss Mollie came into her room, dressed in her blue suit and wide-brimmed hat, Carlin swallowed. She looked so unfamiliar, so separate already.

"When does your train go?" she demanded.

"Eleven ten. James is driving me to the station in an hour."

"First you go home to New Orleans," Carlin said and watched as Miss Mollie sat down on the leather footstool, facing Carlin in the chaise longue. "Then you'll come back to Greenwood in September and begin your new job at the school. Is that right?"

"Yes. I'll spend the summer with my parents, and then I'll come back and I'll be out to see you right away."

"I'll miss you," Carlin began. "It'll be so boring doing lessons without you."

"But you've been doing very well, Carlin. You've gotten a lot of reading and writing done since you've been better. I don't see any reason why you can't complete all the sixth grade work and be ready for the seventh grade by the end of summer. You're really well ahead of most seventh-graders, you know. And, just think, you might begin school in town next fall, and then I'll see you every day."

"Oh, I hope so," Carlin said, but the fall seemed a long way off. "I. . . ." Carlin felt the blood rush into her face and she clutched the copy book in her lap. "I wish you could stay another month. Stay with us for the summer." Carlin felt her lips tremble as she stared at Miss Mollie's silk shirtwaist under her blue suit jacket, a shirtwaist she had always saved for Sunday.

Miss Mollie reached across and patted Carlin's arm with one gloved hand. "I do too, Carlin, but it isn't possible." She looked down, and Carlin saw that her face was sad. "I'll miss you all," she said. "I've loved Rosalie." She turned Carlin's hand in both of hers, avoiding her eyes, and Carlin felt her smooth kid-covered fingers on her palm.

"Mama told me you said that I was quite precocious, and I looked that word up. But she said that you said that because I was precocious, I could have difficulties."

Miss Mollie laughed uneasily and looked out of the window.

"Well, I don't remember my exact words, or why your mother. . . ." She paused. "You're a wonderful, bright family, and you and your brother and Evie all have gifts that you must use. I didn't mean to sound critical. I just meant that it can be hard for intelligent people when they don't use their intelligence. They can get restless and bored." Miss Mollie took Carlin's hand again and squeezed it. "I'll come right out and visit when I get back," she said again. "All right?" She swallowed and looked down at their hands.

"All right," Carlin said, realizing that Miss Mollie was almost as close to tears as she was. "I'll go on with my British history," she promised, making her voice practical, "and I'm going to help Mama teach Evie her grammar." Carlin lifted her gaze and took in the familiar freckles on Miss Mollie's nose, the blond hair, tucked in neatly now.

"Miss Mollie." Aunt Ceny was at the door. "James have got your trunk in the buggy, and he say you better come quick now. That train gonna leave in just an hour."

Miss Mollie rose and took her handbag from the bureau. She smoothed her long blue skirt and turned back to Carlin. "Goodbye, dear. Get completely well and write me soon. And, Carlin," she took a step back toward Carlin. "Keep on reading, you know, and keep on writing too." She hugged Carlin's head against her waist, but Carlin swung her feet to the floor and rose.

"Oh, I'll miss you so," she said and threw her arms around her teacher in an unsteady embrace. "I'll count the days until you come back to Rosalie."

Mama settled beside Carlin on the front gallery that afternoon, and Carlin heard her sigh as she took out her sewing. "This heat," she said and lifted one hand to fan herself. "I don't envy Mollie. That stuffy coach and all those stops. Maybe New Orleans'll be cooler, though I don't suppose so." She sighed again and held up her needle. "I'll miss her." Carlin watched her mother thread her needle and prick the hem of the skirt she was letting down. "Mollie was definitely the best teacher we've ever had for you children."

"Then why did you let her leave?" Carlin's voice was querulous. "She could have stayed the summer. She doesn't start teaching at the school until September." Carlin paused. "She really loves all of us, you know, and Rosalie."

"I know she does," Mama said. "But she had to leave because. . . ." Mama frowned, and Carlin waited. "She had to leave because your papa couldn't afford to pay her anymore," Mama said. "Papa wouldn't want me to tell you this maybe, but you're a big girl now and your long sickness has made you older than your years. With the weevil back, the harvest won't be good this year, and well. . . ." She stopped and Carlin looked down at the wooden floor of the gallery. Rosalie was failing. She had known that and not known it for a long time. There was the sale of Grandfather's telescope months ago, the ring, the loan, and then the weevil's return. She had known it for months, and yet she had not known it at all.

"The gin needs repairs again," her mother continued. "We can't keep taking the cotton over to the Grove. We need money for another plow, another team. Eight of the field hands have left already, and more may leave before picking. We just couldn't afford to keep Miss Mollie on. That's the real reason, dear. I'm grateful to Miss Percy for hiring her to teach eighth grade at the school. Mollie's a fine teacher. She'll be a real addition there. And this means she'll stay in the area for a while, at least, and visit us often." Mama reached for her thimble. "Emmy's going to let Tommy take lessons with Hugh, you know, and, between us, you and I will teach Evie her letters until we can find some better arrangement."

Carlin stared. "Is Papa going to sell Rosalie?"

Her mother put down her sewing and walked to the edge of the gallery, where she stood silent a moment, looking out. "Selling would be a solution, maybe, but it's gotten difficult to sell plantations nowadays. So many are failing. People just abandon them sometimes—leave and hope they can come back when times get better. Your father says we might rent some fields. I say rent all three fields, if we have to, and move in town until things improve. But I'm not sure your papa would ever do that."

That was the difference between her parents, Carlin realized all at once. Mama thought they could solve their problems by renting the fields and moving to town, but for Papa, leaving Rosalie would be like abandoning a child. The sudden perception seemed to light up the space around her mother as Carlin sat staring at her back.

"Your papa couldn't grow enough cotton to make ends meet before, what with this depression in cotton, and now with the boll weevil again. . . ." Mama turned to Carlin. "We can't afford anything beyond the basics."

"What about the loan from Uncle Will?" Carlin asked and sucked in her breath, realizing that was information she wasn't supposed to know.

Her mother sat again, and picked up her sewing. "We can't keep borrowing. Besides, things haven't worked out with Will the way your father hoped. Right now your uncle's more interested in politics than planting, it seems."

"I know," Carlin said, thinking of the peddler's talk. She watched her mother press her fingers to her forehead. Did she feel a headache coming? Maybe if Carlin changed the subject—"Miss Mollie is so wonderful," she said. "But it's sort of sad that she has to teach in Greenwood."

"What?" Mama gave her head a little shake and picked up her needle again. "Oh, Mollie, you mean."

"I thought her family was rich, Mama. I mean, her father's a cotton broker, and he and her mama went to Europe, and they bought that talking machine. Does she really have to teach school?"

"Well, in the beginning," Mama said, "I think Mollie just wanted to earn some money of her own. But her situation's changed now. This cotton crisis is hard on the brokers too. She needs to earn some income."

Carlin looked out at the field. It seemed to her that a huge brown river of trouble was spreading out around them all, oozing over the fields, its muddy churning waters covering the towns as well, the banks and churches, and even the brokers, like Mr. Betts, way off in New Orleans.

"Do you think she'll ever fall in love again, Mama?" Carlin asked, turning from the scary image. "I mean she's so pretty and smart." She paused and added. "I think she'd really like to marry someday."

"Well, prettiness helps, certainly," Mama said. "But intelligence can be a problem for women, especially in the South." She frowned. "Still the Greenwood School is one of the best grammar schools in the county. It's not a bad job."

A rattle of glasses came from the dining room, and Carlin turned to watch Aunt Ceny put a goblet at each place, a knife, a spoon, a fork, and then a napkin, each one rolled into its own silver ring. How could they leave these routines that went back through all the days of her life? She looked out at the garden where the sun was slanting through the chinaberry tree, making the same lacy pattern of light on the red brick walk that she had seen for years.

"Mama," she said and stopped, ashamed of the broken sound of her voice. She had known this for months, she told herself again, but she said, "We can't just *leave* Rosalie."

"Don't you worry." Her mother put one hand on Carlin's knee. "Don't worry."

"I won't," Carlin said. She looked into her mother's dark brown eyes and understood with a sudden clarity that huge changes lay ahead.

※

Carlin came out to the gallery, holding her copy book, and sat down beside her father, who was reading the newspaper by the glow of the lamp on the wicker table. "Papa, could I read you a story I just finished?" she asked.

Her father took off his steel-rimmed glasses and looked over at her. "Well, yes, darlin'." He folded the paper, crossed one leg over the other, and leaned back. "I guess you could."

The story was about a beautiful young woman named Carol, who started a school on her father's plantation to which the colored children came each morning, eager and happy. They not only learned their letters, but they learned poetry and Shakespeare and all about modern agriculture. Then Carol wrote about what she

169

had done at her plantation school, and her book was published in New York City. Many plantation owners all over the South read the book and started new and better schools on their plantations, and everybody was happy, and everyone thought Carol was wonderful.

"The End," Carlin read. She raised her head and looked over at her father, who was sitting with his arms folded over his chest. "What do you think, Papa?" Carlin felt flushed. The story of Carol was the longest she had ever written. Gazing across at her father in the lamp light, she noticed the tired lines around his mouth and the sagging skin beneath his eyes.

"It's good, darlin'." Papa tugged at his moustache. "I just wish—"

Carlin drew in her breath. Only last week Mama had talked to her of Rosalie's problems, of renting fields, of moving into town someday, even. "I'm sorry, Papa," she said. "I didn't mean. . . ." She hesitated. How stupid she'd been to read that story.

"Don't you worry, darlin'." Papa's face moved into its gentle smile. "It's a lovely story. I enjoyed every word."

Carlin looked down. Maybe, she thought, if she simply asked him about Rosalie. "Papa," she began, "I'm worried about . . ." Carlin felt her father's gaze grow stern and she gulped back the word "Rosalie." She was not Mama, nor was she a friend of Papa's in whom he could confide, she realized suddenly. She was simply his little girl. "I worry," she began again, masking her thought quickly. "Because I think I want to be a writer when I grow up, but I worry about whether I could ever be good enough. Do you think I could?" She let her breath out silently, relieved that she had not mentioned the huge problem that surrounded them all, the problem she had been warned repeatedly not to worry about.

"Well, writing's hard work," Papa said. "But it seems to me, darlin', that you've got a lot to say."

❧

Carlin glimpsed the Grove surrey coming up the drive as she sat on the front gallery, and she leaned forward in her rocking chair to look out. Uncle Will had come at last. She watched him throw his reins to Eben, step down, then stride up the brick walk to the gallery.

"Carlie," he said, looking down at her. "How're you feeling?" He looked curiously formal in a white linen suit, and he was carrying a new leather case. Carlin stared up at him, aware once again that her uncle was a handsome man.

"Fine. I'm almost well. That's a nice suit. Is it new?"

"Do you like it?" Uncle Will straightened his shoulders and tugged at the vest.

"Yes." Carlin felt her face grow hot as she sat smiling up at him.

"It was expensive," Uncle Will told her. "But you have to look right in Jackson." He raised one arm to check the gold cufflink on his sleeve. "I'm learning a lot up there, Carlie." He pulled a rocking chair from the row and sat down facing her. His tanned hands looked dark on his white knees. "Things are happening in this country now. There's a man at Princeton University that I've got my eye on. Wilson, his name is. Woodrow Wilson."

"Wilson?" Carlin hoped her cheeks didn't look as red as they felt, and she covered them with her hands. "What will he do?"

"He might run for president. At least that's what a lot of us are hoping. He's a Southern gentleman, Carlie, and he's bright and understands our problems." Uncle Will leaned back, making the rockers rise. "There's so much to do in Mississippi. But if we could get a sympathetic man like Wilson in the White House. . . ." He leaned forward, pushing the rockers down again. "He would see the need for a scientific approach to agriculture. That's what's so important right now." Uncle Will raised one hand. "Food crops and corn," he said, pointing his forefinger at her. Carlin nodded. "Hogs are crucial. We need to establish a cycle of corn and hogs."

Carlin held an alert look on her face as she gazed back at him. What did he mean by a corn-hog cycle? She didn't want to interrupt to ask. He was talking to her like a friend, a fellow politican in Jackson almost.

"It's a difficult thing, getting anyone to listen, getting any action." Sam groaned in his sleep and stretched his graying legs on the floor. "Nobody's enthusiastic," Uncle Will said as he reached down to pat the dog. "Any change is suspect in Mississippi, you know. But I'm going to keep on listening to these agricultural scientists, and talking to them too. You see," Uncle Will said, "with these changes in the wind, the possibility of Wilson's candidacy, and. . . ." He paused. "I mean, it's just possible I could have some influence up there myself."

"Oh, Uncle Will, it would be so exciting if you got into politics." Carlin stopped. That's not what Mama and Aunt Emily thought. She drew in her breath, remembering the sound of her aunt crying. But, but . . . Mama and Aunt Emily didn't know everything. Uncle Will could make a difference. He would.

"I want to help Mississippi, Carlie. I want to help us turn away from cotton to fruits and vegetables and livestock. But we've got to have better transportation. See? Better ways of getting produce to the northern markets."

"Trains, you mean?" Carlin said.

"We need to adopt commercial fertilizers to replenish the soil," Uncle Will went on, ignoring her question. "We've got to change our methods so that we can lift up out of the slavery of this sharecropping system. These systems are ingrained, passed down from father to son over generations, and nobody tries to change. And yet people can learn. We must learn if we are to survive."

Was he talking faster than usual, Carlin wondered? Was this how politicians talked? Now he was telling her about something called nitrogen. She gripped the arms of her rocker. He had lost her, but he mustn't suspect. She wanted to be his listener, his friend.

"I've created this perfect schedule for myself," he said. "I get up at quarter of five every morning, ride for an hour, then after breakfast on Monday, I ride into town and take the train to Jackson. I go to the sessions all day, talk to people, and then read into the night. I stay there through Wednesday, then Thursday I'm back at the Grove, reading, checking my experimental crops, going through the journals. There's so much to learn and assimilate. There never seems to be enough time and yet, yet . . . I mean, if I can just stick to this schedule. . . ." He glanced around him suddenly.

"My God, Carlie, how I go on." He cocked his head and looked at her stack of copy books on the table. "You've been writing, haven't you? It looks like you've filled all three of those books. Have you written stories or essays or what?"

Carlin smiled happily and pulled the copy books into her lap. "Stories mostly," she said. "I've invented this heroine, Carol. She lives on a plantation, and she brings about all these good changes and everything. I copied the best one for you last night." She took the folded pages and held them out, but her uncle did not take them. He looked at the field beyond her and frowned.

"Sometimes I feel as though I'm racing, Carlie—my mind, my talk. There's so much I want to do." He glanced down at the pages Carlin was holding out to him without lifting his hand. "Time. It's all a question of time, Carlie. I've got to find more hours somehow."

"Will you read my story?" Carlin persisted.

"I'll read it on my next visit. All right?"

Uncle Will rose. He took his gold watch from his vest pocket and peered at the face. "I'll be back soon. I've got to go find your papa now. There's something I need to talk to him about."

"I copied it," Carlin said. "You can take it with you." She felt her hand tremble as she continued to hold it out.

"Don't give it to me now, Carlie. I might lose it, and I don't want that. Save it. All right? I'll be back next week or the week after, anyway."

"But. . . ." Carlin thought of how she had rushed to finish copying the story last night. She needed to know whether Uncle Will thought the plantation reforms Carol was advocating fit with his idea of a better South. He couldn't just leave without taking the story. But he was. She watched him pick up his leather case and tuck it under his arm, then move to the door.

"I'll be back soon."

Carlin let the story drop on the stack of copy books as she felt tears start. Uncle Will's visits shouldn't be so important, she told herself. But they were.

Carlin sat at the piano playing a Bach partita while her mother rubbed rosin on her violin bow. "You play with more passion than precision, Carlin," Mama said and smiled as she lifted her violin to her shoulder. "Now that you're able to practice every day, you'd do better to spend more time at the piano and less time reading."

"I don't like practicing, Mama," Carlin said. "I just like playing with you."

"Well, you can't play without practicing, Carlin. Playing the piano well is an important accomplishment for a young girl."

Carlin tipped her head back and studied her mother, who had lifted the violin from her shoulder and was looking at the strings. "It was more than just an accomplishment for you, Mama."

"Well. . . ." Her mother looked down at her. "You're right. It's been a passion with me. But the passion grew out of my practicing, you know."

Carlin shifted as her mother sat down beside her on the piano bench, holding the violin.

"Give me a G," Mama demanded, and twisted one of the black pegs at the end. "All right, now G, D, A."

Carlin played the notes and watched her mother's long fingers touch the strings, then enclose the carved black scroll at the end. "Did your playing help make Papa fall in love with you?" she asked suddenly.

"What?" Her mother stood. She started to settle the violin on her shoulder, but held it up a moment and looked down at Carlin. "What made you ask that, dear? What have you been thinking about?"

"Love, I guess," Carlin said. "Babies. Growing up."

"You really are feeling better, aren't you?" her mother asked.

"Well, I'm going to be a woman pretty soon, Mama, you know."

"True." Her mother put her violin down on the piano top and glanced at the gold clock on the mantelpiece with its cracked cover. "Shall we talk a minute before we start?"

Carlin nodded, and her mother sat down on the wide arm of the horsehair sofa beside the piano. "I know all about it really," Carlin began. "I've seen Reggie do it to Martha in the barn, though bulls and cows are different, and, when he was younger, Sam used to do it to Bessie."

Her mother shifted and glanced a moment at the closed door. "It's gentler and subtler with people, Carlin. It comes more slowly, and if you're lucky—and I have been—it can be a happy experience."

"Even for a woman?"

"Well, it can be. Not always. You want to be sure you love the man you marry. Your papa and I took our time. It wasn't just poetry and violin music, you know. We talked and talked." Her mother glanced at the closed door again. Aunt Lucy, Carlin thought. She would disapprove of such a conversation. "There are hard times in any marriage, of course." Mama looked at the window. "But if you wait, things often shift and you go on."

"You and Papa will have been married fifteen years in August."

"Yes. A long time." Mama glanced at the book of Bach partitas, lying open on the music stand. "I used to think happiness just came, that it dropped down on you like a bouquet and you caught it or you didn't. But now I think that was wrong. I think happiness, especially happiness in marriage, is something you work at, like the piano maybe, or the violin. You keep trying, practicing, and it gets easier. It gets better, more of a habit as you go along."

"Practicing happiness?" Carlin said slowly, and squeezed her elbows against her sides. Mama had been in love with Papa and loved him still, she thought. But when you marry a man, you marry his plantation too, and Mama hadn't always been in love with Rosalie. Carlin could remember when her mother had practiced all morning behind the closed library door, leaving Carlin and Tommy to Aunt Ceny or the teacher, letting Aunt Lucy arrange the menus and the chores. There had been weekends when she had simply ridden off to spend a night at the Grove, maybe two. But that was years ago when Carlin was little.

"Practicing happiness meant a lot of settling for you, didn't it, Mama?" Carlin asked, and sucked her breath in sharply. There were Aunt Lucy's long visits, the evenings listening to the men talk cotton, and always there was the isolation of Rosalie.

"Settling?" her mother said. "You mean compromise?" She glanced at the window and then back at Carlin. "You can't do much of anything in this life without some compromise, you know."

Carlin looked down at the keyboard. Maybe that was true, but she wouldn't make the compromises that Mama had made, she resolved. She would. . . . She paused. She didn't know what she would do, but it would be something else. She let her breath out slowly, aware once more of her mother sitting just beyond her, waiting to talk. Her own life was going to be different, she thought, and the idea seemed to burn in her suddenly like a lighted rod. Different somehow from this.

※

It was a hot night. Mama and Papa had gone to dinner at Elmcrest, and Carlin and Tommy were sitting on Carlin's bed talking. There was a sudden rattling noise on the balcony beyond the open window, and they turned their heads to look. A squirrel? A possum maybe? Carlin looked over at Tommy, who stood and went cautiously to the windowsill.

"Hey there, Tom," a familiar voice called out from below. "Let me in. The front door's bolted." Carlin rushed to the window and looked down. In the light from the lamp on the front gallery, she could make out Uncle Will, smiling up at them from the walk below.

"Uncle Will," she shouted. "What are you doing here?"

"Mama and Papa are over at Elmcrest," Tommy called down.

"I know. I came to see you all. I just threw some sand at the window. I came to hear your story, Carlie. Will you read it to me now? Will you let me in?"

They bounded down the stairs, and Tommy pulled the brass bolt on the door. Carlin could feel the blood pounding in her temples. Uncle Will had come to read her story. He had come to see them, not Papa, not Mama, them.

"It's very good, Carlie," Uncle Will pronounced, when Carlin had finished reading. "You've got a lot of ideas there."

He lay on his back on the parlor rug, his arms under his head.

Tommy was sitting just beyond him, leaning back against the horsehair sofa.

"What I want to know," Tommy said, "is where did Carol get all these notions?"

"She reads, Tom," Uncle Will put in. "She knows other people interested in reform. Right, Carlie?" Carlin nodded. The fact that both her uncle and her brother had listened to her writing and were talking about it made her feel dizzy with attention. "Now, I like all the stuff about her teaching, but I'm wondering what that school would look like. Suppose Carol got her Papa to build a real French *lycée* in gray stone with a courtyard in front."

"It'd have to have a tricolor flying above the door," Tommy said.

"Definitely, and I see a bust in the courtyard. Voltaire maybe." He laughed.

"Sometimes I think France is more real to you than Mississippi, Uncle Will," Carlin said and leaned back in the big armchair.

"Maybe it is, Carlie. At times, at least. But you keep Carol in Warrington County, hear? That's where she's needed." He got up from the floor and stretched, then moved to the piano and sat down on the bench. "How about a song?" he said, running his right hand lightly over the keys. "We're all alone. We won't disturb anybody." He began to play.

> *Farewell and adieu to you ladies of Spain,*
> *Way down Rio.*

He sang out, and Carlin and Tommy leaned close to him, joining in. Carlin gazed at her uncle's face in the light behind the piano, then at her brother's. She would remember this night all the rest of her life, she resolved. Years later, when she was grown, riding in a trolley car maybe, wearing a hat with a veil, she would think back to this magic time in the parlor with Tommy and Uncle Will, the window open to the summer night, the crickets outside in the hot dark, and the three of them singing,

> *Farewell and adieu to you ladies of Spain*
> *Way down Rio.*

And fare ye well my pretty young girls,
For we're bound for the Rio Grande.

Carlin sat by her bedroom window, reading in the steamy August evening. She was aware of her parents talking on the front gallery below, but their voices were muted. Her mother's voice lifted all at once, distinct and sharp. "But it isn't as though it would cost us extra money, Thomas. She could stay with Tazey during the week, and you'd bring her home each Friday."

Carlin sat forward. They were talking about her. "We've been over all that, Belle."

"Well, we need to go over it again."

"She's been so sick," Carlin heard her father say. "Sending her into town now to go to school with all those others and live with just her Aunt Tazey—it'd be such a big change for her. I mean, what's the hurry? She's only twelve. Why can't we wait and send her next year?"

"The hurry is because she wants and needs to go now."

"I don't want her to go, Belle. I really don't." Her father's voice was sad. "She can stay home another year and build up her strength. She reads all the time as it is." There was a pause. Carlin heard her mother clear her throat. A cricket sang. "She'd be home with you and Lucy. She'd learn more about housekeeping and sewing. Skills she's going to need later. You might even try and start her on the violin."

"Carlin's a pianist, not a violinist. And those housekeeping skills. . . ." Mama's voice was hard. "Thomas, I don't want Carlin limited to just that. She's a bright girl, and we need to give her a chance." Carlin clutched her arms about her, listening.

"I know that. I know. But the fact is, I'd miss her." There was a pause. "I'd miss her. I just don't want her going now. She came so close to dying. Not once but two, maybe three times. I don't want her going yet." His voice was muffled as though he had cupped one hand over his mouth. "Don't let's talk about it any more, Belle, please. Her going makes me feel old, and I feel tired and old enough as it is right now."

Carlin waited. She heard the squeak of a rocker and then the sound of the evening paper being unfolded. Were they simply going to stop, she wondered, put this huge question of her life aside for a day or a week or two? Should she just wait and pretend she had never heard?

She went downstairs slowly, stepped over Sam lying in the doorway, and walked out onto the front gallery where her parents sat. She glanced at the empty rocker beside Papa, but did not sit down. She leaned against the balustrade instead and looked at her parents in the glow of the lamp on the table.

"I've been thinking about school," Carlin began. She squeezed one hand within the other. "I heard what you said, actually. I was listening upstairs."

"Oh, Carlin." Her mother shook her head. Carlin looked down at the floor, awaiting a reprimand, but when nothing came, she looked up again, determined to talk.

"Papa," she began. "I really want to go. And once I begin, it won't seem so lonely and odd. It'll be natural. I'll be home every Friday, and we'll have all those nice long buggy rides together, going in and out of town." She paused, feeling her jaw tremble. This was so important, so crucial to everything. "Two buggy rides a week, Papa," she added carefully. "Lots of time to talk."

"You could go just as easily a year from now, darlin'," her father said. "September, 1912. What about starting then?"

"I want to start now, Papa. This September." Carlin clutched the balustrade behind her as she waited for her father to meet her gaze, but he lowered his eyes to the gray wooden floor. "Uncle Will says we Southerners have to get educated so we can make the South new and. . . ." Carlin let her voice trail. Maybe it wasn't a good idea to pull in Uncle Will right now.

Her father said nothing. Mama was hemming very slowly, raising the needle and pausing before she lowered it and pierced the cloth again. Carlin thought of the argument of Amy, leaving soon for her second year away in school, but that also seemed inappropriate right now. "I mean, I know I can go on reading alone and Mama will correct my sums. But it gets boring with Miss Mollie gone, and . . . I just want to go to a real school, Papa," Carlin began again. "I'll never stop loving you or Mama or Rosalie." She heard her voice shake and stopped.

Her father looked up at her and then down at the floor. "All right. Here's what I'll do," he said. "I'll stop by Miss Percy's house when I go into town Thursday, and we'll let her decide."

Carlin drew in her breath and glanced across at her mother. That meant it was done. Miss Percy, the principal, would be glad to have Carlin. She had told Mama so. Mama looked at Carlin and smiled.

"Well, that's settled," she said and stood up quickly. "I'm going to get us all some iced tea. The heat's terrible tonight." Carlin saw the triumphant way Mama tossed her sewing in her chair and stood looking out at the drive a moment before she turned and went into the hall.

Carlin clapped her hands together. "Oh, Papa, thank you. Thank you." She knelt by his chair and put her arms around his neck. "Papa, you fix everything. You really do."

She pressed her head against his chest and felt it swell then drop as he sighed. "I wish I could, darlin'," he said and put one arm around her. "I just wish I could fix everything."

***

Miss Percy, the tall imposing principal of the Greenwood Grammar School, sat at the library table, sipping tea with Carlin and her mother. "As I said," she repeated, "if Carlin reads all the books on this list during the next month, she'll be eligible for the seventh grade in September." She reached for her pince-nez, which hung down against her flat front between a loop of yellowish pearls. "She must also submit four compositions." Carlin glanced at the list on the table, trying to read it sideways and listen too. She had read *Treasure Island* and both the Dickens novels.

"From what Miss Mollie tells me, you're behind in arithmetic and ciphering," Miss Percy said. "You'll just have to work harder in that." Carlin nodded. What would the seventh-grade school room look like? Which desk would she have? She knew Robbie, the postmaster's daughter, but she didn't know any of the other girls. Would they be nice or would they be snooty? Would they think she was too skinny, a dumb girl from the country, a plantation girl? She would need new shoes, and Mama just must buy her a hat.

Miss Percy was talking about the importance of reading American history when Mama interrupted. "I can't think why you'd want the girls to study the history of the United States when they could be learning the history of Greece." She held the silver teapot in midair a moment before she refilled Miss Percy's cup, then added, "Surely Greece was the great civilization that everyone should know." Carlin stared at her mother, but Mama talked on. "When I was young, we had to read all about the Peloponnesian wars and learn the names of the famous warriors."

"Well, unfortunately, we can't cover everything, Mrs. McNair," Miss Percy said. "Nowadays we feel it's important to give the girls some understanding of their contemporary world." She turned back to Carlin. "We're going to begin with this *History of Our Country*," she said, tapping a brown book with her long forefinger. "You would be wise to read through those first four chapters on your own. The colonial period is not easy."

"I remember learning about Athens," Mama went on. "The Golden Age of Athens when Pericles reigned and Socrates was surrounded by all those bright young men."

"Mama." Carlin frowned at her mother. What was the matter with Mama anyway? Miss Percy had driven out to Rosalie to bring assignments and make sure Carlin would be ready to enter the seventh grade. Why was Mama talking about her own schooling, which was years ago? Miss Percy put her teacup and saucer on the table and leaned forward to gather her large reticule, preparing to leave.

There was a knock at the library door. Aunt Ceny stood in the doorway, squeezing her hands. "Miz Isabelle," she said. "I'm sorry to interrupt you all, but. . . ."

"What is it, Ceny?" Mama demanded. "We're finishing our tea."

"It's Ella Mae, ma'am," Aunt Ceny said. "She just come up from the quarters. She's brung her babies. Her new little twins. And she want you to name 'em, Miz Isabelle. Give each of them one of your fancy names."

"Oh, Ceny. Not now." Mama turned back to her visitor. "I tell you, Miss Percy, there's nothing like a plantation for interruptions. Nothing in the world. Now there's this, and in another minute, it'll be my sister-in-law coming in to look for her crochet hook, or the cook will be in asking about pecans for the cake she's making. Carlin will begin playing the piano, or, I don't know. Now it's these babies waiting out there in the kitchen courtyard. I tell you, I could write a book." She shook her head and turned back to the door. "All right, Ceny," Mama said. "Tell her we'll be there in a minute. We'll all come."

"But Mama," Carlin protested. "Mama, Miss Percy only came to. . . ."

"Nonsense," her mother said, rising. "Miss Percy would love to see those cute little babies. They're only a week old, maybe less." They rose, Mama leading the way, Miss Percy following. Carlin sucked her breath in, dreading the scene to come. What would Miss Percy think? She could already see that Rosalie was old and shabby. The upholstered arms on Papa's library chair, in which she had been sitting, were frayed, and the monotonous green row of Dickens and the dark red one of Sir Walter Scott in the bookshelf opposite were not interrupted by new paperbound books, like those that arrived at the Grove from Paris. Miss Percy probably thought they hadn't read anything new in years and had checked them off as an ignorant, country family.

Carlin followed Miss Percy down the gallery steps and around to the kitchen courtyard. Ella Mae, a thick young woman with a halo of curly black hair, sat on the bench beside the kitchen house door, holding one baby in her arms, while Aunt Georgia stood rocking the other. "Morning, Miz Isabelle," Ella Mae said, rising. Her eyes traveled over Miss Percy, taking in her large dark hat and the pince-nez hanging down. "I weren't meanin' to disturb you when you had company," she began. "I was just hopin' you could. . . ." Her smile was hesitant. She glanced down at the little face gazing up at her. The infant made a sucking movement with his mouth and turned his head to her blouse.

"You'd like some fancy names for your twins, wouldn't you?" Mama moved close. "They're beautiful little boys, Ella Mae. May I hold one?" Ella Mae smiled and held out the baby, and Mama settled him in her arms. His dark little body was wrapped in a frayed blanket, and his head had a thin covering of crinkly black hair. "Just look at those intelligent eyes," Mama said, smiling down at him. She turned to Aunt Georgia. "Hand that one to Miss Percy, Georgia. Unless he's damp."

Carlin bit her lip as she watched Miss Percy take the baby and give him a self-conscious smile. "He's very sweet," she said to Aunt Georgia, "but I. . . ." She was holding the baby away from her body, as though afraid to bring him any closer. The baby kicked at his blanket, exposing his dark stomach. Miss Percy tried to pull the blanket back in place with one hand as she held the child with the other.

"Here. I'll take him back," Aunt Georgia said.

"I'm afraid I'm not very used to babies," Miss Percy confessed.

"They's messy at this stage, I tell ya." Aunt Georgia wrapped the blanket around the child. "I don't want him stainin' your dress or nothin'."

The baby in Mama's arms began to squirm. She shifted him to her shoulder and patted his back. "Now what names shall we choose?" she said. "There are twins in some of Shakespeare's plays, aren't there, Miss Percy?"

Carlin glanced at Miss Percy and then down at the brick courtyard where a few brown berries from the chinaberry tree had drifted into little mounds. How awful this was. She should tell Tommy about those berries, she thought, trying to distract herself. They were ready to use in his slingshot.

"Yes, I think there are several sets of twins in Shakespeare," Miss Percy said and hesitated.

"What about *The Comedy of Errors*?" Mama said. "There're twins in that. Now, what are their names?" she challenged. Carlin tucked her elbows in against her sides to make herself smaller. Mama was just showing off. "Ephesus," her mother said. "That's one, and the other's Syracuse, isn't it?" She turned to the teacher triumphantly. "How about that, Miss Percy? Ephesus and Syracuse. Am I right?" Her eyes were shining.

"You probably are, Mrs. McNair," Miss Percy said. "That's not one of the comedies I know well."

"But wait." Mama lifted the baby from her shoulder and settled him into the crook of her arm again. "I don't think this little one looks quite like an Ephesus somehow." She rocked the baby, twisting her hips, so that her long dark skirt rippled around the tops of her boots. "Maybe they should have some names from history instead." She turned to look at the infant Aunt Georgia was holding. "What about Gladstone and Disraeli?" Mama looked back at Miss Percy. "Those are big distinguished names for little boys to grow into, don't you think?"

"They're long," Miss Percy said. "But they're certainly distinguished." She looked at her hostess. Carlin stared at a powdery ant hill beside the mound of chinaberries, wishing that this could be over, that Miss Percy would just turn and leave or that Aunt Georgia would do something to change this moment.

"Do you like those names, Ella Mae? Disraeli and Gladstone?" Mama asked.

"Yes'm," Ella Mae answered. "They's real purty. I like 'em fine." She hesitated. "Kin you. . . . Would you kindly . . . ?"

"Write them down?" Mama looked over at Carlin. "Run inside and get a piece of paper, Carlin, and the pen and inkwell."

Carlin took a sheet of paper from her father's desk with the black lettering, ROSALIE PLANTATION, at the top and arranged it on a leather-covered tray with a pen and the cut glass inkwell. The paper made a blinding white rectangle in the afternoon sun as she stepped down into the courtyard, but Mama, who had given the baby back to Ella Mae, sat down and drew the tray across her lap. "William Ewart Gladstone," she wrote carefully in large flowing letters and underneath it, "Benjamin Disraeli." "They were both famous prime ministers," she explained, turning to Ella Mae.

"They worked in London, England. They were on different sides, but they were both great leaders."

"Thank you, Miz Isabelle." Ella Mae's dark face had gone lax a moment with the weight of the brief lecture, but now it was alert again. She took the paper, folded it over, and fitted it into the pocket of her skirt. "They's real purty names and I'se much obliged."

※

"Mama, why did you do that with Ella Mae's babies?" Carlin demanded. She was holding up her forearms as her mother wound the blue yarn looped around them into a ball. The question came out loudly, and her mother stopped winding the yarn to look at her in surprise.

"Do what, dear?"

"Give them names, with Miss Percy watching and everything." If she had to sit here in Mama's room doing this boring task, she could at least try to make her mother see how awful that time out in the courtyard with the babies had been an hour ago.

"But she enjoyed it, Carlin. I know she did. And those babies are so adorable."

"Oh, Mama." Carlin twisted to one side, but she had to go on holding up her forearms with the wool.

"What?"

"Well, you know Ella Mae can't read or write."

"Of course not. Only a few of Rosalie's colored folk can. Reverend Ambrose reads the Bible a little, and several of the children do. Feely writes quite well, Aunt Georgia says."

"If Ella Mae can't read and doesn't know anything about English history," Carlin continued, "why would she want to name her babies Gladstone and Disraeli?"

"She likes the idea of fancy names from the big house, Carlin. They all do. That's the way Hamlet and Feely got their names after all."

"But Mama. . . ."

"What?" Her mother's voice was sharp.

"She can't pronounce the names, much less understand them and yet . . . yet you think it's funny." Carlin felt the blood pour into her face. The yarn itched on her bare arms. She shouldn't be talking to her mother this way.

But Mama only sighed. She put the ball she had wound on the table beside her and stood. "You're right in a way," she said. She went to the window, pulled the blind partly up and stood staring out. "You're right," she repeated with her back to Carlin. "Do you know the word 'condescension'?" she asked and looked straight at Carlin. She nodded and her mother turned back to the window.

"There's no easy answer," her mother said, looking at her again. "The whites treat the colored people like children, and as I often tell your father, by treating them that way they keep them that way." She hesitated. "I'm among the worst offenders. You don't need to point that out." She breathed out and turned back to the window. "When I first came to Rosalie, when I first married your father, I'd been teaching school, you know. I planned to give lessons to the help here. Your Papa let me fix up the cottage for anyone who wanted to come up and have lessons in the evening after work." Her mother paused. "It sounds noble and fine. But I was lonely. Rosalie seemed so far away from anywhere, even the Grove." She sat down again and picked up the ball of yarn, then put it down. "Nobody came much. Folks were tired. And they didn't know what to think of a master's young wife who wanted to teach the hands to read. Only one or two came. Your Uncle Will tried to help me. He drove around and brought me another two pupils. But then I had a miscarriage and I was sick a long time. Then you came and, well, I didn't go on."

There was a long pause. Carlin watched her mother settle in the chair again. "I liked teaching. I'd hoped to give music lessons. But Rosalie's a long way out of town." She picked up the ball of yarn again and began winding.

Carlin breathed in slowly. "Mama," she started. "If you hadn't had a family—me and Tommy and Evie, I mean—would you. . . ." She hesitated. "Would you have liked to have been a principal like Miss Percy—a principal, or a concert violinist perhaps?"

"Oh, Carlie, Carlie," her mother said. She put down the ball of yarn once more and reached over to lay one hand on Carlin's knee. "You and your brother and your little sister, and your papa, of course, you are the most precious things to me in the whole world."

The Saturday before Carlin was to leave for school, she rose early and ran to the stable, wanting to take one last ride with Papa. She was riding Star, her mother's Morgan, who nudged up close to Graylie as they started down the usual path toward the north field. Picking was almost over, and only a few hands were in the field. The vines on the fence were wet with dew, and a flock of sparrows flew up as they approached. Carlin sat forward in her saddle, proud that her father was letting her ride Star instead of her pony.

Graylie snorted and Lady, Papa's bird dog, loped along beside them. They rode past the field, then up to the pine ridge, and Carlin turned in her saddle to look back. This was the best view of Rosalie. There was the big house with its galleries and the kitchen house beside it, the stable, the barns further back. The quarters lay to the right, partly obscured by the pecan orchard, and on the left was the road to the gin. This had been her world as long as she could remember, she thought. But by this time next week, when she returned to Rosalie, she would have lived in town for a whole week and by then she would be a student in the seventh grade.

"Why don't you trot Star around the meadow?" Papa suggested. "She needs some exercise, and Graylie'd like to rest."

Carlin tightened her knees and pulled in the reins. She had been practicing her trot and now she could show off to Papa. She straightened her shoulders, concentrating on the movement of the horse's body, trying to feel it in hers. She ducked to avoid a hanging vine and trotted on. Papa would see how good she was getting, how she kept her chin up and her heels down. She made a long oval in the meadow, rounded a clump of goosebery bushes, and started back up the rise to the pine ridge where Graylie was waiting.

"Is that good trotting, Papa?" she called out as she rode toward her father. Her father had turned away from the meadow and was staring out at the long drive, and something about the sag of his shoulders kept Carlin from calling again. She pulled Star into a walk and moved toward her father quietly. "Papa?" Her father turned, and Carlin drew in her breath. There was a wet line along the side of his nose, and a drop was clinging to one nostril just above his moustache. Something terrible had happened. Papa was crying.

Was it the harvest? she thought. Had the weevil destroyed so much that the harvest would be even worse than he had feared? Was he worried about borrowing from Uncle Will and Aunt Emily again? She brought Star up close.

"We're going to have to leave Rosalie, darlin'," her father said. "I've been putting off telling you. We're going to move to town next winter. Next spring, anyway. We'll rent a place, maybe the Watson house."

"Leave Rosalie?" Carlin repeated, but her shock was mingled with the relief she felt at her father's quiet, practical tone. Papa might be sad, but at least he wasn't crying.

"It had to be," Papa said. "Rosalie's been losing money for a long time." Something enormous was happening, Carlin realized, and looked down, half-expecting to see the dirt road split into a yawning chasm just beyond them.

"We won't leave for a few months, maybe more. Plenty of time to get things ready, say our goodbyes." Carlin nodded. What could she say?

"I tried to sell," Papa continued. "Mr. Marvin at the bank said . . . but. . . . At least I can rent the pond field, maybe more. We'll see."

"We'll live in town, Papa?"

"Yes. We'll take Georgia and Ceny with us, if they'll come." He leaned back in his saddle and turned his head. Carlin followed his gaze across the field to the cow barn and the broken mule cart, standing near the fence. "I never was a good businessman," Papa said, "though I tried. Things went against me, the cotton depression, the weevil and. . . ." He let the sentence trail. "Rosalie was my father's plantation, your grandfather. I would have given anything to keep it going. But it turned out anything wasn't enough." He raised one hand to his eyes, and Carlin tensed. Don't cry again, she thought. Please, Papa. I don't know what to do.

"Mr. Baxter says he can use me in his drugstore," Papa went on calmly. "He needs another helper." Carlin breathed out. Papa's voice was firm again. "You'll be all settled in school by the time we move. Tommy'll go to the school, too, next year, and Evie. Your Mama can give music lessons. Maybe she'll teach at the school some, too. We'll see."

Carlin saw them in the Watson house. It was big, with its wide wrap-around gallery, and it had a little room at the top, which Carlin would claim for her own. If they moved in January, she would be able to have friends over before school started up again, if she had any friends, that is. She could go to parties on Saturdays maybe, and when the fair came to Huntsville she would go with Robbie.

Carlin drew in her breath. What was wrong with her? She was thinking of fairs and parties, when right beside her, her own papa was telling her that he had failed with Rosalie.

"You haven't failed, Papa," she began. "You just, just. . . ." But what could she say? He had spent his whole life at Rosalie, and now he was going to Greenwood to work in Mr. Baxter's drugstore. "It'll be all right," she mumbled, not knowing what she meant.

"God will help us," Papa said. "He will give us the strength to find our way."

Carlin gazed down at the big house with its galleries. She could feel Papa's sorrow beside her like a huge dark shape, and yet there was all that newness twinkling beyond.

"Come on, darlin'," Papa said and slapped his reins. "We've got to get back."

"Hey, folks," a voice called. Carlin looked up and saw Uncle Will riding across the ring below them on Johnny Boy, the brown stallion. He was wearing his wide-brimmed hat, and he looked large, she thought, his brown boots bearing down in the stirrups.

"I'm borrowing Johnny," he called. "Fancy's laid up for a day or two, and I have to ride into the depot. Train for Jackson at ten. I'll bring him home tomorrow evening." Uncle Will swept off his hat, and Carlin saw his hair pressed down underneath like a dark cap.

"All right, Will," Papa called back. "But don't ride him too hard, please. He's not as young as he once was."

"None of us are." Uncle Will laughed. "Things are getting exciting up there in Jackson, Tom. We might get some legislation through about this crop business. You oughta come up and listen to a session. Bring Carlie. She'd learn a lot."

Papa nodded. "Just don't get too wrapped up in all that, Will," he said. "Politics can be tricky, you know."

"Yes, but if you sit around worrying about all the angles, you never do much at all. Right?" He glanced back at the stable, where the big sliding door hung crooked. Before she was sick, Papa had talked of getting a man from Port Daniel to come fix that door, but he never had. "You can just stay stuck in the same old barnyard, unable to change or improve, unable to make your own plantation pay, even."

What? Carlin clutched the reins. That was an insult to Papa. You can't say that, Uncle Will. You have to apologize.

"Well, I'm off," Uncle Will shouted and turned Johnny Boy toward the gate.

Maybe he didn't know what he'd said, she thought. Maybe he didn't know that they were going to leave Rosalie. Leave Rosalie. The idea smacked against her chest and she jerked back. How could they leave Rosalie?

"See you tomorrow night," Uncle Will called.

Carlin felt her eyes smart, and she bunched the reins in her hands as she watched her uncle disappear into the tunnel of live oak trees that lined the drive. Was it possible to love someone, she wondered, and hate them too?

3

SCHOOL was to begin on a Wednesday in September, and since picking was over, Papa took the morning off on Tuesday to drive Carlin to Aunt Tazey's house in town. Carlin hugged Mama first, then Tommy and Evie on the front walk as Papa settled her trunk in the back of the buggy. "You'll be home Friday," her mother said, sounding matter-of-fact, but she caught her bottom lip between her teeth. "That's only three days off."

Carlin nodded. All at once, the week felt long and scary. She climbed into the buggy and looked back. Mama was standing beside Evie, and Tommy was waving from the gatepost. She looked at the house behind them, the gallery, the fan window over the front door, and felt clutched by a sudden desire to jump down and run back. It was all a mistake, insisting on going to school. Stop, she wanted to shout. Her father settled himself and gathered the reins. "Giddyap," he said. Yes, yes. This was what she wanted, she told herself: school, adventure.

Aunt Tazey helped Carlin unpack her trunk in the narrow spare room at the top of the stairs. Then all at once there was nothing left to do. Carlin went searching for the cat. Later she took a book out into the yard to read, but she kept thinking of what Aunt Georgia would be doing now in the kitchen house, peeling sweet potatoes maybe, or cutting up the chicken. Was Mama practicing or was she sitting on the front gallery sewing? She thought of Tommy trotting on Lightning and Evie swinging slowly by herself under the live oak tree.

The next morning Carlin arrived early at the schoolhouse across the square and waited beside a large camellia bush, hoping Miss Mollie would appear. Girls in pigtails and new dresses ran up, calling to each other, some with lunch baskets. They were talking busily after the summer weeks apart, or without the school routine at least, for it seemed to Carlin that all the town girls knew each other and saw one another almost every day. The boys talked less and punched each other's shoulders a little as they waited for the school door to open. Two teachers moved past her, but no Miss Mollie. She climbed the front steps finally, following the others. She had been told to go directly to Miss Percy's office, but where was it?

Miss Percy came into the hall, wearing a dark skirt and shirt-waist. The black cord of her pince-nez hung down against her thin chest, half-tangled with her string of pearls.

"Ah, there you are," she said, seeing Carlin standing by the wall. "You're to go straight to Miss Stark's room. The seventh grade."

"Miss Stark?" Carlin whispered, aware that a talking group of girls beyond her had quieted to watch.

"It's two rooms down. The brown door." Miss Percy turned to the girls. "You, Mary Beth." She pointed imperiously. "This is a new girl over here, Mary Carlin McNair. I want you to show her to the seventh-grade room. Find her a desk near yours and show her around."

"Yes ma'am," the girl said. She nodded at Miss Percy and led the way down the hall. Carlin followed. Mary Beth would resent being ordered to show her around, Carlin thought, and so she would probably dislike her.

Mary Beth pushed a door open at the end of the hall, and Carlin stood beside her looking in at the empty classroom. There was a long window on the opposite side with a green roller shade hanging partway down. A dry geranium plant stood on the sill beside an uneven stack of workbooks. The wall at the front of the room was partly covered by a grayish-green blackboard, and in front of it was an important-looking desk that must belong to the teacher. There were two lines of wooden seats, which seemed to be nailed to the floor. All of them had curving arms, some of which had ink stains, and the one nearest her had initials carved into the wood.

Carlin moved over to look at a map of the United States on the wall. It was bigger than the one in her atlas, but it was faded and the labels were harder to read. The superior quality of her own map filled her with a sudden confidence, and she turned to survey the room again, taking in the dusty United States flag furled in the corner and a picture of General Lee on Traveller tacked to the wall. The room smelled of chalk dust and the heavy oak floor.

"You come from one of the plantations, don't you?" Mary Beth said, studying her. Carlin nodded. "Can you read well? Can you cipher? Do you have a best friend?" Carlin answered "yes" to all three questions. Mary Beth need not know right now that her best friend was a colored girl, at least the person who had been her best friend until she got sick. If only she could see Miss Mollie at recess, or at lunch anyway. She would rescue Carlin from this scary awkwardness.

"You can sit here," Mary Beth said. "I'm going to sit there." She pointed to a chair near the wall. "I'm saving that seat for Sallie Lou." She pointed to the seat in front of hers. "We always sit together, that is, if Miss Stark will let us." Carlin sat down uneasily and tucked her knees in. It might be nice sitting close to Mary Beth, if the teacher would let them.

A loud bell sounded nearby. Carlin started. "That's just Miss Percy ringing the bell to begin," Mary Beth said. "You'll get used to it. She rings it a lot." Voices came closer. Girls and boys poured into the room. There must be ten people, maybe more. Carlin glimpsed Robbie close to the front and waved, but Robbie was talking to another girl and didn't see her.

A large woman in a flowered dress, with curly hair pulled into a loose knot behind, moved to the front desk. That must be Miss Stark, Carlin thought. The teacher opened a dark green notebook and started down the aisle, looking to the right and left, making marks in the book.

"Hello, Richard. Susan. Mary Beth. You're Mary C. McNair. Is that right?" Miss Stark asked, stopping in front of Carlin. Carlin felt as though every head in the room was turned towards her, watching. "Welcome, Mary. We're glad to have you."

Carlin's face grew hot. She stood up suddenly and looked straight at the teacher. What she had to say was urgent. "The C stands for Carlin," she began and heard her voice shake. "That's what I'm always called. I mean, I'd much rather you call me Carlin than Mary." She waited, enveloped in a hot haze, and it seemed to her that the class waited too.

"All right," Miss Stark said. "We'll call you Carlin then. That's simple." Miss Stark patted her shoulder, pressing it a little to indicate that Carlin should sit down again. "Now," she said turning, "we've got two new boys as well."

As the boys were introduced to the class, Carlin caught sight of Owen smiling at her from the second row. She smiled back, then concentrated on Miss Stark again. They began with a story about Jefferson, which was easy enough, and went on to arithmetic. Carlin studied Mary Beth's bent head in front of her. She wore plaid bows on the ends of her braids. Did Aunt Tazey have any plaid ribbon, she wondered. Would she let Carlin cut it up for bows?

At noon, she sat on the steps outside the school, eating her lunch with Mary Beth and Sallie Lou. "Have you ever fainted?" Sallie Lou asked. "I have."

"No," Carlin told her, "but I had typhoid. I was sick a whole year, and all my hair came out."

"All your hair?" Mary Beth's eyebrows lifted. "Were you bald?"

"Yes," Carlin nodded. "My mother wouldn't let me look in the mirror for a long time."

"Why?" Sallie Lou asked.

"She thought it would scare me." Carlin paused. Is that what Mama had really thought? It was so long ago.

"Did it? I mean when you finally did see yourself."

"Some, I guess," Carlin said. "But I was really too sick to care."

"Ooh, I'd hate to be bald. I hope I never lose my hair," Mary Beth said.

"My Papa said I was lucky not to lose my life," Carlin went on, feeling hot in the focus of their attention. "The boy I was playing with when I caught it died."

"Ooh. He died. That's terrible." Carlin leaned back against the step above her. Those long months of typhoid, even Hamlet's awful death, were suddenly proving useful.

⁂

Carlin saw Mary Beth sitting on the school steps when she arrived the next morning, and she joined her to wait for Sallie Lou. Suddenly Miss Mollie came striding toward them across the grass. "Miss Mollie," Carlin shouted, running toward her. "I'm here! I've already had one day. My mama and papa send greetings, and Tommy said to tell you he's finished *Treasure Island*."

Miss Mollie smiled. "That's fine, Carlin. It's good to have you here. Come down to my classroom after school. We'll talk then. All right?"

"How do you know Miss Betts?" Sallie Lou asked.

"She used to be my teacher. She lived at our plantation almost two years."

"Two years? Why did she leave?" Sallie Lou gave Mary Beth a look. Did they know about Rosalie, Carlin wondered.

"You're lucky to have her for your teacher," Mary Beth put in. "My sister has her for eighth grade this year, and she says she's really nice."

"Oh, she is," Carlin said. "She's wonderful." She looked from one face to the other. She liked Mary Beth, but she wasn't sure about Sallie Lou. "Miss Mollie, Miss Betts, I mean, is a real friend," she added.

※

"Is your plantation failing?" Sallie Lou asked Carlin at recess. "My papa says a lot of people are crowding into town now because their plantations have failed."

Beneath the uneven fringe of her blond bangs, Sallie Lou's blue eyes had a mean glint. "No," Carlin said and tipped her head back. "Not really. I mean, we've had the boll weevil, but we're going to be all right." She thought of Papa and what he had told her at the pine ridge last Saturday. Were they just one more family from a failed plantation, crowding into town? Maybe. But she wasn't going to admit that to Sallie Lou, not now.

※

Miss Mollie's eighth-grade room was much brighter than Miss Stark's room, since it had windows on two sides. Miss Mollie had tacked a row of postcards of Europe along one side of the room—villages with medieval church spires sticking up, sheep in a green pasture, a bridge over a river. Carlin stood in the doorway looking around. Miss Mollie was still thinking of Paul and Europe, yet she looked settled, sitting behind her big desk in her blue shirtwaist with her locket hanging down and a miniature gardenia in a vase beside her.

"Come sit down, Carlin," she said. "I want to hear all about your summer, how your parents are, and Tommy and Evie. What are you reading now?" Carlin crossed the room and sat.

"I'm so glad to be here," she said, "here with you in your classroom, I mean." She turned and gazed around her. "I like school, really. But it's hard making friends. I mean, everything's so new."

※

Arithmetic was not too bad, Carlin reported to her parents her first weekend home, and English and History were easy. She told them about Mary Beth and Sallie Lou, and about her talks with Miss

Mollie. Miss Mollie wanted Mama to know about a performance of *Aïda* she had seen in July.

"It's exciting," Carlin told Tommy the next morning as they hung in the swings talking.

"Isn't it scary though?" Tommy asked. "Don't you miss Rosalie?"

"Yes, in a way," Carlin confessed and looked up into the dry oak leaves, remembering her homesickness when she had arrived at Aunt Tazey's. "But I try not to think of you all," she said. "I mean, I try to keep the pictures out of my mind, you know—the kitchen house, the creek, and the animals. If I do that, I'm all right. And now that I'm getting some friends, I don't think about here so much."

Tommy studied her. "It sounds hard," he said and swung out a little. "I wouldn't want to do it. I'm not that smart."

Carlin frowned. "You're plenty smart, Tommy. You're just. . . ." She stopped and sucked her breath in as she looked down at the scuffed earth, irritated to have to remember the differences between them.

"I'll have to do it myself next winter when we move to town, if we do," he said.

※

The second week of school went by, and then the third. Aunt Tazey was kind and chatty, but Carlin always felt a surge of relief each Friday afternoon when Papa appeared at the front door to drive her back to Rosalie for the weekend. Tommy and Evie were usually with him. They squeezed onto the buggy seat, Tommy beside Papa, Carlin on the other side with Evie on her lap. They pulled the faded carriage blanket across the bumpy row of their knees, for the late October afternoons were growing chill. Papa clicked to Johnny Boy, and the old reassuring clip-clop of his hooves began.

When they got beyond the church, Papa went fast over the bumps, and they shouted as the buggy bounced high, and collapsed into laughter when it banged down again. Sometimes Papa had to tell them to stop bouncing and sit up straight lest they damage the seat. He sounded stern, but when they pleaded with him, he would sing.

Come and sit by my side if you love me.
Do not hasten to bid me adieu.

Carlin and Tommy and Evie tipped their heads back, shouting the chorus into the Spanish moss above them as they rode by.

But remember the Red River Valley
And the girl who has loved you so true.

The sound trailed after them down the dirt road out of town, catching on the shaggy bushes that stood on either side of the road shrouded in dry honeysuckle vines.

When they turned into the long drive, Carlin shifted Evie and rose a little to catch the first sight of the house ahead. The fanlight above the front door was glowing in the evening dimness and the library window was lighted, for Mama was probably practicing as she waited for them to arrive. Rosalie, Carlin thought, my Rosalie. And yet it would not be their Rosalie for long.

✿

Papa announced that he was postponing the move. They would stay on at Rosalie through the spring. Another loan? Carlin wondered, but she did not ask.

When Carlin returned to school after the Christmas holidays, Miss Percy asked her to come to her office. Carlin sat down on the hard chair opposite the principal's desk and squeezed her hands together. What had she done wrong, she wondered? What was Miss Percy going to do to her? Had she decided that children from the plantations were no longer welcome in the school? Miss Percy's wiry gray hair was piled on her head, the usual wisps sticking out on either side. White powder clung to the side of her long nose, and her pince-nez hung against her flat front on its black velvet cord. Carlin looked down at her hands in her lap. One forefinger was dark with ink. She covered it with the other hand and clasped them together again. Would she have to leave?

"I'm going to change you to another class, Carlin," Miss Percy announced. "I'm going to put you into the eighth grade."

"The eighth grade?" Carlin sat forward. Was Miss Percy going to make her go into that senior grade room with all those girls she barely knew, and those boys? She'd have to leave Robbie and Mary Beth. "Oh, but. . . ." Carlin stopped and clutched the edge of her seat.

"You're way ahead in English and History, you know, and you've made real progress with Algebra. You're lucky that you had Miss Betts as your teacher those years at home. You've had a far better start than most." She put the pince-nez on her nose and glanced down at the papers in front of her, then looked at Carlin again. "Now, I've talked to Miss Betts and shown her some of your recent compositions, and she agrees with me. I want you to go straight up to the eighth-grade room this morning."

"But. . . ." Carlin thought of Maclin, the friend she had made in December. They had walked home together three times, and she and Maclin were going to eat lunch together today. "But I. . . ." She stopped and squeezed her ink-stained fingers together again. What could she possibly say? Miss Percy had power over everything.

"You know Miss Betts well, Carlin," Miss Percy said, "and she's eager to have you."

"She is?" Miss Mollie would be glad to have news of her family and Rosalie, Carlin thought, but did she really think Carlin could do eighth-grade work? All that hard math, she thought. Maybe she did, she told herself. Miss Percy said that they had talked. "The only thing is," Carlin said in a low voice, and lifted her head to look at Miss Percy again, "I won't have any friends."

※

Carlin felt like an intruder when she first joined the eighth-grade class. The group had been together all fall, and everyone knew each other and who was best friends with whom. And yet Lolly, a big, laughing girl, offered Carlin one of her sugar cookies on the second day and told her she had eyes like an actress. Mary Beth's sister, Stella, asked Carlin if she would like to help her write the class poem. "Oh yes," Carlin said. "I'd love to." Yet she felt tall and different among these pretty chattering town girls, who had known each other all their lives. She curved her shoulders to hide her height and smiled often to mask her nervousness. A week went by, then two. She and Stella worked on the class poem during lunch period, then Stella invited her to her house after school to continue.

She was beginning to have friends, she told her mother, but the times after school with Miss Mollie were the best. Carlin would wet the sponge and clean the blackboard with sweeping strokes while Miss Mollie talked. At first they discussed Dickens and social reform; later they talked about what the South needed, and Carlin told Miss Mollie about Uncle Will's trips to Jackson and his ideas about new crops to plant. "I think Uncle Will's planning to go into politics," Carlin said, turning from the blackboard to look at Miss Mollie.

"Do you think that would be a good idea?" Miss Mollie asked.

"Well," Carlin hesitated. "I think it would be good, but I don't think my aunt would like it, or Mama or Papa either." Miss Mollie nodded. "I just feel so sad for Papa," Carlin went on. "He inherited Rosalie, you know, and. . . ." Carlin hesitated again. "I mean when my grandfather owned Rosalie, he was kind of rich. Not *rich* rich really, but very comfortable, and now Papa's too poor to go on. He's going to have to work in the drugstore." She looked back at the blackboard. "He feels he's failed." She paused. "That's what he said to me."

Miss Mollie brought in a newspaper article that told about the long term depression in the cotton industry, discussed the weevil blight, and listed the plantations for sale. Papa was not the only plantation owner in trouble, Carlin realized. "The South is in crisis," one of the newspaper writers said. Carlin whispered the phrase to herself: The South is in crisis. Uncle Will was right that it needed change. Uncle Will had a vision. He knew the South, and he would help it grow.

⚎

Carlin hummed to herself as she came down the school steps, carrying her books in a leather strap. It was almost four. She had been talking with Miss Mollie after class again, and her friends had left. A man in a wide brown hat came out of Mr. Mitchell's photography shop across the square holding a large rectangular package under one arm. Carlin stared. "Hey," she shouted and waved her arm. "Uncle Will."

He had begun untying his horse from the hitching post at the curb, but he turned and looked back. "Carlie," he called back. He tied Fancy up again and hurried toward her. "It's late," he said, coming up to the steps. "I thought you'd be at Tazey's by now."

"I stayed talking with Miss Mollie. What are you doing here? What's in that package?"

"Listen, Carlie." Uncle Will glanced around him quickly. The square was quiet, the street abandoned. A brown dog lay sleeping on the sidewalk outside the feed store. "I've got some big news."

"What? Want to sit down?" She glanced at the dusty steps behind her.

"First, let me show you these." He put one foot on the second step, leaned the big package in its brown paper wrapping on his knee, and untied the string. "Look at this," he said and held up a large yellow sheet of cardboard with a photograph near the top and writing underneath.

Carlin stared. The photograph was of Uncle Will. His face was slightly shaded by a wide-brimmed hat, and he was smiling, his chin thrust up. VOTE FOR CHANGE AND PROGRESS read the large black letters, and below, "William C. McNair, Special Election, House of Representatives, July 23, 1912." There was more writing in smaller print underneath, but Carlin let her breath out in surprise and stood staring at the first two lines.

"Oh, Uncle Will," she said. "You're going to run in an election?"

"Yes. Candidate for the Mississippi House of Representatives. You see, Benson Walker, an old fellow who was the representative from our county, died right after Christmas, which leaves his seat open. There's a terrible man, Gravitt, who's going to stand in his place. But he's a race baiter and a demagogue. Nobody in their right mind would vote for him." He leaned forward, smiling. "This is my chance, Carlie. This is what I've been planning for. It's my big chance."

"Oh, Uncle Will." Carlin looked up at her uncle and then at the poster again.

"It's an off-year election, see, and people don't usually go out and vote in those. The campaign'll start officially at the end of April, which gives me almost six weeks more than you get in most of these off-year campaigns. I've got a lot to get organized first. But I figure if I work really hard . . . if I campaign all over the county . . . make speeches at fairs, at stores, you know."

"It's going to be hard, isn't it?" Carlin thought of the peddler's warning.

Her uncle enclosed her in an energetic smile. "Carlie, those fellows in Jackson, the ones who are encouraging me, say I can scoop up this vote like a kitten off the roof of a necessary. No trouble at all." He wrapped the paper around the posters again, leaned over to dust off the middle step with his pocket handkerchief, then waited for Carlin to sit down. When she sat, he settled beside her and rested the package of posters against his knees.

"What about the supervisor of Greenwood, Uncle Will? Is he for you?"

"Norris, you mean? Not at the moment, Carlie. Nor Haynes, the justice of the peace either, though I've got the constable's vote, I think. But I figure the others have got to come around. I mean, I'm going to talk change, Carlie. Change and the New South."

She nodded. The family would worry, she thought, and Aunt Emily would be lonely. But he would win, and he would bring about changes and they would all be proud. "You won't allow the poll tax, will you, Uncle Will?" she asked, thinking of the peddler again.

"Good Lord, Carlie." Her uncle stared at her a moment. "You pick up a lot, don't you?" He gazed down at his boots, then looked at her again. "I'll have to go along with that to begin with, probably. But I don't like it, and, believe me, when I'm elected that's going to be one of my reforms."

He picked up the hat again and spun it on his forefinger. "There's so much to do. This crop diversification is vital, getting more livestock, more corn, crimson clover, cowpeas, bringing in new agricultural methods. Do you know that a crop of crimson clover will furnish the cotton crop with over forty pounds of nitrogen per acre for the next year?"

Carlin nodded, but she had forgotten to look up nitrogen. "The cotton planters are making their soils poor to enrich the fertilizer men," Uncle Will went on, "when they might be gathering all the nitrogen they need from the air. You see, if we can get federal support for crops other than cotton. . . . If we can get compensation, capital, to make change possible then. . . . Change, you see. That's going to be the heart of my campaign."

He gripped his hat in both hands and laughed, then reached for her strap of books. "What are you reading, Carlie? Hey, Shakespeare." He pulled the thick blue book from the clump and opened it. "Where's *King Lear*?" he demanded. "Have you read that one yet?" Carlin shook her head. "Oh, you've got to read that. It's the best one, really." He whipped back the pages. "Ah, here we are. Here." He turned some more pages. "I think of Lear a lot these days, and of Kent too. Listen to this. This line comes right toward the end. Kent says it.

> *I have a journey, sir, shortly to go;*
> *My master calls me, I must not say no."*

He paused and looked at her. "Isn't that great?" he said. "You'll see how it fits when you read the whole thing." He pushed the book back between the others and handed her the strap. He was quiet a moment, then he said, "You see, Carlie, I feel I have a journey too. I mean these economic improvements, these agricultural changes will eradicate the awful poverty around us, help lift the hate and prejudice. They could make Mississippi a great state once more."

He stood up suddenly, tucked the posters under his arm, and put on his hat. "There's so much to do. I've got speeches to write and meetings to arrange and fellows I've got to get in touch with right away."

"Oh, it's so exciting." Carlin slung her strapped books over her shoulder and stood beside her uncle a moment, gazing at the quiet square. When Uncle Will was elected, he could change so many things. He could get the street paved in Greenwood maybe, and find jobs for some of the dull-eyed colored men who spent their mornings leaning against the front of Mr. Baxter's store. She looked at Uncle Will, wanting to say something admiring, but the enormity of all he was attempting made her dizzy, and she asked, "Where did you get that big hat?"

"I bought it in Jackson the day I decided to run. That's the hat in the photograph."

"It's fine," she said. "It makes you look taller."

"The hat's a part of my plan." He raised one hand to the brim and pulled it to a jaunty angle. "The winning candidate in his winning hat," he said. Carlin smiled as he shifted the posters to his other arm. "I'll see you soon, Carlie." He bent and brushed her cheek with a kiss. "Wish me luck."

"I do," Carlin said and felt her throat tighten. "I wish you the very best luck possible." She stood watching as he crossed the square and untied Fancy. How could any man not vote for Uncle Will?

⚜

Carlin sat at the table in the kitchen house on a Saturday afternoon, shelling peas with Aunt Georgia. She broke open a pod, crooked one finger to pull the peas free, and let them drop into the tan bowl in front of her.

"Did you know Uncle Will's running for the legislature?" Carlin asked.

"Mmm-hmm," Aunt Georgia said. "Not much surprise in that. He been wantin' to run a long time now, I 'spect. Your mama and papa's been talkin' 'bout it."

"I don't think they like it," Carlin said. "At least I think they're worried."

"Well, they's so many changes goin' on around here, it's just one more thing. Can't worry about Mister Will too much when you got a whole plantation to close up and a household to move into town."

"But that's not going to be 'til summer now. Papa said so." She pushed her legs out under the table. "That's still a long way off."

"Not that far. Violet's gone, you know. She got herself a job at the hospital up in Memphis." Aunt Georgia raised her head to look at Carlin, then down at the mound of pea pods beside her. "Me and Feely's goin' up to join her, come summer."

"You're what?" Carlin clutched the pod she was holding and stared across the table. "You're going to Memphis? To live? But you said . . . I mean, I always thought. . . ." She sat, pressing the pea pod against her chest. "Papa said you were coming to Greenwood with us, you and Ceny."

"Well, looks like things is gonna go different, what with Violet gettin' this job." She looked straight at Carlin. "I want to be with my family, Carlin."

"But I thought we were. . . ." The idea felt clumsy all at once. Carlin stopped, embarrassed. "I see," she said.

"We'll keep in touch. Memphis ain't the end of the earth, you know."

Carlin looked down at the pounded dirt of the floor. Memphis was far enough apart for two friends, especially if one of them could neither read nor write. Maybe Carlin could write Feely, who would read the letters to her grandmother, but, but. . . . No. It was over, she realized. This ending was as final as Hamlet's dying, or Paul's, and for her it was worse. Carlin glanced around the kitchen, taking in the line of copper pots, the iron skillets, the straw broom beside the stove. All this would soon be over. "When will you go?" she asked and her voice was tight.

"July maybe. Soon's Violet finds a place where the three of us kin live." She stood, lifted the bowl of peas Carlin had shelled, and poured it into her own. "It'll be way different," she said and put her hands on her hips. "We all know that."

"July," Carlin said. "I graduate in June, and then just one month more." She stopped. A copper pot on the stove blurred. Why did Aunt Georgia have to leave and go to Memphis? Why couldn't she come to town with them the way they'd imagined? "Couldn't Violet," Carlin began, "couldn't she get a job in Greenwood?"

"Well." Aunt Georgia hesitated, then lifted her chin. "She wants a new life, a better life for her and Feely and. . . ." Aunt Georgia looked straight at Carlin. "You been sittin' there lots of times talkin' about better things for us colored folk. Those books you gonna write and all. Well, now we's gonna try to git it." She paused. "You gotta be with us, like the Bible says, not agin us, you know."

Carlin nodded, but she could feel tears dribbling down her face. Aunt Georgia wiped her palms on her apron and came around the end of the table. "Oh, honey," she said and pressed Carlin's head against the white apron covering her breasts. "The feelin's ain't just one way. I'm gonna miss you somethin' terrible, too."

❦

Aunt Tazey kept careful track of Uncle Will's campaign travels and his speeches. She cut out every mention of him from the *Greenwood Courier* and pasted each small clipping into a black scrapbook she was making. Every Friday when Papa appeared to take Carlin home, Carlin had to wait, hanging around on the gallery while Aunt Tazey talked to Papa about Uncle Will.

He had given a speech at an agricultural fair in Elton the week before about poverty in Mississippi, she announced. Did Papa know what he'd said? He'd said that Mississippi was the poorest state in the Union and needed the government's help. Was that wise? Would it get votes? What if someone should stand up in one of those crowds and shout at Will, some dreadful uncontrolled country fellow. What if he had a gun? Carlin, who was stroking Aunt Tazey's large gray and white cat with its double paws, straightened. Shoot Uncle Will? The thought ran through her like a shudder. She stared at Papa, then Aunt Tazey, then at Papa again.

"Come on, darlin'. Get in the buggy. We've got to go."

"Papa, are you worried about Uncle Will?" Carlin asked as her father guided the buggy out of town to the road home.

"Not in the way your Aunt Tazey is," he said, and Carlin waited but he did not go on.

When they turned into the drive at Rosalie, Carlie stood up to see the lighted house. "There it is," she said and turned back to her father. But he was sitting forward, holding the reins in one hand, his face settled into sadness.

"Papa," Carlin said and put her hand on his arm. "It's going to be all right, Papa."

He turned his head to look at her. "My sweet girl," he said.

※

Carlin stood in front of the long mirror in her parents' bedroom staring at herself in her white graduation dress. The high neck ended in a band of scratchy lace under her chin, and the wide ribbon sash gave her a real figure, almost. She turned and caught sight of the big bow, drooping down in back, then glanced at her mother, who stood by the bureau, her head tipped to one side, judging the length of the unhemmed skirt.

In just one more week Carlin would graduate from the Greenwood Grammar School. She stared at herself again. Her breasts were barely defined under the white bodice, but her long thin body had a lithe look. Carlin gave the girl in the mirror a tentative smile, then curved her shoulders. She was definitely too tall.

Her mother took an apple-shaped pin cushion from the bureau and lowered herself heavily to the rug, bending to one knee, then the other. "Stand up straight," she commanded. She was holding several straight pins between her clenched lips, and her voice was tight. "Don't slouch."

Carlin straightened and gazed out the window at the cotton field, then let her eyes steal back to her reflection in the long mirror. Her graduation dress was one of the most important dresses of her life, she thought, and yet she looked so unnatural. She watched her mother fold the white material at the hem and jab it with a pin, then move along a little way and jab it with another.

"Oh, Mama, what's the point in fussing over this?" Carlin cried out all at once. "I'll never wear it again after Saturday. There's nobody in Greenwood I want to walk out with, even if I could, and nothing to do there anyway." She twisted her hands, as she stared at herself and waited, not expecting, not even wanting, a response.

Her mother rose, half-stumbling on her housedress with its faded blue flowers. She jammed some pins into the red cushion, plumped it on the bureau, and put her hands on the shelf of her hips. Carlin stared at her mother's reflection behind her in the mirror. Mama had grown heavy in the last year, she realized suddenly, puzzled that she had not really noticed that before.

"Listen to me, Carlin," Mama began. "The South is no place for a bright young woman. I've known that for a long time."

"What?" Carlin turned to look at her mother directly. "What do you mean, Mama?"

"You have to get out of the South," her mother said. "After high school, you must leave. The Huntsville High School is not bad, but after that. . . ." She paused, still clutching her hips, her elbows jutting out in angles on either side.

"I have a little money put by. It's not much, but it could help get you to college. Virginia maybe, or somewhere not deep in the South. It'd be a start at least."

"But Mama. . . ."

"Now when the time comes, don't let on that this was my idea. Your papa'd be sad. He loves Mississippi, you know." She glanced from Carlin to the silent valet beyond the fourposter bed, where Papa's black suit coat hung like a mute presence in the room. "You pretend it's your idea. It will be, anyway. Going away to college."

"I'm good in English and History, but I'm not much good in Algebra."

"You're good enough. You have imagination and courage, and you're a hard worker when you want to be." She stopped again. "I only wish someone had said this to me twenty years ago." She paused. "The South has many problems. I'm not telling you to run away from them, Carlin. I'm just saying you need a wider look. You need to see other things, get some perspective. Then you can make up your own mind about what kind of a life you want to live, and where."

"I . . . I. . . ." Carlin stood staring at her mother. "I wish you could come too, Mama," she said.

"So do I, dear. So do I." Mama sighed and leaned against the window frame. "Sometimes I wish I'd gone away long ago." She paused and looked down at the garden. "But I've got loves here now, and duties. Besides, it's easier for me these years than it was earlier. Still I don't want you to make. . . ." She paused again. "Carlin, I want you to lift up and get out, for a time at least. You understand me?"

"Yes, Mama. That's what I want too. Miss Mollie went to college in the North, you know."

"That would be expensive, and a long way off. But we'll see. There are ways, if you try."

"Oh, Mama, I'll write you every day."

Carlin glanced back at her reflection. Her cheeks looked flushed suddenly. She turned, but her mother was still staring down at the garden.

The deep leaden sound of the bell began in the kitchen courtyard, signaling the noontime break.

"Quick," her mother said and stooped down again. "Let me finish pinning up that hem before we go downstairs. And remember, don't say anything about this to your papa."

⚒

The big eighth-grade room at the front of the school building was decorated with pine boughs and white rambler roses for graduation day. Carlin sat in the second row of seniors, but she had to rise and slip around the others to go get the English prize while everybody clapped. Miss Percy, who looked almost regal in her black velvet dress and long rope of pearls as she stood on the platform at the end of the crowded room, announced the History prize and once again she called Carlin's name.

Carlin stood and made her way past the row of knees and up to the platform once more, flushed and anxious now, lest some of her classmates feel angry that the new girl was taking all the prizes. But if they were annoyed, they didn't show it. People clapped and called her name. Stella hugged her afterwards and told her she was a genius and would surely be a great writer someday. Carlin smiled and kept saying "thank you" to students and parents, "thank you very much." Mama and Papa, who moved outside into the yard with the others for the reception, were saying "thank you" too, as was Aunt Emily.

Uncle Will had come in late. Carlin had glimpsed him standing in the back, when she took the bound book of Shelley from Miss Percy, which was the English prize. "Will you come walk back to Fancy with me?" he asked as the others stood drinking punch and eating cookies outside beside the big magnolia tree. "I've got a present for you in the saddlebag."

They stopped in front of Fancy at the hitching post, and Uncle Will reached into his coat pocket. "I'm sorry I didn't have time to wrap it." He pulled a little square box from his pocket. That was an excuse about the saddlebag, Carlin realized, and glanced back at the thinning crowd in the school yard. Aunt Emily had already given her four monogrammed handkerchiefs, and Uncle Will had probably not wanted her to know that he was giving his niece something else too. She took the box and opened it slowly, half hoping that it would be something funny that didn't cost much. But a small pearl rested on the cotton inside with a gold chain.

Carlin sucked in her breath. "Oh, Uncle Will." She looked up at him, then down at the box again, flattered but worried. "Is it all right?" she swallowed. "I mean, this is so expensive." A gold chain. The only girl in the whole school who had a gold chain was Sally Archer, and she didn't have a pearl to hang on it, not one that Carlin had ever seen. She put the cover back on the box and stared at the name—Shephard's Precious Jewels, Natchez. Precious meant expensive, and even at the Grove they didn't have money for extravagant presents. Aunt Emily kept the accounts, but she couldn't know about this, Carlin thought, and felt the blood rush into her face as she looked up at her uncle again. And yet, she wasn't going to be guilty.

"Each time you graduate," Uncle Will said, "I'll give you another pearl." He stroked Fancy's nose. "And each time you get another prize, you get an extra pearl. It's a darn good thing I didn't make that promise before today." He laughed. "How could I know you were going to carry off the two best prizes? My God, I'd have broken the bank and cleaned out that poor Natchez jeweler."

Carlin smiled as Uncle Will turned to the saddle and pulled one stirrup down. "Do you really have to leave?" she asked, knowing the answer. "Aunt Tazey's made lunch for the family, and Miss Mollie's coming. I'd love for you to talk to her. It's been a long time since you've seen her, and I keep telling her all about you."

"Ah." Uncle Will laughed. "Then I'd better be off, if that's what you've done." He started to mount, then glanced back at Carlin. "I didn't have time to write a card. I'll just inscribe the box. All right?" He took a pencil from his pocket and wrote "To Carlie." The letters were shaky, and Carlin noticed that his fingers were trembling. He clenched his hand a moment and shifted the box. The writing spread out over the top. "With all my love, Uncle Will," Carlin read.

A hot, tender feeling spread through her, and she felt her cheeks burn as she looked up at him. "Thank you," she whispered. "I will keep this for the rest of my life." She tipped her head up to kiss his cheek, but he moved his head so that her lips touched his ear instead. He smiled, then mounted quickly. The big hat was hanging from the side of the saddle, she saw, and he unhooked it and put it on. "I'm proud of you, Carlie," he said, as if relieved by the distance between them. "Whatever happens. Remember that."

Carlin smiled back, squinting in the brightness. Whatever happens. The words snapped her out of the hot maze of her prizes, the praise, and her dizzy wonder at his gift, and she looked up at him with a sudden urgency. "Only seven more weeks until your election," she said.

"Things aren't going wonderfully," he started, then threw his head back and gave her a wide smile. "It's not a big election, Carlie. But I'm going to win. This is my good luck sign. Remember?" He touched the brim of his big hat and slapped the reins. "You wait and see," he called back to Carlin as he turned Fancy into the street. "I'm going to make you proud of your uncle yet."

I'm proud of you now, Carlin wanted to call after him. I'm proud, and I don't want anything bad to happen to you ever. But Uncle Will was already trotting toward the depot.

※

In July the town librarian offered Carlin a job cataloging some crates of books the library had acquired from a failed plantation nearby. Carlin was delighted. Her parents agreed to let her do it, and once more she was to live with Aunt Tazey in town during the week and come home to Rosalie on weekends. The pay was slight, but it was the first money Carlin had ever earned, and she imagined turning it over to Papa proudly. The cataloging, which was to take two weeks, stretched into three, then four when more crates of books arrived from another plantation.

Each Friday when Carlin returned home, she was reminded once again of the huge changes that were coming to Rosalie. The library looked strange. The shelves on one wall were bare. Mama and Aunt Ceny had packed half the books, and Papa took crates with him each trip he made into town. The stable was growing empty too. Lightning had left, sold to a family in Natchez. Johnny Boy had been sold and would leave later, and two of the mules were gone. The quarters were quiet. Four cabins had been abandoned as workers moved on to other plantations or up to Memphis.

The plan was that Mama and Tommy, Carlin, and Evie would move into town the first week of September, so that Tommy and Evie could start grammar school in town and Carlin could begin high school in nearby Huntsville. Papa would commute until the picking was done, then in October, he would begin work at the drugstore. "He could just as easily leave with us," Mama told Carlin. "There's only one field left to harvest, and it'll be almost done by September. It's just that he can't stand to leave."

Sundays went on as usual, despite the other changes. There was the trip to town for the morning church service, then Bible reading at home and a return to town for evensong. Carlin dreaded the buggy rides in the heat. Her stockings made her legs itchy under her stiff petticoat. Mama let her hold her hat in her lap for most of the drive, but after they passed the Magruders' gin, when the church came into view, Mama signaled her to anchor her hat on her head and pull on her gloves.

Papa's father had been the first steward of the Methodist church in Greenwood, and Papa often told how his father had picked the site for the church on a steep rise in the town and had helped design the building. Its sturdy steeple with its tall weathervane could be seen for miles around, and its big iron bell was the first to break the Sunday morning quiet on the square, the Baptist bells ringing soon after. Inside the church, rows of low dark pews faced the carved pulpit. The arched windows were clear glass, letting in the morning sun, and there was a balcony at the back, originally designed for slaves, which some of the young families used when they had to bring their children.

If Carlin had been able to join the choir, like Lolly and Stella, it would have been better, she thought. But Miss Hunt, the choir director, had pronounced Carlin tone-deaf. Even so the hymns were a welcome break, for Reverend Burden, the stern new minister, often preached for more than an hour.

"Couldn't you suggest shorter sermons, Papa?" Carlin asked. "My bottom gets so sore."

Papa, who had been a steward in the church for over twenty years, studied his daughter. "If you would think less about your body, Carlin, and more about the Reverend's message, you could improve yourself." Carlin nodded. Religion and the Grace Methodist Church were about the only subjects in which she couldn't cajole her father. Church was not a duty for Papa. It was the center of his life.

"He's always asking us to turn from sin and be delivered from evil," she said. "But, Papa, no one here is really that bad."

"Sin is with us all, Carlin," he said. "Pride in self, lust, greed. Think about your Sunday school lessons."

"Yes, Papa."

"Carlin," her father said one Sunday, as they drove to church. "This election your uncle's running in. . . ." He hesitated. Carlin looked up, surprised that Papa would mention the subject on a Sunday. "It's a difficult business, winning in an off-year election, you know. You mustn't be disappointed if. . . . Just don't get your hopes up too much, is all I mean."

"No, Papa. I won't."

Carlin looked down the pew when they had settled. Aunt Emily was there, but Uncle Will was once again not with her. He was off campaigning probably. What would God think of his absence, Carlin wondered. Would He understand? Would He let Uncle Will win?

She glanced at the faces of the parishioners as they lined up to shake hands with the minister at the end of the service. "Lovely sermon," Mrs. Watson said, extending her black-gloved hand. "So full of meaning." But Carlin suspected that Mrs. Watson was as relieved as all the others to emerge from the church to the sloping green lawn outside, leaving the organ music pulsing behind, and the lines of hard pews. The shouts of the Sunday school children came from the yard next door and the heavy sweetness of honeysuckle drifted toward them. Everyone was relieved to escape the stern church, Carlin thought, to breathe in the outside air and think of the baked ham and sweet potatoes waiting at home for Sunday dinner.

※

"Baptism Sunday's comin' soon," Aunt Georgia told Carlin.

"But will you be here for it?" Carlin asked and heard the sullen note in her voice. She had told herself that Aunt Georgia's move was a courageous decision, and yet secretly she still felt mad, cheated almost.

"This year what with folks leavin' and all, we'se goin' have our baptism Sunday in July." She slipped a spatula under a freshly baked cake and moved it from the pan to a wide tin plate. "This be my last Rosalie baptism." Aunt Georgia nodded to herself and plunged a knife into a bowl with peaks of white icing.

"Will Reverend Ambrose do it?" Carlin asked.

"Oh, yes. He's our own Rosalie preacher, not that I wouldn'ta like to seen some of them travelin' ones that comes up the river preachin'. But the Reverend Ambrose know us all—our trials and troubles—and our worries now as we'se fixin' to leave."

"Does he dunk people in the creek?" Carlin asked and sucked in her breath, worried that the term "dunk" might seem insulting to Aunt Georgia.

"That's our way. Immersion, some calls it, and it's mighty nice for us having Carter's Creek close by."

"You don't swallow it, though?"

"Oh, no. Ain't no danger of sickness down in the big middle fork where the water's runnin' fast. It's them little pasture trickles what's so bad." She paused and glanced at the door, and Carlin could feel her thinking of Hamlet. "It be Feely's time," she said, looking back at Carlin.

"To be baptized?"

"Yes, and she be all ready. Violet's home, and she's makin' her a lovely dress. We'll have a good time Sunday. First the baptism, then the picnic." She looked down at the bowl. "Ain't got enough sugar for two icings, but I'se gonna bake a sponge too. Your Mama said it was all right. We still got enough eggs and flour for that, thank the Lord."

"You always seem to have fun at your church," Carlin said. "Sundays are happy days for you." She took the long wooden spoon Aunt Georgia handed her and began to lick its covering of icing slowly.

"Yes, we enjoy ourselves," Aunt Georgia admitted. She ran a wide knife lightly over the cake, creating a little white curl on the top. "But that's not the only thing we do."

"Whites hate church," Carlin announced. "The only reason they go is because they're afraid of each other, or afraid of the man in the family that says they have to go."

"Now, Carlin, your papa doesn't go to church because he's afraid. You know that. He believes in God and he wants his children to believe too."

"I know. That's not what I meant." Carlin paused, not sure what she did mean. "It's . . . it's. . . ." She gazed around her at the familiar kitchen house. "I'm worried about Uncle Will," she said and looked up into Aunt Georgia's face. "If he loses this election. . . . It's this Tuesday, you know, and. . . ." She hesitated. "Some people think he's going to lose. I try to pray for him to win, or at least for him to be happy. But I don't know. Our God, the Reverend Burden's God, that is, doesn't seem interested, at least I don't think He would understand how important it is for Uncle Will to be happy."

"Well, I always say," Aunt Georgia began, "there's your church God and then there's your own private God. You know what I mean? I prays to my own God a lot more than I prays to the one at the church, though He's a good God too."

"Yes," Carlin said. "I just hope my private God'll help."

"You's real worried about your uncle, isn't you?"

"Yes," Carlin nodded. "I'm scared he'll lose."

Aunt Georgia put both hands on her hips and stood looking down at Carlin a moment. "I tell you what," she said. "Whyn't you come to the baptism with me and Violet Sunday? Feely'd like it, having you there, and it might soothe you some. Baptism's a soothin' happy time, you know."

"Oh." Carlin felt a rush of embarrassment. She had known about the baptisms each summer, of course, but she had never been to one, and she didn't know of any white person who had. "That's sweet of you, Aunt Georgia, but. . . ." Carlin glanced at the open door. Her sudden polite-sounding voice saddened her as she searched for an excuse. "It'll be on Sunday, you see." She clutched at that realization with a relief. "And Sundays I have to go to our church like always," she said. "Papa would insist, you know. But thank you anyway."

※

The voting booth was in the schoolhouse. Carlin met her father in the town square and looked eagerly at the steps by the front door. Only white-haired Mr. McGowen stood by the railing talking to Mr. Baxter. No one else was around. "I thought there'd be a crowd, Papa. I thought a lot of men would come."

"Might be more towards evening, darlin'. We're coming in the heat of the day." Carlin stared at the schoolhouse again. What did the booth look like inside? If she were a man, she would be able to vote soon and see.

Mr. Marvin came down the steps of the bank and saluted Papa, who bowed. "What do you think of your brother's chances, Mr. McNair?" he asked. Papa nodded but did not reply. "Some people around here were surprised that you would let him try," he said.

"William makes his own decisions," Papa said. "If elected, he'll make an excellent representative, I'm sure." He paused and fingered the brim of his hat. "Good day," he said. He bowed again and moved on.

"I don't like that Mr. Marvin," Carlin whispered.

"You'd better get back to the library now, darlin'," her father said. "I'll see you later." He turned, but Carlin caught sight of his white, closed face as he walked on toward the schoolhouse.

⚘

Carlin went out on the front gallery the evening after the special election. Papa was sitting with the *Warrington County Crier* open on his knee.

"Did he lose, Papa?" Carlin said and sucked in her breath, realizing that she should have asked, "Did he win?"

"Yes, he lost, and I'm afraid he's going to be mighty disappointed, darlin'."

"Then it was a bad loss, Papa?"

Her father studied her a moment, then nodded. "Yes, darlin', it was very bad. Your Uncle Will has had a humiliating defeat. Wasn't but about forty-two fellows voted for him in all of Warrington County." He recrossed his legs and gazed out at the long drive, then up at Carlin. "He's going to need our reassurance, darlin', and our love."

"Yes, Papa." Carlin stood for a moment, looking out at the north field. Lost. She saw the brand-new posters again, and the big hat. How could he have lost?

⚘

"I feel tired and saddened by the whole thing," Papa said to Mama that evening as they settled on the front gallery in their rocking chairs, "even though there were a lot of folks who thought Will's candidacy was ill-fated from the start." Carlin looked up from the book she was reading. She wasn't eavesdropping, she thought, if they went ahead and talked in front of her. Perhaps they wanted her to hear.

"Oh, I know. I feel so sad too," Mama said. "So upset. I keep going back over things. I think of how he tried to get his architectural practice started in New Orleans. But money was already scarce. People just weren't able to afford those lovely Greek-revival houses Will wanted to build. And then there was his enthusiasm about running the Grove and that scientific agriculture business, all that talk about crop diversification, and those trips to Jackson, his ideas about the corn-hog cycle, and then this whole long campaign."

"He never had the Greenwood politicians behind him. Norris and the others." Papa sighed. "You can't get anywhere without their support. But Will thought he could bring them around and. . . . And yet to think of that Mr. Gravitt's victory. That's hard." He sighed again.

"It's all so hard," Mama said. "No wonder they called Will the corn-pig candidate."

The corn-pig candidate, Carlin thought and squinted, feeling tears come.

"Well, corn and hogs may prove to be Will's salvation," Papa said. "Cowpeas too. He's already expanded his corn crop at the Grove, and he's bought more livestock. Now he can test and experiment and do a little writing about it, maybe."

"Maybe," Mama said. "But to think of all he's been through and put Emmy through too. I mean, he began that campaign way back in April. All that time and expense, and it ended just exactly the way we all thought it would."

"It did?" Carlin stood. "You mean you always thought he'd lose?" She stared at her parents through her tears. Papa had warned her against disappointment and yet . . . yet. . . . "I can't believe they called him the corn-pig candidate," she shouted and turned and ran up the stairs.

❦

Carlin rode over to the Grove on Star a few days later, but Uncle Will was not there. She wrote him a note and went upstairs to see Amy, who was home from school.

Amy was sitting at her dressing table, and she turned to look back at Carlin, holding a brush in her raised hand. She was wearing a white camisole, and her blond hair hung loose over her shoulders. Carlin had been over twice to visit since Amy had returned, but now she glanced around her impatiently, wondering why she'd come again.

The blinds were closed at the window, but the room, like the day, was hot.

"You came to see your uncle, didn't you?" Carlin nodded and felt Amy study her. "You've been sweet on him for years, Carlie." She clutched the silver-backed brush against her chest. "You ought to get yourself a real boyfriend, you know?"

Carlin glanced down at the floor, feeling heat pour through her. Sweet on Uncle Will? Was it true? She sat down on the bed.

"I have a boyfriend at school," Amy went on. "His name is Edward. He's really handsome, and his father has a motor car. One that works. He likes me. He told me so. Next year he's going to take me to a dancing party."

Carlin frowned at the pink swirls in the rug and lifted her head. "I have a boyfriend too," she said.

"Who?"

Carlin pulled in her breath, seeing the back of Owen's head, the way his black hair bounced up in back, the weave of his blue sweater, his eyes, and his long hand, months ago, holding the scraping knife in the chicken house.

"Who?" Amy asked again.

Carlin shook her head. Was Owen a boyfriend? Maybe not. But she had other dreams besides Uncle Will, and she wasn't going to tell Amy about them.

"Do you love him?" Amy asked. Carlin looked down at the rug again. "I love Edward," Amy went on. "I'm going to marry him someday."

"How do you know that?" Carlin demanded, suddenly cross.

"I don't know," Amy said. "But I might. Look." She turned back to her dressing table and lifted a little blue bottle. "Mama brought me this perfume from New Orleans."

Carlin rose and stared at the bottle. "Here," Amy said and daubed some on Carlin's wrist.

Carlin raised her arm to sniff it, then gazed around the room again, letting her eyes move from the school pictures to the row of china-headed dolls, back to the closed blinds at the window, as the thick sweetness of the perfume enfolded her. "I've got to get home," she said suddenly. "I've got things I'm supposed to do."

※

Uncle Will and Aunt Emily were coming to dinner, and Carlin was picking blackberries for a pie. She stooped over the tangled vines near the path to the pond, dropping the berries into the small metal bucket that dangled from her arm. Her fingertips were stained a dark purple, and she had a long scratch on her arm. She reached for a vine above her, adding the dark berries quickly to the mound in her pail. In the stillness of the hot afternoon, the only sound was the hum of a dragonfly in the weeds close by. Suddenly she heard a cough. Carlin whirled around. Uncle Will was standing bareheaded just a few yards away.

"Hullo," he said. "I got your note." One hand was sunk in the pocket of his jacket, and he looked down.

"Good." Carlin stared. She had not seen her uncle since the election. His face looked gray, and he stood with his shoulders hunched. "I'm glad you came early," she said, embarrassed by her stare. "I'm picking blackberries for a pie." But that was obvious, she thought.

Uncle Will nodded and moved past the tangled vines to the opening to the path that circled the pond. "Come sit under the willow a moment." He held up a long branching vine with briars. Carlin stooped and passed underneath. Was she sweet on Uncle Will, the way Amy said? Being sweet on your own uncle was bad. Strange, anyway.

"I love this place," Uncle Will said and sat down under the shaggy willow tree. Carlin settled her bucket carefully and sat beside him. "I used to think about this pond sometimes when I was in France." He shaded his eyes and squinted at the smooth water. "It made me feel I had a home."

"That's nice," Carlin said and paused, not sure what to add.

"So long ago," he went on. "So many choices made or not

made. I was a bachelor then, and an architect. Then I married your aunt and became a plantation owner. Then I plunged into politics and. . . ." He stopped a moment and broke off a piece of grass. "I was going to rescue the South, you know."

Carlin sucked in her breath. This was the time to say how proud she was of him, despite his defeat. But Uncle Will went on. "I've always talked to you about my plans, Carlie, my life. I used to tell you about my architectural studies when you were only six." Carlin smiled and waited. "How long has it been?" he asked and turned to look at her.

"You mean, how old am I?" Carlin said. "I'm thirteen now." She waited. The silence lengthened. "I'm really sorry about the election," she started as she watched Uncle Will bend the long blade of pond grass back and forth into accordion-like folds. If only he would turn his head and look at her again, she might know what to say. But he went on folding the piece of grass. "Papa says lots of people don't even vote in off-year elections, and after all, now that you've learned so much about politics and agriculture and everything, you can do something else to help." Her long speech sounded silly and she sucked in her breath, mad at herself for saying it and at him for allowing her to.

Uncle Will let out a long sigh and flung the grass away. "I never thought they'd abandon me, Carlie, my fellow Mississipians, even the fellows right here in Greenwood." He paused. "It's so strange. You think you can do something, help in some little way. But in the end there're all these other things. I mean, it's not just the habits of the electorate or the one-crop economy. It's. . . ." He stared out at the water again. "I don't know," he said slowly. "I don't know what it is."

Carlin waited once more, feeling the silence prickle around her. A long interval crawled past. She should say something. "Mama thinks I should get out of the South. After high school, I mean." She waited. The comment seemed self-centered, but maybe he hadn't heard it anyway. He was staring out at the pond.

"I get dark and gloomy sometimes, Carlie," he began. "I have for years. I don't know why. I used to say the black beast was on me. Sometimes I think it's gone, that I've seen the last of it and can live my life like anyone else. And I do for a while, but then it comes back again." He stopped and stared at her as if surprised she was beside him. "We'd better get those berries back to Aunt Georgia." He stood up abruptly and brushed at his trousers. "She'll be wanting to make that pie."

✻

"Shall we do one more, Emmy?" Mama stood beside the piano with her bow lifted and leaned over Aunt Emily who sat on the bench.

"Oh, I'm afraid I can't," Aunt Emily said. "I'm too full of that delicious dinner." She patted her satin belt. "That pie."

"What about you, Will?" Mama asked. "Why don't you take over? There are some nice old French songs here." She nodded at the book of music on the stand.

Carlin glanced at her uncle, who sat on the horsehair sofa beside the piano, and watched him shake his head. "Not now, Belle," he said and smiled weakly. Carlin, who was sitting on the leather hassock opposite him, put one hand to her neck to touch her pearl on its gold chain. Maybe he would see it, she thought, and crossed her legs cautiously. Maybe he would even smile back at her, but he was looking down at the rug.

Aunt Emily settled in the rosewood chair across from the sofa, and Mama sat down beside Uncle Will. "Baptism's tomorrow morning," she said.

"Oh yes, and our people are all excited," Aunt Emily added. "But I tell you, I'll be glad when it's over. All this talk of sin and salvation is wearing me out." She laughed. "The sooner we get those dunkings done, the sooner they'll all settle down to work." She looked at Mama. "They'll be joining yours tomorrow morning down by the creek."

"Baptism always used to come in lay-by time," Mama said. She gazed at the French doors, which stood partly open to the evening air. "But this year they decided on July. I suppose it has to do with Georgia's leaving, and James." She lifted her eyes to her husband, who sat with his back to the marble fireplace. "It feels odd to me." She gave a little laugh and looked toward the doors again. "But then, right now a lot of things feel odd."

"Well, it's the same big job for us at the Grove, thank goodness," Aunt Emily said. "We're very grateful that we escaped that weevil, aren't we, Willy?" She glanced across at her husband, who was scratching at a small stain on one trouser knee with his forefinger.

He dropped his hand and lifted his head, as though suddenly aware of the group. "The boll weevil could be a blessing in disguise," he said slowly and turned to look at his brother as Carlin drew in her breath. "It could force plantation owners to change from cotton at last."

"Oh, Willy, dear." Aunt Emily glanced at Papa, then Mama. "Willy, what a thing to say, especially to Thomas." Carlin waited. Was Uncle Will going to turn to Papa and apologize? But no. He sat staring down at the rug, white-faced and silent.

"Willy's planning to increase our vegetable crops in the spring," Aunt Emily told them. "I mean, with his passion about diversification and all, he really must." She was quiet a moment, then looked at Mama and said, "You know I was thinking, wouldn't it be lovely if we could all go up to Jackson for Thanksgiving? It would please Father so, and we could take Aunt Philadelphia along so we wouldn't be a burden. We could have some old friends in and make it a real visit." She paused and waited.

"Maybe," Mama said. "Let's see when the time gets closer."

Carlin studied her aunt. She was pretty in her yellow dress with its high lace collar. Mama looked older, not fresh like Aunt Emily. But she had a kind of fierceness that Aunt Emily lacked. There was something soft and vulnerable about her aunt, she thought, something sad.

"I've been telling Willy that his campaigning has a silver lining," Aunt Emily went on, as if she recognized that her plan for a Jackson visit was an inappropriate topic right now. "I mean, he can try out some of those reforms at Felicity Grove—the cowpeas, the crimson clover, and the livestock, you know. He can do it right there where it'll make a difference, just the way he wants."

"That's right, Will," Papa put in and leaned forward. "You can make the Grove a kind of example. You can apply these scientific methods and write about them."

Carlin glanced at her father, then back at Uncle Will. His mouth seemed to tremble a moment and his face had a scared look.

"Maybe," he said. "I don't know."

"You've always been good at writing," Papa went on. "I bet *The Progressive Farmer* would be delighted to have anything you wrote."

Carlin watched. She could feel the group waiting. Her uncle was staring in her direction now, but his gaze seemed to move through her to the fern at the window, then out into the night. A shudder shook Carlin and she pressed her elbows against her sides. For a moment no one spoke, but it seemed to her that a cold chill had run through them all.

"I had a dream about Uncle Will last night," Carlin announced the next morning at Sunday breakfast. "It was strange." Carlin looked at her mother and stopped. The images had faded, actually, but a sense of sadness hung around her still. She put one hand to her forehead. "It gave me a headache," she said. "I don't think I want any sausages."

Carlin saw Mama look down the table at Papa and meet his eyes. They were talking in their silent language, Carlin thought, discussing her worry about Uncle Will, her headache.

"Well, darlin'." Papa lifted the cover from the copper chafing dish in front of him and peered at the sausages. Holding the cover in one hand, he studied Carlin. "Why don't you stay home this morning and rest. You don't have to go to church today. You can read your Bible, and we'll be home as usual by one o'clock."

Carlin glanced from her father to her mother, then at Tommy, who was staring at his plate, mad that she got to stay home from church probably, while he would have to go anyway.

"Thank you, Papa." Carlin folded her napkin. "I think I'll just go lie down a while. May I be excused?" Papa nodded.

Carlin went upstairs to her room. She kicked off her shoes,

pulled down the mosquito netting, and slid onto her bed. She wasn't sick, and it wasn't really a headache, she thought. She felt a queer fullness in her lower body, as though she were waiting for something. It must be the dream, she thought. It had left her with a vague, dizzy sense, even though it seemed far off. She looked around her room, at the bureau with its pictures, the washstand, the armoire. She had visited the Watson house a week ago with Mama, and it was not nearly as big as she had imagined. She would have to share a room with Evie, Mama said, and it would be crowded.

Mama came in to say goodbye. There was the usual talk below as the family crowded into the buggy, then the sound of hooves in the gravel. Carlin rolled on her side and watched the buggy disappear into the dusty tunnel of live oak trees. She would read, she told herself. She glanced at her Bible on the bedside table.

There had been water in the dream, or something dark. Carlin sat up quickly. The dream would keep coming back if she stayed in bed. She swung her legs over the side and pushed back the mosquito netting. She went to the bureau and brushed her hair. That was better. Leaning on the windowsill, she looked out at the lawn. Soon Aunt Georgia and Feely and the others would start down the path at the side on their way to the creek for the baptism. Aunt Georgia had said this was her last baptism at Rosalie. How many Sundays were left before they would all be leaving? Seven? Eight?

Carlin turned and looked back at her bureau. How many more times would she stand there brushing her hair? A hundred, two hundred? Someday a second-to-last time would come, and then that last time that she would brush her hair in her own room at her own bureau before they left Rosalie for good.

Carlin felt her mouth tremble and looked down the drive again. She should have gone to church. She didn't have a headache, and she didn't want to be here alone. A sob began in her throat. She thought of Uncle Will. He had been defeated, but at least he didn't have to leave the Grove. He could start making those changes Aunt Emily had spoken of, and writing about them in that magazine. Maybe part of his sadness was the fact that they were leaving Rosalie so soon. Leaving. It was only a month now or a little more.

Her shoulders shook suddenly and she covered her face, feeling the tears slide out between her fingers.

"Carlin?" Aunt Georgia stood in the doorway, wearing her blue church dress and her big straw hat. "What's you cryin' about, honey?" She crossed the rug in her heavy uneven walk and leaned down to put her arm around Carlin's shoulders.

"I don't know. I had a dream about Uncle Will and. . . ." That was part of it, Carlin thought, but there was more.

"Aw, honey. It ain't gonna help your uncle none for you to sit up here cryin' all alone. He's takin' that election business real hard, but he gonna be all right." She straightened and glanced back at the door. "I tell you what. You come along with us to the baptism. It's pretty down there by the creek, and cool, too. You'll see Feely and Violet, and then we'll have a nice picnic. We'se fixed some real good food. Never mind them shortages. That pecan cake and that potato salad with walnuts what you always like."

Carlin looked up at Aunt Georgia. Her broad dark face was framed by the straw hat, and there was a moustache of perspiration above her upper lip. This might be one of the last times they would be together, she thought, and glanced around her room. If she stayed here alone, she would just be sad and bored. She looked at her lap, surprised to realize that she was still wearing her Sunday dress with its blue and yellow flowers. Her gloves lay on the bureau, but she probably wouldn't need them for the baptism. Still I'll be the only white person there, she thought. Did they really want her? Yes, Aunt Georgia did. She had invited her last week after all.

"Oh, thank you," Carlin said, and stood up quickly, then stooped and grabbed her shoes from the rug. "I'd love to come."

Violet and Feely were waiting in the kitchen courtyard. Violet, who had come back from Memphis for the event, looked large in a bright teal blouse, and Feely stood beyond her, tall and remote in her white dress, the long skirt hanging down around her dark ankles. Carlin stared. Once she would have run down to Violet's cabin to see the new material and discuss the pattern. Now the dress was all done.

"Hey, Feely." Carlin smiled at her friend, feeling shy. If they had still been close, she might have told Feely about her library work or Miss Mollie's visit. She might even have talked to Feely about Uncle Will. But now. . . . Carlin caught her bottom lip between her teeth and waited. What was left of their old friendship, she wondered?

"Hey." Feely nodded at Carlin and looked away.

Is it all right for me to come to your baptism, Carlin wanted to ask her. Do you want me to? The questions crowded into Carlin's mouth, but she remained mute, waiting while Violet and Aunt Georgia divided the things to be carried among them: the pail of potato salad for Violet, the two straw bags for Feely. Aunt Georgia picked up the cake basket and would have taken the quilt too, but Carlin clutched it, insisting on carrying something. Mama and Papa might not like her going, she worried. This was a ceremony for colored people, after all. But it was too late now to turn back. They joined the line moving across the end of the north field toward the creek.

Aunt Julia, tall and majestic, with a maroon skirt over her layers of petticoats, and a rooster feather in the brim of her straw hat, stopped near the ridge and waited for them to catch up with her. "Nice, hot Sunday. Just right for a baptism," she said. The others nodded. There was a soft neighing beyond them. Aunt Julia turned. Star and Johnny Boy stood close together at the fence, gazing across at the passersby. "Them two horses is gonna miss each other," Aunt Julia said. "Johnny Boy's been sold to a man in Natchez. 'Course, that Star, she's your mama's horse, though you's the one what rides her the most now, so your papa can't sell her. But them two horses, they's been together all their lives. Ain't that right, Miss Carlin?"

"Yes," Carlin said, and gazed back at the horses, seeing their deep brown eyes and the soft hair of their ears. Star was named for the white mark on her forelock, while Johnny's forelock was black. They both stood sixteen hands, and for years now they had grazed together part of the day and all through the summer nights under the stars.

Aunt Julia turned from the horses to look back behind them. From where they stood, they could see the big house clearly, the kitchen house beside it, the rose arbor, and part of the long drive. "Lotta changes ahead," Aunt Julia said. "Won't nobody be in that house come November 'cept a few mice maybe. Few roaches in the kitchen."

"Aw, Julia. You stop that." Aunt Georgia laughed and looked back too. "Ain't no roaches in my kitchen."

"Won't be your kitchen no more, Mama," Violet spoke up. "Won't belong to nobody then."

"What you mean?" Aunt Georgia said. "That Mr. Young, the man what's gonna rent the fields for timberin', he might live in the house. Mr. McNair say so. Besides, Mr. McNair, he be there hisself right through pickin'."

"He be all alone though," Aunt Julia continued. "No buggies rattlin' up the drive, no family comin' and goin', no little cousins flyin' around, and no children ridin' crazy on their ponies right smack into the clean washing on the line." She laughed and looked over at Carlin.

Carlin smiled briefly, then glanced back at the house. Aunt Julia was right. It was all coming to an end. Carlin had known that for weeks, months really, and yet it was only today that she seemed to feel it. How could that be? She had been so excited about the library job, the money she had given Papa. But Rosalie would soon be gone. It was their world, her world, and it was about to end.

Carlin wheeled around to Aunt Georgia and started to clutch her arm. Don't let it go, Aunt Georgia, she wanted to cry out. Do something. Please.

"Oh, Lord." Aunt Georgia lifted the cake basket. "The icin' on this cake is rubbin' off. We's gotta git goin' or it won't look like nothin' when folks is ready to eat."

They joined the others, moving along the path. Everybody was dressed up. Two of the men wore ties, and Eben wore a pair of red suspenders. All the women were wearing dresses. Some had lace collars, and most wore hats like Aunt Georgia's. Everyone was carrying something: picnic baskets, quilts, crates to sit on, and the familiar palmetto fans inscribed, "Collins Funeral Home, Jackson, Miss."

They started down the bank to the creek, through the dry cattails and the hanging willow branches. Violet cautioned Aunt Georgia about the briars on the vines as they made their way down to the water. Below them a voice lifted and a spiritual began.

> *We are climbing Jacob's ladder.*
> *We are climbing Jacob's ladder.*
> *We are climbing Jacob's ladder,*
> *Soldiers of the cross.*

Aunt Georgia and Violet opened the quilt between them and spread it over a stretch of dry sand and stones a few feet back from the water. "Sit down, Carlin," Aunt Georgia said. "Make yourself comfortable. The preacher's gonna do the baptizin' first, see? Then we'll have our picnic."

Carlin knelt on the quilt and waited uneasily for the others to sit down beside her. Violet sat, then Aunt Georgia. She saw Feely eye the bodies on the quilt, taking in a space near Carlin, but she chose one beside her mother instead. She's mad, Carlin thought. She doesn't want me here.

"You likin' your town job, Miss Carlin?" Violet asked, and pulled her fan from the basket.

Carlin stared at Violet for a moment, startled by her formality. Had she become a stranger to them all? "Oh yes," she said. "It's very interesting." But that sounded even more formal. "You ought to come see me sometime," she began, looking across at Feely. "Maybe you could bring those children you look after, and we could go walking some morning, maybe."

"Mornin's I gotta wash and sweep," Feely said in a low voice. "With them three babies, I ain't got no time for visitin' or walkin' neither." Carlin swallowed and looked down. That was it. Their friendship was over. "Besides," Feely added, "colored folk ain't real welcome at that library, you know, even just stoppin' by." She stretched out her legs and patted her dress down around her calves.

"But in Memphis, where we's goin', they treat colored folk like people. Ain't that right, Mama?" Feely turned to Violet.

"That's what we heared. Seems kinda true so far. That's what we's hopin' anyway."

"Good," Carlin murmured weakly. "That's good."

"I be so glad to bust out of this old plantation, this Rosalie, and that stupid little town," Feely said. "I can't wait, I tell you. I just can't hardly wait."

"It's gonna be different than here. That's the truth," Aunt Julia said from her crate close by. "Not like a little old cotton plantation what's failed. No ma'am."

Oh Lord, Carlin thought and looked down at the frayed edge of the quilt. Rosalie, failed? But it was true.

Sinners do you love your Jesus,
Sinners do you love your Jesus,
Sinners do you love your Jesus,
Soldiers of the Cross.

The voices were strong, despite the noise of talk and people calling to each other. Carlin felt enveloped in the sound. If only she could believe like this, she thought, maybe all her churning sadness would dissolve. If only she could know this God and believe.

"This be the last baptism here at the creek," Aunt Julia said, half to herself as she waved her fan. "Where we's all gonna be this time next year, only the good Lord knows."

Reverend Ambrose stood up. He wore his long ministerial coat and white pants. His good broadcloth Sunday pants were to be spared a dunking, Carlin realized. Aunt Ceny rose and helped him out of his coat, first one arm, then the other. She folded its black shoulders together and laid it on the quilt. Carlin sat staring up at the Reverend in his white shirtsleeves as he folded his hands across his stomach in a reverent gesture and turned to the water.

The talk around them began to subside. A voice sang out, "Oh brother, don't you want to go?" Aunt Georgia joined in, then Violet and Ceny, their voices strong. Carlin sang softly, embarrassed that she didn't know the verses.

Oh brother, don't you want to go?
Don't you want to go down to Jordan?

The singing grew louder as the Reverend crossed the sandy area and started out into the water, moving cautiously over the stones. It wasn't deep, Carlin thought. She and Tommy had often gone out into the middle to cast their fishing lines. She imagined the feel of the cool brown water as she watched it envelop the Reverend's legs in his white pants. Tyson called something to the Reverend, then waded in and handed him his black Bible. The Reverend opened it, holding it high above the water. "Dear friends," he started. "Here we are once again before God and Jesus in this place." Carlin closed her eyes and clasped her hands. Please make it all right that I'm here, God, at a baptism for colored people. I know it's not usual. But make it all right. Please.

Eben ushered a thin young woman in a long white dress out to the Reverend. "That's Sarah Ann," Aunt Georgia whispered. "Luther's wife. She and him's leavin' Rosalie next week, but she wanted a creek immersion before she left." Carlin nodded and bent her head, then raised her eyes cautiously. She could see the young woman standing between the two men, her head bowed, while the Reverend prayed over her. Then Eben took the Bible while the Reverend put his hands on her shoulders and pushed her down into the water. Carlin watched. The interval seemed long. Was she all right? The woman came up dripping, her dress sticking to her body and her black hair hanging around her face in wet strings. The singing changed, swelling out to greet her as she moved back across the stones to the bank. "Hallelujah. Amen. Amen."

Feely stood, and Carlin looked up at her. Violet rose, then Aunt Georgia stood up heavily, leaving Carlin alone on the quilt again. Violet smoothed Feely's hair quickly, and Aunt Georgia straightened her sash. Feely picked her way over the outstretched legs to the water's edge, where Eben and Tyson waited. She looked slim in the white dress, and Eben smiled at her as she grasped his arm and stepped into the water. Carlin watched her cross the slimy stones. With Eben beside her, she would not stumble as they had done so often together when they were fishing, clutching each other and squealing as they splashed down.

The brown water sucked at Feely's skirt, which Aunt Georgia had probably ironed that morning, and it clung to her thighs. Her sash floated on the surface a moment, then sunk out of sight. She moved in further, but her small breasts, her shoulders, and her upper arms were still dry. Feely stood before the Reverend with her back to Carlin. Carlin saw the Reverend smile and raise one hand to touch her cheek. Aunt Ceny and the Reverend had lived in the corner cabin next to Aunt Georgia and Violet ever since Feely and Hamlet were babies. Feely had known him all her life.

"Do you, Ophelia Thomas, desire to be baptized?" Carlin could hear his voice clearly, but Feely's murmur was lost in the singing that had begun again a little way down the creek bank.

> *Oh, sister, don't you want to go,*
> *Don't you want to go to Jordan?*

"Almighty God, we thank you for the gift of water." A large jay landed in the tree across the bank and called loudly to its mate so that the Reverend's words emerged in broken phrases. "Sanctify this water. . . . Cleanse. Rise in Jesus and. . . ." There was a pause. The jay was silent, and Carlin heard the words, "I baptize you in the name of the Father, and of the Son, and of the Holy Ghost." The Reverend put both hands on Feely's shoulders, but Feely seemed to dip down in front of him in a curtsy. The water closed over her. Carlin shut her eyes. Feely would be seeing the long slimy grass below the surface, the bubbles rising, a school of minnows maybe. But she would not be scared. She emerged and stood, wet and smiling. "Amen, my dear," the Reverend said. "In the name of the blessed Jesus, Amen."

"Amen," Aunt Georgia said.

"Amen," Violet shouted, and Carlin heard the amens rise around her. The men ushered Feely back to the bank, where she stood on the sand with water dripping from her dress and the curly ends of her black hair. Violet stood up and kissed her, and Aunt

Georgia flung a towel around her shoulders, then took her face between her large palms and kissed her forehead.

Carlin sat looking up, feeling tears start. She bent her head, worried that Feely would notice, and stared at Aunt Georgia's feet beyond her in the sand. She was wearing Mama's old black cloth shoes, in which she had cut holes at the sides to make them fit her wider feet.

Carlin felt tears running down one cheek, leaking over her chin. She raised her hands to cover her face. Why I am crying? It isn't Feely. She doesn't even want me here. It isn't the baptism. She glanced around her and caught her lower lip between her teeth. It's the way everything is rushing toward an end, the way nothing will ever be the same anymore.

She moved and ran her hand over her buttocks. Feeling something slimy, she looked down. There was a dark red blot on the quilt, a stain from something on the sand underneath, she thought. She looked out at the water again. This was not her world, this dunking and singing. And yet she had lived beside it all her life. She thought of the Reverend leaning on his hoe in his garden, of Aunt Julia milking with her petticoats dripping down between her knees, of Aunt Georgia in the kitchen courtyard, sewing the black and white stocking dolls. Carlin mopped her nose with the back of her hand, then pressed the space underneath her nostrils, but the tears kept coming.

She squinted up into the willow branches, desperate to distract herself from this awful crying. If Feely turned, she would see, and so would Violet and Aunt Georgia when they came back to the quilt. The wrinkled water was glittering in the sun. She turned to glance back at the path above them and at a cotton shed beyond. Soon all of this would be gone. Gone. Carlin felt as if a huge hand was pressing on her chest and she brought her arms up in front of her to push it back. Stop. Go away. She got up, staggering a moment on the quilt. Something was oozing down between her legs. She twisted, pressing her thighs together. What was the matter? She must leave. Get back to the house. Oh, what was the matter with her, anyway?

Aunt Georgia turned back to Carlin. "What is it, honey? You lookin' bad."

"I . . . I have a sort of headache and. . . ." Carlin stopped. She couldn't lie to Aunt Georgia. "I don't know what's the matter. I. . . ." She stood staring up at her friend, feeling tears tremble in her eyes.

"Turn yourself a little, honey," Aunt Georgia directed. Carlin turned partway, keeping her eyes on Aunt Georgia, who stared a moment, then nodded. "Lissen, Violet," she said, leaning toward her daughter. "We'se goin' back to the big house. Jest for a minute, Carlin and me. We be right back." Violet turned, studied Carlin, and nodded.

Aunt Georgia took Carlin's hand, and they started up the creek bank together, then dropped hands to hang onto the willow roots as they pulled themselves up. At the top, Carlin turned to look back. Down below, people were opening picnic baskets as children scampered toward the bank and began to wade.

> *Sit down servant, I can't sit down.*
> *Sit down servant, I can't sit down.*
> *My soul's so happy that I can't sit down.*

Aunt Georgia turned to the path. "Come on, honey," she said. "We'se gonna get you fixed."

Carlin stopped and twisted to look down at her back, where a dark red spot had spread out on her dress. She knew what that was, she realized. That red, that oozing, that was her own blood coming out, washing away her eggs that hadn't been used. That blood meant she was grown up now, and it would come every month, the way it did for Mama and for Aunt Georgia too, she thought, staring at Aunt Georgia's broad buttocks in her blue Sunday dress, as she walked up the path ahead.

Aunt Georgia turned back, as if she could feel Carlin's eyes on her. "Keep on," she said, and Carlin followed. She had been lifted up into a new group, she thought, a sorority of grown women.

Carlin paused when they reached the field and stood staring at the cotton plants. The tight choking sense of loss pressed against her chest again. This oozing blood was part of the whole huge sadness that was enveloping them all, Carlin thought, part of all the loss, the waste, and shame.

She stood by the washstand in her room as Aunt Georgia helped her out of her flowered dress. "Now, don't you worry none about this. I kin get them stains out." Carlin nodded. She had not been thinking about the stains. Aunt Georgia went down to her mother's room and returned with a stack of folded cloths and some pins. "You'se a woman now, Carlin," she said. "A real grown woman, and this is a happy day."

"It is?" Carlin let out a moan. "It doesn't feel happy." She stepped into the clean underpants that Aunt Georgia had lined with rags and pulled on the dress she held out. "I don't know," she said. "I feel like everything's sad—leaving Rosalie, this." She looked down at her body. "Everything."

"Things end, Carlin," Aunt Georgia said, and folded her arms over her heavy breasts. "But things begin too. Remember that. We'se leavin' Rosalie, but now you'se a woman, and we'se all startin' a new life."

Carlin looked down, feeling her tears begin again. Aunt Georgia was right, of course, and yet. . . . "Oh Aunt Georgia." She moved close and buried her face in the damp, dark neck. I don't want things to change, she wanted to cry out. But she only stood huddled against her friend, dampening the lace collar of Aunt Georgia's Sunday dress with her tears.

※

The summer seemed slow and hot to Carlin. There were mornings when she felt bored sorting the stacks of dusty books and longed to be home at Rosalie, riding Star or fishing in the cool creek. And yet everyone seemed to assume she could tolerate the tedium of work like any grown-up.

The door to the town library opened one afternoon, and Carlin, who was bent over a box of books, straightened and looked up. Miss Mollie stood in the doorway, smiling. Carlin smiled broadly and felt herself flush. Her sleeves were rolled up and her face felt sweaty.

"When did you get back?" she cried. "I didn't think you'd come until almost time for school."

"I have some preparation to do, so I came back a little early," Miss Mollie announced. "I heard you had a job working here. Good for you."

Carlin pointed to the solitary chair in the small room and began unrolling her sleeves. "How was New Orleans?" she asked. "Did you go to some concerts? Some plays?"

"Well, we can't do so much of that now. But my parents were fine and glad to see me. They want me to go on with my education, finish a graduate degree—later that is, when there's a little more money." She peeled off her gloves and laid them across her knee. "Their talk made me think of you and your education."

"My education?" Carlin settled herself on a packing box across from Miss Mollie and looked at her questioningly.

"Have you ever thought about college, Carlin?"

"A little," Carlin said. "I mean, Mama's really anxious for me to get out of the South. After high school, that is. She wants me to go to college somewhere outside the South, the deep South anyway."

"Have you ever thought of Radcliffe?"

"Radcliffe College in Cambridge, Massachusetts? Like you?" Carlin smiled a moment, then frowned and rose. She walked to the window and stood staring out into the empty street. "You want me to be like you." She turned back to Miss Mollie and frowned. "But I'm not you. Don't you see?" She waited, but Miss Mollie did not answer. "You expect too much of me, you and Mama. I'm not as smart as you think, or as brave either." She stopped again, then went on. "Papa doesn't expect all that. He just wants me to stay home."

"Is that what you want, Carlin?" Miss Mollie asked. "To stay at home?"

"I don't know. I don't know what I want. It seems so far off."

"You're right," Miss Mollie said. "It is far off. You have high school to think about, and right now you have this job."

"Uncle Will studied in Paris, you know," Carlin said. She moved from the window and stood looking at Miss Mollie with one hand on the desk. "You know about his defeat?"

Miss Mollie nodded, and Carlin looked down at the floor, feeling that heavy subject rise up again. "I didn't mean to be rude," she said, wanting to hold onto Miss Mollie's attention. "I mean I'm grateful to you for thinking about my education. I've thought about Uncle Will studying in Paris and you in Germany and. . . ." She hesitated again. "I'd like to be adventurous the way you were," she went on, "not just stay around Greenwood, waiting to get married. But I don't know."

"You'll be adventurous, Carlin." Miss Mollie stood and pulled on her gloves. "I don't worry about that." A mule wagon passed outside with the heavy clopping noise of hooves on the packed earth. Miss Mollie turned to the door. "There's plenty of time to think about college later." She opened the door to the bright hot morning outside. "I'm glad you're not worrying about your uncle anyway." She paused a moment on the top step. "I was afraid I'd find you brooding over that."

⚜

Carlin was back at Rosalie on Saturday. She paused, hearing footsteps behind her as she walked down the back road from the stable.

"Hey," Owen said, catching up.

"Hey." Carlin looked up quickly, then down at Owen's bare feet on the dusty road.

"How you likin' your job at the library?" he asked.

"Fine." Owen seemed taller than she was all at once, and his dark workshirt made his black eyes look big in his long face. "Fine," she said again.

"You checking all those books that folks bring in?"

"Yes. That's what I do mostly." Carlin wanted to tell him something more, but she couldn't think what. Would he be going to high school? Would he ride in a buggy, or would he walk like her?

"You'd be good at that," he said and turned to the path to the barn. "Bye."

"Bye," Carlin whispered, but Owen had already gone.

⚜

Carlin trotted down the drive one early Saturday morning and reined in Star by the pecan orchard, hoping to see a deer. But nothing was moving in the silent woods except a sparrow singing on the branch of a redbud tree. Carlin turned and stared at the pond field which stretched out on her left. At the rise of the hill, she could see an old chimney, the last of the Dougal plantation which her grandfather had bought after it burned. Once there had been a big house there, and stables probably, a gin, a barn, and quarters. Now only the chimney was left.

Carlin began trotting again and rode all the way down to the fence by the county road. She reined in Star and looked down the dirt road, expecting emptiness, but was startled to see a short man coming toward her, moving in an even, sturdy walk. It was Mr. Mishkin, the peddler. His black pack rose up behind his shoulders, and his bowler hat was pulled down low.

"Miss Carlin," he said and smiled. He raised one hand to lift his hat, pushed at his pack with the other, as he moved toward her. "You're up early. How are you? Well, I hope."

The little man's formality confused Carlin for a moment and she leaned forward in the saddle, uncomfortable at her elevation above him. Did her riding pants and the high black boots that used to belong to Mama give her a pretentious air? "I'm very well, thank you," she told him. "Have you just been at the Grove? You must have left early."

"I did. I have a ways to go today." The peddler put one hand behind him and massaged his back.

"Aren't you going to spend the night at Rosalie?"

"No, unfortunately. I've gotta keep going. Just stopping by for some of that good coffee your cook makes. See if I can sell a few things, then I'll push on."

"Oh, well, if it's such a short visit, I'll walk up the drive with you." Carlin slid down from her saddle. "Come on, girl," she said to Star and folded the reins in one hand. "We're going to walk with Mr. Mishkin."

"Where are you headed from here?" Carlin asked. "Why are you in a hurry this time?"

"Well," the peddler began. "I figure this'll be my last peddling stop." He paused. "I'm going to try and get me a regular job in a store in Natchez, maybe."

"You're going to get a store job?" Carlin turned to look at Mr. Mishkin full in the face. He seemed older this time, smaller and more bent. The deep creases in his face, which had once given him a foreign, almost handsome look, pulled his mouth downward now in tired lines.

"A lot of the plantations are closing up around here," he said. "Nobody to sell to, no place to stay."

"You can't make a living?" Carlin asked.

"Not by peddling. This county's changed. So much around here has changed. I used to look forward to coming into Warrington County. It's different from other Mississippi counties, you know, with the woods and the hills." He paused and smiled at Carlin. "Parts of it remind me of the country around Odessa, you know? I mean, there are beautiful old places there, like the Grove. I think that's why I always liked coming here. Your family, your uncle and aunt, the food, the talk in the kitchen houses. I'll remember that. Peddling was a pretty good life here ten years, even three years ago. But now with that depression that hit cotton growing, and then that weevil. Folks'll tell you it's the one-crop system, but I say it's the international market. Cheaper cotton coming in from abroad. People don't have money to buy the little extras, whites, nor colored folks neither. They're scared, a lot of them. They don't even have time now to talk."

"That's sad," Carlin said. "But will a store job be any better?"

"Maybe. Maybe not. At least it'll keep me fed a few months until this cotton crisis eases some."

"We won't see you anymore then."

"No. But you'll soon be leaving here yourselves, they say."

"Yes." Carlin looked down at the dusty toes of her black boots on the sandy road. "We're not leaving till August, though and. . . ." She stopped. A rifle shot sounded somewhere in the undergrowth beyond the pecan orchard. "What was that? Papa didn't take his gun."

"Your uncle probably. He was up time I was. Going hunting, he said."

"Uncle Will hunting? He never hunts. I don't think he even owns a rifle."

"Oh, he does now. A nice new Winchester. Showed it to me last night. Shot a fox last week, he said."

"That's funny." Carlin frowned and looked off into the pecan orchard, but the woods were silent once again. She felt the peddler turn his head to watch her. She wanted to ask if Uncle Will had told him when he had bought the Winchester, but she smiled at him instead, as it seemed to her Mama might do. "Tell me more about this job you're going to look for, Mr. Mishkin," she asked. "What kind of a store would you like to work in?"

❦

Carlin stood inside the riding ring watching her sister trot around the dusty oval. "Up, down, up, down," Carlin called. "That's right, Evie. Good." She pulled herself up on the fence and perched on the top rail in the noonday sun. Evie was doing remarkably well. She really didn't need riding lessons, and she certainly didn't need to be watched every minute.

Papa rode up on Graylie and stopped beside Carlin. "She's a natural-born rider," he said. "Moves right along with the horse." Carlin nodded. Had she ever been called a natural rider, she wondered, as she looked back at Evie, neat and self-contained in her overalls, with her pale pigtails bouncing on her back.

Papa rode off, and she stared down at the dusty weeds beside the fence. Did Papa like Evie better than he liked her? She blew her breath out in a long exhalation. How silly. He loved them both for different things, in different ways, but she wanted to be her father's only love. His favorite. Was this the way Tommy had felt about her, she wondered, and saw herself all at once, talking away at the dining room table, making Papa smile, while Tommy watched, his eyes dull with an old jealousy.

Carlin looked up at Evie again. "You're doing beautifully," she called out.

Carlin was home for the weekend again and lay on her bed, writing in her diary. The heavy noonday heat had enveloped them, and all of Rosalie seemed drugged with sleep. She heard a yell from the woods, then the noise of dogs barking. Bessie and Blue were scrapping, maybe.

She flipped to a new page and wrote on. There was another volley of barking outside, then a shot. Carlin sat up. Was that really a shot? She folded her journal shut, the pencil inside, and stuffed it under her pillow. What was happening? She lifted the mosquito netting, bringing the room into clear focus, and slid down from her bed.

"What's all that noise in the woods?" she asked, standing in the doorway of Tommy's room. "I thought I heard a shot." Her brother, who was leaning on the sill of his open window, staring out, turned to look back at her.

"You did," Tommy said. "One of the dogs has rabies, I think." Carlin crowded in beside him at the window. Tyson emerged from the woods, a dark red kerchief tied around his head. "Mad dog. Mad dog," they heard him yell, as he ran up the path toward the quarters. "Mad dog." They saw Aunt Georgia come out of the kitchen house and grab Dodie, her grandson, who was playing in the courtyard below. She yanked him by the arm, pulled him inside the kitchen house, and slammed the door.

"Which dog is it?" Carlin squinted, dreading the sound of another gunshot.

"Bessie or Blue maybe," Tommy speculated. "Eben had his shotgun. I saw him go into the woods."

"Oh no," Carlin groaned. "I hate this."

"If one of them's gone mad, they have to kill him, Carlie," Tommy told her. "Remember Little John, that big dog at the Grove? Hugh said he had long strings of saliva hanging down. Holton had to shoot and. . . ."

"Don't. I don't want to hear about it." Carlin covered her ears, then lifted her hands. "Did they kill him?" she asked.

"They had to," Tommy said. "If it's a mad dog, he's rabid.

Rabies comes in the saliva." Tommy opened his mouth and pointed to his tongue.

"I know what saliva is," Carlin said irritably, and turned back to the window. There was silence in the quarters now. Carlin thought of the shut doors, the deserted vegetable gardens, and the people inside, waiting.

"If a mad dog bit you," Tommy said. "you could go mad yourself. That's why Tyson's warning everybody. That's why that dog, whichever one it is, has to die."

"I know," Carlin said. "I know. I just don't like it. That's all."

"Look. There's Thadeus and Eben coming up from the woods now," Tommy said. "See? That must be where he is or was, rather—in those trees."

"Poor thing," Carlin said. A second shot sounded and then another. Carlin bit her lip. "That didn't sound like the stable shotgun," she said. "The one Eben has. It makes a crackety noise. That sounded like Papa's rifle to me. Is he in the woods too?"

"I don't know," Tommy said. "Maybe."

The men stood waiting on the dusty path. Papa appeared behind them, carrying his rifle. He looked strangely unfamiliar in his white shirtsleeves, without his jacket. Carlin stared. He moved to the men, nodded, then walked slowly ahead of them up the path toward the kitchen courtyard.

Aunt Georgia came out of the kitchen house, holding a copper stirrup cup by one of its brass handles. She watched Papa mop the perspiration from his face with a handkerchief, push off his braces, then take the cup by its second handle and nod to Aunt Georgia. Was he drinking spirits in the middle of the day?

It was Lady. The fact fell open before her all at once. Lady, Papa's beloved old bird dog, had been rabid and Papa had had to shoot her with his own rifle. He had told Mama last night that she seemed tired, maybe a little sick, Carlin remembered. But rabies? The mad dog, the one with the dangerous spittle swinging from her mouth, had been gentle, loyal Lady. Papa had bought Lady the spring she was born, she remembered, and now he had had to shoot his companion of almost thirteen years.

As Carlin watched her father take another swallow from the stirrup cup, she felt a knot in her throat. Should she run down to him? What should she do? Mama came down the gallery steps and crossed the brick courtyard. She reached up and touched Papa's cheek, then put her arm around his waist. Her father handed the stirrup cup back to Aunt Georgia, and Carlin watched her parents walk slowly to the gallery stairs.

"This is a terrible summer for Papa," Tommy said. "He has to leave Rosalie. Uncle Will lost the election, and now he's had to shoot his own bird dog. This must be about the worst time of Papa's whole life."

"Yes," Carlin said and felt a chill run through her. "Yes." It was terrible about Lady. And yet. . . . She had been afraid of something else, she realized, something more terrible than rabies and mad dogs. She gazed out at the cotton field. What?

When Carlin came home from town the next weekend, she was startled to learn that Uncle Will was staying at Rosalie. She sat at the end of the bed in the guest room, watching her mother stack a pile of tablecloths and napkins in a double row along the middle of the bed. "He needed to get away from the Grove for a few days," Mama explained. "He's been feeling sad, you know, and we thought a change of scene would help."

"What about Aunt Emily," Carlin asked. "What does she think?"

"It was her idea. She and your papa and I talked it over, and Will agreed."

"But. . . ." Carlin stopped. Her mother's head was bent and when she raised it, Carlin saw the deep vertical crease between her brows. "Hand me that white tablecloth at the end, Carlin." Mama took the folded cloth and opened it partway. "This red stain has been here for years. I ought to have cut this up for napkins or given it to Georgia long ago. But I don't know. It belonged to my mother and. . . ." She held it against her for a moment and sighed. "I tell you, moving is hard. Very hard."

When Papa came to pick Carlin up the following Friday, Aunt Tazey confronted him with questions that Carlin would have asked if she had dared. "But Thomas, why is he staying so long? He's already been there ten days, and Isabelle has so much on her hands right now. Do you think this visit is really helping him?"

"Oh, Will's no trouble. We always enjoy having him, you know." Papa paused suddenly and straightened. "He's getting better, Tazey," he said in a different voice. "I can see some change. Don't you worry. Pretty soon he'll be back to the old Will once again."

Carlin sat beside Papa in the buggy, enjoying the quiet of the ride, since this time neither Tommy nor Evie had come along. When the buggy approached the big magnolia tree near the town cemetery, Papa slowed a moment and pointed at its large white flowers, poised like open hands amidst the dark leaves. "That is one of the most beautiful sights in the world," Papa said.

"It's lovely," she agreed. "But Papa you've only been outside of Mississippi three or four times, not counting your trips to New Orleans, I mean." She sucked in her breath, worried all at once that she might have insulted her father and destroyed the easy intimacy of their ride.

"You mean because I haven't seen the whole world, I can't know that that magnolia is beautiful?" Her father patted her arm. "In the world I know and love, it's beautiful, darlin'. Beautiful to me."

Carlin nodded and thought of Uncle Will, who knew Paris so well. She thought of him silent and sad at Rosalie, and all at once she had a plan.

"Papa," she said, turning to face her father. "I'm going to talk to Uncle Will about Paris when we get home. I'm going to ask him about the Sorbonne and the Left Bank. That'll get him talking, don't you think?"

"Well, darlin', it might." Papa looked down at Johnny Boy's wide back. "But just don't. . . ." He folded the reins in one hand, hesitating. "Don't expect too much of your uncle right now."

Carlin hurried across the wide hall to the door of the parlor and looked in. Her uncle sat on the smooth horsehair sofa, his elbows on his knees, his head in his hands. Carlin turned the brass door handle a moment, making a noise, but he did not look up.

"Uncle Will?" He raised his head. His gray eyes took her in without surprise. She was just there, his gaze seemed to indicate, another detail in the household routines going on around him. But she was going to change his mood, Carlin resolved, and sat down in the chair opposite him. "Uncle Will, I've been thinking about Paris," she began and crossed her legs as she leaned toward him.

"About what?" The whites of her uncle's eyes were webbed with red blood vessels, and his face looked gray, almost unshaven.

"Paris. Someday I want to go to Paris." She watched her uncle's face and waited, but his expression did not change. "You see," she continued, feeling clumsy, "I've been thinking about when I finish high school. I mean, I know that's a long way off and everything, and then college, I hope, somewhere. But then. . . ." Carlin heard the shake in her voice. "*Je pense que peut-être je peux aller à Paris et*—" She stopped. Her French was terrible. This whole idea was false. Maybe she'd never finish high school, much less go to college. How stupid and conceited she must seem, asking about Paris. She forced herself to finish the sentence, moving into English, since she knew so few French words. "And study at the Sorbonne, like you." But the plan was limp now, bereft of any conviction. "I thought maybe I could go to Paris the way you did."

"Paris? What about Paris?" Her uncle's eyes moved partway up her shirtwaist, not reaching her face. He glanced at the rug and sighed. "Carlie, I'm sorry. I can't talk right now." He pushed one hand up over his forehead, raking his fingers backwards through his hair. "Another time. All right?" The arm flopped down and Carlin saw his hand, lying white and long on his dark trousers. He lifted his head briefly. "I'm sorry. I just don't feel much like talking today."

"Of course." Carlin nodded. Once you would have talked to me for hours, she thought. Once you would have been excited if I had said that I wanted to imitate you. She stood and smoothed her skirt. "I'm sorry," she said. "I'm sorry to bother you."

She rushed out into the hall and started toward the kitchen house. But Aunt Georgia had gone. She and Feely had left from the train depot last Saturday. The sight of them waiting on the platform in their straw hats, Feely with the baskets pulled close, Aunt Georgia sitting on the steamer trunk, came back to her with a vividness that hit her stomach like a fist. Aunt Georgia was gone. Carlin could no longer run to the kitchen house to talk about Uncle Will. She let out a little moan, then plunged toward the staircase, determined to get to her room before anyone saw that she was crying.

❧

Uncle Will was still at Rosalie when Carlin returned the following weekend. She came downstairs on Saturday morning and found her mother talking to Aunt Ceny in the front hall. "Did he eat any of his sausages?" Aunt Ceny shook her head. "What about his eggs?"

"Just a little, Miz Isabelle. I scrambled 'em the way he likes, and he ate a forkful—maybe two or three. It was more than yesterday anyways. Seem to me his color's a little better this morning too."

"And he went out on Fancy right after breakfast? Was he riding down the drive or toward the pine ridge?"

"The ridge, Miz Isabel. But he weren't carryin' his gun."

"All right, Ceny. Thank you." Mama sighed and turned to the dining room. Carlin sat down at her place and watched her mother pour herself a cup of coffee at the sideboard. She started toward her chair at the end of the table, then, holding her cup and saucer, she moved to the window instead and looked down the drive.

"Uncle Will seems to be on everybody's mind right now," Carlin said as her mother sat down. "Don't you trust him, Mama? Can't he do anything without you worrying about him all the time?"

Her mother gave her a sharp look and raised her cup, then lowered it into her saucer. "Carlin, don't criticize. Please." She pulled the pitcher toward her and poured some cream into her cup. "You're away all week, you know, and you don't understand everything."

❧

The family had gathered in the dining room for supper: Mama, Papa, Tommy, Evie, Carlin, and Aunt Lucy. Papa glanced toward the hall and waited, but Uncle Will did not appear. Papa bowed his head. "For these and all Thy blessings, Lord. . . ." Uncle Will came in quietly and went to his chair.

"I'm sorry, brother. I. . . ."

"Perfectly all right, Will," Papa said. He finished the grace, stood, and bent over the ham that Aunt Ceny put down in front of him. James would have waited quietly beside Papa with a white napkin folded over his arm, ready to pass the plates, Carlin thought, but James had left Rosalie. Aunt Ceny hovered near the sideboard looking frayed and confused. The fact was that Aunt Ceny was now doing both James and Aunt Georgia's jobs.

"Looks delicious," Papa said and gave Mama a tired smile as he picked up the carving knife. He served Mama, then put a slice on the plate beside him and began cutting it into small pieces.

"I can cut up my own meat now, Papa," Evie protested.

"Yes, darlin', I know," Papa said and continued to cut. "Now you, Will. Here's a nice tender slice."

"Nothing for me, brother." Uncle Will raised one hand in front of him, palm outward, as if to ward off the meat. "I'm not hungry tonight." He looked down at the tablecloth.

"Just a little sliver for strength," Papa coaxed and put a thin strip of ham on the plate. Carlin, sitting directly across the table from her uncle, lifted her eyes to study him. He looked vaguely disheveled. His white collar was limp and his string tie was pulled out of line, as though such things were not important anymore.

"Did you see Rick Magruder on your ride this afternoon, Will?" Papa asked. He had finished serving the stacked plates, and he put several slices of ham on his own plate and sat down again.

"No. I didn't go that way. I rode toward the woods."

"I see. Well, you must stop and see him soon. He said he was looking forward to talking with you." Carlin watched her father, aware of the self-conscious cheer in his voice and the weariness.

"Have some mustard with that ham, Will," Mama urged. "It's not French, of course, just good old Rosalie mustard." She laughed, but the sound hung around them unanswered. Carlin glanced at the others, feeling a clutch of embarrassment at her mother's tired pleasantry. She turned. The light had caught on a single hair, protruding from her mother's chin. She thought with a shock of Mama sitting on the front gallery with Uncle Will in another summer, laughing happily at some story he had just told. "Do have some of these black-eyed peas at least," Mama urged, but her voice dipped down, expecting defeat.

"They're good," Tommy said and moved his fork to his mouth in an exaggerated gesture, trying to help his mother. Even Evie was eating with deliberate care now, her resentment over the cut-up meat forgotten in the tension that enveloped them all. For a moment Uncle Will's face moved into a tentative smile, then it faded. He shook his head at the china serving dish and looked down once more.

Carlin felt herself growing hot. She squeezed her napkin together in her lap and leaned forward. "Uncle Will." She pushed back her chair and stood. "Please stop being sad. We all love you, you know, and you love us, so don't be sad. Please."

Heat poured through her as she felt the family's startled stares, their faces turned toward her around the table.

"I mean, it's not just you, you see. It's sad for us when you're sad, because we love you."

Her face was on fire. From the corner of her eye, she could see her mother lean forward, felt her hand on her arm.

"That's enough, Carlin," she whispered. "Sit down."

"I'm sorry, Will," Papa said, turning to his brother. "She's just a little upset, a little. . . ."

"She's right, Tom," Uncle Will broke in. "Carlie's right." He put his napkin on the table and stood. "I know I've made you sad with my sadness. All of you. I've held you prisoners with my gloom, and I'm sorry." He bowed to Carlin and left the room.

"Will. Brother." Papa pushed back his chair and hurried after him.

The room seemed strangely empty all at once. Aunt Ceny opened the door, looked in, then closed it again.

"Oh, Lord," Mama murmured and clasped one hand in the other, holding them close to her chin.

"I'm sorry, Mama. I . . . I. . . ." Carlin's bottom lip was trembling and she caught it between her teeth.

"What you said was right." Aunt Lucy turned to Carlin with a stern look. "You have no need to apologize, Carlin." Her face looked pale and strained as she held herself straight in her familiar black dress.

"It's true." Mama put her hand on Carlin's arm again. "We all love Will. We just want him to feel like himself again."

"There they are." Tommy pointed to the long window as the two men came into view, walking together down the drive. They could see Papa's brown back and Uncle Will's slightly taller black one beside it, their heads bent.

"I only meant to tell him that we love him," Carlin said, turning back to her mother.

"You did," Mama said. "And it might help. Now turn around everybody and finish your dinner."

⁂

If only Aunt Georgia were still here, Carlin thought as she sat down on the bench in the kitchen courtyard after supper. If Carlin could visit her in Memphis, maybe. She leaned back and gazed up into the chinaberry tree.

"Carlie." There was a step on the brick surface of the courtyard. Carlin turned and saw her uncle. He smiled and moved over to the bench.

"Uncle Will. I'm sorry about what I said at supper. I only meant. . . ." Explanations crowded into her mouth, awkward and overdone. She stopped and sat silent as she watched him sit down.

"Remember how we used to talk about the South and its problems?" Uncle Will asked.

"Oh, yes," Carlin said. "I remember all our talks."

"There's going to be a lot of crop diversification right here in Warrington County pretty soon. Corn's coming in, you know, and people are going to buy more livestock."

"Corn's always useful," Carlin said. She felt so warmed by her uncle's presence that she was barely aware of her words. "I mean for cattle, and things."

"Diversification, Carlie, and crop rotation. That's what will save the South." He took his pipe from his jacket pocket, put it in his mouth, then pulled out his tobacco pouch and unrolled it slowly. Carlin watched, smiling. She hadn't seen Uncle Will smoke his pipe in weeks, she realized. He packed the bowl, then struck a match, making a tiny flare of orange in the dark. He was better, she thought, as she watched the bowl grow red. He was like himself again, smoking, talking. What Papa had said to Aunt Tazey was true. He really was getting well.

"Uncle Will," Carlin began and stopped, not knowing what she wanted to say. Her uncle looked at her, then tipped back his head and blew out a stream of smoke, that drifted slowly upward into the chinaberry leaves, dissolving in the evening air.

"I'll see you later, Carlie." He rose and walked across the courtyard, smoking his pipe.

※

Carlin rolled over on her back and stared up into the mosquito netting. She had been dreaming about Uncle Will again. He had leaned down over the bed and whispered something. Was it, "Good night"? She wasn't sure, but he was all around her in the room, the smell of his tobacco and riding boots. She groaned, remembering the scene in the dining room. She had said things awkwardly, had embarrassed them all. And he had said that awful thing about keeping them prisoners. But he had forgiven her, hadn't he? He had sat with her on the bench in the kitchen courtyard and they had talked about . . . what? Crops. Diversification. Something like that. It had been quiet and gentle, like the old times. She curled on her side, pulled her knees up under her nightgown, and slid down into sleep again.

She sat up frowning. Had an hour passed since her dream? Twenty minutes maybe? She stared at the window. It was gray outside now, but soon it would be light. Maybe she hadn't dreamed that face. Maybe Uncle Will had actually come into her room.

Perhaps he had wanted to talk. Perhaps he couldn't sleep. She found her shoes, pulled on her overalls, stuffing her nightgown down inside. She hurried along the hall. Uncle Will's door was open, his bed empty. Yet he often roamed around the house, she knew, even around the garden at night. Carlin started down the stairs. She could wake Papa. But if she had only had a dream about her uncle it would just worry him. Uncle Will wasn't in the library or sitting on the front gallery rocking.

She ran across the dewy bricks of the kitchen courtyard and up the path to the stable. The smell of hay and manure rushed toward her. She saw the door was half-open and she ran down the aisle. The stall at the end that Uncle Will had been using for Fancy was empty. Carlin put on Star's bridle and led her out into the yard. Should she go back for Papa? No. Uncle Will was just out riding somewhere before dawn. He had done that before. She mounted bareback and trotted down the path toward the pond. That's where he would be. It was his favorite place. The woods were silent. No birds called, no tree frogs chirped. She would find him there, she told herself, as she rode along beside the cotton field. He would be sitting on the bank under the willow tree wearing his big hat. She would sit down beside him, and they would talk about the corn and cowpeas and the crimson clover that he might experiment with at the Grove, and the articles he'd write.

As she approached the pond, she glimpsed Fancy's buttocks, then his long swishing tail near the blackberry vines at the end of the path. He was not tethered, Carlin saw. He was dragging his reins. Carlin stared, then slipped down from Star and caught them. The big horse whipped his head up and yanked back. He was nervous. He wanted his breakfast. Uncle Will had tied him loosely, and he'd pulled away from the fence. Coaxing him, Carlin managed to tie Fancy and then Star.

She ducked under the blackberry vines and ran along the muddy bank toward the willow tree. She saw her uncle's boots all at once, the black soles exposed, the toes pointed up into the tree. His head was hidden under the willow leaves. He was lying on the moss, looking up into the sky. Carlin felt relief flood through her.

It was all right. All right. "Uncle Will," she called softly, uneasy about disturbing his meditation. The sky above him was lightening now and would soon be striped with purple and orange clouds.

"Uncle Will." She drew closer, then stopped several yards away. His long body looked familiar in the dark trousers and tan shirt. Beneath the leaves she could just make out his big hat. She lifted her eyes to the blackberry bush beside him and saw red glints among the leaves. Holly berries, she thought. Holly berries? Here? A rivulet of red was running down through the moss. She saw the rifle lying beside him in the weeds. The hat was ripped, his head torn.

"No," she breathed and heard the shocked sound of her whisper in the early morning silence. "It can't be. No." She turned, stumbling first, then running, down the bank, under the blackberry vines, back to the fence. Her hands were shaking so hard she could barely untie Star's reins. She had to push Fancy away with one arm, then pull herself up on Star's back. "No, no," she kept saying to herself as she trotted, then galloped down the road under the dripping moss to the north field. When the gullies along the side slowed her, Carlin jerked at Star's reins and turned her straight through the field, riding fast, heedless of the ripening cotton plants they trampled, riding though the barnyard, past the rose garden, to the front of the house, to the open window of her parents' bedroom above. "Papa. Papa," she yelled. "Papa, it's Uncle Will. Uncle Will. He . . . he's . . . oh, Papa. No."

🙴

Carlin could hear the uneven rattle of her teeth, which were still chattering as she sat at the dining room table wrapped in a blanket. "Mama." She looked up at her mother, sitting beside her. "He put the rifle into his mouth, didn't he?" She clutched herself and rocked. "I dreamed he came and leaned over my bed. I thought it was a dream and then, then. . . . I thought maybe it wasn't, maybe he was telling me goodbye and I went to follow him and. . . . I meant to come get Papa, wake you both, but. . . ."

"Shh, shh. It's going to be all right, dear. It's going to be all right." Carlin felt her mother's arm around her shoulders, felt her pull the blanket up, as her sobs began again.

There was a sound at the door. Several people were talking in the hall. It was not yet breakfast time, but the house felt tense with activity. She could hear Aunt Lucy giving Aunt Ceny directions in the hall. Eben and another man were hammering something near the gate, and from the sound of the voices, there must be a dozen people in the courtyard. Carlin could see a strange horse tied to the hitching post. Someone had come from town already, and Papa had just come back from the Grove.

The door opened. "Belle, dear. I've brought your sister," Papa said. He stood in the doorway, looking pale and strained. "You go to her now. I'll sit with the child."

Carlin clutched her arms around her, rocked by another series of shudders. She looked up, barely comprehending, as her mother stood and her father sat down at the table beside her.

"Take another swallow of this brandy," he urged her, lifting the teacup.

Carlin sipped the fiery drink, then stared at the bowl of wax fruit in the center of the table—a yellow pear with freckles, a red apple, a banana with brown lines. She had looked at those objects every day of her life, and yet now she felt she had never seen them before. "If only . . . if only I hadn't said what I said to him last night, Papa." Carlin stared at the pear. "But he came and sat on the bench in the kitchen courtyard with me and we talked. We talked like. . . ." Carlin covered her face, as sobs began shaking her again. "It was like old times, Papa, before."

Her father leaned close and put his arm around her. "I know, darlin'. We had a nice walk after supper, he and I." He inhaled, a long, shaky sound.

"It was me that made him say that about his keeping us prisoners."

"No, no, darlin'." Papa's voice had a sudden severity and he pulled back to look at her. "Nothing you did or said last night had anything to do with your uncle's death. Do you understand? Nothing."

Papa bent so that his face was close, his serious gray eyes staring into hers. "Your uncle was in a deep melancholy mood. This was the only way he could see to get out. It was his choice." Papa stopped and folded his hands together. "God in His great mercy will understand, for Will is with Him now."

Carlin looked at her father and felt another rush of sobs coming. She laid her forehead on the table and cried again, hiccupping with the strain. She felt her father's arm around her shoulders, his hand patting her back, but she did not stop. She would just go on crying and crying, she thought, gulping down more and more attention.

"Stop, darlin'. Please try to stop." She heard the fear in her father's pleading and lifted her head. There were tears in his eyes, and his lips had a strange blue look. She saw him swallow. Uncle Will was Papa's only brother, and Papa had felt responsible for him. A shudder went through her, and she felt her father tug the blanket up around her shoulders again.

"It's terrible for you, Papa. Isn't it?"

"It's terrible for all of us. I loved him. We all did. Poor Will." Papa's voice wavered again. "He only wanted to escape his suffering. He didn't see any other way."

"Did he tell you that, Papa?"

"In a way he did. Yes."

"Was it the election?"

"It was a lot of things, darlin'. The election was the final straw. All that work, and then that humiliation."

Carlin looked up at her father. His lips were trembling, and she knew he might cry. "He told me about his black beast, Papa. The beast that came and haunted him."

"Yes, yes. That terrible melancholy. We just kept hoping it would go away, your mama and I and Emily, of course. But it didn't and Will, poor Will. . . ." Papa's voice shook again and he put one hand over his face. "He's been tormented all his life," Papa went on after a moment. "He just felt he couldn't go through that darkness again."

Carlin watched her father and waited. "He was my friend," she began slowly, as if she were talking to herself. "A friend all my life. Even when he was talking about things I didn't understand or wasn't interested in, he was talking to me like a friend, another grown-up."

"He loved you very much, darlin'." Papa lifted his handkerchief and blew his nose.

A stern familiar voice sounded in the hall outside. "That's Dr. Dabney, darlin'. I have to go." Papa stood and started toward the hall, but stepped back to face her again. "Carlie, darlin'. . . ." He did not go on. But something urgent in Papa's white face made Carlin stand up beside him, clutching the blanket around her. "I know he loved me, Papa, and you do too." She was crying again, but she could feel her father's arms around her.

✿

Carlin sat straight up in bed and stared. The shadowy room seemed to shake with her scream. "No, no. It can't be. No!" Someone lit a lamp close by. Carlin clutched herself and closed her eyes. This had happened once before, maybe twice. Once her mother had appeared in the doorway holding a lamp. Once, or maybe it was the same time, Papa had come in wearing his tobacco-smelling robe.

"Hey, Carlie." That was Tommy's voice. Carlin squinted up at her brother as he bent over her holding the lamp.

"You?" she said. "Where were you? Was I so loud that I woke you in your bed?"

"Uh-uh. I was here." Tommy nodded at the chaise by the window.

"What? You've been sitting there?" Carlin pulled herself up to a sitting position and stared at him. "You've been sitting over there waiting for my nightmare?" She gaped at her brother.

"I didn't want Mama and Papa to wake."

"Good Lord, Tommy. Did you sleep? Haven't you gone to bed at all?"

"I've been sleeping here." He jerked his thumb at the chaise. "Slept as much as you, or more. Want this?" He pulled a shawl from the end of the bed as Carlin shuddered again. She nodded, took the shawl, and clutched it around her.

255

"You're amazing," she said and let her breath out slowly. "You got to me before Mama and Papa heard." She stared out into the dark hall, but it was still empty. "You fixed it so they'll have a full night's sleep before the funeral."

"They need it." Tommy plopped down on the bottom of the bed and leaned back against the footboard.

"I promise you these nightmares'll end," Carlin said. "This screaming. I mean, it wasn't so bad tonight."

"Oh, you're about over 'em," Tommy said.

"You're sure I didn't wake them?" She looked out into the hall again, but no one was there, and there was no sound of footsteps. She didn't want to wake her exhausted parents, and yet a childish part of her wanted them close. "It's terrible when that moment comes back and back," she said. "The way he looked and everything."

"Listen, Carlie," Tommy said. "It's not just you who sees it. We all do, in our minds at least. Everybody at Rosalie saw it then, and we keep seeing it too."

"But. . . ." Carlin started to point out that she had been the one who had actually found her uncle at the pond, then stopped.

"You know what I think you should do?" Tommy said.

Carlin shook her head. She thought with a sudden longing of her mother's arm around her shoulders and yet, of course, Mama should sleep.

"What I think you should do," Tommy went on, "is choose a picture of him when he was strong and happy. I see him leaning back at the dining room table one evening. Not this summer, but last summer when he was happy. He's wearing his white suit and laughing because he's just said something funny, and he has a wishbone in his hand. I've got that picture all filled in almost, the way his hair pops up in back, the way the bone looks with little bits of chicken sticking to the top. I get it all clear in my head, and then I quick slap it down over the other. See? And it works, kind of. Aunt Georgia taught me that trick when Lady died."

"Aunt Georgia?" Carlin's voice trembled. "Oh, if only she was here. If only. . . ."

"I know. Mama says that too. If Aunt Georgia was here, we'd all get strong faster. That's what Mama says."

"But she had to go to Memphis," Carlin pointed out. "She had to go with her family."

"I know. But I miss her." Tommy covered his mouth with one hand and Carlin realized with a start that he was afraid he might cry.

"What's the trick with the picture?" she demanded, grasping for some distraction. "I don't understand." She pulled the shawl tighter around her shoulders and glanced at the window a moment, surprised that she was shivering when the night outside was hot.

"Well." Tommy chewed his thumbnail a moment, then continued. "You make your picture and then you slam it down fast over the other and hold it there so it'll stay. You think of your own picture of him."

"All right." Carlin gazed again at the open door. She didn't want to play games about Uncle Will, but Tommy had been lying in the chaise all night. "I see him on Fancy," she started slowly, "wearing his big hat right after my graduation. He's smiling down at me just after he gave me my necklace." She put one hand to her neck and felt for the gold chain. Mama hadn't objected last night when she'd noticed that Carlin was wearing the necklace in bed. The pearl felt warm, and she held it for a moment before she went on. "He's wearing his boots, of course, and he has on a brown jacket and a red tie, I think, or maybe it was that plaid one. I'm not sure."

"That's it," Tommy said and leaned back against the bedpost. "Keep working at it, filling it in. Then you just take and smash it down on top of the other."

"All right," Carlin said. "I'll try." She pulled the shawl up higher and looked around the room. "What time is it anyway?"

Tommy reached into his pants pocket and pulled out a pocket watch slowly. The watch was Grandpapa's, a birthday present from Papa. "Ten after four in the morning," he said. "Eleven after, actually."

"Oh, Lord," Carlin said. "I'm never going to get back to sleep now." She glanced at a dark blue skirt hanging from the back of the straight chair. I've got to finish letting down that hem," she said. "I have to wear that to church tomorrow."

Tommy slumped down on the chaise. "Finish it now if you want. I'm going to sleep."

"Go back to bed. You'll feel terrible tomorrow."

"I'm all right. I don't mind sleeping here." He swung his feet up onto the hassock and lay back, letting his breath out noisily.

"I guess I could finish that," Carlin said, glancing at the skirt again. She slid out of bed, gathered the skirt, took her wicker sewing box from the top of the bureau, and returned to her bed. "Might just as well hem at four in the morning as four in the afternoon."

Tommy rolled his head and watched her. "You know, it's funny." He tipped back and stared up at the long crack in the corner. "His funeral reminds me of his wedding in a way."

"What? What do you mean?" Carlin stared at her brother. "That's a shocking thing to say."

"I know, but it's just that there's something so big about it," Tommy continued. "Everybody's involved, here at Rosalie, over at the Grove, and in town, too. Everybody knew him. They all need to talk about what he did."

"Oh, Lord." Carlin turned and looked out at the black night beyond the open window. "What if they say he committed a sin in the eyes of God?"

"Some will. But Papa doesn't say that, and he's a better churchgoer than most of them."

"I just don't want people accusing him of sin," Carlin said. "Papa says that he couldn't see any other way out of his blackness."

"I know that, but. . . ." Tommy bit at his thumbnail and looked over at her again. "There's a part of me that feels really mad, though. Don't you? I mean, I want to yell at him and . . . and . . . I don't know. I just wish he hadn't picked that way."

"Yes." Carlin nodded slowly. "I know. I want to yell at him too."

Tommy put his legs on the floor so that he was straddling the footstool at the end of the chaise. "I was jealous of the way he made a princess of you."

"A princess?" Carlin looked across at Tommy. "You were jealous? I didn't know that." She paused. "I mean, I guess I did know it, but I didn't want to." She put down her needle and picked up Mama's little crane-handled scissors to snip a thread. "I wish I didn't have to wear this stupid skirt tomorrow." She looked over at Tommy again. "I know it wasn't fair. He knew me first, of course. But the fact is, I loved being his favorite, going for walks with him, listening to his talk, getting the best presents when he came back from New Orleans or when he came back from Paris. Remember when he came back from his wedding trip?" She rested the needle on the dark cloth, caught the pearl, and pulled the chain up over her chin. She held it there a moment, thinking that she might start sobbing again. But she was all cried out for now.

"I never worried much about you or Evie, really," she went on and glanced at the window. "But after he married Aunt Emily, I did feel guilty about Amy. I mean, I knew she must feel hurt sometimes when he paid more attention to me than her." She held her needle up and looked at her brother. "I felt guilty, but I didn't know what to do about it."

"Oh, well," Tommy said and pushed out one leg to look at his boot. "You couldn't help it. It's just the way it always was." He looked at her suddenly. "I wish you weren't going away, Carlie."

"What do you mean?" Carlin said and cocked her head. "I'm not. I'm going to move to town with you and Mama and Evie and start high school."

"I know, but you'll go away later on. You've always said that."

Carlin looked at her brother and then out at the night again. "I'll come back," she said. "I won't leave forever."

"If you do come back, I might be right here at Rosalie." He looked around the room. "If I can raise the money. . . . I mean, if they develop a really good spray for weevils. I'm going to learn about corn and alfalfa, and other crops too, at college. I don't know. I just bet you I could make this a working plantation again. I mean, that Mr. Young, who's renting the pond field for timber . . . he's not rich. I bet I could buy him off someday and plant that field with corn, maybe."

"I bet you could, Tommy." Tears had gathered in Carlin's eyes, but they weren't even talking about Uncle Will. "I bet you can do just about anything you put your mind to," she added and heard her voice shake.

"You almost finished?" Tommy asked. "I could doze a little now, if you'd blow out that light."

"Just a minute," Carlin said and hurried, but she was almost done.

Tommy was right in a way, Carlin thought. The tension in the crowded vestry the morning of the funeral was curiously similar to the tension of that afternoon three years ago when she and Amy had waited in their flower girl dresses, clutching their baskets of rose petals before the wedding. Once again the church was filled to overflowing, not with wedding guests in pastel silks and white vests, but mourners in blacks and grays.

The room was hot, and Carlin moved to the window to look out. "Carlie." She turned. Amy was at her elbow, looking thin in her gray dress, its wide white collar seeming to exaggerate the fear in her face. "Oh, Carlie. I can't believe it. I just got home from Memphis last night, and I still can't believe it."

"I know." Carlin saw Amy's red-rimmed eyes and put her arms around her cousin. "Neither can I," she whispered as she felt Amy's mouth press against her neck.

"You were the one that found him," Amy said, leaning back to look at Carlin. "His body, I mean."

"Yes, but I. . . ." Carlin hesitated. "Papa says we have to think that now he's with God." She looked down. The phrase sounded vaguely embarrassing.

"I wish I'd been home," Amy said. "I wish I could have done something." Tears filled her eyes and spilled over, starting down her cheeks. She fumbled in her pocket for a handkerchief and, not finding one, wiped at her face with her curled hand.

"Here." Carlin raised the handkerchief she was clutching and wiped Amy's cheeks, then feeling her own tears begin again, she wiped her face as well. "Keep it," she said, pressing the handkerchief on Amy. "You mustn't worry about not being there," she went on and felt her lips tremble. "He was at Rosalie anyway. He was. . . ."

"Come on, girls," Mama said, turning back to them. "You've got to get in line now."

They moved to the cluster of family at the door. Papa was standing in front holding Aunt Emily's arm. "You'll walk with your brothers, Amy," Mama directed. "Just behind your mother."

"I hate this. I just hate it," Amy whispered to Carlin. "All those people staring and talking about him." She bit her lip and raised the handkerchief again.

"Don't worry," Carlin said. "It'll be over soon." But her voice shook as she spoke, and she could feel her nose beginning to run. "Let me have it back a second." She blotted her nose with the handkerchief, then handed it to Amy. "It's communal," she said and put one arm around her cousin's waist as they turned to the others.

"All right, dears," Mama said. "Now Amy, here, and Carlin here with Tommy and Evie." Carlin gave Amy's hand a squeeze and they separated to take their places.

There was another wait. Mama stood behind Aunt Emily straightening the folds of the dark veil that hung from her wide black hat. Under the shadowy netting, her aunt looked small and fragile, Carlin thought, as she waited passively for Mama to finish. She seemed to have shrunk in the past two days since "the accident," as everyone was calling it. Papa patted her hand tucked against his arm, then pushed the door open. The organ music enveloped them as they started into the church. Faces turned back to look. The storekeeper, the feedstore man, Miss Giles from the post office. Everybody was there. Carlin walked stiffly beside Tommy holding Evie's hand.

She sat down in the front pew between Mama and Evie, and bowed her head. When she lifted her eyes, she saw her Grandfather in his frock coat, standing behind the polished coffin holding a Bible. "We beseech you to mercifully pardon all his sins." Carlin stared down at the hymnal in her lap. There were people here who thought Uncle Will had committed a sin.

To everything there is a season,
and a time to every purpose under the heaven.

Carlin unclenched her gloved hands, eased by the familiar verses which Papa must have chosen.

A time to be born,
and a time to die;

Long ago when she smashed the picture above the front stairs, Papa had made her memorize those lines. She had been so angry then. Had Uncle Will been angry? Angry at himself?

A time to plant,
and a time to pluck up that which is planted.

She drew in her breath with a shudder. It had not been time to pluck up Uncle Will. He should be here with them still. Someone was sniffling nearby. There was the snap of a clasp as someone else reached into a purse for a handkerchief. "Receive him into the arms of Your mercy," Grandfather said. Her father raised one arm to wipe his cheek, and Carlin saw her mother put her gloved hand on his knee. Oh, Papa, she thought, and felt her eyes fill with tears again. She raised her hand and pressed the space beneath her nose with her forefinger, needing the handkerchief. "May his soul rest in peace."

There were sounds of movement in the pews behind them, some blowing of noses, then Aunt Tazey, who was sitting on Papa's right, began crying audibly, trying to get up as she did so, dropping her handkerchief, stooping down to find it. Papa put his arm around her and walked her down the aisle with Aunt Emily on his other side as the organ music began again.

It seemed to Carlin, glancing around her, as she went down the aisle with Tommy and Evie, that everyone she had ever known or seen in her life was in the church that day. All the pews were filled, and people were standing along the wall at the back. Out in the vestibule, people shook her father's hand as Carlin and Amy stood beside him. People nodded, muttering consolations, then moved onto Mama and Aunt Emily who stood on either side of Grandfather, stern-faced above his clerical collar and beard. "So sad." "God's will." "In God's hands now." What could people say? That he had been a good man? That everyone had loved him? That he shouldn't have died? That was the mute scream rising from them all, Carlin thought. She clasped her hands together as a shudder went through her. He shouldn't have died.

❧

The long, sad weeks after the funeral moved slowly, Carlin felt, despite the work of packing and the inevitable approach of the day when they would leave. A month passed, and all at once there were only three more days before they would move to town. Carlin was supposed to be in her room packing her clothes, but she ran outside to the stable instead, deciding to ride into town and get the mail. Nobody would mind, she thought. It would save Papa the trip later on.

Carlin had thought about the move for so long that part of her yearned to have it over and done. She was tired of listing her Rosalie memories: the times she and Tommy used to ride home with Papa on Graylie in the evening, watching the lighted house grow close, the times the peddler came, the times they had fished with Hamlet and Feely in the creek, the time of Uncle Will's wedding, and the time. . . .

She stood on the post office steps, glancing through the packet of mail. There was a square smudged envelope addressed to "The McNair Family" in a round hand. Carlin stared. Was it from Amy in Jackson, where she and Aunt Emily were living with Grandfather now? But why would Amy write to "The McNair Family"? Besides, the postmark was Ohio. She was one of the McNair family. She had a right to open it, she decided, and slit the envelope.

Dear Mister McNair and family, the letter began. *We were real sorry to hear that Mister Will died. We hope you all is starting to feel better now.* There were two crossed out words then, *My grandmother sends her special sympathy. Ever yours, Ophelia Powell."*

Carlin stood staring at the short message and the odd, unfamiliar look of the signature. How had they learned about Uncle Will, she wondered. When? His death was over a month ago. Aunt Georgia must have been horrified. "My grandmother sends her special sympathy." The formal words seemed completely unrelated to the big warm arms that would have enfolded her and Tommy, and Mama, too, each one in long consoling hugs. Carlin could see the tears running down Aunt Georgia's dark cheeks.

I'll write her, she thought. I'll describe the funeral, how the church was packed. Feely could read it to her. Carlin trotted along the county road, planning her letter. It was odd that she had not thought of writing before. She slid off Star to open the gate to the Rosalie drive, fastened it behind them, then remembered in a rush that she had no address for Aunt Georgia. She and Violet had talked of sending their Memphis address, but they never had and now they were in Ohio, or so the postmark indicated.

Carlin tied Star to the gate and pulled her diary out of the saddlebag. She needed to write, she told herself, now, here, without interruption. No one would notice if she took another half hour. Papa was sorting saddles and leather straps in the tack room, and Mama had to finish the linen closet.

She opened the diary with its speckled black and white cover and wrote in the date. This must be her fourth diary for 1912, she thought, imagining the stack of them at home on the shelf in her closet. "What does it do to a person to lose a friend—just have her or him leave your life?" she wrote. "I have lost Uncle Will forever, and now I think I have lost Aunt Georgia too. I think almost my first memory is being rocked in her lap in the kitchen house, crying about something, yet cuddling against her body. I can see the chipped paint on the arm of the rocker and I can smell Aunt Georgia's apron, her neck. Do I really remember that, I wonder, or did she tell me about it?" Carlin went on writing.

She closed her diary finally and mounted Star. It would be a nice ride home. A breeze had come up, and the usually still air felt fresh. Carlin turned her head. A queer, sharp smell assaulted her suddenly. She frowned and rode on. When she came out from under the first tunnel of live oak trees, Carlin saw a spiral of black smoke rising near the stable and heard the high, frightened scream of a horse. Fire. Had the stable caught fire? She pressed Star into a gallop.

All at once she could see a pillar of red and yellow flames rising to the left of the house. The kitchen house, she thought. It was in flames. Aunt Ceny had left the stove untended or let some pot boil dry. But wait. Was it the big house too? She pounded closer. Not the big house. No. It couldn't be. Heat spread through her, and she felt her heart banging in the center of her chest as she pressed Star on. She could hear shouts. Someone was yelling for more buckets, and as she got nearer, she recognized the crackling, tearing noise of fire.

Star whinnied and tried to rear. "Stop it," Carlin muttered, yanking the reins. But Star swung her head and started to plunge into the field. "Stop." Carlin slid from her back, dragged the big horse to an oak, and tied the reins. "Wait here," she said and began running.

Maybe they could put the fire out with the pond water, she thought. But the pond was almost dry. There was more whinnying and shouting. Her boots hit the dirt making hard slaps, and her heart continued to bang. Had they gotten everyone out? Oh, please God, don't let anybody be hurt.

She stopped on the paved part of the drive and stared around her, panting. Some smoke gushed from the dining room window, but they would need to put out the fire in the kitchen house first. Carlin rushed toward it, stumbled, and fell to her knees on the bricks at the edge of the courtyard. She straightened, startled at how hot they were. She stared. The kitchen house was a burning shell.

She ran around the side of the big house and saw the bottom of a yellow curtain blow out through the library window, then curl up suddenly into flame. There was a bang, then another. A gun? She glanced around her wildly. No, the window panes. The front windows had exploded, raining shattered glass down on the front gallery. She saw Mama standing near the rose arbor with Evie and Aunt Ceny.

"Oh, thank God," her mother said when Carlin ran up to her. She clutched her shoulders with both hands, and Carlin saw the terror in her face. "Thomas," Mama yelled and pulled Carlin forward. "Come back. She's here. Here."

They stopped on the brick walk and Carlin raised one hand to shade her burning eyes as she saw her father back out of the window of her room above. "Good." He waved, then pointed. "I'm going to get your violin," he yelled. "Your violin."

"No, Thomas," Mama shouted, "Don't. Don't go back in there." But Papa had already climbed through the window. There was a wild whinny. Tommy was pulling Graylie across the drive toward the field. She whipped her head and pulled back as she saw the burning house. Tommy stopped and peeled off his shirt with one hand, wrapped it around Graylie's face and led her on. She could help with the horses, the mules, Carlin thought. But Papa. He had gone back into the house to find her—now he was looking for Mama's violin.

A ripple of little flames had started along the gallery floor. Through the far window, she could see a moving orange wall inside. Carlin gaped. Papa mustn't go down into that. The whole downstairs was in flames. No, Papa, no. Come back.

Carlin twisted her hands. If she rushed up those steps and reached through the window. . . . She knew where the violin was. She started forward, but the heat hit her once again and she fell backward, bumping into a line of flower pots. "Carlin, come back here," her mother ordered. "For heaven's sakes, stay back."

Carlin retreated. Eben rushed past her with a pail of sloshing water. He stepped up on the burning gallery and flung the bucket at the orange mass beyond the window frame. It hissed a moment, then roared on.

She turned. If the column on the end caught fire and fell . . . if the gallery roof tipped . . . Oh, God. Papa would have to jump over its flames. She watched him crawl out through her window again. He was all right. He hadn't gone down. He could still jump. There was time. Now. Now. The flames were starting up that column on the end.

Her father moved to the balustrade and looked down. There was a crackling noise close by. Oh, no. The flames were circling the column. He must jump. "Jump, Papa. Jump," she shrieked.

The column bent outward suddenly and toppled into the ivy below, causing a smoky fog of sparks to rise. Wait. He could jump over it. All at once the whole garden was a sea of flames.

She must do something. Anything. He was still safe on the gallery roof. She fled across the rose garden to the oak tree. She yanked and pulled until the looped end of the rope fell from the tree, pushed off the swing seat, bunched the rope under her arm, and ran.

She leapt across the burning ivy to the big maple tree that Mama had often said was much too close to the house.

"Carlin." She turned, hearing her mother's scream. "Don't." Mama was standing on the brick walk, her hands raised.

"I'll be all right," Carlin yelled and grabbed the first of the old wooden footholds she and Tommy had nailed into the trunk years ago. Hurry. She fitted her feet onto the holds and pulled herself up to the first fork. Hurry. The soles of her riding boots were slippery. She scrabbled as she climbed.

Another cloud of smoke rose. She slapped at a spark on her shoulder and climbed on. Her eyes were streaming. Where was Papa? Where was he? How could she throw the rope so that he could see it? Sparks pricked her arms, but she must climb higher. Her stupid boots kept slipping on the branches. The bark cut her hands. She pulled herself to the next fork. This must be high enough.

A thick stump of a branch stuck out just beyond her. That was it. That would hold Papa's weight. He could jump and swing out. Her hands shook as she knotted the rope in a loop and fastened it around the stump. Maybe he'd already jumped. Maybe he was all right. But if he was still there at the balustrade. . . . There was a knotted ball at the end of the rope where the swing seat had been. Carlin grasped it. "Papa," she yelled. There was no answer, only the roaring sound of the flames and the shouts below. "Papa," she screamed.

"Here." Her father's hoarse voice sounded close. Carlin flung the rope out. It thumped the side of the house. But it was still loose in her hands. She had missed her father. Oh, God. God. She leaned back, swung the rope again, and waited. The rope tightened. Papa had caught the other end. She saw him raise his arms to clutch it. "I've got it," he shouted and leapt. Carlin squinted, feeling her eyes burn. A cloud of smoke rose, covering him. He must have swung beyond the burning area. He must be safe. Make him safe, God. Please.

A horse whinnied somewhere below. Whose? Tommy and Eben must have gotten all the animals out of the stable by now. Shouts rose from below. It was Mr. Magruder and his son maybe.

"I'm down," Papa called. Thank God, she breathed. Thank God. The Magruders must have seen the smoke and ridden over. Maybe there were other neighbors down there, too.

Carlin stared down, then backed to the trunk. There was a rumbling below her. "There goes the floor," someone shouted. "Right down into the cellar." Carlin jumped from the last foothold on the tree trunk and leapt back from the burning ivy. It was so smoky now that she could barely make out the group of men as she stood beside them, coughing, and rubbing her eyes.

"My girl," Papa said as she pushed up beside him. He put his arm around her and pressed her against his side in a fierce hug.

"Wait." Carlin pulled back to slap at her father's shoulders, then his back. "You've got sparks on your shirt."

"Carlin, are you all right?" Her mother ran a hand over her hair. Her voice trembled. "Are you sure you're all right?"

A roaring began and they all stumbled backwards, half crawling over the burning garden as the roof crashed down with a thundering noise. Carlin saw one orange wall sway like a living thing, then drop into the burning below. Evie gave a cry and Mama pulled her close, shielding her face against her breast.

"My God," Mr. Magruder said. "That fire's gone faster than any I've ever seen. No possible way of fighting that, McNair. Nothing we could have done. Nothing at all."

Carlin stood holding her hands to her burning eyes. She wanted to close them but felt hypnotized by the sight. Without the roof, the back gallery was strangely exposed. Another column wobbled and fell forward. "Oh, sweet Jesus, save us," Aunt Ceny moaned.

❧

The town fire wagon arrived in the afternoon, its clanging faint as it turned in from the county road far off. By then the fire had dissolved into a series of smudges around the blackened foundations of the house. The house and the kitchen house behind it, the stable, and the barn had burned to the ground. The volunteer firemen walked around the rubble with Papa and several neighbor men talking. Carlin followed at a distance. An acrid smell lay over everything, enveloping them like some nauseating gas. She bent to look at a piece of the dining room highboy. A shattered mirror was jammed upright beside it. The piano had toppled backwards, one burned side exposing a chaos of wires and hammers within. "But no one was injured," Papa told the men. "Not in the big house, the kitchen house, nor the quarters, and all the horses and mules were saved." Carlin turned. The post for the front gate, that Toe used to open to let them in, was still sticking up, a blackened pot hanging from the top.

❧

They moved into town the night of the fire, and two weeks later Carlin rode out to Rosalie on Star. She had come out with her parents several times before, but this afternoon she was alone. The three brick chimneys, the ones from the library, the parlor, and the kitchen house towered over the blackened area. The few pieces of salvageable furniture had been hauled away and the rest picked over. She walked through the rubble, noticing the bits of broken china, the iron hinges, the shards of glass, the nails, and bits of metal.

She sat down on a pile of smoke-stained bricks and looked around her, wondering why she had come. A mockingbird called, and she turned to watch it settle on a branch of the chinaberry tree, which stood unscarred, unlike the maple she had climbed, whose branches were bent and burned on the house side. She reached down and lifted a brick beside her, then another, and saw a gray leather spine. She leaned over and pulled it up. It was the diary

Uncle Will had brought her from Paris, barely damaged, pushed between the bricks, as though between two book ends. Had any of her other diaries survived? She stood and turned back more bricks, looking. But the diary from Paris was the only one. She sat down again and opened the book. "Uncle Will came back from Paris yesterday and brought me this diary," she read. "It is so wonderful to have him home. His coming back changes everything." She closed the book. How long ago that was, how different she had been. She gazed up at the chinaberry tree. She had been a little girl then, not really little maybe, but so much younger, so much more . . . what? Innocent? Isolated maybe? And now? She was older. She had seen things.

She stood, fitted the diary into her saddlebag, and rode to the south field slowly, where the rows of cotton plants that had been picked leaned together, dry now, their leaves brown, as though they too had been wrecked like the burned plantation behind them.

She turned Star and started trotting toward the drive, avoiding the path to the pond, as she had ever since Uncle Will had died. She made a detour to the pine ridge instead and trotted up the hill. At the ridge, she paused and looked down on the wide burned space where Rosalie had been. She could see the foundations of the big house and the stretch of blackened bricks where the courtyard had been, the kitchen house, the stable and its half-burned door, lying in the weeds. She turned to the quarters, where most of the cabins were still intact, then back to the burnt area. "I loved this place," she whispered, and felt self-conscious, hearing her own voice in the quiet. "And I was loved here too."

> *Farewell and adieu to you ladies of Spain.*
> *Way down Rio.*

Carlin turned to the drive and started trotting back toward the county road. She leaned forward, touched her heels to Star's flanks, and cantered through the tunnel of live oak trees and out into the light of the setting sun.